A SOUL LIKE GLASS

KINGDOM OF BETRAYAL
BOOK FOUR

EVERLY FROST

When the first light shines, hope is born.

PART ONE
THE SECRET IN THE SHADOWS

TAMRA SILVERSPUN - FIVE NIGHTS AGO

CHAPTER I

TAMRA SILVERSPUN

With every hateful word I prepare to speak, I wish I could separate from my body.

I need, desperately, to distance myself from the pain I have to cause my sister if I'm going to protect her.

Asha's face is already strained. The strands of her previously silver hair are tarnished nearly black, like a silver pot that got too close to the fire.

Her skin, where it's visible around the black evening gown she's wearing, is discolored, as if she has been painted with gray ash, a dark contrast to the love that shines from her eyes.

Unbreakable love for me and Gallium, who is our brother and also my twin.

It was love that caused Asha to give up her freedom and wager her life for ours.

For ten years, she sacrificed her freedom so we would be protected from the humans who would have killed us. She shielded us with her ferocity and her audacity to hope that we might one day be free.

Now it's my turn to protect her.

Gallium has already stepped toward her, pulling her into an embrace. "The Vandawolf said it was safe to hug you."

"It is." The tension in Asha's shoulders visibly eases as she accepts Gallium's hug.

The way she closes her eyes tells me how much this moment means to her. How much she needs to know that we won't judge her for what has been done to her.

How much she needs to know that we don't fear the strip of black metal that has adhered to her left hand.

It's metal that once belonged to the cruelest Blacksmith, Malak Ironmeld, and now it's part of her body, appearing so deeply embedded into her palm that it sits flat across it.

We're located in the throne room of the fae monarch, Queen Karasi, where we were all summoned to dinner.

Only two days ago, we finally escaped the human city situated within the land that the fae call *Vadlig Odemark*—the *Cursed Wasteland*. We were separated from Asha at the start of our journey. She went back to help the Vandawolf fight a monster that had risen from the ash. Gallium, Thaden, and I were forced to continue on without her, traveling into the mountains, where the fae found us.

They gave us no choice but to present ourselves to their Queen.

Since then, Queen Karasi has done everything in her power to keep us separated from Asha.

She's finally left us alone.

We are *finally* reunited, and now...

I must tear us apart again.

Oh, my heart. I must become a cold-hearted villain because it's Asha's love for me that I need to use against her now. To stab at her with my voice as sharply as I can and make her believe that I despise her because of her power.

To keep her safe, I will turn myself into her enemy because the real threat... the danger she doesn't yet know about... is standing right beside me.

And she trusts him.

Just as I did.

Thaden Kane casts me into shadow where he stands over me.

I've remained sitting at the dinner table, and his tall, broad-shouldered, muscular frame is an undeniably powerful presence.

His hair is bronzed. His right arm is covered in fine, bronze scales the same burnished shade as his eyes. His clothing conceals the full extent of his scales now, but I've seen the way they extend across his right shoulder and up the side of his neck, as well as down his right side under his arm, stopping only above his waist.

The civilized tunic and pants the fae gave him to wear do nothing to diminish the raw brutality I sense in him. Rather, the tunic stretches tightly around his biceps and the expanse of his chest, sitting snuggly at the edges of his shoulders.

I expected him to focus entirely on Asha, but instead, his focus flickers to me, as if he can hear the hitch in my heartbeat and sense the fear in my blood.

His scaled hand feathers my arm, his forehead gently puckered, a look of concern on his face.

His touch would be comforting if I hadn't seen through his lies.

Since he first arrived in the ashen wasteland outside the human city, he has masqueraded as a human who fell victim to Milena Ironmeld—Malak's only sister.

Thaden told us that Milena killed a dragon and used its spirit to change him, giving him the scales, bronzed hair, and physical strength he now has.

He delivered the Vandawolf a message, supposedly from Milena, warning the Vandawolf that she was coming to claim her city. *She* supposedly calls the city *Svikari Traidor*: Home of Traitors.

But Thaden's story was far from the truth—a truth I've been uncovering and piecing together, fitting the information I've gleaned from Thaden himself with what I already knew from the humans with whom I interacted within the city over the course of my life.

Tiny pieces that all come together to form one inescapable conclusion: Thaden Kane is a Blacksmith.

Worse, he's Malak's own son.

I don't pull away from him.

Rather, I lean in to his touch.

I need him to trust me. By the bright saints, I can't reveal that I know his secret.

Up ahead, Gallium pulls away from Asha. They're standing only ten paces away from us, their interaction clearly visible to me.

Gallium's features are tense again. "The Vandawolf also told me you plan on leaving us behind."

I wasn't part of Gallium's conversation with the Vandawolf just before, so I'm not sure if by 'us' Gallium means just him and me or—*hopefully*—Thaden too.

"Yes." Asha's lips press together, a sign of her determination. "I'm even more certain about it now that I'm aware the humans have dragons."

Gallium nods. "Gliss filled us in. Which is why I don't agree with your decision. You'll need all the help you can get."

Gliss is one of the fae who brought Asha to the castle. Her sister, Elowynn, is the Queen's Champion.

The fae are at war with the humans who live in the west, a conflict that I thought the fae should surely have won by now, given the strength of their elemental magic.

But the humans have powerful allies. They have dragons.

Over the last two days, I've heard the fae whisper fearfully about the might of the dragons, especially the fire dragons, and the devastation that they can cause.

Asha's shoulders slump at Gallium's assertion that she needs our help, but she lifts the tarnished strands of her hair, allowing them to rest across her left palm. "Humans did this to me, Gallium. They're resourceful and cunning. They could do far worse with the help of dragons. Far, far worse with Milena's assistance."

She's talking about the humans back in the Cursed Wasteland. Those humans are not part of the war in the north between the Fae Queen and the human Queen, whose name I've yet to hear.

In fact, the humans in the Cursed Wasteland are cut off from the rest of the world, living in their walled city in the south.

But if those humans, as isolated as they are, managed to inflict such harm on Asha, then I shudder to think what the humans in the west could do with the support of both the dragons and Milena Ironmeld.

Still, I hide my fear for Asha when her focus flickers to Thaden and me, ensuring that my features are stony because that's how I need to appear.

I brace myself for the moment when I can strike...

"Judging by what Milena did to Thaden," Asha continues, her focus pausing on him, "she's a Blacksmith with a heart like Malak's—"

She's given me an opening and I can't waste it, no matter how much it hurts.

I rise from my seat, drawing on every shred of cruelty I can find in my heart and pulling it like a cloak around myself.

"A Blacksmith like you," I snap, my voice overly loud in my ears even as I try to distance myself from what I'm saying.

The blood drains from Asha's cheeks.

The pain in her eyes is instant.

And it hurts me. *Damn*, it hurts. But I can't stop.

I glare at her as I push my chair out of the way with a loud *screech* that I've already calculated will jar her nerves. It will also rankle the Vandawolf, because I saw how he winced at the fae's raucous voices during dinner. His hearing is truly like that of a wolf's. Just as Thaden's hearing is as sharp as a dragon's.

They are both dangerous men.

"Yes," Asha says, her voice strangled as she gestures to the band of black metal attached to her left palm. "With this medallion, I'm capable of great darkness."

She has never been a liar. She has always spoken the truth, even when it hurts her. Her acknowledgment tells me how hard she's fighting the darkness of Malak's metal.

I want to tell her that she could never do what Malak did, that she is nothing like him and never will be.

But I can't reveal my compassion and love for her right now.

I lift my chin and turn my glare on the Vandawolf. He is as much a looming figure at Asha's side as Thaden is at mine.

But he is also changed now. Gone is the sharp tooth that used to protrude between his lips on one side of his mouth. Gone is the wolfishly amber color of his left eye.

I didn't think it could be possible.

When Asha begged me to heal him, I was certain he would only succumb to his wolfish instincts and imprison her again.

I wanted her to be free.

Free of the past. Free of everything that chained her, including him.

How wrong I was.

He looks at me now with a nearly human face. He has intelligent, deep-gray eyes like the color of the sky at dusk right before night falls. His hair has remained the same gray color as a wolf's pelt, but there is no savagery in his jaw. No rage in his face. No anger tightly controlled.

He is an inexplicably calm force at Asha's side and, by the saints, he appears even more powerful for it.

But now I need his anger. I need his fury to rise. I need it aimed at me.

"When you kept our sister away from us," I say to him, "I believed it was because you hated us and wanted to hurt us. But now I wonder if you did it to protect us." I harden my gaze as my focus switches to Asha again. And then I spit the words, "Because she's so much like Malak."

Asha flinches. Her chest stills, as if she's struggling to breathe.

Oh, I've hit her hard.

I fight the voice inside me that wants to scream at what I've done.

Beside me, Thaden is looming even closer, his eyes wide and his hand still, his fingertips frozen against my upper arm.

For a moment, I think he's going to jump to Asha's defense and rebuke me.

Nearer to Asha, Gallium has taken a step back. Like me, he has silver hair and pale-green eyes, which have flown wide.

His lips have parted in apparent shock.

He understood my decision not to heal the Vandawolf, even though he disagreed with it, but he will not forgive me for speaking so cruelly to Asha now.

The Vandawolf's reaction to my accusation isn't what I need.

I want him to react badly to my taunt, especially because I addressed it to him instead of to Asha.

I expect him to rage at me because it's as clear to me as the beating of my own heart that he loves her.

I saw it ten years ago when I first laid eyes on him at the Blacksmith Academy run by my mother. Gallium and I were only nine years old. We had been summoned to the Academy's forge, where the Blacksmith students worked at their anvils, shaping their metal.

Our mother stood in pride of place at the front of the room in all her regal beauty.

The Vandawolf was positioned at Asha's elbow, where our mother had forced her to be. He was gripping a chunk of deadly crimson coal, holding it over the bowl beside Asha's anvil.

I'd caught the fading laughter in the room as the door opened and witnessed my sister with her shoulders slumped. I knew immediately she was the subject of her classmates' ridicule.

Oh, but the look on the Vandawolf's face.

I had never seen him before that moment. Of course, at nine years of age, I didn't have a hope of meeting all of the humans in the vast city.

Even so, the Vandawolf was taller and more muscular than any other human I'd ever seen. Stronger-looking than any human teenager I'd encountered.

He looked well-fed. Determined. And fucking angry.

His gray eyes cast fury at the other students.

Despite the fact that he was dishing out coal that could set him on fire, he seemed oblivious to its danger at that moment.

And then, when the student who was standing at the anvil

directly behind Asha's position used his metal to fashion a spiderweb of sharp blades and spun them at Asha's back, cutting her...

The Vandawolf did something I'd never seen a human do.

He took hold of the crimson coal in his bare hand, burning flames and all.

I thought for an impossible moment that he was going to ram it down that bully's throat. By the saints, I wanted him to.

But Gallium acted first.

My brother snatched our mother's hammer right off her belt and threw it across the room with all his might. He was strong, even then.

The hammer spun all the way to the anvil next to Asha's, hit the bowl of coal next to that anvil, and sent the burning rocks flying through the air.

The explosions that followed took my breath away.

The Vandawolf ran straight for Asha, but she was already racing toward us, darting through the fiery chaos, her ragged, silver hair flying—and all of her determination blazing in her eyes.

She scooped up Gallium and me and tore out of there with us.

The last glimpse I caught of the Vandawolf, he was standing in the middle of the flames, watching us disappear to safety, wearing a breathtakingly unexpected smile on his face.

But there was something else.

A sapphire glow had lit up his body, and it was like nothing I'd ever seen before.

That glow was gone the next time I saw him on the night he was turned into a beast. By then, he had annihilated my people. Killed my parents. And dressed himself in gore.

His hair was dripping with blood, his snarls were far from human, and his breathtaking smile... Well. It was gone.

And so, I thought, was his love for Asha.

In all the years since, I couldn't find out anything about who the Vandawolf was or where he had originally come from. It was apparent that his family had died, but otherwise, his background was a mystery even to the humans in the city.

For ten years, he was simply *the Vandawolf.*

Then, a little more than a week ago, Asha was gored by a monster in the wasteland outside the city. It happened moments before Thaden Kane appeared. The human healers refused to help her, so the Vandawolf called me instead.

It was the first time I had the chance to be near her in ten years.

In the quiet moments after I had worked over her mauled body, my heart in my throat as I did everything I could to save her, I said to him: *"You chose to keep Asha alive. You don't want her to die."*

He scowled back at me and quietly threatened to kill me.

After that, he gave me the task that has brought me to this moment.

He told me to go to the prison beneath the castle where he was holding Thaden Kane prisoner and to extract any truths from him that I could.

Thaden lied to me over and over again, so many times.

But it was what I saw him do on the final night before we left the city that revealed his true identity to me.

I followed him to Malak's orchard, where the apple trees sparkle in the dark, and watched him prowl to the very spot where Malak's private anvil used to rest—a location known only to a few people.

Thaden had crouched and pressed his right hand to the ground, and while the acoustics of the place stopped me from hearing what he said, I read his murmur in the intense twist of his lips: *Fuck you, Father.*

Before I had a chance to speak with Gallium alone, the Vandawolf's guards scooped me up, and I couldn't warn my brother, let alone Asha.

Now, I expect the Vandawolf to rise to Asha's defense. I have accused her of being like Malak—a cruel and unjustifiable accusation.

I *need* him to rise to her defense because I can't pick a fight with silence.

But *dammit*, despite my taunt, he doesn't reprimand me.

I'm forced to escalate all on my own.

Stepping toward Asha but speaking to the Vandawolf, I say, "You tested Asha when you made her pick up Malak's hammer on the night you separated us. I wasn't there to see it, of course, but I heard about it. The way her whole body lit up, the strength she displayed, the awful power she suddenly controlled. You made sure she only ever used that power against the monsters. You controlled her darkness."

As I move toward Asha, both Gallium and Thaden step toward me. Gallium is shaking his head, as if he strongly disagrees with me.

Thaden's hand has dropped from my arm and the crease in his forehead has deepened.

Asha's hand has risen to her heart and her breathing is shaky.

I stop only three paces away from her.

I hold my head high, remaining as cold as I can be. "I have a memory of you, Asha," I say, speaking more quietly now, deliberately using a partial truth against her. "Gallium and I were huddled behind Malak's throne while you fought for our lives and tried to protect us. But you aren't that person anymore. Now I wonder if you ever were."

Her breathing is sharp, her lips pressing together, but I don't stop speaking, continuing to attack her with my voice.

I step even closer to her and fill my words with ice. "The humans didn't cover you in soot, darling sister. They scratched off the shiny surface to reveal what was underneath."

Asha finally flinches back from me.

It's a small action, but it speaks loudly.

Tendrils of both silver and black light spill around her clenched palm, which she holds tightly at her side.

I worry that I've pushed her too far...

But her voice is controlled as she turns to Thaden and does exactly what I need her to do.

"Thaden," she says, her throat visibly tightening. "If you care about my family, please take them somewhere safe. You don't have to tell me where. I don't have to be a part of their lives. But you know this land better than we do, and I trust you to keep them safe."

Thaden's brow furrows as he throws a furious glance at me. I could believe that he cares about her. I could even believe that he's worried about me.

If only it were true.

If only I could trust him.

I maintain my icy exterior, my head held high as I continue to glare at Asha, ensuring she doesn't change her mind.

Her instincts will be screaming at her to stay with us. To protect us. I have to make sure she doesn't.

"Of course," Thaden replies, his expression dark as he throws me another glance. "I'll do as you ask."

Asha takes another step away from me. I'm not sure if she's conscious of the way her right hand seeks the Vandawolf's arm, the way her body language speaks to the connection they share.

"Thank you," she says to Thaden. "That's all I need. We're leaving at first light. I hope you'll do the same."

With that, she turns away from me and hurries toward the exit. The Vandawolf follows closely on her heels.

I catch her quiet exhalation, a sound of pain that stabs at my heart before the door closes behind them and they're gone from sight.

Whatever battles she might now fight, I know that the Vandawolf would give his life to protect her.

He is no longer the beast he was.

I'm certain she will be safe with him.

I'm relieved at the outcome, but I close off my features as I turn back to Thaden and Gallium, preparing myself to be reprimanded for my cruelty.

But—*No!*—Thaden's already stepping past me, a blur of bronze as he hurries toward the door after Asha.

I can't let him talk her out of separating from us!

But it's already too late.

The door swings shut behind Thaden, closing with such a loud *thud* that I jump.

Damn.

I fight my frustration and my fear as I drop my head into my hands.

All my cruelty can't be for nothing.

Please don't let him talk her out of separating from us.

Gallium is at my side within a heartbeat. "Tamra?" His pale-green eyes are full of concern. "What's going on?"

I can't say anything. Thaden will hear.

"Please don't hate me," I whisper.

"Never," he says.

His focus passes to the door through which Thaden passed and then back to me.

He gives me a determined smile.

My eyes widen. *Does Gallium know? Has he figured it out?*

He inclines his head, a small nod, and my legs nearly buckle with relief.

Gallium wraps me up in a hug, his voice the barest breath of sound at my ear. "Be careful."

When he pulls back, his determined expression reminds me of my own resolve. The warmth of his hand on my shoulder speaks to the unbreakable bond of family that will always give me strength, no matter how dark our fate seems.

I press my left palm to my hip a little above the location of the belt I've wrapped around my upper thigh. It's impossible to see beneath the flowing folds of the overly decorative dress Queen Karasi gave me to wear.

My hammer is strapped to my left thigh and my medallions are wrapped around my left calf.

The fae won't have realized that I'm carrying my tools. The contact with the metal may light up my eyes and hair, but my glow is easily overlooked under the bright lights in this place, especially since the Queen overloaded me with powders and serums to accentuate the contours of my cheekbones and the color of my pale-green eyes.

Thaden may well have sensed that I'm carrying my tools, but I'm certain he will now attribute it to my fear of Asha.

I only wish I could have brought Gallium's hammer, too. He doesn't exactly have a long gown to hide it under.

He gives me a crooked smile and doesn't try to conceal his speech. If Thaden's listening, I'm certain he'll interpret it as Gallium simply siding with me.

"Always remember," Gallium says. "I'll fight beside you."

I turn back to the door, waiting for it to reopen and for Thaden to reappear.

I make myself a promise: If he threatens Asha, we will kill him.

No matter the cost.

CHAPTER 2

Five tense minutes later, the door opens.

Thaden steps back into the room, pausing as the door closes behind him, an air of calm about him that I consider with misgiving.

Is he about to tell us we will go with Asha after all?

There's a part of me that desperately needs to stay with her. Facing Milena Ironmeld will be a dangerous task for her. But again, I remind myself Asha is strong; she is prepared for Milena's enmity, and the Vandawolf will fight at her side.

It's Thaden who could truly hurt her.

By keeping him away from her, I've removed the greatest threat to her.

"Thaden?" Gallium prompts. "Is Asha okay?"

Thaden's expression is troubled. "I sent Asha in Milena's direction, but I also promised Asha I would do what she asks," he says. "I'll take you to my old village in *Myrkur Fjall*, where you will be safe from the fight between fae and humans."

Myrkur Fjall is a human village that sits in the shadow of a mountain somewhere in the north. Supposedly. I only have Thaden's description of the village and its location, none of which might be true.

Still, I'm intensely relieved at the confirmation that Asha is safe from him for now. Even if I can't show it.

Then he continues. "But she agreed with me that I ought to find her as soon as I can. She needs me beside her in the fight against Milena."

His gaze is distant, and the tension around his mouth is growing. I wish I could read his thoughts and make sense of the web he's trying to weave right now.

My jaw clenches, but I try to hide my frustration.

I should have anticipated that he would try to join her again on his own—after all, *I* was the one who pushed her away, not him. What irks me the most is that he makes it sound as if *he* is all she needs.

If I weren't pretending to hate Asha right now, I would make it clear to Thaden that Asha needs *us* at her side. She needs her family.

Together, our power would be unbeatable.

Which... now that I think about it... Thaden might very well be aware of that.

It could suit him to leave us in some village and pursue Asha on his own...

I find his gaze on me and I'm worried I haven't controlled my expressions.

He shakes his head at me. "Why would you hurt her like that?"

The rebuke I was expecting. The response I prepared flows from my tongue. "Because she's dangerous," I say with all the conviction I can muster. "You may feel safe around her, but I don't. My power isn't like Gallium's and it's certainly not a match for Asha's power. I'm a healer. I can't fight. If the darkness overcomes her, she could kill me at a moment's whim."

Thaden's expression softens. "You're hurting, Tamra. You must feel like you lost your sister when you were finally reunited with her."

I let my eyes fill with tears because now I have an excuse to shed them without betraying my true emotions. "I hate what this power has done to her," I whisper, speaking the truth this time. "I hate all of it."

He nods earnestly. "Of course you do." His thumb brushes my cheeks, easing my tears away. "Nobody wants to feel powerless. But I promise you we will reach safety soon."

With that, he turns to Gallium. "We need to move quickly if I'm to have any chance of doubling back and catching up with Asha. The journey to my old village will take three days each way, so my chances are already slim. I don't have time to waste."

I don't want Thaden to reach Asha at all and I'm certain Gallium won't, either.

I consider coming up with an excuse to delay our departure, but the reality is that there are threats here, too.

Asha made a deal with Queen Karasi to secure our safety: Asha would hunt and kill Milena Ironmeld, and in exchange, the Queen's healers would save the Vandawolf's life. Asha also bargained for our safety. We are free to move around the fae castle and encampment and to leave whenever we want.

But the fae made it clear that Blacksmiths have been their enemies ever since Malak himself assassinated their former Queen.

Now that Asha is leaving, I don't doubt that Queen Karasi will have plans for us. For the last two days, she has been whispering poison in my ears about Asha—which Thaden is fully aware of, so at least he can assume my apparent hatred toward my sister was encouraged by the Fae Queen.

Gallium speaks up before I can interject. "The sooner we leave, the better," he says. "The fae play games with each other. We can't risk getting caught up in their trickery."

Just this evening, we witnessed the game they played with one of their own: a fae woman named Dusana attacked Asha out in the mountains. The attack happened after the Queen had given Asha amnesty. Instead of punishing Dusana when she returned to the castle, the Queen invited her to dinner, gave her a beautiful dress to wear, and had her beaten in this very dining room when Dusana didn't see it coming.

If it weren't for the fae who cleaned up, there would still be blood on the floor.

But, oh, how it must be stabbing Gallium's pride to continue subduing his strength. To play to Thaden's intentions and allow him to take the lead when Gallium's true power is...

Breathtaking.

Gallium hasn't shown Asha even a tenth of what he can do.

I sometimes wonder if he has even shown *me.*

"Thank you," Thaden says to Gallium, giving him a quick nod, and then he casts me a quick look. I read the assessment in his eyes. He's analyzing me so closely that I can hardly breathe.

"The sooner I leave my past behind, the better," I say, my shoulders slumping as if I were defeated.

Some of the sharpness in Thaden's expression fades. "Then we're agreed. Let's move."

Half an hour later, we've navigated the castle's vast corridors and managed to evade any inquisitive fae on the way back to our rooms.

Gallium and I have our own separate rooms side by side, but mine adjoins Thaden's with an interconnecting door between his room and mine.

The Queen, it seems, thought that Thaden and I might appreciate that. She seemed disappointed when it became clear that the door between our rooms remained closed at all times.

Thaden himself made a show of pulling a piece of furniture across the door on my side, blocking it from being opened from his side. It was right after the Queen had shown us to our rooms, and she'd watched him do it with pursed lips.

After which, he murmured to her, *"With respect, Queen Karasi, don't make assumptions."*

Only moments after that, a swarm of fae staff confiscated the packs we'd brought with us and all the supplies within them. They called it 'tidying up,' although it was clear that they didn't want us to have what we would need to easily leave this place and venture back out into the dangerous wilderness beyond these walls.

Gallium was not deterred.

He located the fae's armory and has been gradually raiding it —not for weapons, but for supplies.

While the Queen was obsessing over me, constantly dragging me to her side and seemingly determined to poison me against my sister, Gallium was able to slip away multiple times.

Twice, he was worried he might have been spotted by the Queen's Champion—the fae woman called *Elowynn of the Dawn*. But if she did see him taking supplies, she didn't try to stop him.

Gallium also managed to hide packs in the forest to the west of the castle. He left them where Asha and the Vandawolf could find them. I'm certain he gave the Vandawolf directions to the packs during dinner.

Now, I step quickly into my room and head straight for the bed, kneeling and reaching under the overly soft mattress for the objects hidden beneath it.

I pull out from under the mattress a pair of long pants, a long-sleeved tunic, and a pair of high boots that will be far more practical than the dresses and slippers Karasi gave me to wear.

The clothing is a mottled brown color. When Gallium first brought it back to our rooms to hide it, I was surprised to see the color and texture of the weave. The fae wear sleek armor that's form-fitting. They would never wear items as simple and drab as these.

At the time, Gallium was grim. "Taken from dead humans," he said. "The fae use this clothing when they send spies into human territory. I heard them talking about it."

As much as my own feelings toward humans are complex because of their hatred of me, I would die to protect the two humans who raised Gallium and me.

Kedric and Maybelle treated us like their own children. They put themselves in terrible danger when they took us in. They raised us with kindness and empathy and more love than I'd ever thought I could receive from people who were supposed to be our enemies.

Leaving them behind in the Cursed City was one of the hardest things I've had to do.

Slipping into the bathroom, I change quickly, unstrapping my hammer and medallions before I dress in the human clothing.

Then I head straight for the little table on the far side of the bed, farthest from either door.

While the fae may have confiscated our old belongings, what they wouldn't touch were our toolboxes.

They're clearly afraid of our tools, as they should be.

I now face the dilemma of deciding whether or not I should continue carrying my hammer close to my body.

At dinner, I needed to conceal it because otherwise, it would appear that I was threatening the fae. Much like attending a dinner with a dagger on my belt.

But now...

I quickly reconsider if I could continue concealing it so I could keep it close.

As far as Thaden knows, I wouldn't be able to do much with it. My Blacksmith power is unique. Unlike all other Blacksmiths, I can't transform metal. I can't create weapons or change a medallion's shape.

I can only use my power to heal others. By placing a medallion onto my right palm, I can create a conduit between my power and a person I need to heal. Or a plant I need to change.

Now, I consider if I can slip my hammer and medallions under my cloak...

But the way my hammer makes my skin luminous will be obvious out in the darkness of the mountains. A layer of material between the metal and my skin isn't enough to stop my skin, hair, and eyes from glowing with power.

We need to be stealthy. I can't be a beacon in the dark.

I return my hammer to my toolbox, promising myself I won't be powerless for long.

~

The cold night air hits my cheeks as I step from the stifling corridor and into the wilderness that lies outside the castle.

Gallium steps out ahead of me while Thaden is at my back.

The trees are sparse enough that I can see high into the vast night sky and out across the land. The castle has been hewn into the side of a mountain, and we now stand on a ridge to the side of it.

To our left is an enormous plain across which there are tiny dots of flames from a thousand campfires.

An army of fae warriors camps down there.

Immediately in front of us and to our right is a forest that must stretch across the mountain on either side of the castle.

In the west—the direction we're currently facing—the sky is lit up with lightning, but it isn't because of a storm.

The fae ride creatures called *thunderbirds,* whose wings can make a cracking sound like thunder and whose bodies light up with magic that appears like lightning in the sky. The thunderbirds can also dull their magic until they disappear into the night sky, becoming nearly imperceptible.

Their lightning now is a warning to the humans who live in the west to stay clear of the fae camp.

As I step out into the night, I'm unsettled by the fact that none of the fae intercepted us on our way out of the castle, let alone here at the exit. Granted, we were careful to creep through the maze of corridors and halls without drawing attention, but it felt too easy.

Gallium seems to think so, too, quietly voicing the same question that I have. "Where are the guards?"

Thaden shakes his head, the bronze scales that extend up the right side of his neck catching the moonlight. "I agree. That was too simple." Then he inhales audibly, his head tilted as he points. "Asha and the Vandawolf came this way. Maybe she threatened the guards to stay out of her way."

I don't question Thaden's ability to track my sister with his dragon's senses.

If I were to touch my tools, I could sense another Blacksmith—provided they're also using their tools.

But without our tools, we may as well be human. Unless I reach for my hammer, I won't know where Asha is.

I give a huff. The exhalation helps me calm myself while my instincts continue prickling. "Of course she would use threats to make her path easier."

Gallium presses his hand to my shoulder. "Well, if there's one good thing to come of it, *our* path should be easier." Then he turns to Thaden to ask, "Which way did they go?"

"West," Thaden says.

"Good. That's where I hid the packs," Gallium replies. "We should collect whatever packs they didn't take with them."

Thaden nods before he gestures in the other direction. "To get to *Myrkur Fjall*, we will need to head east—the opposite direction to Asha—and then south. But it shouldn't take us long to double back after we collect the packs."

He hurries in the direction Gallium pointed, and I follow closely, but my brow has creased. "I thought you said your village was in the north?"

"It was," he replies, throwing a soft smile back across his shoulder. "When we were in the south, it was north." He points past the encampment. "But from here, it's to the east and then south."

A worry settles at the base of my stomach, and it isn't because of Thaden Kane.

The land in the east is dangerous.

A shudder passes through me as I glance back in that direction.

Even from here, I can see the dark clouds that obscure the sky in the east. I can almost smell the scent of blood that I'm certain will fill the air there...

Thaden Kane promised to take us to safety, but I'm certain it will be a lie.

He will take us into danger.

CHAPTER 3

Within minutes, we locate the remaining satchels that Gallium hid in the forest.

He left four packs here, and only one is missing. Assuming Asha and the Vandawolf were the ones who took it, I'm concerned that they didn't take two, but I can only hope they had good reasons.

The satchels contain food, water flasks, some spare clothing, and fur pelts, which we'll need to stay warm. Gallium deposits his toolbox into the pack he chooses, and I do the same, aware of the glance he throws me since his hammer is in my box.

"We have a choice now," Thaden says, slipping the straps of one of the packs over his head and surprising me by not immediately commanding us to plow ahead. "We can evade the fae encampment by heading east, back along the mountain, and then turning south once we've cleared the location of their army. Or we can pass directly through the encampment—that is, go south first and then east along the mountain range there. That's the quicker but more dangerous route."

"More dangerous because of the fae?" I ask. "Because of passing through their encampment?"

"Yes," he replies. "And then there is the danger of the blight in the east."

"Which we'll encounter either way?" I ask. "Given that we have to travel east for either option."

He nods, continuing to study me with his bronzed eyes.

It suddenly feels as if he's testing me.

As if the option I support will tell him something... *But what?*

"You would prefer the more dangerous option?" Gallium asks him.

"I think we can handle the danger," Thaden replies swiftly. "I don't like the delay in reaching Asha."

I turn to face the south, even though I can no longer see the fae encampment from this location.

Thaden seems confident they won't pose a threat to us and if I don't support him, I'm worried it will be obvious I don't want him to reach Asha to "help" her.

On the other hand, I've already shown him that I no longer care about her safety.

Or... if he thinks I'm acting out of hurt because I believe what I said about the darkness of her power... Is he trying to *make* me care about her?

My forehead creases as I peer back at him, aware that he has the ability to hear how fast or slow my heart beats.

It's just as well that I learned to live a life of subterfuge. Humans taught me to hide my emotions, to blend in and disappear. For many years, Gallium and I even dyed our silver hair to brown, so we didn't stand out. We both learned the value of being invisible and compartmentalizing our emotions to control our responses.

Where he stands, now behind Thaden, Gallium gives me a shake of his head, his green eyes conveying his worry. "It's a choice between our safety or Asha's." He arches his brows at me. "I know which choice she'd make for us."

"The safer path," I murmur.

But which would *I* choose if I were really angry with her?

I tip my chin. "Then we take the so-called dangerous path. We go through the fae encampment."

Thaden's eyebrows rise. He looks genuinely surprised. "You would choose that path just to spite your sister?"

"No." I turn the corners of my mouth down. "Because it's the smarter path. I've spent the last two days in Queen Karasi's pocket. She has showered me with gifts and treated me like some sort of pet. I don't fear passing across land controlled by her army. And as for the rest of the journey, we don't know what else lurks in these mountains. The wasteland around the Cursed City taught me that the environment is constantly changing. The longer we're out in the open, the more dangerous it will be. So, to my estimation, going south first is safer."

If the blight that exists in the east is anything like the Sunken Bog outside the Cursed City, then it's far more dangerous than any fae.

By the way Queen Karasi described the blight that had taken over her lands, it's far worse than the Bog. She showed the first signs of real emotion, true horror, when she spoke of it.

The longer we take traveling through it, the more dangerous it will be. Thaden is stronger than I am—and Gallium is stronger as well. I need to be smart in my decisions.

I can't help Asha if I'm dead.

I tip my head at Thaden. "Why are we still standing here? I thought you wanted to move fast."

His forehead creases as he peers at me for another moment. There's a question in his voice. "I was certain you'd rather leave your sister to her fate."

I press my lips together again. "Just because the best option for her is also the best option for me doesn't mean I'm choosing it for her."

He tilts his head, an acknowledging gesture. "Okay, then."

Gallium points in the direction of the encampment. "Let's at least pass on the eastern side of the camp. Going through the center would be foolhardy. I scoped out pathways leading from the castle yesterday. There's a narrow pass farther along this way that circles behind the castle and then leads back down the mountain. It's winding and dark, and I don't think the fae use it, but by my calculations, it should let out on the eastern side of the fae camp."

Gallium's eyes meet mine as he passes me, already headed in that direction.

His fleeting smile tells me he trusts me.

My heartbeat calms again.

My brother has always been a source of strength for me. His unbending belief in my strength and intelligence has kept me alive even at times when I struggled to believe we could survive.

Not for the first time, I remember the way he looked up at Asha when we huddled behind Malak's throne, waiting for the Vandawolf to come and end us.

I'll fight beside you.

Gallium has lived his life to that creed.

I hoist my chosen pack over my shoulder and follow closely behind him, conscious of Thaden's presence at my back.

The path through the forest behind the castle grows darker where the trees thicken and then even darker still when we reach the opening to a gently sloping corridor down the side of the mountain.

"This is it," Gallium says, his voice hushed. "The way the dirt along the bottom is undisturbed tells me the fae don't use this path. Probably because they don't need to. They can ride their thunderbirds down to the plain."

"Are you certain it lets out below and doesn't come to a dead end somewhere?" I ask.

He shakes his head. "Not completely. But when I scouted for ways out of here, I didn't see any other safe paths down this mountain."

"How nice to have a thunderbird," I murmur, knowing that we will need to keep an eye on both our path and the sky above us, since the birds can camouflage themselves against the night sky when they want to.

Thaden steps into the pass, studying the rock walls that curve up and over it. "I'm willing to take the chance. These walls are solid. They won't collapse on us."

Gallium and I follow, descending into the corridor. The farther we go, the higher the rock curves up and over us on both sides until only a slip of sky is visible above us.

The farther down we go, the darker it gets until Gallium dislodges stones with every step and whispers to me to watch where I walk.

It gives me an idea, an opening I can't pass up.

A moment after Gallium's warning, I allow myself to trip and stumble, making a lot of noise about it before I veer sharply to the side of the rocky corridor and press against it, my breathing unsteady.

Thaden is immediately at my side, and in the darkness of this cave-like corridor, the scent of dragon fire that radiates from his body is overwhelming. "Tamra?"

"It's too dark," I say, squinting at him in the gloom. "I don't have your eyes."

I'm too fucking helpless.

Or that's what I want him to believe.

"You should get out your hammers," he replies, faster than I thought he would. "Accessing your power will sharpen your eyesight, won't it?"

As he speaks, I make out the turn of his head, but I can't see exactly where he's looking, only that his dragon scales seem to be catching the light right now, and his focus isn't entirely on me.

"Good idea," I whisper. "I don't want to trip and break my neck. Gallium, do you agree?"

I wait for my brother to reply, his outline approaching me in the dark. He'd made it a few extra steps ahead of me when I tripped.

"Agreed," he says. "We should carry our hammers into the fae encampment, too. Concealed under our clothing, of course. We don't want it to look as if we're about to attack them."

I slide carefully to the ground, reaching for his arm before I drop my pack onto the ground between us and huddle over it. He places his pack beside mine, also huddling over, our heads nearly side by side as we retrieve our tools.

For the last ten years, we got very good at hiding the fact that we had access to our parents' hammers and medallions. When I first picked up my mother's hammer, I was terrified that her cruelty would have been imbued into the metal like Malak's had been imbued into his hammer and medallions.

But the metal obeyed me, almost as if it had been *relieved.*

Its reaction to my touch made me wonder if the hammer might have originally belonged to my grandmother, since she'd fought against Malak when he'd first risen to power. From the little our mother had mentioned of her, I knew enough to recognize that she had been an incredibly powerful Blacksmith. It was only because our mother had betrayed her that she had been defeated and killed.

Within moments, Gallium's copper hammer is in his right hand while my silver hammer is in mine. The copper hammer was our father's and Gallium has struggled with it. Our father's House was Copperstream, and the Blacksmiths of that House did not share the kind of compassion and hope that our grandmother had.

My eyesight immediately sharpens, and I'm aware of the luminous glow emanating from our skin. Gallium's eyes are now alternating between shades of blue and green and even purple. The same way my own eyes must be shining with power.

Gallium and I both inherited our mother's silver hair and took the name of her House, as was our peoples' custom. Although we inherited our father's pale-green eyes, the way our eye color changes when we have access to our power seems to be unique to us—and Asha. Her eyes do the same.

An impossible calm fills me. A control that I was barely clinging to before now comes easily.

I reach for my medallions next. Each toolbox contains three of them. They're strips of metal about an inch wide and five inches long.

They can be transformed instantly into weapons. Our parents wore their medallions on their biceps or forearms or even as jewelry. But always, the medallions were in contact with their skin. Once we put the medallions away from our bodies, they become dormant.

To wake them, we must tap them with our hammers.

I do that softly now, listening to the gorgeous chime each one makes as it wakes up. Followed by the melody of Gallium's medallions also waking up.

He positions his medallions onto his left forearm, one above the other, before rolling his sleeve back down.

I do the same.

Then we slip our hammers into the inner pockets of our fur coats. They're a little lumpy, but it will have to do.

Of course, now we will both have to work hard to constrain and conceal the mental and physical strength that our tools give us.

My eyesight is enhanced, and so is my hearing. Along with the whisper of the breeze in the distance, I'm finally able to make out the sides of the corridor we're passing through.

Now I can see what Thaden was looking at.

This is no ordinary path.

CHAPTER 4

Runes are carved in the walls in a snaking line all the way along the corridor as far as I can see.

My voice is breathless. "What is this place?"

Even Gallium looks surprised, but then, the runes weren't visible from the entrance, and I'm not sure exactly when the carvings started.

"These are Einherjar runes," Thaden says, moving closer to my side and reaching past my shoulder to point to the particularly ornate carvings on the wall directly beside me.

The scent of his fiery skin fills my chest, seeming stronger than before as he brushes his fingertips across the runes.

"Einherjar?" I ask carefully, glancing at Gallium, but he shakes his head. He hasn't heard that word before, either.

"They are a brutal people who now live in the far north," Thaden says softly. "They believe in the gods—in titans and Valkyries and jotnar."

"Jotnar?" I ask.

"Plural for the jotunn." Thaden gives me a smile that speaks to danger. "Giants of ice and fire and rock."

He releases me from his gaze to press his palm fully against the next rune before running his fingertips lightly across the ones beside it. "The Vandawolf was born into an Einherjar clan."

My eyes fly wide. "What?"

Thaden glances at me, nodding before returning his attention to the wall. "When Milena was torturing me, she told me what she knew of him. She met his father—and him—when he was a small child. He had a younger brother. They lived high in the mountains to the west of the Cursed City, hidden from the Blacksmiths and other humans. Somehow, Malak must have found out about them. She didn't know how."

Thaden's hand flexes against the wall before he takes a sharp breath and steps back, swiftly changing the subject. "According to the story inscribed on this wall, this corridor belonged to a god: the World Serpent." He trails his hand along the runes, seeming to read as he goes. "The World Serpent unfolded from around the world, descended from what was called *the Earth Sea*—that's the sky—and chose this place to hibernate and transform. When it awoke, it emerged from this cocoon in the form of a human male whose power was inked into his body in the shapes of black serpents."

Thaden reaches the end of that line of runes and then turns to arch an eyebrow at me. "If you can believe it."

I purse my lips. "You can read their runes."

Thaden nods. "My village is populated with those who have escaped other places and wish for a new life. I've learned from them—everything they were willing to teach me."

I consider the circular shape of the corridor and the way it gently curves back and forth. It certainly makes me imagine an enormous serpent hibernating within it. And then slithering out again, changing as it goes, leaving the corridor behind it like a shed skin...

I shake myself, focusing on Thaden's eyes.

His smile softens, and he continues before I can reply. "You can see better now. I can tell because you're looking at me." His eyes narrow just the slightest. "For the first time in hours, actually."

Looking at him is a dangerous thing.

Too easy to get drawn in by his strength and power.

Too easy to be beguiled.

Too easy for me to believe his openness and doubt that he's my enemy...

He inclines his head toward the corridor. "Let's go."

He turns away, breaking our gaze, and I draw a shaky breath.

Gallium draws level with me and I make myself focus on the power around him. Calm and steadfast. Honest and true.

I tell myself I know what I'm doing.

I know the path I have to take.

Soon enough, the downward slope through the corridor eases and the tunnel lets out onto level ground.

Cold wind buffets my hair, bringing with it the scent of campfires and ash before settling down again.

The corridor hasn't let out far enough east that we can avoid cutting across at least some part of the encampment, which extends from this side of the valley all the way to the base of the mountains on the other side.

Countless white tents have been assembled across the plains, and even though it's past the middle of the night, there is a hum of activity.

Guards are positioned at intervals all around the space, and I'm grateful for my enhanced eyesight.

No matter their Queen's orders, all of them are our enemies.

While Thaden takes the lead again, proceeding more cautiously than I thought he might, Gallium continues to walk at my side.

I don't miss the way he has positioned himself so that he is between me and the nearest fae guards.

He is now gripping his hammer in such a way that his closed fist rests around its head while the handle is tucked up under his sleeve.

His hand is so big that the hammer isn't visible.

My hand is smaller, so I can't conceal my hammer that way. But then, I'm short and petite, so I expect that the fae won't see me as much of a threat, anyway.

And it's true that I won't be.

I may be nimble and know how to evade a punch, but judging by what I saw of the fae's combat training over the last few days, any one of them could knock me flat in seconds, hammer or not.

The four guards nearest to us are certainly wide awake, their sharp eyes following our every step. I'm not surprised that all four guards are female. Only women are allowed in their army.

They're all wearing raven-black armor that blends seamlessly with the tops of their boots so that it appears as if they are wearing a single suit from their toes up to their necks.

Every fae warrior carries weapons that conform completely to their armor. They call them *liquid blades*, and we won't know exactly what kinds of weapons they are—swords, daggers, or something else—until the women pull the blades from their armor.

The style of their hair is also uniform, each one wearing their hair in a single, tight braid, but that's where the similarities end.

The fae have skin in varying shades, ranging from dark brown to fair, and hair colors in pinks, purples, and blues that remind me of flowers.

As we approach, their reaction to us is anything but subtle.

Within moments, the woman standing farthest ahead of us steps directly into Thaden's path, and the other three circle around to flank us on each side, forcing us to draw to a stop.

"We know who you are," the first woman says to Thaden. Her skin is light brown and her hair is pale blue. "You aren't welcome here."

"Then you'll be happy to know we're leaving," Thaden replies.

The guard narrows her blue eyes at Gallium and me. "The only thing that would make me happy would be to see those two Blacksmiths dead." Her sharp gaze returns quickly to Thaden. "And you, a human beast. I would see you in chains."

My heart sinks as she raises her hand to her shoulder, reaching for her weapon.

Thaden tenses.

I can't see his expression because he's facing away from me, but the Blacksmith magic within him is flaring like a flame around his silhouette.

I sense his inhaled breath and anticipate his anger.

The situation is quickly deteriorating, and I can't let a fight break out.

CHAPTER 5

I speak before Thaden can respond, raising my voice at the guard. "You haven't told us your names."

The first woman barely spares me a glance, but I don't let that deter me.

"There's one name I know very well," I say quickly, and then I enunciate carefully, "Dusana of the Dusk. Have you heard of her?"

The fae standing on either side of me stiffen. So, I sense, does the woman standing behind me.

"Please tell me your names," I say, more loudly, "so that I may repeat them to your Queen."

The guards glance at each other. The first woman has stiffened, her jaw clenching.

"Or perhaps you would rather let us pass," I say.

With a huff, the first woman flicks her hand, at which the others step back from us.

Ahead of me, Thaden doesn't waste a beat, striding past the first woman and paying her no further attention.

Gallium and I keep pace with him, but I'm very conscious of the hate-filled glares the women cast at me as we pass.

The first woman spits in the dirt when I reach her.

I don't rise to the insult, but it draws my attention downward, and I notice for the first time how bare the ground is. There's very little vegetation here. From above, the encampment appeared almost sparkling. But now that we're down here...

In the distance, a child cries.

I'm suddenly conscious of the hacking cough coming from another tent. Then, the quiet weeping from the tent beside that.

The flap of that tent is partially open, and I catch a glimpse inside, where a fae woman with golden hair leans over a child who is lying on a stretcher. A male fae kneels on the other side of the stretcher, his hand covering the child's. Tears glisten on their cheeks.

My heart wrenches to see them.

Clearly, the child is gravely ill, cheeks and lips tinged with gray.

From behind me a voice calls, and I glance back to see that it's the same blue-haired fae who stepped into Thaden's path.

"This is what Blacksmiths have done," she says, her brow furrowed and jaw tight. "Are you pleased with yourselves, Blacksmiths? Are you happy with the suffering you've inflicted on our children?"

One of the other guards—a woman with golden eyes—quickly takes hold of the blue-haired woman's arm and pulls her away, shushing her.

My heart sinks even further.

A glance at Gallium's pale face tells me he feels their pain as intensely as I do.

"Our people have a lot to answer for," he growls beneath his breath, a hint of anger in his voice. It's so unlike him to feel rage, but it's justified.

"Not us, Gallium," I whisper. "We didn't do this. We weren't even born when Malak and his followers turned the earth into a wasteland. We were children. Powerless children."

Despite my assertion, my legs feel heavy, as if my heart has descended so far to the ground that it's nearly impossible to keep moving.

"Could your power help them?" Gallium's focus falls to my arm, where I have concealed my medallions. There's a spark of hope in his eyes. "Could you try healing them? Do some good—"

"*Do not try.*" Thaden's voice is shockingly cold, his presence at my side, sudden.

My focus snaps up to him and my eyes widen. I struggle with my own anger now. My disbelief at his command. "How could you tell me not to try?"

His shoulders slump and his voice softens. "Because your power will only make their illness worse."

"How?" I ask, struggling to understand.

His broad shoulders sink even further and his expression is now bleak. "It is because of magic that the blight spreads. You will understand once we get closer to it."

He turns away from me, his back stiff, his gaze turned toward the mountains that sit in the distance. "You will see soon enough."

I don't want to believe him.

I want to help the fae. To prove to them that Gallium and I are nothing like Malak and his followers. But there's something about Thaden's posture...

Just as I have learned how to recognize the smallest changes in his behavior, the tension around his eyes and mouth, the quickly hidden clenches of his jaw, and the tightness in his voice that tells me when he's lying, I can also discern when he's telling the truth.

"There must be something we can do," I say. "If not now, then we need to find a way."

Thaden gives me a nod. "For all supernaturals. Not only the fae."

Without another word, he continues ahead.

Once more, Gallium and I follow, as we will continue to do for now.

We walk to the sounds of misery. Tents filled with illness and sorrow. Softly crying fae. Coughing children.

By the time we reach the other side of the encampment, my eyes are downcast.

I glance back once more at the tents.

Queen Karasi spoke proudly of an army and I saw for myself the warriors training within the castle walls. I saw the women flying their thunderbirds and spent the last few days surrounded by the Queen's favored fae—all of them healthy and physically strong.

But now I wonder at the true extent of her army and if it's mostly a bluff?

Thunderbirds positioned strategically in the sky in a way that makes it look like there are many of them...

Fires are kept burning in the encampment to appear as if a thousand warriors are ready and waiting to strike...

Even the mountaintop castle that makes Karasi's position appear lofty and dominant...

All of it is designed to give the appearance of strength when the reality is that her people are suffering.

My focus rises to the castle we left behind, the eastern side of it now lit with the first rays of dawn.

How the Queen's desperation must be growing. Assuming she actually cares beneath her self-centered façade.

A feeling of dread settles at the base of my stomach.

Desperation can drive even good people to do terrible things, and a monarch like Karasi is already primed for cruelty.

It takes us an entire day to climb the top of the mountain at the edge of the valley.

A sparse forest sits across it, made up of scraggly trees with leaves that appear brittle in the fading light.

The wind whistles past them, making their boughs creak and groan, and I find myself shivering, not from cold, but because the air is weirdly heavy up here.

We traveled at an angle, heading upward but easterly, and as we pick our path through the fallen vegetation—old branches and crackling twigs—my skin prickles.

From up here, I can see that this mountain range sits farther north of the mountains that circle the Cursed City. I can nearly imagine it in the distance, but I can't be completely certain how far away it is.

Thaden is relentless, pushing onward even as night falls.

He glances back regularly to check that I haven't fallen behind.

I don't complain. Or try to slow us down. Although that strategy does occur to me.

The farther we go, the more I find myself studying him.

The air around him is changing.

Maybe it's the way he carries himself, more upright. Maybe it's the expression on his face when he looks back—the little tension lines around his eyes and mouth that have eased somehow.

The way his breathing sounds different... Deeper, maybe.

There's a scent in the air.

Of copper and... something else...

Something not quite right.

I can't quite put my finger on it, but I know that Gallium is aware of it, too, because every now and then, his hand brushes my arm. His focus will glide from Thaden's back to a point in the environment around us, as if he wants me to take note of it.

A tree with oddly black bark extending up one side of its trunk.

A fallen branch with trails of a dark, goopy substance crisscrossing all over it.

The faint rustle of leaves when the trees appear to shiver as we pass them by, except that it isn't caused by the wind because it happens when the breeze *dies down*.

Finally, when the moon sits high in the sky, Thaden draws to a halt. He studies our surroundings, his head held high as he draws an audibly deep breath and then nods to himself.

"It's safe enough to stop here, but not for long," he says. "We'll need to take turns keeping watch."

"What makes it safe here and not elsewhere?" I ask, keeping my voice to a low murmur.

He gives me a grim smile. "The creatures in this forest wake up at night. I think you noticed the black bark and the trails of slime?"

The fact that he was aware of us doing so concerns me a little.

Nothing seems to escape his notice.

"The beasts of this forest sleep within the trees during the day," he continues. "They wake up at night. But there aren't any nesting in this location."

I take note of the tree trunks and undergrowth, all of it brittle and brown. No black trails in sight.

"We should sleep while we can," Gallium says. "I'll take the first watch."

I'm so tired I can barely nod.

It's only because of my power that I've kept going, and I'm certain Gallium is the same. We haven't slept for the last thirty-six hours and we can't ignore our sleep deprivation much longer.

Thaden, too, wears dark circles under his eyes, but he shakes his head at Gallium's suggestion. "I can draw on the dragon's energy to stay awake longer," he says, dropping his pack at the base of the nearest tree. "I'll wake you in three hours to take over the next watch."

Allowing Thaden Kane to guard us while we sleep isn't a good option.

I was already sliding my pack from my back and now I grip the handle, desperately trying to think of an excuse to stay awake, too.

A brief glance at Gallium and the close-lipped smile he wears tells me it's no use.

"Thank you," I say to Thaden. "Both of you. Wake me if you need me."

Within minutes, I've settled against the tree nearest to Gallium, eaten a little of the food in my pack, wrapped my fur around me, and tucked my hammer firmly against my side.

My eyes close.

What feels like seconds later, I wake to a light touch on my cheek.

My eyes fly open, but I relax to see Gallium crouching beside me.

"It's morning," he says.

My brow creases as I take in our gloomy surroundings. "But it's still dark."

He gives me a firm nod. "Yes."

As he rises to his feet, moving back through the undergrowth, I untangle myself from my fur, my hammer firmly gripped in my hand.

Around me, the trees are shrouded in shadows. Not a glimmer of sunlight makes it to the ground, even though the canopy of branches is sparse.

Black clouds boil above us.

The air smells like copper, filled with the heavy scent of blood.

I gasp. "If it's morning, where is the sun?"

On the other side of the clearing, Thaden Kane stands with his head tilted to the sky.

"The blight is surging," he says, his voice sharp.

He turns to me, his gaze piercing and the tension around his eyes growing. "Your presence is drawing the darkness to us."

CHAPTER 6

My presence?

For a moment, I think Thaden means both Gallium and me, but his focus is so finely pinpointed on me that I'm not sure...

I take a deep breath, only to inhale the heavy scent of copper again. *Blood.* It coats my tongue and makes breathing difficult.

Every instinct in my body is telling me to move, to get away from the copper scent in the air as fast as we can.

"We need to move faster." Thaden bursts into action, striding toward me, pulling the fur from my stiff shoulders and rolling it up. "There's a rocky path along the mountain ridge up ahead. We can follow it."

I don't hesitate, reaching for my pack and slinging it across my back, already moving in the direction Thaden pointed.

An hour later, we step out from the forest and onto a ragged mountain's edge—a barren ridge that extends for hundreds of paces to my left and right and stretches far into the east.

The sight in the distance snatches the breath from my chest. "Damn."

Crimson clouds boil in the distance, turning the landscape

beneath them to red. A wasteland of ash spread far, far into the east, as if crimson snow has fallen.

Dust storms swirl across the plain, the ash lifting and whipping across the flat land, all the way up the visible sides of mountains in the east.

Despite my need to hurry, I've missed a step.

Thaden slows a little, allowing me to catch up while Gallium follows close behind me.

Thaden points. "There used to be a fae city at the edge of the plain over there."

I follow the direction indicated by his hand, making out the silhouettes of what could be crumbling stone structures in the distance.

"Then the blight took over," he says. "Their animals died and their children got sick. If you look carefully, you can see a lake."

I peer into the distance, locating the shiny, oval surface on the eastern side of the rubble. "I see it."

"The water became poisonous," Thaden says, shadows growing in his eyes. "Much like the lake near the Cursed City."

"The Toxic Thirst," I murmur. "Ingesting its water kills you."

He nods. "The exodus of fae from the east began soon after that. Queen Karasi won't admit it because she wants to cultivate the belief that there are many more fae ready to be called from the east, but what you saw back on the plain—that's the entire fae population." He gestures into the dark distance. "There are no living fae in the east now. Only bodies that continue to feed the blight."

"What do you mean, *feed*?" I ask.

It's always been a mystery to me how the blight spreads. Even more so, the way the wasteland outside the Cursed City would give rise to monsters that would attack the city—monsters that Asha was sent out to kill.

I know that Blacksmith magic, and all the experiments Malak and others conducted, led to this, but I don't know *how*.

Of course, everything Thaden tells me could be a lie, so I

watch him carefully as he answers, trying to separate fact from fiction based on his facial expressions and body language.

"I, too, wanted answers," he says.

Truth.

"When I had the chance to gain information from Milena after she captured me, she said that the rot started with the murder of other Blacksmiths thirty years ago."

Truth. Maybe. But also... *not* truth.

I fight my frustration at how smoothly he speaks and how faultless his features remain. I can't be certain how to unpick what he's telling me into its truthful and untruthful pieces.

All I can do is listen.

"Apparently, when Malak slaughtered the Blacksmiths who opposed him at the beginning of his reign, he disposed of their bodies by burying them deep within the earth that is now the wasteland on the northern side of the Cursed City."

The environment around the city was treacherous for as long as I knew it. On the northern side is an expansive wasteland of white ash that stretches all the way to the first ring of mountains. On the eastern side is a dangerous marsh the humans call the *Sunken Bog*, filled with malformed trees, deadly snakes, and mud that's constantly sinking in on itself.

The western and southern sides remained somewhat untainted—that's where the humans grow their crops—but only because they built stone walls around those areas to keep the rot out.

Beyond those walls, the mountains grew wild.

"Milena thought that the creation magic had leached from the dead Blacksmiths' bodies into the soil and started an unstoppable chain of events," Thaden says.

My forehead creases as I maintain a quick pace to keep up with Thaden. "But Blacksmiths have died and been buried before, haven't they? Why would this cause a problem?"

Thaden shakes his head, his eyes gleaming at me. "Burial is a human tradition. I imagine it's all you knew since you grew up surrounded by humans. But, no. Blacksmith bodies must be burned."

My lips part with surprise. "What?"

He gives me a cold smile and a firm nod. "Any flame will do, but a pyre built of crimson coal is most effective."

Crimson coal is the special coal that was mined in the eastern mountains and used in Blacksmith forges. It's the same scorching substance that the Vandawolf gripped in his hand on the day I first saw him at the Academy.

After the Vandawolf took control of the city, he forbade any person to be in possession of crimson coal. He also destroyed all hammers and medallions—except ours—although I never saw the destruction happen, and I still don't know how he did it.

"When Malak chose to bury his enemies, it would have been an overt act of disrespect," Thaden says. "Akin to leaving the bodies out to rot. And *rot* is what they caused."

"I didn't know that," I whisper before turning to Gallium, who is a step behind me.

I meet his grim eyes. We were young when our people died. I don't recall my parents ever mentioning this custom—or witnessing it.

Of course, it's possible that Asha knows about it. Maybe she went to a mourning ceremony when she was younger. Maybe she heard or read something. There were books in the library, but after the Vandawolf rose to power, we were not allowed to access them. We also couldn't ask Asha because we had no contact with her.

Or maybe it isn't true at all. Thaden could be lying about all of it.

"Over the course of thirty years after that," Thaden continues, "the Blacksmiths used that same burial ground to try to expand their power. They experimented on living things—animals and plants. They started drawing on dark magic, which drains life, and that, too, soaked into the soil. With every failed experiment and every dead thing they discarded into that same ground, the layers of creation magic and dark magic grew. It created a never-ending circle of dark life and dark death."

Thaden falls silent, his boots crunching on the brittle ground, snapping twigs and what looks like burned moss.

I don't have time to study the debris carefully, but the rocky surface appears blackened, and when I take a moment to peer closer...

I don't think it's moss, after all.

Is it ash?

Little flecks of it are caught between the uneven, rocky formations and protected from the wind so they don't blow away...

The farther east we travel along this mountain ridge, the more barren the ground has become. But only immediately around us along the long stretch of the wide path we're walking. In contrast, on each side of the ridge, right at the edge, there are trees. Black, misshapen ones, creaking and groaning in the wind.

I've fallen back a step, drawing level with Gallium, and I nearly miss what Thaden says next. "There's a very good reason why Blacksmiths can't access their magic without their tools."

"Why?" I ask.

"Because creation magic must be constrained. It *must* be limited." Thaden draws to a sudden stop and points. "This is what happens when it isn't."

I follow the direction of Thaden's upheld arm through the gap in the burned trees.

Out in the far valley, dust storms rage, just like the ones I saw yesterday.

From a distance, they looked small.

Now, I can see that they're *enormous*.

Tornados of alternating white and crimson ash crash across the valley and up the side of the far mountain. I'm alarmed to see that they always head southwest. If I had to guess, the Cursed City is in that direction.

Each tornado smashes into the side of the mountain, falling away and shattering into dust again right as it reaches the top of the peak.

But that's far from the worst of it.

Dark forms clash in the middle of the plain. Crimson ash streams across them, the flow so thick that I can't make out more than their huge silhouettes. Maybe they have horns. Maybe they have giant paws and shining, metallic bodies. Maybe they have enormous mouths full of teeth.

They're fighting each other, slashing and clawing, on and on. When one of them crumbles, a river of ash streams across its body, and within moments, another rises to join the fight.

My heart is in my throat; my blood, pounding in my ears.

I press my hand to my chest, trying to calm myself.

Beside me, Gallium has frozen, but I don't miss the way his hand has tightened around his hammer.

Thaden's voice sounds close to my left shoulder, a soft growl in my ear. "Do you see that mountain ridge? The one the dust storms can't seem to pass?"

My throat is constricted and all I can manage is, "Yes."

"The fire dragon Graviter Rex burned that ridge," he says. "Just as he burned this one."

Thaden points to the path we've been walking along.

"By burning all living matter along both ridges, he stopped the blight from spreading in either of these directions."

"It spreads through living things?"

"No." Thaden's voice is harsh. "It spreads through *dead* things. That's the problem. Anything dead that was once living has the potential to feed the rot."

I sense the blood draining from my face. "A living tree drops leaves that then decompose."

"Exactly. Even a leaf that may still appear green is already dying." He nods, his face stony. "But it's dead, magical beings that really feed the darkness and help it spread."

I exhale slowly, trying to stop the sinking of my stomach. "Fae magic is connected to nature."

Thaden nods. "They draw on their environment when they use their magic. They literally drew the blight into their bodies.

And when they died, their magic fed the darkness like no other supernatural's body could.

"Layer upon layer of magic has built up where the fae cities used to exist—creation magic, dark magic, elemental magic. Humans, on the other hand, have very little magic in their bodies, which is why the blight has not raged out of control in the south or west. But here..."

His eyes are shadowed and dark. "The fae were doomed as soon as the darkness entered the soil, water, and even the dust in the air. Now their land is pure chaos. Magic is building on itself without an end."

I'm tense with a new worry as I turn to Gallium, my fears forming words that tumble from my mouth. "Ten years ago, when the Vandawolf killed over a hundred Blacksmiths, did he bury the bodies? He hated our people, but he would never stoop to disrespecting the dead. He would have considered burial *respectful*. Do you know where he—"

Gallium reaches for me, gripping my shoulder with his free hand. "He burned them, Tamra."

I take a shaky breath. "Are you sure?"

Gallium nods. "I heard Maybelle and Kedric talking about it. He made the humans build pyres. It took them two days. Many of the men were angry about it. They wanted to rebuild their homes. Braddock was the most vocal."

I shudder at the memory of the human named Braddock, who had called for our deaths on the night our people died.

"They were even angrier when the Vandawolf collected up all of the crimson coal and used it to burn the bodies. It's how he destroyed all of the tools..."

Gallium's gaze is suddenly far away, and I study him closely. "Brother?"

"I snuck out in the night," he says quietly. "After I heard Maybelle and Kedric talking. You were asleep. When I got out there, the pyres were already lit. The humans were staying away. The Vandawolf was in the middle of the field, standing in front of a bowl of blazing crimson coal and he was burning tools. One by one. Putting them into the fire. Making sure they burned to ash." Gallium focuses on me again. "I'll never forget the look on his face."

"Anger?" I ask softly.

He shakes his head. "Grief."

I'm quiet as Gallium turns back to the dark plain in the east, clears his throat, and says, "The Vandawolf had no part in this."

My worries now grow for another reason. I gesture to the dark environment in the east. "Thaden, if your village is close to the heart of the damaged land, how is it safe from this?"

His expression softens a little. "It's sheltered by barren rocks that curve around it in a near-complete circle. It sits, quite literally, in the shadow of the mountain and also, remarkably, protected by it."

"But..." I reach out to him, my fingertips hovering above his scaled arm. "You said that our Blacksmith magic was drawing the darkness."

I'm suddenly overly conscious of where I'm standing and the fact that I'm wearing my medallions and accessing my power.

"Blacksmith magic is drawn to itself," he says, his voice hollow. "You are not dead, and yet the darkness is drawn to you because of its origins."

A sudden chill passes down my spine.

That scent in the air that I inhaled when we first headed east... A whisper in the breeze like dark voices calling...

My fear grows as I whisper, "It *wants* us dead."

CHAPTER 7

Gallium's hand on my shoulder anchors me, and I let out my held breath, but I have to speak my fears. "Thaden, we could draw the blight to your village."

Thaden's jaw clenches. His focus is on my hand, where my fingertips hover above his arm.

I've never touched him.

Oh, he's touched me. A hand on my shoulder, a brush of his non-scaled arm against mine. But I've never reached out to him before. And never when I was accessing my power.

The *pull* is strong.

Blacksmith magic attracts itself.

"We shouldn't go to your village," I say, plowing on. "I shouldn't go there. Gallium shouldn't go there. And now that you're changed, neither should you. We all carry Blacksmith magic that could endanger your people."

His jaw clenches again. "It's a risk I have to take."

"Why, Thaden?" I ask quietly, needing an answer even as my hand continues to hover above his scaled arm, and he doesn't try to move away. "Because you promised Asha? Surely, there are alternative places you could take us?"

Now, he steps back from me, his focus rising once more to my face, but his jaw is no less tight. "There are other reasons. You will see."

He turns away from me, as if it's settled.

"But, the risk—"

"You will see!" he snaps back at me, a deep growl in his voice.

For an instant, the cloak he wears over his emotions disappears. It's fleeting. But I see it, the face he hides.

The face he has masked with bronzed hair, scales that glitter, and a presence that radiates with the strength of a dragon.

There's a look in his eyes.

It's the same wild, intensely angry look Malak Ironmeld gave me when he strapped me to his anvil—

I refuse to revisit those memories, that trauma. I shut it away as I have so many times before, but I can't stop my shudder.

Thaden doesn't see me shiver. He has already turned away and is now surging ahead along the burned-out path, determination in his every quick step.

For the first time, I wonder...

If getting back to Asha isn't the only reason he's so anxious to reach his village, then what else is he hiding?

Gallium's hand tightens on my shoulder, and when I look at him, he gives me a determined look.

No matter what lies ahead of us, we will protect each other.

By the time we stop to rest and eat, breathing has become difficult.

The heavy scent in the air is overpowering, a combination of burned ash and fresh blood. The sky has remained dark, so it's impossible to know if it's daytime or the middle of the night.

All I know is that I'm exhausted.

Even Thaden seems to be struggling with his breathing, using gestures instead of words to indicate where we should lay our furs.

"Safe here," he rasps, minimizing his speech while he indicates the bare stretch of blackened rock, not a hint of a dead leaf or branch in sight. "Should reach village tomorrow."

I want to ask him if he anticipates we'll get there in the morning or later, but my mouth is too dry to speak. Sipping water does nothing to help, and worse, our water supplies are running low.

My power is keeping me going.

But it's also a danger.

Within the breeze is the same *pull* I experienced when I reached out to Thaden.

I drop to my unrolled fur and extend my right hand into the wind. The air changes direction, swirling around my fingers, circling faster like its own little storm—

I snap my fist closed and lower my arm.

Gallium gives me a grimace. The wind plucks at his hand where he grips his hammer and at his arm where the medallions are nestled. He folds his arms firmly across his chest when he sits down, but he's forced to unfold them when I hand him food to eat.

He stares at it before he nibbles the edge of the apple-like fruit, barely touching it.

I understand his reluctance to eat. Our bodies are working hard, running on power alone. The thought of swallowing food... I'm sure I'll only bring it up again.

We're caught now in a dilemma with no good outcomes.

Without our power, our bodies would be stretched beyond their limits, and we'd face collapse. With our power, we're becoming targets for the environment.

I leave my medallions where they are nestled around my arm and take careful bites of the apple that Gallium hands back to me. I can't eat much more than he did.

After that, I offer to take the first watch—a suggestion that basically consists of me tapping my chest and saying, "First."

I'm surprised when Thaden doesn't argue. His shoulders are hunched, and the rings under his eyes are darker. He finishes the apple-like fruit he was eating, core and all, gives me a nod, and then lies down on his fur with his back to me.

Gallium is slower to agree, but it doesn't take him long to

reach for his fur, pull it over himself, and close his eyes, facing me, his eyelids slowly closing.

It's only once they're both asleep that I realize we didn't agree on who would take the second watch, but it's the least of my concerns.

When the wind dies down, I can hear more clearly the sounds from the distant plain.

A mournful call.

A soft cry.

A high-pitched shriek cut short, and then another eerie call.

And within all of the sounds, a rhythmic clanging that takes me back to the day my people died. Students were hammering their medallions out in the wasteland. My mother's commands cut through the air, carrying the force of her power.

"Forge!" she screamed. *"You will forge until your hands bleed and your muscles break!"*

I pull my knees to my chest, wrapping my arms around them.

I never forged my own medallions. Was never given my own hammer. Instead, my power was taken.

But it came back. It resurged.

I am not that powerless child anymore.

Pulling my fur up around my shoulders, I resist the urge to raise my hand into the wind again, to let the air play around it.

Blacksmith magic... Creation and darkness...

With that thought, I can't help but focus on Thaden.

When Asha, Gallium, and I die, our people will be extinct. Or so I always thought.

It isn't lost on me that Milena Ironmeld is out there somewhere, and now Malak's own son lies sleeping only a few paces away from me.

It takes both a Blacksmith father and mother for a child to be born with Blacksmith power.

If Thaden were someone else...

In another life...

But our people should never rise to power again. After what

that power has done to the fae and even to the humans, it's for the best that we will be the last of them.

For hours, I sit, my thoughts whirling around in my mind like the dust storms out in the darkness.

Until the air changes.

It happens imperceptibly at first, a small shift in the heaviness, a subtle change in the acidic scent...

And then, suddenly, my chest burns, and I can't breathe.

A gust of wind billows across the barren range, bringing with it the heaviness of blood and death, snatching the air from my chest.

I grab hold of my fur to keep it from being ripped from my shoulders, my focus flashing to my left—the direction from which the wind is gusting.

Clang!

I jump as the sound of a hammer hitting metal rings in my ears, whirling around and around me, a disorienting hum of noise.

I don't know where the sound's coming from. I don't know what's making it. It sounds muffled and eerie and... *wrong.*

Clang!

I jump to my feet just as a dark tornado of wind and debris and crimson ash appears at the edge of the ridge, only fifty paces away.

A dust storm!

My heart thuds, and fear shoots through me.

It will stop. I tell myself it can't pass the edge. There's nothing here for it to feed on. Nothing dead. Only the echo of my dead mother's commands and the beat of long-ago hammers.

Then, to my shock, the dust storm pushes forward another foot, edging toward me, as if it's found something to feed on, something to let it approach me.

At the same time, it thins and begins rising up and up, an elongating tornado of ash and darkness before its uppermost half begins to curve down, arcing toward me across the distance.

It doesn't need to move its base if it can reach me this way.

"Thaden!" My screams tear from my throat. "Gallium!"

Gallium leaps up first. He was already facing me, and he's instantly awake.

I catch the desperation on his face as he launches himself up from his lying position, his muscles pumping as he throws himself toward me.

His strong hands collide with my side, shoving me out of the path of the descending wind tunnel.

I hit a solid surface—Thaden's chest. He must have lurched to his feet a moment after Gallium. His arms close around me, and he whisks me to the side, propelling me away from my brother, who now stands directly in the path of the storm, and no matter how fast Gallium moves, he won't evade it.

Fear for my brother fills my heart, and in that moment, there isn't time to scream.

There's nothing I can do to stop the dust storm crashing down on him.

Gallium's form disappears within the dust storm.

My scream is whipped away in the wind that crashes across the clearing, forcing me into a crouch with Thaden's body curved around mine even as I shout at myself to get back to my brother.

The raging ash has formed visible ropes within the swirling tornado, each one appearing covered in sharp, thorny barbs, all of them writhing and flailing. The mire is so thick that I can't make out Gallium at all.

Then there's a bright flash of copper. A streak of metal cuts through the mire, and my breath stops.

"Gallium!" I scream against the wind, my voice snatched away, and my hair whipping sharply across my face.

I make out another slash of copper within the storm and then another. Each one faster than the last.

Gallium.

And then—

Light explodes between the dark ropes, and I can see my brother's silhouette backlit in a copper glow. He's rising up within the darkness, his entire body covered in copper armor that flows around him like liquid skin, protecting him.

My eyes widen as I realize that he must have made that armor from a single medallion.

He grips a dagger in each hand—undoubtedly formed from his other two medallions—and he's whirling, the blades flying back and forth, cutting through the storm, slicing across the ash ropes, piercing the darkness. Faster than I've ever seen him fight.

Just as the ash thickens again, he drops to the ground, crouches, and then leaps directly upward.

Up through the darkness and into the sky above the tornado.

High above it.

In an instant, his daggers transform into swords, both of them pointed downward. His biceps are bunched—every muscle in his body is tense and strong. The sheer concentration on his face, his pure determination, takes my breath away.

And in that moment, I truly believe he has a chance.

He soars downward, gravity taking him back to the storm, but this time, he's arcing toward its stem—closer to the edge of the ridge.

His blades slash downward.

At the last moment, the tornado splits into two, forming a second, thick rope that swings across the air.

It smacks into his side and the *thud* it makes is as if the tornado is made of solid wood and not ash.

Gallium shouts, and I can only watch as pain floods his face and his body flies backward.

Out into the dark sky.

And then he's gone. Over the edge.

CHAPTER 8

"No!" My scream is full of desperation, my arms reaching toward the spot where Gallium fought the darkness only seconds before.

My cry is drowned in the wind, but only for a moment.

Then the storm rapidly recedes. The entire tornado retracts, disappearing so quickly that I lurch to the ground, my hands slapping the cold rock now that the wind is no longer pushing against my body.

The silence is loud in my ears.

I can't hear Gallium falling.

I can't hear anything except the blood pounding in my ears and Thaden's soft breathing as he holds me close.

"Gallium!" My cry echoes around me as I shove myself from Thaden's arms, fighting his hold so hard that his grip loosens.

"No, Tamra!" Thaden's alarmed cry washes over me as I race to the edge of the cliff, heedless of the danger of the waiting darkness.

"Brother!" My cry falls into the terrible silence below me.

The darkness is so thick that I can't see a thing, even with my enhanced eyesight.

Oh, please...

Just as I prepare to scream into the darkness, a flash of lightning bursts across the air, streaming in from my right.

Amethyst-colored energy explodes through the air, dazzling in its intensity.

A mighty bird with inky-black feathers and a dark-purple beak soars across the darkness, swooping downward, the lightning surrounding its body lighting up the space around it.

A fae thunderbird!

And there, finally, I can see Gallium's falling body, his form lit up within the explosion of light.

He's throwing his daggers upward, the metal they're made of extending like ropes from his fingertips and forming hooks at the end, but they scrape uselessly down the side of the rocky cliff face. He can't slow himself down.

The thunderbird spears toward him in a near-vertical dive, its rider a mere silhouette clinging to the bird's back with impossible strength.

I recognize this bird, and my heart leaps.

Her name is *Concord*. She belongs to Elowynn of the Dawn, Queen Karasi's fierce and formidable Champion, who commands the fae army.

Gallium rode this bird when he went with Elowynn to bring Asha back to Karasi's castle.

As another burst of lightning explodes around Concord's body, I can finally make out Elowynn on her back.

Elowynn's hair is the darkest black, with deep-purple highlights, and her violet eyes gleam in the amethyst energy bursting around her.

The immense strain is visible on her face as she clings to her bird.

Concord is plummeting so fast that I barely hear Elowynn's scream. "Gallium! *Reach for me!*"

He retracts his weapons, the copper metal streaming back to his arms as he stretches to his left, his hand reaching, *reaching...*

My heart is in my throat.

I can't do anything but watch as they drop for another heartbeat... and another... and another...

And then, with a scream, Elowynn throws herself off her bird's back, leaping into the space between her and Gallium, her body arching with the force of her jump.

Finally, her hand closes around Gallium's.

Her momentum knocks him sideward.

Concord sweeps her wings and somehow—impossibly—carves across the air beneath them.

Elowynn reaches for the bird's neck and then she's pulling herself and Gallium both onto its back, where they land, their arms entangled.

Concord soars back up into the air, sweeping her wings with powerful beats that carry them back up the cliff face.

I nearly drop to the ground with relief. Then I remember that I'm in a terribly dangerous location.

Already, I can sense the air moving below me, the scent of blood growing, and the rushing sound of a dust storm building once more.

No doubt it will come for us again.

"Tamra!" Thaden shouts from behind me. "We need to move!"

His voice is rapidly coming closer and my attention is suddenly split between him, where he's running toward me, and my brother, who is safely on Concord's back and is soaring up toward me.

With a *whoosh*, Concord flies up and over me, gaining height with every beat of her wings.

I catch Gallium's shout as they fly higher above me. "Set me down!"

"No!" The fear in Elowynn's reply hits me hard, clear in her voice, even though I can't see her face now. "We can't land. The blight will kill us."

As the bird circles around, turning toward the west, Gallium leans out to the side, and I catch the flash of fear and tension in his face.

For a moment, it looks like he might choose to leap from Concord's back, but even with his power, he would break his legs from that height.

As the bird carries him away, it looks like Gallium shouts back to me, but this time, his words are snatched away by the wind.

I can't hear him. And already, Concord is disappearing along the mountain ridge, soaring higher as she flies into the west.

In the next moment, Thaden's hand closes around my arm, his snarl sounding in my ears. "She was following us."

He scans the sky, turning in a slow circle. "If there are others, they're staying high enough that I can't sense them."

"But it's dangerous up there."

His eyes narrow at the boiling clouds. "They must be desperate."

I'm not sorry that Elowynn was following us, given that she saved Gallium, but I don't understand why they'd risk following us here.

My forehead creases. "What could be so important that they'd risk their lives?"

Thaden's jaw clenches. He shakes his head. "We need to move. The darkness is building again. Between the blight and the fae, we won't be safe until we reach my village."

Now that my heart rate is settling, new fears grow.

My brother is no longer at my side, and I'm not sure if he'll be able to make his way back to me. It could be incredibly dangerous for him to try.

I can hear the dust storms rebuilding, and I know they could crash up to the edge of the ridge at any moment. I've already passed the point in the landscape where I could travel on my own. As much as I'd like to believe I could do it, my chances are better with Thaden.

Maybe.

I want to rage at the uncertainty of my path and all the dangerous choices in front of me.

Concealing my fear is too difficult, so I don't try as I turn my face up to Thaden's.

His expression softens, his scaled hand rising to my shoulder as he speaks with conviction. "I won't let anything happen to you, Tamra. I promise."

To believe him would be foolhardy, but by the saints, I wish I could trust that he won't lead me to my death.

I nod, my mouth dry and my voice a whisper. "Let's go."

He rapidly scoops up the fallen furs, along with Gallium's pack, while I quickly retrieve my own pack.

As I hurry back to him, my gaze passes over the edge of the ridge where the dust storm attacked—the spot where it progressed closer to us than it should have been able to.

My heart plummets to see what lies near the edge of the ridge.

I nearly miss a step before I force myself to continue, wiping my expression clean before Thaden glances back at me.

My mind whirls as we set off at a jog.

I wouldn't have been able to see this without my power—I wouldn't have had a chance with human eyes—but I spot three discarded apple seeds.

Little, dead things lying on the rock behind me.

I tell myself they can't be from the apples we ate tonight, even though I know full well that Thaden would have had many chances to flick the seeds across the stone when Gallium and I weren't looking...

The leaf may be green, but it's already dying.

I concentrate on controlling my breathing as I follow Thaden Kane Ironmeld through the darkness.

CHAPTER 9

For hours, I jog beside Thaden, my feet hitting the rocky ground, my legs aching with every step.

Breathing has become nearly impossible, the air rasping against my throat, burning with every inhale, freezing with every exhale.

At some point, the incline begins to descend—or rather, the path does—while a wall of rock increases beside us until it is chest height, as if the path we're now following cuts down across the mountain ridge.

The stone is still too low to provide a windbreak, and finally, I stumble.

Veering to the right, I knock into the low rock wall before my knees give way, and I find myself sliding down it, trying to stop myself in a half-crouching, half-stooping position.

"We have to keep going." Thaden veers back to me, reaching for my arm. "I can help you—"

"No!" My cry sounds before I can stop it. At some point, the shield I've kept around my true feelings has crumbled.

Exhaustion has finally taken its toll.

He pulls to a stop, his right arm extended—the scaled one. "Tamra?"

I know from what Gallium told me that Thaden used his right hand to help Asha forge weapons for the humans back in the Cursed City.

It makes sense to me that he would cover his powered hand in dragon scales.

After all, to render a Blacksmith completely and permanently powerless, all you have to do is cut off their powered hand.

The dragon scales protect Thaden from that.

There is no blade in the world that can cut through dragon scales.

His hand remains only inches away from my shoulder.

My eyes meet his, and I can't stop my fear from rising; can't stop my pounding heart.

He looks down at me for a long moment, his expression slowly wiping clean. "You don't trust me."

My breathing is too rapid, and I can't seem to calm it. "How can I when you've lied to me about who you are?"

He takes a step back, and his arm falls to his side.

Again, he takes a moment. When he speaks, his eyes are hollow and there's a bleakness in his voice that I wasn't expecting. "You know who I am."

My throat constricts, but I force myself to speak. "I do."

"Then say it." He remains motionless, his eyes hollow. "Tell me who I am."

I try desperately to bring moisture to my lips.

I have nowhere to run.

At my back is a darkness that wants me dead.

In front of me is Thaden, a man as strong and powerful as the Vandawolf.

Thaden may not be carrying a hammer right now, but he could easily take mine and use it to destroy me.

I exhale, knowing that speaking his true name aloud could be my end.

"You're Thaden Kane Ironmeld," I say. "You're Malak Ironmeld's son."

He takes another step back, his expression withdrawn, his arms loose at his sides, and his shoulders slowly hunching.

"I won't let you destroy my sister," I snarl. "I care about her too much."

His brow creases, and now he seems confused. "But back at the castle, you said—" The furrow in his brow eases. And then, "You were trying to push her away."

"I was protecting her from *you*." I press against the wall at my back, forcing myself to be more upright. "I won't let you hurt her."

"'Hurt her'?" His mouth is downturned. "I have no interest in hurting Asha. I *need* her." He takes a step toward me. "I came to the Cursed City because I need her help."

He takes a step toward me, and even though it's a quiet step, it feels angry.

"I need her help," he repeats softly. "And I will do whatever it takes to get it."

"Why?" I ask, pushing myself fully upright. "Why do you need her?"

He shakes his head at me, his bronzed eyes flashing. With rage or desperation... I'm not sure.

"You will see," he says.

That was the answer he gave me when I told him we shouldn't go to his village or we'd endanger the people who live there.

"No." I maintain my upright position, even though my legs are screaming at me for rest. "I won't see."

His eyes narrow at me. He doesn't have to ask me why for me to continue.

"Because I'm not going with you," I say. "I'm not going any farther than this. I won't take the darkness to your village—"

He lurches toward me, a sudden step that brings him within inches of me before he stops, his gaze blazing down at me.

His eyes are suddenly hollow again. His voice is a bare whisper. "I thought you might be different, but you're just like all the others. You've already judged me."

How could I not?

I snarl back at him. "I've judged you on your actions, not your name!"

"What actions?"

"You lied to me. From the very beginning—"

"How?" he demands to know. "What lie?"

"You told me you were human," I say, my head tipped back, my voice biting. "You acted as if you hate Blacksmiths."

"I *am* human," he snaps back. "And I do hate Blacksmiths. Every fucking one of them."

I narrow my eyes. "Including me, then."

"Except you," he snaps back. And then more softly. "And your brother." His jaw clenches. "And even Asha. I no longer hate her."

Other than moving closer to me, he hasn't made any move to bridge the gap between us.

His arms remain at his sides.

"But you..." Confusion is like lava within me, burning through my thoughts. He claims to be human. He claims to hate Blacksmiths. But he's a Blacksmith, not a human. "But you're..."

Still trying to lie to me.

Allowing my anger to rise and give me the strength I need to push away from the wall, I step in far closer than is safe and pin him with my gaze. "You're Malak's son. You're a Blacksmith, not a human."

"That doesn't mean I don't hate them."

I'm close enough to him now that I could collide with him and still, he makes no move against me. "You aren't human."

He exhales softly, what sounds like a carefully controlled breath. The tension in his jaw eases as his focus passes across my earnest face. His lips part, then press together, the slightest movement.

Is he weighing his answer?

Is he trying to devise a lie?

Or is he preparing to tell me the truth?

For a long moment, silence passes between us, broken only by the heavy breeze.

Then, he says, "I have always been alone."

I wait for him to go on, but he studies my face, giving me a chance to speak, as if he expects me to refute him again.

When I don't, he continues. "I was surrounded by humans and raised by dragons. I learned their ways. I forged bonds with them. But always, I was alone. And always, Milena was never far away.

"All my life, she watched me. Waiting for signs of my father's cruelty. And soon enough, I realized that the dragons were watching me, too. All of them waiting for me to turn to the same darkness that my father welcomed into his heart."

Thaden stops again, as if he expects a retort from me, but I remain silent. Not because I won't act or because I believe him, but because the more I know about his beliefs, the more knowledge I can gain. The more knowledge I have, the safer I'll be.

"Just as you're watching me now," he says.

He raises his right hand, turning it over in the dim light. He's close enough to me that he could wrap that arm around me.

Or break me with it.

"Even when it became clear that I wasn't left-handed, the scrutiny didn't ease. Milena didn't hold anything back about my father and the things he'd done. She told me everything. The dragon king himself, Graviter Rex, made it his mission to ensure I was aware of Malak's every dark choice.

"But one day, Milena told me a lie. She found me sitting at the edge of a cliff when I was ten years old. I asked her if I could make wings out of metal and fly away. I wanted to leave my name behind. Find a place where nobody had heard of Malak Ironmeld, and I could be free of his legacy." Thaden's voice softens. "Do you want to know the lie she told me?"

"You're going to tell me anyway," I say.

He nods. "She told me that my father loved me."

I blink at Thaden. I don't know enough to refute Milena's claim. "How do you know it was a lie?"

He gives me a cold smile. "Because you can't love something when you don't know it exists."

"Are you certain Malak never knew about you?" I ask. "Surely, your mother—"

"No." His rebuke is soft, but the growl in his voice tells me I'm in dangerous territory. "If he knew my mother had given birth to me, he would have killed her."

My forehead is deeply furrowed. "But... why? Malak used everything for his own purposes. If he was worried you could challenge him, he would have done to you what he did to us and stolen your power. I can't see him killing—"

"Because my mother was human."

I blink at him, frozen to the spot. "That isn't possible."

His lips twist. "Which is almost certainly why he didn't think twice about the chance of a pregnancy."

My eyes are wide. "Both parents must be Blacksmiths." I try to fight through the whirlwind of confusion within my mind. "Well... Who was she? Your mother?"

His jaw clenches. "I saw her when I was there," he says softly. "When I went to your Cursed City." The tension in his features eases, and he gives an exhalation like relief. "She was alive and healthy."

"Her name, Thaden," I say, a demand for an answer.

"*Alive and healthy,*" he repeats, the tension washing across his face again. "Because nobody knows who she is or the fact that she brought Malak's son into the world. And for that same reason, I didn't speak a word to her."

"You're protecting her," I say, my eyes widening.

"Of course I'm protecting her!" He shakes his head at me, an intensely angry movement. "Even Milena only spoke my mother's name once. And even then, it was in a whisper. When she was certain the dragons couldn't hear.

"I want to believe there was a small shred of goodness in Milena that compelled her to keep me and my mother safe. But I know she only did it because she wanted to use us as leverage against Malak. Her knowledge was her power over him."

Thaden's presence is now overpowering. His eyes glitter down at me. "So you see, Tamra Silverspun, I didn't lie. I am human."

"And what of the rest of your story?" I ask. "Did Milena really change you into a dragon against your will?"

He is silent.

For a terrible moment, I actually want him to lie to me. To tell me a story that I can willfully believe.

All because of that look in his eyes when he told me he's human. A painful hope, as if he wants more than anything to *be* human.

For myself, I don't know what happened to the dragon. I only know that it makes no sense for Milena to have killed one when she's clearly allied with the dragons. There's no reason for her to anger them like that. I don't even know what dragon was killed.

Of course, dragons could have enemies amongst themselves...

I'm certain Thaden could concoct a believable story.

Instead, he says. "Milena didn't kill the dragon."

I wait for him to continue, barely daring to breathe, praying now for the truth.

"It was..." He shakes his head. "A tragedy that..."

He closes his eyes for a long moment.

I want the words he isn't speaking. I need him to fill the silences with explanations, but he doesn't.

"I had no choice," he says, his forehead creasing and his eyes squeezing harder closed. "I had to make myself as strong as possible for the battle I knew was coming for me."

He opens his eyes, and now they're hard, gleaming bronze and filled with fire.

"I have no choice but to become what Milena and the dragons feared," he snarls. "To protect what I love, I will embrace the dark."

CHAPTER 10

I can't fight the shiver raging down my spine.

I take a step back, but this time, Thaden follows me, his arms finally rising as he reaches for me.

His scaled arm slides easily around my back while his left hand slips across my cheek and to the side of my neck.

I'm frozen in his arms, fighting the push and pull of my feelings, the need to stay where I am, colliding with the knowledge that I'm most certainly in terrible danger.

Despite the ferocity of his admission, he speaks softly now. "Only days ago, you told me that I am not a beast. You said you understood the battle I fight with the dragon whose soul I carry. You told me that since I came into your life, you have hope."

His expression softens further. "I knew you were lying. I could tell from your heartbeat. You simply wanted your sister to understand your reasons for refusing to heal the Vandawolf."

I'm stiff as I wait for him to continue, aware of the medallions sitting on my arm and the hammer resting in my pocket.

His thumb brushes my cheek. "But even in your lie, you gave me hope."

"Hope of what?" I whisper, my voice a bare rasp.

"Come with me to the Shadow Beneath the Mountain," he

says. "Let me show you why the dragon died. Let me show you why I came to the Cursed City. Once you've seen, then you can pass judgement on me. I will welcome whatever justice you deem necessary. All I ask is that you give me this chance."

I told him I wouldn't go any farther with him, but the reality is that the alternative is death.

I have no water left.

I won't survive the trek back along the mountain range.

I suppose I could scream at the sky in case there are still thunderbirds following us... even though I doubt they'd descend to scoop me up. It would be dangerous for them to do so, and they have no reason to help me.

As if he reads my thoughts, Thaden glances upward. "If I could pull a thunderbird down for you, I would."

His eyes lower to mine as he continues. "I will carry you if you need me to, Tamra. I will do anything to get you to my village. I will fight whatever battles I have to fight and embrace any darkness I need to embrace so that you can see what I've been protecting."

"What about my sister?" I ask. "You sent her in Milena's direction. Where did you really send her?"

When he hesitates, I harden my voice. "Do not utter another lie, Thaden Kane Ironmeld. No matter how difficult it is to speak the truth, you will speak it, or I will choose to walk into that darkness rather than stay at the side of a liar."

He exhales quietly and gives me the barest nod. "I have sent Asha into a trap designed to protect her from the wrath of the dragon king."

My throat is tight, and my eyes narrowed. *A helpful trap?* Is there such a thing?

"Explain," I command him.

He takes a deep breath. "It isn't a short explanation. You're thirsty. You need hydration—"

"*Explain*," I repeat, grinding the word between my teeth.

"Okay," he says softly, his hands raised, placating. "First, you need to understand what I can do. I'm not left-handed like my father. I can't wrap a medallion around my hand, touch a living thing, and command it to change its shape or nature.

"But when it comes to working metal and creating metallic objects of extreme intricacy, I excel." His voice is matter-of-fact, not a hint of boastfulness in it, which surprises me. "I long ago surpassed Milena in metalworking skill. She said that I may have even surpassed my father in that regard. But even with that level of skill, I couldn't do what he did. I couldn't use my power to transfer the soul of a creature into metal and then transplant that metal into another living being."

My thoughts are whirling. "But then... how did you take on the soul of the dragon?"

His expression becomes blank, wiped clean. "Dark magic."

I try not to recoil, but it isn't any use. I've flinched away from him, and he won't have missed my reaction.

His voice becomes a deep growl, and it's as if I were listening to the dragon himself when Thaden says, "When the fire dragon died, I had a heartbeat to make a choice. I knew that the dragons would come for me, and they would kill what I was protecting. The only way I could protect what I love was to turn to the darkness. To call on malice and cruelty and embrace Lysander's death. With a single piece of twisted metal, I captured his soul.

"Then I used my hammer to fashion that metal into the shape of a dragon, and I hammered it into my own chest."

My eyes are wide, my breath still.

Thaden's jaw is so tight that I'm surprised he hasn't cracked his teeth.

"I forced myself to stay awake for long enough to drive the device deep into my heart before I passed out."

He lifts his right hand. "This hand... It is no longer peaceful."

He closes his fingers into a fist.

"I knew that Graviter would sense his son's death and come looking for me, so I left the village as quickly as I could. I went straight to the clifftop where I used to meet Milena, and there she was, waiting for me.

"I tried to explain how Lysander died. I tried to tell her I had no choice, but she wouldn't listen. I tried to ask for her help, but she refused. I told her she should have made Asha a hammer, and that was when she flew into a rage and cut off her own hand. She was the last hammer-maker. She did it just to fucking spite me."

His voice becomes a snarl. "She believed that I had *chosen* to become like my father, and indeed, by then, it was true. I used one of the devices I'd created on the lone tree that grows on that clifftop. It trapped Milena within a spiderweb of branches. It would trap any Blacksmith who stepped close enough to it. So that is where I sent Asha."

I draw back a little, horrified. "How would caging her like that protect her?"

"Because I know Graviter Rex. His fury knows no end. He will seek justice by killing every living Blacksmith, no matter how innocent they are. That includes Asha. And you. And Gallium."

I gasp. "Gallium!"

"Will be safe with the fae. But Asha isn't. As soon as she promised Queen Karasi that she would go west, she was in grave danger. If I could have gone with her—" His jaw clenches. "But I couldn't. So I sent her, not straight into the heart of danger, but to the only location where she might be safe."

"But... what will stop Graviter Rex from burning down that tree with Asha trapped inside?" I ask, horrified.

"Because Milena is also inside it," he says.

My forehead creases. "Why would that make a difference?"

"Because the dragon Milena rides—a forest dragon named Torva Viridia—witnessed our battle. She loves Milena and will not leave her. She's bound to try to free Milena, but she won't succeed. The dark magic in that tree will keep her at bay. Most importantly, however, she won't allow Milena to be burned alive."

I shake my head. "That is a terrible gamble."

"Which is why I need to get back to Asha as soon as I can." He searches my eyes, a painful desperation entering his expression. "But I won't abandon my promise to her, either. She will never help me if anything happens to you. *Please*, will you come with me?"

He drags in a breath, his chest pressing to mine as he inhales deeply, and his voice softens. "You will be safe in *Myrkur Fjall,* and maybe, once you see what I'm protecting, you'll stop looking at me as if I'm your enemy."

I can't breathe. Can barely think. But even if I could think clearly, I doubt it would help me right now.

No matter how much I wish I had a choice, I don't.

"I'll come with you." I fight a sudden and unexpected sense of anticipation as I continue. "I will see what you want me to see."

The tension in his body vanishes.

His thumb brushes my jaw, and a smile touches his lips.

"I promise you, Tamra Silverspun," he whispers. "It will explain everything."

PART TWO
THE FIRE IN THE SNOW

ASHA SILVERSPUN – PRESENT DAY

CHAPTER II
ASHA SILVERSPUN

The echo of my scream fades, and a cold silence settles around me, broken only by the icy breeze.

Erik rests in my arms, his head cradled to my chest, his left hand dragging in the snow beside him as I try to hold him close.

The light is gone from his eyes.

The breath has left his chest.

No longer will he tell me that I am limitless.

No longer can he tell me that he loves me.

A new scream builds within me, a powerless scream filled with rage. *"Erik!"*

I have nowhere to put my grief.

Nowhere to place my fury.

All I have is this cry that tears across the snow-filled clearing in which I kneel.

The clearing extends for a hundred paces in each direction between a forest of trees on my left, a cabin on my right, and a small forge directly in front of me. The cabin is sheltered beside a massive rock face that extends to the top of a mountain.

Erik brought us here. This place was once his childhood home. Only hours ago, he told me all his stories. He finally spoke about how we first met and everything he lost to keep me alive: his family, his home, and even his identity.

He told me I was his destiny.

Now, a new cry surges through me, a wail of pain that's filled with all the darkness in my heart, but instead, the air brightens at the sound.

I'm suddenly aware that my left forearm has brushed the hammer Erik forged for me, and now a burning sapphire light bursts into life around me.

The hammer rests in the snow, its block-shaped head sunk into the icy powder. Its black handle is barely touching me, and yet its power is undeniable.

My power is undeniable.

Erik gave his life for this hammer. He poured all of his life-sustaining deep light into the metal so I could finally access my true magic. He emptied himself into the task, draining his own life with every moment of the forging.

He made me a war hammer unlike any Blacksmith hammer before it, and he asked me to take it, claim it, and accept it.

But I don't want it.

I don't need it.

I need *him*.

I need his ferocity, and his quick mind, and his determination. I need his belief in me and his perseverance. I need his constancy. I need his ability to see all of the moves and countermoves, the threads of possibility, and the plotting and scheming of others.

I need his *need*. I need his fire. I need his heart.

For years, he was the Vandawolf, a beast created in an act of pure malice, whose wolfish mind was in constant turmoil.

Not long enough was he Erik, the man he'd been born to be. The man who loved me but didn't show me until I healed his body with my power, merging the wolf's mind with his once and for all.

I gave him back his freedom to choose his own path.

A path that led to his death.

My shoulders slump, and my tears drip on his quiet face, droplets sliding across his cheeks as if they were his own.

A murmur sounds behind me, the quietest growl. "Bright Heart. It is done. You must come away now."

My arms only tighten around Erik's body before I twist slightly to see the golden fire dragon whose large body takes up much of the space in the clearing behind me.

He is the dragon king. Graviter Rex. He vowed to end all Blacksmiths after his son, Lysander Rex, was murdered. But I made peace with Graviter. I convinced him that I am not his enemy, a feat that was only accomplished after Erik convinced the great dragon to listen to me and hear me out.

My voice is a rasp, my vocal cords raw from my screams. "The metal Erik used to make this hammer... You gave it to him, didn't you?"

My voice carries no accusation. Only sadness. I understand that the dragon must walk his own path—the path that is best for other dragons. But without that metal, there would have been no hammer and no chance for Erik to die.

The handle is formed from half of one of the onyx spears Erik and I brought with us. Those spears are unbreakable, but Erik must have found a way to snap one of them in half.

The hammer's head is a double-sided block, evenly balanced and carved with runes. I recognize them only because these same runes are etched into various parts of the nearby cabin. They have meanings that Erik described to me when he told me his story only hours ago.

"I gave him the gold for the hammer's head," Graviter admits softly. "It's dragon's gold. I hoarded it for centuries to give it living properties and make it receptive to forming a bond with another being of pure light. I had intended to give it to my son. For that reason, it contains only love and hope."

His voice becomes raw as he speaks of his son. He, too, has known terrible loss and deep grief.

But the conviction in his voice doesn't waver as he continues. "The metal for your hammer was freely and willingly given, as it needed to be. It was the right metal for your hammer. The right metal for you to access your true power."

"'The right metal,'" I whisper; a hollow sound.

I understand the dragon's intentions.

For years, I had no choice but to use the hammer of Malak Ironmeld, the only other left-handed Blacksmith in my people's history.

His hammer and the medallions that went with it—strips of black metal that could be transformed into weapons—were filled with hatred. Every time I picked them up, I fought the malice within them, fighting to maintain my own thoughts and heart and not lose myself to the intoxicating power of his tools.

I feel none of that malice in the hammer that rests at my side.

All I feel within it is...

Love. Hope.

Everything Erik wanted for me.

I squeeze my eyes closed, unable to still the flow of tears. I have no choice but to let them fall.

Erik and I once stood across from each other on the balcony outside the tower he kept me in. Blood-red raindrops fell between us, marking the invisible barrier that existed between us at that time.

Even then, he was part of my life. Even with that invisible and seemingly unbreachable boundary between us.

"The right metal?" I repeat, opening my eyes and twisting further toward the dragon. "Nothing is right now that Erik is gone."

How can I function when it feels like I've lost a part of myself?

My arm shifts away from the hammer, and the clearing goes dark again.

The contrast is startling.

The moon is shining at its fullest, moonbeams filling the clearing, and yet it's the weakest light compared to the brightness of my magic.

Even so, the sudden dullness of the air brings other things into view.

A small orb of light floats close to Graviter's shoulder, becoming clearly visible again now that my magic has faded.

When the orb first arrived at this clearing, Graviter explained that it was a magical being called a *Celestial Star*. It's a living creature, but it doesn't speak. Instead, it seems to communicate through movement.

It danced at Graviter's side, flitting here and there, trailing light wherever it went. There was a happiness, a joyfulness, about it.

Now, its light has dimmed, and its movements are subdued.

Can it feel my sadness?

Does it know my grief?

Graviter lowers his head even further toward me, a slow and careful movement as if he would nudge the tip of his nose to my side. "You will be whole again, Asha. I have seen it."

When Graviter Rex first came upon us on the snowy mountain east of here, and after we fought him and survived, he ate a leaf from a monstrous tree that I healed with my power.

It was baffling to watch him pop that bright-blue leaf into his mouth and chew. But then he exhaled burning-blue flames, and his words struck me with foreboding.

He said that the magic in the leaf—my magic—had shown him all my memories. But more than that, it had shown him all that will be. My future and beyond.

He said that there will be a war in which dragons, humans, Blacksmiths, and fae will stand across a battlefield from one another and be tested. A war that will only be the beginning of other wars.

But he also said that without a beginning, there can't be an end.

Now, the mighty dragon edges so close to me that the heat of his fiery breath warms my cold cheeks.

His earnest eyes are huge in my vision. "You must take the hammer and use it—"

"I don't want it."

Graviter's expression hardens, a frightening sight, given how close his mouth is to me. "You must move away from Erik—"

"Do *not* tell me to let him go." I bare my teeth at Graviter, as if

I were the beast that Erik once was. "Don't tell me to give him to the ground."

Graviter doesn't flinch or retreat, no matter how fiercely I return his stare. *Why would he?* He is the strongest of all dragons, and I am refusing the power that would give me the physical strength to challenge him.

I am refusing to pick up the hammer.

Surprisingly, his voice softens. "I will not tell you to let him go, Asha Silverspun. But for now, you must move away from him so that his soul can be claimed as is the custom of his people."

My eyes widen as I realize what Graviter means. "A Valkyrie will come."

Erik explained to me that he was born into a clan of humans known as *Einherjar*. Members of the clan spend their whole lives building and cultivating their deep light—a spark of magic that exists in all humans, but few know how to harness it, let alone how to increase it.

An Einherjar's greatest ambition is to burn out their deep light in battle, giving themselves incredible strength and speed. By burning out their light, they trigger their own death, but that is not what matters. What matters is that they achieve a glorious death in battle.

The Einherjar believe that if they die this way, a Valkyrie will come for their soul and deliver them to the Hall of Warriors.

I twist away from Graviter Rex, my focus now drawn to my left.

Not ten paces away from me, there is a stone statue.

It is the statue of a man, frozen mid-battle. His left leg is forward, his sword raised and poised to strike. In the moonlight, I can see every detail of the statue's face and the resemblance of its features to Erik.

The man within this statue was once Erik's father. Malak Ironmeld turned him to stone in a fight that happened because of me.

Erik's father is a powerful figure, although slightly narrower in the shoulders than Erik. The blade of the sword he's holding catches the moonlight and reflects it. Despite the years the weapon has been exposed to the elements, the blade shines a bright steel-blue.

Erik described to me his deep sadness when his father's soul was not claimed by the Valkyries. Erik's theory was that his father's soul couldn't be claimed because it was trapped in stone.

My eyes slowly widen.

And then my shoulders slump.

I, too, have the power to turn living things to stone. Although... I'm nearly certain I can't do it with a hammer alone. Each time I did it, I used a medallion—a strip of specially forged metal—that was wrapped around my left hand and gave me access to my power.

But I could never do that to Erik. Not to selfishly preserve his body.

I tell myself to unfold my arms from around him.

I tell myself that I can lay him down in the snow because this is what he would want.

And yet...

I *can't.*

I can't release him.

Opening my arms means acknowledging that he's gone. It means taking my body heat away from him and allowing him to grow cold.

I look up again to Graviter, my eyes welling with tears. "I don't know how to do this."

His expression remains calm and soft, his breathing slow. "You must find a way. And quickly. Because the Valkyrie can't be far away now, and she will fight you for him, Asha."

Graviter's warning isn't lost on me. I've never met a Valkyrie. Just as I had never met a fae before I had to fight a group of them in the mountains. All I know is that the Valkyries have silver wings. But it isn't hard to imagine that any creature whose purpose is to ferry the souls of warriors into the afterlife must be terrifyingly fierce.

Graviter confirms as much as he continues speaking.

"Whichever Valkyrie they send for him, she will have no mercy for your grief. The Valkyries are a race of women who deal in death and can deliver it within a heartbeat."

Despite my logic, my fear vanishes, and a reckless need rises within me. "Let her fight me. I won't let him go any other way."

Please let her fight me.

Please let her force me to open my arms.

Because I can't...

I try to breathe, try to drag freezing air into my chest, try to convince myself that there isn't a part of me that has died with him.

The only way I can give Erik to the ground is if someone physically forces me to do it, and it seems Graviter Rex isn't prepared to swipe his paw at me, or he would have done it already.

His brow furrows at my rash response, but at the same time, his skin flushes pale, somehow less golden, and now I'm not sure what to make of his expression.

Is he... afraid?

"Do not think you can win against a Valkyrie," he says. "They are invulnerable to all magic. *All magic,* Asha. Not even Blacksmith magic can hurt them. Not even with your hammer could you defeat her. And make no mistake: They will send their fiercest warrior to claim a man like Erik the Vandawolf."

My heart thuds in my chest, but it's slow and heavy.

Perhaps I should be horribly afraid, but there is no fear in this world that can overcome my sadness.

Graviter persists, and now I have no doubt about the depth of the fear in his voice. "She will kill you, Asha Silverspun."

"Then let her!" I snap back at him.

He recoils sharply at my shout. I give him a vicious smile.

"It will be a glorious death," I say. "Will it not? The kind that might allow them to ferry me to the Hall of Warriors with him."

It's an irrational statement—I'm not an Einherjar—but I don't care.

"No, Bright Heart." Graviter edges forward again. "This is not how you're meant to die."

The moment he speaks, he swallows visibly and withdraws a little, as if he regrets his words.

I stiffen as the full extent of his meaning sinks in. The implication that I'm going to die. Just not in this way. "How I'm *meant* to die?"

He pales even further but doesn't respond.

A feeling of dread swirls at the base of my stomach, but even my growing sense of foreboding isn't enough to still my tongue or stifle the bitter taste in my mouth.

"How difficult it must be for you now, Dragon King," I say. "To have seen it all. To carry the burden of what you should or shouldn't speak aloud."

"Bright Heart—"

"If this is not how I'm meant to die," I challenge him, raising my eyes to his, "then I have nothing to fear."

Even as I speak, I sense a far-off energy in the air. A rush of wind across my cheeks icier than the breeze that whispers across the snow-filled landscape.

The faint beat of wings reaches my ears, and I'm drawn to the sky behind the dragon. To keep my eye on it, I'm forced to twist even farther away from my hammer, hunching over Erik's body to keep him close.

At the movement, a sharp pain pricks my chest, making me gasp.

I risk taking my eyes off the sky for a heartbeat.

Before he died, Erik extended his claws and one of his hands is now wedged dangerously between us. The tip of one of his claws has pierced through the fur cloak I'm wearing and presses against my ribs.

His claws can pierce even a dragon's hide.

He told me to cut off his claws and use them, but I could never do such a thing.

I adjust the position of his hand, ensuring it won't hurt either him or me.

Within the space of those seconds, the air behind me has become fraught with an energy I've never felt before.

It is both alive and deadly.

A powerful, rushing wind billows my silver hair about my head, and the sound of wings intensifies to the point where I can't hear anything else.

I fight to keep my head raised and to open my eyes, preparing for the arrival of the woman who will take Erik from me once and for all.

I focus on the sky behind the dragon, only for the breath to stop in my chest.

There is not one woman raging through the air toward us...

There are three.

CHAPTER 12

The trio of women spears through the air toward me, their silver wings catching the moonlight in painfully sharp flashes.

They follow an arc that allows them to avoid Graviter Rex's position before they soar across my head and drop to the snow between me and the forge.

To keep them in my sights, I twist away from the dragon again, once more facing forward, my hold on Erik even tighter now.

The Valkyries land in a neat cascade, each one folding her wings to her sides to make room for the next woman, who drops to the ground with breathtaking precision.

They're astonishingly beautiful, their skin flawless, their hair sleek and shiny, and their figures lithe, their muscles clearly honed.

Each one wears armor made of intricate plates of metal in a deep-purple color and carries a sword at her back.

Until they draw their weapons, I won't know exactly what threats the blades pose, but the swords have similar-looking slender handles that appear to be wrapped with some kind of cord. Not a style of handle with which I'm familiar.

Interestingly, when they fold away their wings, the energy

around them fades, and when their wings have fully retracted, it's as if they're completely human. There is not a single shred of the supernatural about them.

It's similar to the way I am like a human when I don't have physical contact with my tools. Although, unlike me, these women no doubt remain just as dangerous with or without their wings spread.

They step toward me without hesitation, each one surveying the surroundings as they move, their gazes moving from the hammer at my side—currently not touching my body—to the dragon and the Celestial Star who have remained at my back. Finally, to Erik.

"Move aside, Blacksmith," the woman in the center commands without breaking stride.

She's tall, and her shoulders are broader than the other two. Her black hair is tied back in intricate braids, and she wears a sneer on her face that cuts through her beauty.

As she continues speaking, she gives a dismissive flick of her hand, as if I were nothing more than a pest. "We have come for Erik the Vandawolf, and you would be wise to get out of our way."

"I will not move," I whisper, my throat suddenly dry.

For a heartbeat, it seems that none of them heard me.

I suppose they're unaccustomed to being disobeyed.

Then the woman to my right pulls up sharply, speaking in a warning tone. "Sisters, she means to defy us."

That woman has auburn hair tied in knots across her head. Her eyes are sharp and her figure is as muscular as the central woman's. Her right hand rises to the handle of the sword at her back, but she doesn't draw it yet.

The other two are quick to halt, although it's the woman on the left, the one who has yet to speak, who takes one step closer than the others. She has the brightest green eyes and mahogany-brown hair that's also tied back in braids, but she's more petite than the other two.

I don't plan to underestimate her despite her size.

The central woman snarls. "Impudent Blacksmith!"

The woman on the left with the bright green eyes holds up her hand. "Perhaps she doesn't understand that it's impossible to stand in our way. Even a Blacksmith as powerful as she is."

The black-haired woman responds with a huff, but the green-eyed woman persists. "She is one of the last of her kind. It would be a shame to kill her if there's still a chance we can reason with her."

The auburn-haired woman gives a heavy sigh and lowers her hand from the handle of her sword, looking at the black-haired one, who now folds her arms across her chest and glares at me.

I suppose that's her way of acquiescing because she doesn't voice a further objection.

"Do enlighten her, Sister," the auburn-haired one says, casting her sharp gaze over me. "Before we are forced to take her life."

The woman with the bright green eyes takes another step toward me. She appears far more cautious of me than the other two—despite stopping closer to me to begin with.

She slowly lowers herself to the snow opposite me, taking up a kneeling position a full three paces away from me, her legs tucked under her and her hands folded in her lap.

She looks serene even as her breath frosts in the freezing air, and she doesn't seem to notice the cold that must be seeping through the plates of armor covering her legs.

"I am General Glass," she says, her gaze steady. "This is General Griffin and General Glaive." She indicates the woman with black hair first and then the one with auburn hair. "We serve the Valkyrie Queen and are entrusted to command the three sections of her army."

I study General Glass closely. She can't be more than twenty years old. Maybe only a year older than my sister, Tamra, and my brother, Gallium, who are twins. My heart wrenches to be reminded of them, even if Tamra is angry with me. I need to get back to them. They're in terrible danger, but I can't help them until I deal with the threat directly in front of me.

Glass continues speaking, her voice cautious and her gaze seeming to take in every small change in my expression. "It is a great honor for an Einherjar's soul to be claimed by a Valkyrie general," she says. "Even more so that their soul will be collected by not one, but all three of the Valkyrie Queen's generals."

Her expression remains earnest. "I promise you we will carry his soul with the greatest care and respect back to our Queen. She, herself, will lay him to rest at the head of the Hall of Warriors. These honors have never been bestowed on any Einherjar before. It is the greatest glory an Einherjar can ever achieve."

It's everything his people believe in. But Erik left that life behind.

"He didn't die for glory," I say, my voice a rasp.

He died for me.

He died *because of* me.

Glass's focus slides to my hammer, her gaze lingering on its head, where it's partially immersed in the snow.

"Bravery," she whispers, her focus now passing across the runes etched into the hammer's head. "Loyalty, strength, perseverance, and hope. Those are powerful protective runes, and each is filled with his deep light."

Her focus returns to me. "He carved those for you. They are his wishes for you."

My eyes burn with tears. Erik's body is becoming heavier in my arms and it feels...

I gasp against the pain.

It feels as if he's pulling away from me.

He's leaving me.

"If you take his soul, what will you do with his body?" I ask.

"We will take that, too," she replies. "So it can be burned on a sacred pyre, as is the way of the Einherjar people."

I drag air between my lips, tipping my head back to the clear sky, trying to fill my chest with oxygen before I suffocate.

There will be nothing left of him but ash.

General Glass's voice softens. "You're grieving." She refolds her hands in her lap, and there's a catch in her voice as she continues. "I understand your pain, Blacksmith."

I find myself focusing on her features more closely, on the tension around her eyes and the press of her lips.

"I, too, have experienced loss," she says quietly. "It encompasses my every thought and overwhelms my every instinct. But with every breath I take, I must fight it."

As she speaks, Glaive steps farther to my right while Griffin moves to my left, both of them moving to flank me.

"We are a fierce race," Glass continues, her voice hardening now. "We have very little room for compassion and no room for weakness."

Her jaw clenches as her gaze flickers meaningfully to the other two generals, who continue to move until they are positioned mere paces from each of my shoulders, perfect locations to strike me down.

I imagine they can easily lop off my head from where they now stand.

They don't seem to be paying any attention to Graviter Rex until he edges toward them, his big form moving at the corner of my eye and the heat from his fiery mouth puffing across my back.

He doesn't have the chance to speak before Glaive snaps at him, her auburn head tilted to him even while she keeps her sights on me. "Do not interfere, Dragon King! You know well enough that no creature on this Earth, however powerful, can withstand our magic. Not you. Not that Celestial Star. And certainly not this Blacksmith. If she wishes to die beside her love, then we will oblige her."

I don't have the chance to gauge his response because Glass continues speaking to me, her voice sharp now. "You must move away, Blacksmith, or we will kill you. We will not return to our Queen empty-handed. Not when there is a soul such as Erik's to be claimed."

He is more than a soul to me.

My focus falls to Erik's face. To the snowflakes that rest on his cheeks and no longer melt. To the blueness of his lips. The paleness of his cheeks. The way he is turned toward me.

I remember when he was dying after the fight outside the

human city, the hollowness of his voice when he first spoke of snow.

"I'm tired of digging in the snow. Let me sit beside you, where it's peaceful. Let it end here with you and me. In the snow."

Glass's voice is beyond harsh. "We will not tolerate a challenge of any kind," she says. "To challenge us is to challenge our entire race. Do you wish to start a war with us, Asha Silverspun?"

It's the first time one of them has called me by my name.

My focus snaps up to her.

I asked Graviter a similar question about war. I told him that if my enemy could find a way to kill a dragon, then I could, too. I told him that if he wanted a war, then let it begin here and now, with him and me.

Do I fear a war with the Valkyries?

No. I do not.

"Asha." Graviter's voice cuts through my dangerous thoughts. It's filled with warning—and coming from farther behind me. I can no longer see him from the corner of my eye, indicating that he's moving as far as he can away from the Valkyries. "Do not make enemies of the Valkyries."

The sound of ringing steel fills the air.

Light flashes across their curved blades as both Glaive and Griffin draw their weapons. The angle at which they're standing allows me to clearly see the weapons, and the tips pointed at me.

I've never seen swords like these. They are sleek, curved, and so sharp that the edges reflect the moonlight.

"Move aside," Glass commands me, rising to her feet where she has remained opposite me.

She hasn't drawn her weapon yet, and she takes several steps back, so I presume she will allow the other two the honor of killing me. Based on her present position, I guess she doesn't want blood splatter on her armor.

She waits another heartbeat while I remain exactly where I am.

I am where I belong. Beside Erik.

A short, frustrated sigh escapes her lips. "Such a waste."

Then she gives a nod to the other two generals, who raise their swords, their postures filled with purpose as they prepare to swing at my neck.

It will be a swift execution.

Judging by the way they're holding their blades, the black-haired Griffin will cut my head from my neck while the auburn-haired Glaive will drive her sword at an angle through my shoulder and down into my heart.

My mind fills with the memory of Erik's voice.

"Let me sit beside you, where it's peaceful."

"Let it end here with you and me," I whisper.

The air moves across my back as the two razor-sharp blades swing toward me.

CHAPTER 13

ut not today.

I drop and twist, my left hand snapping out, my fingers closing around my hammer's handle.

My forward drop takes me down onto Erik's chest and out of the path of Griffin's blade, which sails harmlessly through the air where my neck was located only a heartbeat earlier.

Glaive's blade was a second slower than Griffin's—not because she's weaker, but because that's undoubtedly how they time their executions.

But it gives me the barest moment to twist out of her path.

Only just.

The blade's edge slices across my fur coat, cutting open the material and letting the freezing air in.

Then the hammer is in my hand and I'm swinging it upward.

Its handle clashes against the edge of Glaive's sword, knocking it away from me.

The moment the hammer is in my hand, my power explodes across the clearing, lighting it up so brightly that the Celestial Star's now-distant form disappears completely.

Strength floods me, every muscle in my body firing.

Swinging the hammer is effortless. Even though I'm aiming it backward, a move that would ordinarily be difficult and carry less power. But the hit I land against Glaive's sword is so powerful that she's knocked backward, stumbling and then sliding to right herself.

Her eyes have flown wide.

Now that I have full access to my power, I can sense everything within the clearing.

The gasp that leaves Glaive's lips is a sound of both pain and shock as streaks of energy from my hammer ripple along her arm and chest.

I sense every shift of air, calculating that it will take Griffin another few heartbeats to recover her balance since her blade didn't meet the resistance she was expecting.

It's Glass I need to worry about in these next few seconds.

I swivel back to her as she launches herself at me across Erik's body.

Oh, she's fast. Much faster than the other two women, her body flying across the air even without her wings.

The compassion she revealed to me earlier was not weakness.

She leaps with incredible strength, her sword effortlessly drawn, and I picture the clean cut she intends to make through my neck.

She must intend to end this quickly.

I don't need to adjust the trajectory of my hammer, allowing it to follow through so that it carves the air across my head and then forward.

With a shove, I allow it to fly forward and the handle to slide through my fingers.

The hammer's large head smacks into Glass's stomach, right against her lowest ribs, before I close my grip around the handle once more, ensuring I don't lose control of it.

The impact of the hammer's golden head against her armor makes a *clang* so loud that without my power, I'm certain my ears would bleed. As it is, energy splashes across her body, and she flies backward. Her sword's momentum brings its tip swinging wildly close to my face, but I lean back, evading the steel.

It comes so close, I can almost taste the metal her sword is made from.

It's clean and pure, and my instincts are suddenly firing.

Every piece of metal these women are wearing and the swords they're wielding are susceptible to my hammer.

My power may be more extensive than that of other Blacksmiths, but I am like other Blacksmiths at heart: I was born to beat metal into submission.

Glass corrects her balance midair, landing lithely, but the force of my hit sends her sliding farther away from me than I'm sure she would like.

Griffin has now recovered and is coming at me again, this time with a wild swing, as if she intends to slash at me wherever she can make contact. The savage arc of the blade indicates she's given up on a clean kill.

I rapidly adjust my hammer's trajectory, jabbing it at her sword, aiming for a full hit of the hammer's head against the side of the blade.

At the instant of contact, I send a command through my hammer and into her blade.

Submit to my will.

Energy shoots through the sword from my hammer, a stream of golden power.

The blast knocks Griffin backward, causing her to gain air as her body crashes across the clearing.

Her sword is ripped from her hand, spinning wildly away from her.

She crashes into the snow, her landing digging a turret in the white powder.

Her sword lands several paces away from her, neatly dropping to the ground, its tip driving deep into the snow, where it remains upright.

I don't wait for her groan of pain to reach me.

I swing backward, this time blocking Glaive's downward cut from behind me—another slashing cut, this one an underhanded strike at my exposed back.

Her blade meets my hammer's head.

I send another command through the metal.

Obey me.

Her sword flies directly backward, ripping from her hand and swinging in such a violent arc that it nearly slices across her own side. Not that her armor wouldn't protect her, but the shock on her face is gratifying.

I don't slow my attack, punching the hammer's head at her chest.

My power connects with the metal plates.

Get away from me.

Energy splashes across her torso, rippling out through her arms and up her neck, accentuating her wide eyes and open mouth a split second before she crashes back through the snow, tumbling gracelessly through the powder.

I swing back to Glass.

Oh, but she's observant.

She must have figured out exactly what I'm doing because, with a heave, she drives her sword down into the snow and leaves it there.

Then she begins rapidly peeling off her armor.

The groans of the other two women reach me across the distance, and I'm aware that they're trying to get up, but even Glaive—whose armor I didn't directly command—is struggling. The metal in their armor is now weighing them down.

They both begin trying to crawl through the snow toward me, inch by painful inch, but they aren't making it anywhere fast enough to concern me.

"We can't go back to our Queen empty-handed and defeated," Glass says, and I'm surprised by the tension around her eyes now, the hint of fear on her face.

If I were willing to leave my current position at Erik's side, I could easily launch myself across the space between us and attack her before she could get her armor off.

But my right hand remains resolutely pressed to his heart.

I haven't broken the connection between us once so far, using only my left arm to defend myself and twisting at the waist to angle my hammer as I need.

The other two Valkyries must have taken note of Glass's actions because they've stopped trying to crawl toward me and are now attempting to push off their armor. It's clinging to their bodies as if by invisible strings, making them grunt and heave with effort.

Despite the freezing cold, Glass doesn't seem bothered by the snow as she pulls off her boots. Her bare feet sink into the powder, but she doesn't wince.

She's now dressed in nothing more than strips of black material wrapped around her breasts and stomach and a pair of short, tight pants in a style I've never seen before: cut high at the hips and with a waist that extends upward to meet the bottom of the wrapping around her breasts and upper stomach.

Her sharp gaze rakes across me. She clenches and unclenches her fists as she stretches her neck and rolls her shoulders.

"Will you spread your silver wings, General Glass?" I ask her softly.

Her focus flickers to my hammer, and she gives me a little smile. "Not a chance."

She takes a deep breath and focuses back on my face, her concentration intense. Only her right hand moves, her fingers unfurling from the fist she made with them.

My heart begins to race as I wait for her to make her move, painfully aware that the other two have now succeeded in pushing off half of their armor.

Farther behind them, Graviter has shrunk up against the trees on the other side of the clearing. There's only so far he can go, but with my enhanced senses, I can feel his growing fear, the way it seems to increase with every new twitch of Glass's fingers.

I adjust my hold on my hammer, allowing the handle to slide through my fingers so I'm gripping the handle right beneath the head.

As my fingers brush the underside of the golden block, my power sparks again, flickering around me in bright streams.

My hammer will be my fist, and if I have to shatter her, so be it.

My other hand remains resolutely on Erik's chest.

I raise my chin at her. "Come on, Glass," I whisper. "Let's find out which of us will shatter."

She moves in a flash.

Taking a quick step back, she launches herself at me, her feet leaving the ground. She gains air, arcing down toward me, her left hand formed into a fist that will surely break my jaw.

But she's left her right side exposed.

My left hand sweeps across my front, and my stomach muscles bunch, allowing me to lift without losing contact with Erik.

I'm ready to ram the hammer up beneath Glass's chin and break her face.

At the last moment, she changes direction, an impossible shift of balance that takes her toward my left side. She half-spins, like a spear turning in the air, taking her out of the path of the hammer's head and directly toward its exposed handle.

Both of her hands close around the onyx shaft.

That's when she spreads her wings.

They ram into my body, her feathers cutting across my chest like knives. As she wrenches my hammer upward, the impact of her wings knocks me backward.

For the first time since the Valkyries arrived, my right hand leaves Erik's heart. My body is wrenched away from him, and my legs out from under him.

Within my mind, I'm aware of the pain and damage to my body, but all I can focus on is the way his head and torso hit the snow without me to hold him. The way he's facing away from me.

The lost contact feels like I'm being ripped apart.

I must be screaming. I must be bleeding. My instincts are raging as I try to pour commands through the hammer.

Break! Shatter! Burn!

Destroy her wings!

But my grip on the hammer loosened the moment I gained air,

and just as I tried to scream commands through it, my hand opened.

There's air between me and my hammer. Just enough that I'm not in contact with it.

I fly backward; the wind rushing around my ears before I hit the snow with a hard *thud*, propelled so far from Erik that I'm now a full ten paces away.

I've landed on my back. General Glass drops onto me. One of her knees lands on my chest, and the other on the snow next to me.

My ribs shift under her weight. One of them *pops*.

For those awful seconds when my hand opened around my hammer, the air around me went dark. In the seconds before I scream at my fingers to tighten again, I may as well be human.

In that heartbeat, I catch the desperation in Glass's eyes. She didn't manage to wrench the hammer entirely from my grip, so this heartbeat is all she has before my strength will surge again.

Her wings are spread. Her left hand shoots toward my neck faster than I can send a command to my hand.

Her move weakens her hold on the hammer, but—

Fuck!

My body seizes with shock the second her palm touches my throat.

Pain strikes through me from my heart, a horrible burning agony that pulls and *pulls* out from me.

Above me, Glass's lips are pressed together into a hard line, and her eyes gleam as silver as her wings.

My left hand is still wrapped around my hammer and now her wings are vulnerable, but I can't seem to draw on my power.

I can't move.

I gasp, choke, and try to breathe, unable to scream as my life streams away from me.

CHAPTER 14

She's killing me.

And all it took was a touch.

The last of my logical thoughts are cynical. If she can kill with a single touch, then it's no wonder Graviter has remained at the edge of the clearing. Even now, despite lurching toward me, he hasn't intervened. But his body is shivering, ripples flowing through his scales, and heatwaves flow across the air above my head.

I'm certain that he wants to help me.

But I chose this path.

I couldn't let Erik go. And now his sacrifice for me will go to waste.

As death darkens the edges of my vision, I seek Erik's still body across the short distance between us.

I can't reach him.

I've lost him.

With that final thought, I exhale and stop struggling, sinking into the memories that I can cling to until my final moments. All the good and all the bad.

The way he shouted at me when he was dying.

"You were meant to leave me."

The way he whispered...

"I wanted to do one good thing."

"You did," I say within my mind, unable to utter the words, my vision blurring as the memories take over.

I'm standing opposite Erik on the balcony outside my tower, the wind plucking at my transparent robe, its white sash flying from his fingers, his body pressed to mine while the sky weeps blood onto us.

And now, again, the sky is weeping.

A cold droplet of rain falls onto my cheek, slipping across my skin like an icy finger trailing down my cheek.

I follow it down to the little body held carefully in my arms.

She has the smallest and most perfect fingers and toes, but her tiny lips are turning blue, and her chest is struggling to rise and fall.

She's too quiet.

She hasn't cried.

My baby girl has barely taken her first breaths. She's dying in my arms, and I can't save her...

With a sudden, startling clarity, I realize that these are not *my* memories.

Power pushes at my consciousness—my own power—and my left hand twitches around my hammer, the first movement I've been able to make.

The darkness clears from the center of my vision, and Glass's face comes back into focus.

Her brow is deeply furrowed, and beads of sweat rest on her forehead.

Tears stream down her cheeks.

Her sadness pours through me.

The loss of her daughter is raw and recent and overwhelming.

It's a terrible, horrible pain.

A pain I could use against her.

Strength streams from my heart, down my left arm, and into my hammer, at which power flows from my hammer back into my heart. Strength and power as I finally accept the gift Erik gave me, the hope he forged for me.

Glass's hand is unbearably tight around my throat, but her wings are fully spread and completely vulnerable, and she doesn't seem aware that my level of wakefulness has changed.

I'm not about to give her any warning.

My left hand shoots upward as I drive the hammer toward her right wing. I allow the hammer's handle to slide through my fist, giving me the reach I need to make contact with her silver feathers.

She seems to become aware of the movement too late, her concentration on me simply too complete for her to notice until now.

Her eyes fly wide as she attempts to jolt backward. Her wings begin retracting, but it doesn't do her any good.

The hammer's head collides with her feathers, and my power sizzles into them.

But instead of commanding her to break, I let my own grief guide me.

Heal.

Accept the sadness.

Move through it.

You can be whole again.

She gasps, and her gaze flashes from her wing back to me.

Her reflexes were already carrying her away from me, her knee rising from my chest and her wings giving a single sweep, but her gaze remains on me as she lands lightly in the snow opposite me.

Her hand flies to her heart. "What did you do?"

I don't have time to answer her.

The other two Valkyries have recovered and are charging toward me.

They've left their armor in the snow and are now both dressed only in underclothes similar to Glass's. Their breasts are wrapped in strips of black material while short, tight pants cover their pelvises. Unlike Glass, their stomachs are bare.

They leap toward me, kicking up snow as they move.

"Glass!" Griffin screams, her determined eyes blazing at her sister. "Seize Erik's soul before it's lost!"

Glass stumbles back toward Erik, but her knees buckle three paces away from him and she falls to the snow, kneeling in the white powder, her wings dropped at her sides.

Tears flow down her cheeks, falling to the snow.

My hammer remains extended in the air.

I have only seconds to defend myself.

I swing toward the other two Valkyries, seeking any metal on their bodies, but there's none. They've abandoned their weapons, and I'm certain they won't spread their wings.

As they rush at me, I take note of the way the black-haired Griffin comes directly for me while Glaive circles to my right. I'm certain that Griffin will try to disarm me, while Glaive will seek to use her power on me. Maybe she has to get her hands around my throat like Glass did, but it's also very possible she can kill me through contact with any part of my body.

I'm still in a crouched position.

Instead of deflecting Griffin, I swing my hammer to the right, away from Griffin's grasping hands and toward Glaive's leg.

It's an awkward move, forcing me to twist at my waist and expose my left side, but it keeps my hammer out of Griffin's reach.

Power splashes across the air as my hammer moves, my thoughts radiating out from me as I swing.

Be calm.

Glaive leaps out of the way just in time—the force of the hit alone could have broken her leg—and the hammer arcs downward, hitting the ground instead.

Thump!

The impact of the hammer on the snow is far more intense than I was expecting.

Light streams out from the hammer's head, an explosion of gold and sapphire.

The air *thuds.*

Snowflakes rise from the ground.

Energy ripples outward.

Both Valkyries are thrown backward, Griffin with her fist still raised where she was about to punch my exposed face, and Glaive where she was already airborne, having leaped upward to evade the hammer's strike across her legs.

All I can do is grip my hammer's onyx handle and marvel at the streaks of light radiating out from it through the snowy ground.

Well, what do you know?

Erik truly gave me a hammer like no other.

The hammer should be heavy, but it's as light as air when I heft it upward and swing it again.

This time, I deliberately aim for the ground between me and the two Valkyries, ramming my hammer down onto the snow just as they're regaining their footing.

Be calm.

Energy explodes through the ground where the hammer hits, spearing in all directions across the snow like beams of light from a little sun.

The beams reach the side of the cabin, shaking its walls. They hit the oncoming Valkyries, who throw themselves forward, their wings extending and wrapping around themselves as if they think they can cocoon themselves against the vibrations and cut through the wash.

They make it within reaching distance of me before I ram my hammer down into the ground again, its uppermost rune catching my eye.

Be hopeful.

The hammer's head crashes into the ground. *Thump.*

Icy powder rises from the surface of the snow, dancing on top of the ground as the vibration continues. Around the clearing, the trees shake, spilling snowflakes from their leaves, only for the ice to dance in the air, riding the vibrations of energy.

In the distance, Graviter Rex leaps upward, beating his wings and rising from the ground. He may as well be a moth in the tumult of energy building around me.

"Asha!" he roars, his voice no more powerful than a whisper. "Stop!"

No.

Somewhere between letting go of Erik and feeling my life stream away from me, I bonded with this hammer.

Maybe it was in knowing that grief doesn't only belong to me.

Pain comes for us all—even for a powerful Valkyrie who can deliver death with a touch of her hand.

I spin to General Glass, where she has collapsed in the snow. She alone has remained on the ground, her wings now wrapped around herself, her eyes raised to mine.

I speak directly to her when I say, "Erik wanted me to live." I give her a soft smile. "So I'm going to live."

I'm going to live with everything he gave me.

I will live with loyalty, strength, perseverance, and hope.

But so will *he*.

With that thought fixed firmly in my mind, I raise my hammer above my head.

While power builds around me, swirling and intensifying, growing brighter and brighter around my left hand, I fix a single command within my mind.

Then I ram my hammer down onto the snow with all my might and scream, *"Wake up!"*

CHAPTER 15

My hammer hits the snow.

Golden light streaks across the white powder toward Erik's still form, where he lies fewer than ten paces away from me now.

The explosion of power rages across the snow, sending snowflakes into the air, glittering as brightly as shards of glass.

They rise up around Erik's body like rain in reverse, as if I could turn back every crimson drop of blood-rain that fell on him and me.

Again, I lift my hammer, raising it above my head and striking it down. "Wake up!"

My power thuds into the earth and shrieks across the distance, a golden light that explodes upward around his body, lighting up the snowflakes.

This time, his body rises off the ground, elevated mere inches, his dark hair falls away from his face, and my power turns him toward me.

His eyes are closed.

His skin is pale in death, but I make him a vow: *You will not sleep in this snow.*

Living power pours through me as I raise the hammer

again. I'm vaguely aware that Graviter Rex is roaring from somewhere behind me. The other two Valkyries are silhouettes of silver suspended in the air, caught in the tumult of my power.

I grit my teeth and ram my hammer down again.

My heart is pounding. My breath rasps from my throat, my voice already hoarse from the attack on my throat. Sapphire light burns my palm where I grip the hammer, a beating pulse gleaming with every beat of my heart.

Once more, I scream, "Wake up!"

You will open your eyes.

You will stand up.

You will live, Erik.

Power rages around me in an increasing storm, but it's quiet where I stand. Too quiet.

My ears might be bleeding.

I'm certain they are.

My heart is raw, and my hands are burning.

Through the tumult, a bright glow dances toward me, flitting between the streams of power, somehow finding the gaps between them and darting closer.

It's the Celestial Star.

She dances between the streams of my power; her form glides fearlessly and glows brighter the nearer she gets to me.

I'm not sure how I can tell with so much certainty that she isn't afraid of me. Or how I somehow know that she's...

Happy.

Maybe it's the soft humming sound she makes that—impossibly—I can hear clearly despite the violence of the storm around me.

A gentle song that reminds me of the first sparkle of starlight in the sky before the night falls and the brief calm as sunlight gives way to the moon.

She glides right up to my face, filling my view with her light, and for a moment, it's like looking far beyond the dark sky and at the purest star.

Then she glides to my left, settling into the air above my shoulder, where she hovers.

The hum of her energy gives me the peace I need.

I take a deep breath, ignoring the chaos I've created around me, focusing once more on Erik.

I will hit my hammer to the ground as many times as it takes to bring him back.

Again, I raise the hammer, striking it down into the ground.

And again. And *again*.

At the corner of my eye, the stone statue of Erik's father suddenly cracks, my power traveling from his feet to his head.

The stone begins to crumble.

But I don't stop.

I can't.

"Loyalty," I scream into the storm. "Strength! Perseverance! Hope!"

I raise my hammer one more time, blocking out every doubt in my mind, but this time, I don't shout.

"Erik the Vandawolf," I whisper. "You will wake up and live."

I let my hammer drop to the snow, and I drop with it, falling to my knees.

My power strikes the snow, multiple golden threads shooting up and across the air. Each one curls around Erik's body, one around his chest, another around his neck, another around his legs, winding around and around him before sinking into his body where my power vanishes.

I watch him with all the hope he gave me, aware that behind me, Graviter Rex is slowly lowering himself to the ground, the Valkyries are also returning to the snow, and General Glass has retracted her wings.

While the final streams of my power fade, it seems we are all focused on Erik.

His body slowly lowers to the snow, his face turned toward me, but his hair falls across it.

The silence around me is unbearable as I refuse to let go of my hope, as I *will* Erik to breathe. To open his eyes.

But his chest doesn't rise and fall.

His eyes don't open.

He remains quiet and still where he lies in the snow.

My grip on my hammer's handle loosens as my shoulders slump. Even though my physical contact with my hammer keeps the clearing bright, the light feels dull to me now.

I have nothing but a fading hope that extends into a long moment of silence.

Then there's a soft *crack* on my left, followed by a little *thud*.

A piece of stone falls away from his father's statue.

I refuse to take my eyes off Erik even when there's another soft *crack*. Another quiet *thud*.

More chunks fall away from the statute.

And then, suddenly, the statue crumbles, pieces falling all at once, except for a thin line of stone that extends from the front of Erik's father's foot all the way up to the sword so that, astoundingly, the sword remains extended in the air, even though the rest of the statute has become nothing more than a pile of broken stone.

The air where the center of the statue once stood shimmers.

A spark of light suddenly flares and then grows, other streams of light forming in the air and pulling together.

It's a slow formation, piece by careful piece, until a perfect sapphire orb floats in the air near the sword.

On my right, General Glass takes such a sharp breath that it sounds like an inhaled shriek in the heavy silence.

In an instant, she fully retracts her wings and, keeping me in her sights, darts across the space between me and Erik to reach his father's statue.

I'm aware of the scuffling sounds of the other two Valkyries also lurching forward, both of them coming into view at the corner of my eye.

Glass reaches the orb first.

Her movements slow down so that, despite her former urgency, both of her outstretched palms close gently around the orb.

For a moment, her eyes glow silver, and then the orb seems to anchor to her right palm, remaining attached to it even when she lowers her arm a little.

She gives an audible sigh of relief before she pulls the orb close to her chest, her palm facing upward so that the orb turns gently on the spot in front of her torso.

Despite her external calm, her focus snaps to her sisters far more fiercely than I was expecting. "To claim the soul of Bjarne Haakonsson of the Einherjar is a great honor." Her voice hardens as she stares her sisters down. "It will be enough."

The other two Valkyries are silent for a long moment.

Then Glaive rubs her jaw. "Bjarne's soul was thought to be lost. His seat in the Hall of Warriors has been empty for a long time."

Griffin makes a humming sound in the back of her throat before she purses her lips in apparent thought. "Indeed, our Queen will certainly be very pleased that we have collected his soul."

"Then we're done here, yes?" General Glass asks firmly.

She doesn't take her eyes off her sisters, even though she angles her body toward me.

In response to Glass's statement, Glaive's forehead creases, but she looks more perplexed than angry. "What of Erik the Vandawolf's soul? It should have risen from his body already, but it has not. How is this possible?"

"Perhaps he gave everything into the making of that weapon," Glass suggests, still keeping her sisters firmly in her sights, even though she inclines her head at my hammer.

The other two Valkyries consider me with far more wariness than they did before, their posture becoming tense. I'm not sure why their attitude toward me has changed until Griffin speaks, now in a low murmur.

"If Erik the Vandawolf gave his entire soul into that weapon, then it is to be feared," she says. "As is the woman who holds it."

I have remained slumped in the snow, a quiet emptiness filling me with every passing moment.

I don't feel fearsome right now.

What use is power when it can't save the ones I love?

General Griffin finally gives a firm nod. "Yes, we are done here. Glaive, you will help me collect our armor."

Just like that, the tension around me evaporates.

Without another glance at me, Griffin and Glaive set about retrieving the metallic suits they peeled off and left in the snow, along with their swords.

The Celestial Star darts to my side, where she sways so close to my downcast face that she nearly brushes my cheek. The glow around me has faded so significantly that she is brighter than me now. Her light is cold but somehow calming.

General Glass also approaches me, her footfalls seeming more cautious than before.

I narrow my eyes at Glass as she extends her free hand down to me.

"I wish to go in peace," she says. "Will you allow that?"

I consider her offered hand. Does she really expect me to touch her now that I know how easily she could kill me?

"Or do you consider the Valkyries your enemies?" she asks, her voice tightening.

I'm conscious that the other two Valkyries are eyeing me again—and most certainly listening for my answer—while they busy themselves collecting the last pieces of armor.

"I have enough enemies already," I say, turning away from them. "Go in peace."

I have powerful enemies. The Fae Queen, for one. Even though I completed the deal I made with her, there is no trust between us. She will turn on me when it suits her.

The humans in the Cursed City are also my enemies. They schemed to kill Erik and nearly succeeded. I lived with their hatred my entire life.

And then there's Thaden Kane, who could be my most powerful enemy of all. When he first came into my life, he claimed to be human. He said that the Blacksmith, Milena Ironmeld, had experimented on him and turned him into a beast.

She'd supposedly killed Graviter Rex's son, Lysander, and used Lysander's soul to give Thaden the physical attributes of a dragon.

It was a lie.

Thaden is not human.

He's a Blacksmith, the son of Malak Ironmeld himself. Malak subjected the humans in the south to a thirty-year reign of terror and subjugation.

Thaden pretended to assist me, sending me in Milena's direction, only to actually send me into a trap.

My brother and sister are with him, and my fear for them is constant now that I know who Thaden really is.

General Glass quietly retracts her hand. She turns to leave and then pauses, lowering herself into a half-crouched, half-kneeling position at my side.

She speaks so quietly that I can barely hear her. "It's a Valkyrie's curse to live without affection. We can show it to our daughters, and they can show it to us. But to all others, we are monsters in the dark. I think you understand this."

Her green eyes meet mine, but I consider her with wariness despite the open expression on her face.

"You are a Blacksmith, but not like the others," she continues. "Even in the far north, we have heard stories of how you wield Malak Ironmeld's tools. I think you must understand what it means to be the monster in the dark."

My lips press together. Only a week ago, Malak's metal adhered to my left hand. I couldn't remove it. I faced a constant battle with the cruelty and malice in that metal. I used that power to turn humans into stone and ash and mist. Those humans had been trying to kill me—had tried to kill Erik—and I hit back without mercy.

I take a deep, shuddering breath and then speak quietly, hoping she knows I'm being genuine when I say, "I'm sorry about your daughter."

Her lips press together as she swallows, her throat visibly constricting before she takes another glance at her sisters.

They've pulled on their armor and appear to be ready to leave.

Just as they spread their wings and call her to join them, her focus shifts to Graviter Rex.

I'm surprised when a look of intense fear fills her face.

I'm baffled by the reason for her anxiety, since it's clear she's one of the few supernaturals who could kill the dragon king if she wished.

A heartbeat after her expression changes, she darts toward me, such a sudden movement that my hand closes reflexively around my hammer.

I prepare to defend myself, but all she does is speak.

Beneath the rush of wind from her sisters' wings, she whispers, "Find the one they call Thaden Kane. Protect him. *Please.*"

She draws back as quickly as she lurched toward me, her gaze fixed on me, desperation flickering in her eyes before she wipes her expression clean.

Once more, she is cold and untouchable and completely in control.

She glides to her feet, steps back, spreads her wings, and lifts into the sky, joining her sisters too quickly for me to have any hope of questioning her.

I can only stare up at her disappearing figure in shock.

Protect Thaden Kane?

Protect the Blacksmith who lied to me from the very first moment and now holds my family at his mercy?

What the actual fuck?

All three Valkyries soar across the clearing in a rush of wind.

To my left, Erik's father's sword creaks in the breeze but remains suspended at the top of the column of stone—a column that should have crumbled by now. Somehow, the weapon is defying gravity, its blue blade gleaming in the power that radiates out from me.

I tear my focus from it, once more looking at Erik, but not for long before I lower my eyes to the snow.

It's too painful.

I can't look again.

I sink all the way to the ground, leaning forward over my knees, curling my arms forward, and lowering my hammer's handle so that it, too, lies beside me.

I tell myself I will stand up soon and build a pyre. Graviter can help me. But for now, I'm frozen.

As I press my forehead to the snow, I wish I could numb my sadness and now my growing fear.

I *will* find Thaden Kane Ironmeld. I have to. But whether or not I protect him or kill him remains to be seen.

I thought Erik would be by my side when I had to make that choice. I thought he would come with me on my journey and face that battle with me.

For a very short time, I was certain I was no longer alone.

I close my eyes and tell myself I only need a few moments here, and then I will get up.

I will put away my grief, and I will start again.

"Bright Heart?" Graviter Rex's quiet growl sounds behind me as his footfalls thump softly across the snow. "You must get up."

"Leave me be, dragon," I whisper against the icy ground. "Just a little longer. I promise I'll stand up soon. Just... leave me be for now."

"Asha?" the quiet growl sounds again.

My exhalation carries my defeat, but still I repeat, "Please. Leave me be."

"I would rather not do that," comes the reply. And then, "Precious Asha."

My eyes fly open.

The breath stops in my chest.

Erik kneels in front of me. His dark hair is damp with melting snow, his gray eyes are filled with worry, and his left hand is extended toward me, his fingertips only an inch away from the side of my face.

As our eyes meet, his lips form a soft, fleeting smile that fills my world with light.

"I never want to leave you again, Asha Silverspun."

CHAPTER 16

My heart splinters into little pieces that pull back together in a rush. "Erik!"

I throw myself into his arms, knocking him into the snow, desperate to feel his body against mine, to convince myself this isn't a dream, that his heart is beating, and his chest is rising, and his arms are really closing around me.

By leaping forward, I've left my hammer behind. The light dims around me, but the moonlight has never felt brighter.

Erik catches hold of me, wrapping his arms around me so that we end up in a sitting position, my legs curled around his waist.

"Asha." He says my name, and that's all before he presses his cheek to mine and closes his eyes.

I hold on tightly, inhaling deeply, dragging in his wolfish scent, and at the same time trying to control my ragged breathing and to stem the river of tears flooding my eyes.

It's no use fighting them.

"You died," I cry, weeping against his neck and trying to drag him closer, even though his chest is already plastered to mine and my legs are already locked around his hips. "You died, Erik."

He holds me as I cry, his voice broken as he growls my name over and over again. "Asha... Asha..."

"You chose to die." My accusation is hard and grief-stricken, full of all the pain I thought I could push away.

His response is quiet, his words washing through me. "I never meant to cause you pain."

"It hurt. It tore—" My voice chokes because my tears won't stop. "Losing you tore me apart. I couldn't..." I try hard to speak. "I couldn't breathe. My heart... it broke."

His eyes are closed, but tears leak from them. His hands press against my sides, pressing, moving, sliding up my back to my neck, then my face, cupping my cheeks.

"Never again," he growls, his lips finding mine, a brief touch that isn't enough for me. "I will never leave you again. As long as you want me, I'm here."

I don't wait for him to kiss me again, pressing my lips to his with a hunger born of loss and new hope. My hands tug at the base of his tunic, my fingers seeking his skin, needing to convince myself of his warmth, his *life*.

I'm conscious of the dragon and the Celestial Star, both very close behind us, the Star now dancing quietly at Graviter's side, the energy around her humming happily.

The dragon's eyes fill with tears as he lowers his head in what I can only interpret as a bow. "Asha Silverspun, I have witnessed the making of your hammer and now I have seen what you can do. I will never forget how you used your hammer to bring back life. The dragons will never forget."

He clears his throat and turns away before I can reply.

"The Star and I will leave you to this time together," he says, already moving. "We will return at daybreak."

Daylight can't be far away now. Maybe only an hour.

Time feels even more precious than it did before.

With every second, every heartbeat that I spend with Erik, my awareness of how quickly it could all end only grows stronger.

Graviter sends a storm of wind around us as he rises into the air with a fierce leap, tucking his legs under him to safely avoid colliding with us.

He soars overhead, banks to the right, and heads farther west.

Within seconds, he disappears into the night.

The Star darts toward the forest, as if there were suddenly something very important over in that direction. She also disappears into the night, but I'm certain she'll be back, too.

Right now, my whole world is this moment.

Erik rises to his feet, keeping me close and supporting my legs to remain wrapped around his hips. "Asha—"

"Take me to the fire," I say. "Don't let me go."

Heat bursts to life in his eyes, a desire purer than I ever thought I'd experience.

Instead of carrying me to the cabin, he turns swiftly toward the forge, every step taking us closer to the warmth of the fire that smolders in the bowl beside the anvil.

A single lump of crimson coal rests inside the bowl, its glow gentle now that its fire has died down. The volatile substance will issue a constant heat.

I'm not sure if it will overcome the freezing air, but as soon as Erik steps into the forge, I'm surrounded by warmth.

It's a small building with an open front but with walls on all other three sides, along with a ceiling.

Somehow, the warmth stays in.

His fur coat hangs on a nearby hook, and he snatches it off the wall, dropping it onto the top of the anvil before setting me down on the fur in a sitting position.

I'm already tugging at his pants and then my own, lost in the desire filling my body. His hands slip beneath my shirt and up across my back and breasts, stroking me through the material before he descends lower. I lift my hips off the anvil so he can drag my long pants off before returning to me.

His mouth burns kisses across my pelvis before he buries his head between my legs, his tongue stroking me, making me moan with need.

I take hold of his shoulders, pulling him back up to me. "I want more."

He fills me and then I'm lost to the rhythm.

I refuse to close my eyes as I take every overwhelming, soul-consuming thrust, my mind and body bursting with pleasure until my breathing is ragged and my moans are coming hard and fast.

His lips crash against mine, his growl thrumming through me and pushing me over the edge.

I cry out as the orgasm breaks across me, taking him with me into a release so complete that my arms and legs feel formless, my world breaking apart and coming back together in his arms.

Erik draws me to the floor, our bodies still connected, somehow pulling the coat down first and lowering himself onto it while I rest down on top of him.

That's how we stay for a long moment, where I once again settle my head to his chest and try to fight my fear that his heart will stop beating.

It thumps in my ear, a strong rhythm.

Please, let it never stop.

He speaks first, his voice quiet. "How did you bring me back?"

I lift myself upward, smoothing the dark hair away from his forehead and cheeks. "What do you remember?"

His expression is solemn. Far too solemn. "I remember you calling me 'Vandawolf.'"

He'd asked me never to call him that name again.

I'd screamed it in my grief before he died in my arms.

He strokes my back, as if it doesn't matter. "I chose to leave you. I *was* the Vandawolf at that moment. It was always easier for me to make painful decisions if I put aside my own heart and thought like a wolf."

He falls silent for a long moment. Then, "I never expected to survive any of this. When my father died, I counted my days. When my brother died, I actively wished for death to come for me. When I sent you away from the city, I *planned* to die. I knew the humans wanted to self-govern, as they should. I was ready to die."

His eyes seek mine. "You pulled me back from the darkness then. You kept me alive. And again, now in the snow. The darkness swallowed me, but you reached in and wrenched me back out again."

I try to find the ability to breathe. Even speaking feels impossible while my heart is pounding so hard in my chest.

I'm not sure how I can explain to him how I woke him when I don't really know myself.

"You gave me a hammer," I whisper, as if it were that simple. "So I used it."

I've left it out in the snow, but it's not as if the ice can hurt it.

Erik's responding smile is a little crooked. "You used your hammer."

"I did."

He looks pleased. "Do you like it?"

I burst into tears again. I can't stop myself.

I press my forehead to his, openly weeping while his hands rub my back, then smooth down my arms, then rise to tangle in my hair. His lips find mine, the lightest brush that I can't return because I'm crying too hard.

"I made it for you," he says, nudging my cheek with his. "It's the right hammer."

I swallow hard, needing to speak. "Loyalty, strength, perseverance, and hope."

"And love," he says, brushing his lips against mine. "Don't forget love."

When I don't immediately respond, he cups my jaw with his strong hand, his expression solemn again. "Don't forget, Asha."

"I'll never forget," I promise him.

CHAPTER 17

We stay lying in each other's arms on the forge floor for a long moment.

Too soon, I'm aware of the trickles of cold air defying the heat of the crimson coal smoldering in the forge.

Against my will, I shiver, and that's all it takes for Erik to reach for my warm clothes. He uses his shirt to help me clean up, telling me he can get another tunic from the cabin soon—one of his father's old tunics should fit him—and then we quickly dress.

I don't want to leave this moment, but I force myself to take a step toward the front of the forge, stopping when Erik's arms snake around me from behind.

It seems he doesn't want to leave this moment, either.

He plants a kiss on my neck. "Can you halt time?" he asks at a low growl. "Preserve this heartbeat and the next?"

I wish I could.

I turn into his kiss, my whole body in a state of bliss that makes me want to return to the forge floor. Or maybe to the fur beside the fire inside the cabin...

But then his arms tense, and I'm aware that his focus is suddenly beyond me.

"My father's statue," he says.

I must have been his sole focus before, and he's only now seeing how broken the statue is. I don't know how he'll feel about what happened to it, but I want to speak only the truth.

"I broke it," I say, uncertain if I should feel regret or relief that it happened the way it did. "The rock released your father's soul, and the Valkyries claimed it—"

His focus flashes to me. "The Valkyries?"

"They came for you."

"They?" He considers me warily. "More than one?"

"All three generals. Apparently, it's an honor."

His eyes are wide. He looks baffled, as if he can't imagine why all three would come. "It is."

The corners of my mouth twitch upward at his reaction. "Their Queen has reserved a place for you at the head of the table in the Hall of Warriors."

His eyebrows arch. "Uh...?"

I press my lips together, trying not to smile at how utterly stunned he looks. Not an expression I thought I'd see on his face.

Then his forehead creases again, and his voice becomes wary. "But they didn't take me."

I grimace. It's my turn to struggle with my words. "I... uh... didn't make it easy for them."

"Good." His sudden smile fades, and his eyes fill with sadness. "But my father—"

"They collected his soul."

"What?" He's suddenly gripping my shoulders. "How?"

"It was when I was trying to wake you up," I say, attempting to explain it and failing dismally. "All the power from my hammer... Your father's statue shattered... Somehow, his soul rose from it. General Glass collected it. She promised he would rest in the Hall of Warriors."

Erik closes his eyes with a groan, his shoulders slumping forward, his hands suddenly heavy where he holds me.

I'm tense and uncertain about how to read his response. "Erik?"

He adjusts his position to slide his arms around me again before he lifts me off my feet, hugging me. "Thank you. It means more to me than I can ever—"

His voice chokes, and he shakes his head, placing me back on the ground.

"For years, I've blamed myself for what happened to my father. He died a warrior's death, but his soul was captive, and I thought he would never find rest—" Again, Erik stops to clear his throat. "My guilt showed me no mercy."

Erik told me all about the circumstances of his father's death—how his father had burned out his deep light trying to defeat Malak, only to be turned to stone. "You were not responsible for Malak's actions."

"I told myself that, but my heart refused to believe it," he says. "Now my father will be at peace. I can finally lay the past to rest."

Catching hold of my hand, he draws me from the forge and toward the statue.

When we reach it, he extends his free hand toward the sword.

The moment he touches it, the stone column keeping it suspended crumbles into dust, leaving him holding the weapon.

The steel blade catches the moonlight, glinting at us.

He starts to speak and then stops, staring at his hand. Slowly... very slowly... a sapphire glow builds where he touches the sword.

His eyes are wide as he turns to me. "Asha, you have to tell me what you did when you brought me back because this..." His hands are full—one gripping the sword, the other holding my hand. "This shouldn't be possible."

"What shouldn't be?" I ask, thinking how calm the air feels around us and just how perfectly the light gleams in his eyes.

"I gave all of my deep light to your hammer. All of it. It's why I died. And yet... I can feel it again."

I honestly don't know the answer, and my forehead creases as I try to make sense of it. "Graviter told me that my hammer—or at least its head—is made from dragon's gold that he hoarded for centuries. He said it could form a bond with a being of pure light."

I reach for Erik, brushing my fingertips to his strong jaw. "You gave all of your light into my hammer, but if you *gave* it to my hammer, then..."

"Your hammer could give it back."

I nod. "Is that possible?"

He gives a low chuckle, shaking his head. "With you, anything is possible."

I am limitless. That's what Erik told me before he died.

The notion scares me, but I shake it off, promising myself I will discover my limits soon.

"Will you do something for me?" Erik asks. "Will you pick up your hammer right now?"

I eye him curiously. "Why?"

His eyes crinkle at the corners. "I'd like to see what happens."

I'm not sure what he expects, but I'm not against it. "Okay."

Despite his request, it seems he's unwilling to let go of my hand, walking with me to where I left my hammer in the snow.

I have no objection to his constant touch. I need the contact to convince my heart that he won't leave me again.

My hammer gleams in the moonlight where it lies on a bed of white snow, but it's nothing like the glow of my body when I touch it.

I quickly scoop it up, accepting the power that streams through me and the way it lights up the space around me. Although, it's calmer now that I'm becoming more familiar with it, and it dims when my thoughts settle. The light seems to become more peaceful as it reflects my quieter emotions.

A moment later I gasp in surprise, suddenly focused not on my hammer but on the sword Erik's holding.

Sapphire light like a blue flame rushes from Erik's hand where he grips the sword, all the way across his chest, down his other arm to our entwined hands.

I can feel the deep light flowing from him as if its energy is infinite. Flowing from him to me, back to him, back to me, over and over again in a constant, gentle stream.

His chest rises with a deeply inhaled breath, and the smile he gives me is stunning.

"My light was always drawn to you, Asha," he says. "Right from the moment I first saw you. I poured all of my deep light into your hammer, and now, I believe it's flowing through our bond, making us both stronger."

I let my heart fill with warmth. "We're unbreakable."

Our bond is unbreakable now.

I vow I won't let anything tear us apart.

CHAPTER 18

Erik's smile banishes all of my fears, and I'm not afraid to let go of his hand.

The bright, sapphire light fades from around us, but a glow remains, a haze of gold and sapphire that slowly fades.

I don't want to destroy this moment with new fears, but it's better to tackle them before my sense of strength fades.

I prepare to speak, but Erik gets in first, anticipating me so accurately that my breath is once more snatched from my chest.

"Your family needs you," he says, a new urgency in his voice. "Now that you have a hammer, you can forge your own medallions. With those medallions, you can protect your family against Thaden Kane and anyone else who threatens them."

Every Blacksmith child is given a hammer when they turn five years old. They then have years to practice using it, learning to hammer all kinds of metals until they turn sixteen, when they are allowed to forge their three medallions.

Forging a single medallion takes days. It involves heating a lump of metal in a fire of crimson coal and then beating that strip of metal over and over again to infuse their Blacksmith magic into it.

Once forged, a medallion will obey a Blacksmith's will,

changing its shape into any metallic object with a single thought. A dagger, sword, rope, chains... whatever the Blacksmith needs at that moment.

The medallion can be worn against the skin in the form of an armband or even jewelry, so it can be accessed quickly.

The medallions were basically weapons on command.

But I wasn't given a hammer when I turned five years old. It wasn't until Erik forced me to pick up Malak's hammer that I discovered that my power was like Malak's.

Unlike other Blacksmiths, Malak was left-handed.

And also unlike other Blacksmiths, who were limited to hammering metal and using their medallions to form metallic objects, Malak could use his power on living things.

When a medallion was pressed to his left hand, he could send his power into living things and transform them at will.

Only hours ago, Erik told me the story of how Malak demonstrated his power to Erik by turning an apple into a dripping piece of meat.

Malak was very clever about concealing the fact that he was left-handed. Always making a show of using his right hand while secretly using his left. I never knew his secret. Only Erik discovered it.

As for me, it took me ten years to figure out that if I wrapped a medallion around my left palm—my powered hand—I could alter the nature of living things with a single touch and a single thought. I did it by accident.

But I also did it with Malak's dark medallions.

Now, I need my own medallions.

"To make a medallion, I need the right metal. It can't be touched by anyone's power but my own." I shake my head in frustration. "My hammer is only half of the equation. I can use it to command and shape metal and even, somehow, to share the light you poured into it. But to face Thaden Kane, I need a medallion. And I don't have the right metal to create one. Or the time to create it."

I feel like I've come full circle with my problems and achieved nothing more than to repeat myself in the process, but Erik is listening attentively, the little changes in his facial expression conveying to me the speed of his thoughts.

"Do you remember the story of how Malak changed the tree outside his childhood home?"

I nod, uncertain where Erik is going with this. "My parents told me the story. The tree's branches scraped his window at night. He didn't like it, so he turned that tree into an apple tree. He made its trunk glow so it would sparkle and no longer frighten him."

"How old was he, supposedly, when he did that?"

My brow furrows. "Eight or nine. So I was told."

Erik's lips settle into a grim line. "According to the story you were told, did he have medallions at the time?"

"Uh..." My brow furrows as I try to recall. "He must have. Maybe he forged them early...?"

Erik's gaze softens. "May I tell you the story as Malak told it to me?"

"Please do."

"He pointed to the tree and told me that he was only eight years old when he stumbled out into the darkness. He described his face as bruised. There was blood in his eyes. He held his hammer in his hand and he struck that tree with all his might, wishing only to break it down. Instead, he made it glow."

I'm quiet, somehow more stuck on the bruising and blood that Erik mentioned than I am on the message I believe Erik wants to convey to me: that Malak transformed that tree with his hammer alone.

"You know... Genova said something similar to me that morning she met me in the apple orchard."

Genova is—or perhaps now *was*—the head of the farmers' guild in the human city. I don't know what might have happened with her after a faction of humans led by the metalworkers and carpenters took control of the city.

I remember her grim words as I continue, "She said she never wanted to forget that the seeds of the city's downfall were planted because a boy was forced to deal with his fears on his own. And then she asked me a question I don't think anyone could answer."

Erik gives a quiet nod, as if he knows exactly what that question was, and it seems he does when he murmurs, "What happened in that house that made Malak so afraid of the dark?"

I close my eyes as the question lingers in the air.

Darkness is created. It is *made.*

I take a deep breath, trying to focus on the future. "Is it possible that I can do much more with my hammer than I thought I could?"

"I think you've already demonstrated that you can."

True.

"But I also believe," Erik continues, "that a medallion can be used much more easily and effectively. Consider the way that Tamra used her medallion to heal you. If her power were like yours and all she had was a hammer... well... she couldn't very well heal you by hitting you with her hammer."

Ouch. I can't help my snort. "Right now, she might like it if she could. Hit me with her hammer, I mean."

When I last saw my sister back at the fae castle, she accused me of having a heart as dark as Malak's. She was afraid when I asked her to heal the Vandawolf that he would imprison me and separate me from her again. Her fears were well-founded after all the years Erik had kept us apart.

To her mind, I must have chosen him over her.

I heard the pain and hurt in her voice when she spoke harshly to me on the night I left the castle.

Her words were like daggers pushing me away.

I try to pull my thoughts back to the problem at hand. "Even if I can do more with my hammer than I previously thought, it seems I still need medallions. So I'm back to my original problem."

"Graviter's gold was the right metal for your hammer," Erik says. "When he returns, we can ask him about the right metal for your medallions. We will find it, Asha, I promise you."

He slips his arm around me and draws close, his lips brushing my forehead. "As for the problem of *time*, I understand your worry. But your family is worth far more to Thaden alive."

"I've been trying to tell myself that he won't hurt them, but I can't be certain. Not after he lied about who he is and the fact that he killed a dragon."

"You're faced with a difficult choice, Asha. You can rush back to your family without a medallion and risk that Thaden can defeat you. Or you can wait, forge a medallion, and risk that Thaden will hurt your family."

Erik's kiss eases some of my tension. "Whatever you decide, I'll be beside you," he says. "Whatever you need, tell me. I lost my family. I won't let you lose yours."

The conviction in his voice settles my anxiety. I may not be able to make longer-term decisions, but I can control what happens in the short term.

"In either case, Graviter will return very soon," I say. "I want to be ready to leave when he does—either to find the metal I can use for a medallion or to find my family. I'll decide once I have Graviter's advice about the metal."

"Then let's prepare."

We head inside the cabin and spend the next ten minutes preparing ourselves to leave, including dressing in fresh clothing. We each don long pants and tunics under our warmer clothing so we can remove the heavier furs if we enter a warmer environment.

We brought two satchels when we came here, and mine still contains my old toolbox. Inside the toolbox are Malak's black hammer and three medallions, which includes the medallion that's imprinted with dragon scales from Thaden's palm.

Graviter Rex warned me to never touch Malak's metal again, so I take care when I glance inside the box.

Also within it is the small, metal device that I pulled from Erik's heart—the one Malak used on him to turn him into a beast.

Last of all is my grandmother's silver pin.

It was given to me by a human woman called *Mother Solas*. She is the cousin of the last human king who ruled the Cursed City before Malak rose to power. My grandmother, who fought against Malak, had given the pin to Mother Solas for safekeeping.

When Mother Solas then gave me the pin, she told me she saw my grandmother in me. She promised there was hope for me.

Erik also selects two weapon harnesses from the wall of weapons by the door, pulling one on over his coat before depositing a number of daggers at the front and his father's sword at his back. He also retrieves a bow and a quiver of arrows and positions them in separate slots in the harness.

He helps me slip a second harness around my shoulders and to position my hammer securely within it. Because of the hammer's head, I have to slide it into the scabbard handle-first, so grabbing it will either mean trying to grab the hammer's head—which is too large for my hand to wrap around—or the very top of the onyx handle where it meets the head.

Then he takes another dagger from the wall, holding it almost reverently.

"So long as you don't have a medallion, you might need this," he says, sheathing the blade and handing it to me. "It was my brother's. He preferred a bow and arrow, but he kept this weapon sharp to keep me happy."

Erik told me how he was the one who would fight up close with the beasts his family hunted in the forests of this mountain. His father's words to him echo back to me now, the grim way Erik repeated them when he told me his story.

Erik will do the cutting.

His life was harsh even before he met me.

"Erik..." I consider the weapon for a moment before slipping it into my harness. "Thank you."

He clears his throat. Gives me a nod. And finally turns to the door.

Now that we're warmly dressed and ready to travel, we step from the cabin, the final embers from the hearth fire casting light across the snow before we close the door behind us.

Erik is alert, his head tilted, his gaze vigilant as he surveils our surroundings.

Because of the way the cabin is situated, with the door on one of the shorter sides, it takes a few moments to round the corner back into the clearing.

We're only three steps away from the corner when Erik freezes.

A second later, the sound of beating wings reaches me, a frantic, flapping noise that stops abruptly.

Erik's hand flies to my arm.

"Wait." He is startlingly tense, his eyes narrowed and his gaze distant, as if he's using his wolfish senses. "That isn't Graviter."

CHAPTER 19

I consider the heavy silence with growing dread.

There's a presence out here. I can feel it. But no matter how I search the nearby trees, I can't see it.

I want nothing more than to draw my hammer, but it won't do me any favors to light up like sunlight. The sky is still dark, actually darker than I expected, although I don't have time to ponder why right now.

Slowly, I lower my satchel down onto the snow beside the cabin wall, and Erik does the same.

Then I reach for the dagger he gave me, sliding it from the casing at the front of my harness. I'm forced to recognize how useful a medallion would be in this situation. To be able to transform it into whatever weapon I might need could make a huge difference in a fight.

The frantic flapping noise sounds again.

This time, it comes with a scrabbling sound.

I spin to the cabin's roof, and at the same time, Erik snatches his bow from his back, rapidly nocking an arrow to his bow. He circles out from the cabin, moving away from the cabin into the clearing beyond it.

I follow his path, steering wide into the space the clearing affords us. While I grip the dagger firmly in my right hand, I'm fully prepared to reach for my hammer with my left hand.

A shadow rises up from the other side of the sloping roof.

Its form is so misshapen that I can't immediately make out what kind of creature it is. Only that it's big... or rather... it's *wide*.

A sharp, black beak becomes visible, and black wings extend at its sides, flapping and stretching before it scrabbles in my direction, seeming to follow my movements.

Even though its wings appear to be made of black feathers, its body is covered in fur, like that of a bear or a wolf. Its talons are more like claws, rasping against the wooden paneling on the roof. They're long enough that they could tear through my chest like a sword.

As I back away into the clearing, preparing for the creature to leap from the roof at any moment, it shakes its head at me, a weird, snake-like hiss emitting from its mouth.

Shivers race across its body, and a flurry of snowflakes shake from its feathers and fur, filling the air around it.

The cloud of frozen icicles billows toward me.

Suddenly, I'm inhaling the heavy, copper scent of blood, an overly familiar smell.

It freezes me to the spot.

Erik gives a soft growl, mirroring my thoughts. "There's blood in the air."

As he speaks, one of the snowflakes reaches me, wafting right across the air in front of my face and then through the space between Erik and me.

I don't need powered eyesight to identify that the snowflake is crimson red.

My voice is strangled. "It's frozen blood-rain."

It has never rained blood up on these mountains. Never in the west. Only ever on the northern side of the city down on the plain.

Blood-rain would fall every time a monster was about to rise in the wasteland. It was a warning that I never ignored. Every time it rained, I would go out to fight whatever monster rose from the mud and ash.

The scent comes with an energy that buzzes at the edges of my senses.

I try to make sense of the bird creeping toward the edge of the roof, where it clings with its sharp talons.

If it's a monster, where did it rise from?

The bird shrieks at me, a high-pitched scream. And then it beats its wings once more, this time a strong sweep that launches it from the roof and directly toward me.

As the bird soars at me, lightning shoots through its body.

Its wings crack like thunder and suddenly, I'm frozen with recognition.

It's a fae thunderbird!

But not a natural one.

This bird has clearly been impacted by Blacksmith magic; its fur and feathers and claws are a mix of bear and bird and wolf.

In the seconds as it shoots toward me, its talons extended, my thoughts are rapid, racing through my mind in an instant.

All of the monsters that rose from the wasteland were products of the transformation magic that seeped into the ground. They formed from the bones and bodies of discarded experiments.

There's still a small chance that this beast didn't rise from the wasteland. After all, the wasteland is all the way down the mountain and to the north.

I don't have time to work through the possibilities.

My reflexes take me backward, my leg muscles bunching before I leap. At the same time, I reach for my hammer with my left hand.

The moment I touch its handle, my speed increases, and so does my strength.

I swing the hammer while I'm midair, aiming for the side of the bird's approaching head.

At that same moment, a blaze of sapphire energy streaks toward me from my right.

Erik leaps at the bird from the side, his sword raised, his jump taking him so high that he's soaring down toward the bird from above, the perfect angle to slice through its neck in one, clean cut.

My hammer hits the bird first, my left-handed swing crashing into its head with a *crunch*.

The force of my strike rams it down and to the right, its body hitting the snow so hard and so fast that its body rips through the snow, gouging a deep turret for twenty feet before it comes to a stop.

Erik lands in a crouch a few paces away from me, adjusting his downward swing with apparent ease so that he can spin toward the bird, which is now behind him.

It lies still in the snow.

My hammer shakes in my hand, power surging uncontrollably through me. But it's a punishing sensation.

Within my mind, I repeat the moment it connected with the bird's body, the horrible *crack* it made, and the way my power shot back at me, biting and angry and rebellious. As if...

My eyes widen.

Then I'm running at the beast, unable to deny the overwhelming impulse flooding my mind and body.

Ahead of me, the bird twitches. One of its wings was forced beneath its body by its fall and slide, but its other wing is spread out across the snow, its feathers appearing jagged and sharp up close.

A trail of black ooze lines the turret it made in the ground.

Black blood. I can smell it.

Its eyes are open and it follows my approach but doesn't try to move.

Like every other monster I killed, its eyes are filled with intelligence, the instincts of a predator infused into its mind.

But with intelligence comes pain.

And confusion.

A battle between animal instinct and higher reason.

I drop to the ground in front of the bird's head.

Erik is only a few steps behind me. He stops beside me, his

sword held ready to deliver a killing blow to the bird's neck, but still, it doesn't move.

It simply returns my gaze.

Gripping my hammer in my left hand, I rest the weapon down on the snow beside the bird's head. Then I sheathe the dagger Erik gave me.

I lean forward, my shoulders slumped, as I dare to slide my hammer forward until it touches the bird's neck.

My whispered command is barely audible. "*Live.*"

The bird's wings shiver, but it remains lying broken in the snow.

Desperately, I wish for a medallion because the example Erik gave me only minutes ago has come to pass.

I can't help this bird by smacking a fucking hammer into its body.

I press the metal more firmly against the bird's neck, speaking louder. "*Live.*"

Do *not* die.

Erik is tense where he's remained beside me. "Asha, it's in pain. You have to end it."

My focus lifts to him, and I voice the realization that hit me only moments ago. "My hammer can't kill. It *won't*. I tried—"

My voice chokes, and I struggle to continue.

"I tried to force it to kill. Now I need to fix what I did."

CHAPTER 20

To my surprise, Erik doesn't argue. His tension disappears, and he gives me a smile, that breathtaking smile that makes sapphire light glow in his eyes.

"Malak used death to make himself more powerful," he says. "You are not Malak." He puts his sword away, sheathing it at his back. "Your power is yours, Asha. It's entirely your choice how you use it."

I turn back to the bird, recognizing the aspects of its body that remind me of the thunderbird who carried me to the fae castle.

That bird's name was Concord. She belongs to the Fae Queen's champion, a fierce warrior woman named Elowynn. It was Elowynn and her sister, Gliss, who healed Erik when he was dying the last time.

This bird is not as big as Concord, but when its wings shiver again, small sparks of lightning flicker and glow, seeming to originate from its chest—which is currently obscured from view because of the way it's lying.

I gasp. "Erik! Help me lift it."

His tension returns, his focus on the bird's talons, but he doesn't question me. Without further hesitation, he crouches, reaches around the bird's shoulders from behind it, and hefts it up against his own chest so that it's now lying at an angle. His left arm supports the uninjured side of his head. As strong as he is, there's a strain in his neck muscles as he fights to keep it in that position.

Hefting a thunderbird onto its side is probably something he never imagined himself doing.

I can't help my lopsided smile.

Fuck, I love this man.

With that thought, power surges through my heart and down my left arm.

I quickly lift my hammer and press it to the bird's upper chest, where the flickers of blue lightning dance with every shiver of its wings.

Then I close my eyes and send my impulses through my weapon.

Be whole and live.

I sense the resistance in the metal, not to my impulses, but to the realities of its own form.

Unlike a medallion, this hammer is fixed, not malleable. Even if it doesn't want to spill blood, it was made for hammering, striking, not soothing. Not molding to the shape of a beast's heart or its pain.

A moment later, I sense the bird's breathing stop. Its chest no longer pushes at my hammer with the rise and fall of indrawn breath.

The lightning that danced across my closed eyelids only moments ago has also stopped.

My shoulders slump even further as I berate myself.

I can't save monsters.

I open my eyes, withdrawing my hammer and looking at Erik, preparing to tell him to place the bird back on its stomach, only to be bowled right over.

A giant, feathery form knocks into my chest.

My back hits the snow, and then I can't distinguish between

the flurry of feathers so close to my face, the playful growls filling my ears, or the sizzling energy suddenly flickering across my vision.

Just as quickly, the thunderbird leaps off me, leaving me staring up in shock at the dark sky.

Erik steps into view, his hand extended to me, a grin on his face and a barely controlled laugh in his voice. "Congratulations, Asha. You created a wolf-bird. Get used to being knocked over."

"Um... huh?"

He helps me to my feet since it seems I'm too stunned to get up on my own.

I spin to the creature that's crouched in the snow, only ten paces away from me.

It has four legs. Paws like a wolf. But its wings, body, neck, and face are like a thunderbird's.

It hunches down, its legs and torso visibly tensing as if it were preparing to pounce on me again.

I point my finger at it. "No."

It cocks its head at me, blinks for a moment, and then renews its crouch, its eyes bright.

"No," I say again. "No pouncing."

Beside me, Erik gives a short, sharp growl. It reminds me of the growls made by the dominant alpha wolf we encountered in the mountains on our journey to find Milena.

The bird's focus instantly shifts to him.

It gives him a defiant stare, head raising, lightning suddenly visible across its chest.

He growls again, even more sharply this time, at which the bird slumps to the ground with a soft whine.

It looks so forlorn that I feel bad. For a moment. And then I'm simply relieved.

It's alive.

I'm grateful it's alive, although... I'm not sure what I'm going to do with it since it hasn't given any indication that it's going to fly away.

Erik reaches my side and folds his arms across his chest, but his smile fades as he turns his attention to the sky.

The heavy scent of blood-rain has remained in the air. "Something isn't right," he murmurs.

"I don't understand what's happening," I say. "This creature was clearly impacted by Blacksmith magic, but... where could it have come from?"

"There was never anything like it in these forests when my family hunted here," Erik replies. "And nothing like it in the mountains around the city. I'd never seen a thunderbird until we stayed with the fae."

"Could the fae have created it somehow?" I ask.

"With Blacksmith magic they don't control?"

I shake my head. "If Milena was their ally, and not the humans', it might have been possible, but she wasn't. What about farther east, where the blight has taken over?" I ask. "Could it have flown from the poisoned land out there?"

"Maybe." He rubs his chin for a moment. It draws my attention to the shadow of growth across his jaw and the tiredness around his eyes that I suspect he's trying to hide from me now. "It's a long way from there to here."

I grimace, murmuring, "The chances of it coming all that way are slim."

Erik's lips press into a worried line. "The most likely option is the wasteland."

I turn in that direction, even though I can't see it because of the trees.

"If it came from the wasteland, then it means a thunderbird died there at some point." I shudder. "The fae said that Malak assassinated their former Queen. Could he have taken her thunderbird?"

Even as I ask the question, I don't expect Erik to have the answer. Neither of us was alive when the assassination happened.

To my surprise, he nods. "Actually, he did. He told me so."

I consider Erik's grim expression. On the night I first met Erik, he made it clear that he knew all of Malak's secrets. He forced Malak to tell him everything before he killed him.

I try to suppress another shudder. "So he killed their Queen, took her bird, and buried its body in the wasteland alongside so many other creatures. Quite probably right next to a wolf in this case."

And now they rise.

All of the monsters are malformed by the creation magic churning within that soil.

I consider the bird with a new sense of dread—my focus now on the fact that the city bells aren't ringing, which means this creature didn't raise any alarms.

Which means there's a high chance that it flew straight to me instead of attacking the city.

"Blacksmith magic is attracted to itself. If this bird rose from the ash all the way down on the plain and didn't understand its existence or know what to do..." I cast Erik a worried glance. "Would it avoid the city and seek me out instead?"

My stomach sinks as a horrible realization dawns on me, and I continue speaking before Erik can respond.

"All those monsters... If my siblings and I hadn't been in the city, would the monsters have even attacked? Would they have turned away and come looking for us instead?"

Erik's hands are firm around my shoulders. "You don't know that for sure."

"But—"

"Asha, listen to me." He points at the bird, which has—rather impossibly—continued to obey Erik's command to stay where it is. "This is a creature of the air. It has the ability to fly to you without harming anything along the way. But other monsters— wolves, bears, stags—they could have razed the city on their way to you. Or just because it's in their nature. Trust me." He releases my shoulders to thump his chest. "I know the mind of a beast."

Erik is a wolf.

He's whole now, his mind no longer splintered, but it wasn't always so. He understands what it means to wake up changed and overcome with rage and want nothing but blood.

I push at my fear, trying to find the light in the dark. "Well, other than the time Thaden arrived, at least only one monster has ever risen at a time. And regardless of the reason, this one didn't attack the city, so—"

My speech is cut short by the bird's earsplitting shriek.

I'm startled by the way it jolts backward, its eyes wide, its focus turned to the sky.

A second later, jagged, red lightning slashes across the dark air above us, snapping and snarling like a living thing.

Thunder crashes immediately after it, so loud that I slap my hands over my ears, my cry of alarm drowned out by the noise.

I drop to a crouch, and Erik drops with me as a storm of crimson snowflakes washes across the tops of the trees, heading toward the clearing.

They're swept up in swirling tornados that rage overhead and smash against the rock face behind the cabin.

The bird drops low to the ground, its wings held tightly to its sides, pressing itself down beneath the onslaught like we are.

Despite the raging thunder and the sudden snowstorm, I'm aware of Erik's hand on my arm, anchoring me where he remains crouched low beside me.

His head is turned to the left. The direction of the city.

The lightning, thunder, and snowflakes are all coming from that direction. And they don't seem to be letting up anytime soon.

Beneath the maelstrom of sound and the snowflakes raging overhead, I make out a whisper in the air.

Wake up...

My shoulders tense, and my heart begins to pound as the echo continues.

Wake up, wake up, wake up...

Another sound joins it. Faint and far away, but it makes my heart sink.

Bells are ringing.

Familiar bells.

Singing out into the air like they always would when a monster was about to rise from the wasteland. The humans would hide in their homes, and I would be called to fight the beast.

Only hours ago, I struck my hammer down onto this very snow and commanded the dead to rise.

Wake up, I screamed.

And now I wonder... *What the fuck have I done?*

CHAPTER 21

"The bells are ringing."

I don't realize that I spoke my thoughts aloud—hell, I can't hear much of anything right now—until Erik leans in close, his lips at my ear.

"For years, I forced you to fight monsters," he says, his voice a low growl. "I won't compel you to fight them again. You can leave. Find Graviter. Make a medallion. This doesn't have to be your fight. It's your choice."

I turn to him, searching his eyes, trying to read his thoughts because I don't know why, but I'm certain he was about to end with 'but'...

All around us, the snow swirls. From within it, the bird's silhouette appears. It crawls toward us, remaining hunched down on the ground, no doubt trying to stay beneath the worst of the icy tumult.

Erik returns my gaze, his own steady.

"But *you* will fight," I say.

I can see it in his eyes. He will choose to battle whatever monster has risen, even if he won't ask me to do so.

I want to believe that neither of us owes any responsibility to the humans living in that city. They hated me and wanted me dead. They betrayed Erik and tried to kill him. What's more, they aren't defenseless. I created weapons that will allow them to fight monsters on their own.

But all he has to do is murmur into my ear, "Maybelle and Kedric."

They are the names of the human couple who raised Tamra and Gallium, caring for the twins at great risk to themselves.

With a resigned sigh, I murmur back, "Mother Solas and her granddaughter, Rachel."

Mother Solas was the one who gave me my grandmother's pin.

Rachel was on my personal guard. Erik placed her there so he could keep an eye on her and protect her from the humans who would like to see the royal line extinguished once and for all.

Rachel called me *Lady Silverspun* and treated me with rare kindness. I have never wished her harm.

There's one more name I also say. "Councilor Genova."

She was the one who asked about Malak's beginnings.

She was also the one who warned me that I was in danger before I left the city. On my last morning there, when she walked with me in the apple orchard that Malak had created, she asked me: *"What does a powerful man do to a woman strong enough to challenge him?"*

My answer echoes back to me.

"He destroys her."

At the time, I believed she was warning me about the Vandawolf's motives, but now her words remind me of other dangers.

Thaden Kane is out there, and every minute I delay going after him, I risk my siblings' lives.

But Tamra would never forgive me if something happened to Maybelle and Kedric. Not when I could have kept them safe.

"How long will it take us to reach the city?" I ask Erik.

He grimaces before leaning close again. "Walking, it takes nearly four hours to reach the city's western side. Running, maybe half that time."

It's too much. Whatever monster is about to rise from the ash could decimate the entire city in that time.

I turn my focus back to the bird.

Erik follows my line of sight.

The beast is pressed to the ground in front of us, its face turned up to me, a pleading look in its eyes as if it wants me to make the noise stop.

As soon as it seems to realize it has my attention, it scoots farther forward, aiming its large head for my lap.

I firmly place my palm against its forehead to stop it from knocking me over again. I don't have a hope of shouting commands at it in the storm, but it pauses, nuzzling up against my palm.

I lean in close to Erik. "Do we have another choice?"

He shakes his head.

Dear saints.

The hardest part will be rising through this storm into what will hopefully be a clear sky above it. Or we might encounter something worse up there.

I suddenly gasp. "My satchel!"

It contains Malak's tools. I can't leave them behind. Not because I plan to use them, but because they can't fall into the wrong hands.

"I'll get it!" Erik says.

"No, it's my responsibility."

"One of us has to get it, and you need to stay here and keep Blackbird calm. He trusts you more than me."

I arch my eyebrows. *Blackbird?*

I guess it's as good a name as any.

But also, "He?"

"He," Erik says firmly.

It isn't exactly the most important thing right now, but still, I ask, "How do you know?"

Erik shrugs. "It's a wolf thing."

With that, he propels himself forward across the snow, belly-crawling using only his arms so he stays low to the ground.

Within seconds, he's swallowed up in the storm, leaving me crouched, my heart in my throat with worry for his safety.

Blackbird takes the opportunity to inch forward, pushing his face up to mine, his size dwarfing me and his weight nearly knocking me flat.

He whines in my ear, a worried sound.

You and me both, bird.

Five tense minutes later, Erik reappears through the snow, dragging my satchel at his side.

I reach for him, pulling him close, all my worry rushing away and relief replacing it.

His arms slip around me, even though it's an incredibly awkward gesture now that we're both crouching again—and the bird insists on gluing its head to my free side.

"Hey, it's okay," Erik says, speaking once more at my ear when my arms lock reflexively around him.

Losing him will never be okay.

I take a deep breath as I nestle into his embrace, preparing myself for our next steps.

"Stay low," he says, handing me the satchel. "You go first. I don't want Blackbird to throw me off."

Slipping out of Erik's arms and down into the snow, I maneuver my satchel so that I can slip it over my head and carry it across my body. Then I drop into a belly-crawl like Erik did, moving alongside Blackbird's neck to his wings.

Fae warriors use saddles to ride their thunderbirds. We don't have that luxury. I'll need to pull myself up onto Blackbird's back so that I'm either sitting in front of his wings or behind them. I honestly don't know which would be safest or best, but his neck looks slender, so I opt for a position behind his wings.

Reaching up as best I can, I hoist myself onto his back, trying to keep low. The wind plucks at my back, and for a moment, I'm fearful that it could rip my hammer right out of the scabbard.

In the next second, Erik slips up behind me, pressing in close behind me. He's sheltering me, but that also means he's now taking the worst of the storm.

Blackbird's body shivers, but he doesn't try to throw us off.

"Up!" I scream into the wind. *"Up, Blackbird!"*

He pauses.

Then he leaps upward, and all I can do is pray we aren't headed to our deaths.

CHAPTER 22

The snowstorm hits us.

But Blackbird manages a far more powerful jump than I was expecting, quickly gaining height.

Thank you, wolf legs.

He extends his wings a moment later, and for a second, it feels as if we'll shoot right up into clear air without problems.

My hope is quickly stripped away.

The snow is like glass, icy particles ripping at my face before I bury my head against Blackbird's neck, circling my face with my arms, praying that the fur coat I'm wearing will resist the cutting icicles.

It's nearly impossible to breathe in the force of the wind.

But Blackbird... Oh, he's still fighting to rise up through the storm.

I can't see the tips of his wings, but his lightning surges and thunder rumbles with every beat he makes. He moves with the wind, slipping from stream to stream as if he's reading the air.

If he really was somehow born from the bones of the Fae Queen's thunderbird, then that thunderbird was a powerful creature indeed.

A terrifying second later, we burst up into quieter air.

It isn't *clear* air. Far from it. We're surrounded by churning clouds that flicker with blood-red energy. But we've risen out of the worst of the snowstorm, and it's peaceful by comparison.

As Blackbird finally levels out, both Erik and I no longer need to lean so low.

We adjust our position, neither of us speaking as we drag air into our chests.

Erik's left arm slides around my waist, and he brushes a kiss to the side of my neck. He's still pressed up against the hammer at my back, which must be horribly uncomfortable, and the bulk of the satchel has slipped to my side beneath my right armpit, but he doesn't seem deterred from hugging me.

I close my eyes and hold on to this moment. His touch. His warmth. His scent. And the weightlessness of being airborne, even though there's a terrible storm around us.

Erik is alive.

I will fight any battle to keep him that way.

When another streak of lightning cuts across the clouds directly ahead of us, Blackbird swoops low to avoid it.

I grip with my legs, my stomach muscles straining, as he descends even farther.

Then, just like that, we drop beneath the cloud cover.

The air is tinged with crimson, an awful hue that fills the space in every direction, but we've left the mountain peak behind, and the clouds overhead have yet to open up and release the blood-rain they clearly hold.

The air is heavy with energy, but it's eerily quiet.

The Cursed City comes into view on the plain up ahead.

The city is surrounded by a ring of mountains that closes it off from the rest of the world. It lies closest to the edge of the western mountains, which makes the journey from this direction shorter than it would have been if we'd been approaching from the north.

The city itself is circled by a high stone wall, atop of which have battlements. The wall has only four gates leading to the outside—one each in the north, east, west, and south.

On the northern side of the city is the vast wasteland, which stretches all the way to the northern mountains and is covered in white ash and dotted with skeletal trees.

To the city's east is the Sunken Bog, a writhing swamp in which lies the Toxic Thirst—a poisoned lake—and which I can just make out as a small, silver, oval shape from this distance.

On the southern side is the farming land. The crops and livestock have further defenses in the form of a myriad of high stone walls that cordon off multiple areas.

We're approaching it from the western side, so our view encompasses both the northern and southern sides of the city.

While red clouds boil above us, the bells located on top of the city's wall continue to ring out.

But as we fly closer, my heart sinks.

The stone wall has three gaping holes in it, each one a large, crumbling fissure with piles of rubble within it. Two of the gaps are on the north side. One is harder to see because it's closer to the eastern gate, but it's large enough that I'm not imagining it.

All of the gaps are wide enough that a monster could get through.

Erik must have spotted the gaps, too, because he stiffens, his arms tightening around me.

"What happened there?" I cry, trying to be heard over the wind. "Could it have been a monster?"

It's startling to me that I don't see a beast yet. True, the rain has started to fall, but the wasteland in the north looks far too calm. There are no large figures approaching the walls from any side—or even within the city as far as I can see.

Which makes me think the damage to the wall happened before now. But from a monster or something else, I can't possibly know.

Anything could have happened here since we left.

On my last day in the city, a group of humans betrayed Erik. Nero, the leader of the metalworkers' guild, and Vincent, the leader of the carpenters' guild, stood high up on the northern ramparts, looking down on me. *Laughing* at me.

My former guard, Braddock, stood with them, and he laughed loudest of all, his ruddy face gleaming with triumph.

They had just shot Erik with a giant crossbow bolt that I had fashioned with my own hands.

I had forged for them that crossbow, along with a harpoon, a net, and weighted chains, each powerful enough to take down a monster within moments.

I vowed that I would come back and destroy those humans.

Now, again, I have to remind myself why I'm flying toward this city instead of leaving its people to their fate.

Maybelle. Kedric. Mother Solas. Rachel. Councilor Genova.

Even the Wasteland Warriors who were as loyal to Erik as humans could be. He trained them to defend the city, but they were nowhere to be seen on the day he was betrayed. I have no idea what happened to them.

"That damage looks days old," Erik growls in my ear. "It looks like it was caused by explosions, not claws and teeth. Can you see the burn marks at the edges of the holes? And the rubble in the industrial area to the north?"

I reach back with my left hand, brushing my fingers against my hammer, instantly giving myself the benefit of enhanced eyesight.

I follow where Erik is looking, my eyes widening as I make out the blackened buildings to the city's north. Those buildings are used for metalworking, carpentry, and textile manufacturing.

"Could it have been caused by crimson coal?" I ask.

When the humans tried to kill me, they ground up crimson coal into an explosive powder and set fire to it, creating a blast as deadly as a fire dragon's breath.

"Very likely."

As Erik speaks, lightning flickers again, this time sizzling across one side of the city to the next, bringing the damage into full view.

Many buildings in the north are blackened and burned out, and the carnage continues southward as far as the castle in the center of the city.

I'm surprised to make out a blockade there. It extends out from the side of the castle's walls, cordoning off the southwestern corner of the city. I can't see exactly what that barrier is made out of—maybe stone and wood—but it's clearly made of many objects piled high.

A whirlwind of possibilities flies through my mind, first and foremost that the explosions in the north could have been an accident.

Crimson coal is incredibly volatile. If the humans were crushing it up in the north and a fire broke out, the explosions could have decimated those buildings and blown holes in the city's external wall.

Or... the explosions might have been deliberately caused.

Acts of destruction. *But by whom and against whom?*

It's concerning, but the threat of a monster is more so.

"We need to get these furs off," I say. "They'll be a liability if it starts to rain."

"Agreed."

I lean low over Blackbird's neck, spotting a small clearing in the forest below, still a safe distance from the city's western wall. "Blackbird, take us down."

I have no idea if he understood me, and I'm concerned he doesn't, but then he alters his course slightly, dipping to the clearing like I hoped he would.

We jump off as soon as he lands, stripping off our coats and fur pants and quickly repositioning our harnesses and weapons. My satchel is unwieldy, and the toolbox is beyond problematic with its bulk, but there's nothing I can do about it. I position it at my back, and Erik helps me adjust it so that it doesn't impede my hammer.

Then we're back on Blackbird and rising into the air again.

The bells continue ringing, the sound peeling out through the air.

The clanging grows louder as we near the city's western wall, and now that we're nearer to it, it looks like only the bells on the walls in the west and south are ringing.

The city streets appear deserted. So is the top of the wall in the north and east. There are no guards there.

As Blackbird angles to the left, now heading northward around the city wall, the status of the weapons I forged becomes visible.

Only the harpoon and the net launcher appear intact. Where the crossbow and the launcher for the weighted chains were installed, there is only rubble.

What *has* remained intact is the stone monolith of the last monster I fought. It was a giant wolf with black, onyx tusks protruding from its face. I used my power to turn it to stone near the city's northern gate, where it has remained like a sentinel.

After turning it to stone, I broke off both of its tusks and used them to make a stretcher to carry Erik across the wasteland. He used one of those tusks—half of it, to be precise—as the handle of my hammer.

Now, I focus on the heart of the storm that's building over the northern wasteland.

It's growing worse by the second.

The clouds are thicker there, heavy with rain that has yet to fall, and the lightning is at its brightest.

Lightning was never a good sign in a storm.

A monster that forms from lightning is always stronger and harder to kill. A fact that makes me now wonder...

Does it have something to do with the thunderbird that might have been buried here? Unlike the wolves and bears and birds and deer that were buried here, a thunderbird's body already carries magic. Its strength and magical power could have leached into the soil, combined with Blacksmith magic, and influenced the strength of the monsters that formed.

I watch the flickers carefully, the way they sizzle through the clouds and snap at the air halfway between the sky and the ashen land.

Wherever the lightning strikes the ground, that is where the monster will rise.

Finally, we reach the edge of the city's northern wall, where the scent of blood grows unbearably strong.

I remain focused on the clouds ahead, waiting for them to break.

Waiting for the blood-rain to fall.

I take a last deep breath as the energy in the air increases to the point where it feels like my chest is being compressed. I brace for the freezing cold water to fall, anticipating how cold it will be.

A second later, the downpour starts.

A moment after that, we fly into it.

But when we hit the rain, it's like a trigger.

Lightning explodes across the sky directly above us, splitting into a myriad of strikes that spear down around us.

Blackbird darts left and right to avoid the deadly strikes while I try to keep my eye on as many of them as I can. I sense Erik's tension behind me, catching the way he follows the path of each strike across the air.

We need to anticipate where the energy will hit the ground, but as all of the bright strikes spear downward at an equal speed, my fear grows.

Other than the time Thaden appeared, there has only ever been one monster at a time. Sure, they might be as close as a day apart, but there were never two in a single day.

This time already feels different.

Blackbird must have risen from the ash earlier and found me.

Another monster is already about to rise.

But if more than one beast forms...

My eyes widen when the already splintered streaks of lightning split again.

There are now so many possible strikes that I can't count them all.

I hold my breath, waiting for one of them to hit the ground.

And then...

None of them do.

Every strike stops midair, snapping at nothing before vanishing.

The rain also stops.

A sudden, heavy silence settles around us. Blood-rain drips from my hair and down the back of my neck. If there wasn't a little slit in the bottom of my scabbard, my hammer would be swimming in blood.

Confusion fills me as my gaze flies across our surroundings, and I try to understand what has happened.

Then, from within the silence comes the sound of wings.

I draw a sharp breath.

Oh. No.

Fear is like lava sizzling through my body as I realize I'm looking in the wrong direction.

I tilt my head backward, sensing Erik do the same.

Up.

I look up.

To the swarm of flying beasts descending from the clouds.

CHAPTER 23

There are too many of them.

So many that my heart plummets and panic threatens to choke me.

I thought I knew what I'd encounter: a monster that I could fight on the ground.

I never expected a swarm of airborne beasts that seems to be growing in number with every passing second.

Already, I count more than thirty, and still, the clouds writhe with more.

All of them resemble birds in some way, although none of them look like Blackbird, and none appear to create lightning within its body like he does. It's a small relief that none of them appear to be a thunderbird like him, but that's where my relief stops.

In a flash, I make out sharp teeth, tusks, antlers, and claws. Some have furred legs—two or four or even six legs—and others have scaled, snake-like bodies that writhe in the air. Still others have stingers on their tails like those of insects.

Some of them are smaller, allowing them to dart through the gaps between others' wings. The beaks on those small creatures may not be as large, but I have no doubt they could rip my throat open with ease.

Blackbird reacts faster than I can flinch.

He banks left, avoiding the downward swoop of a feathered creature whose talons would have sliced off my head and tears away in the opposite direction, heading northward across the vast plain.

Bless him, he's luring the creatures away from the city, but the fact that they stream after us tells me we're their target.

"Asha!" Erik is reaching for his sword, but he doesn't slide it free. "I need your permission to kill them."

When I thought we would face one monster, my choices were simpler. My chances of saving it were higher. But not so for a swarm.

"You need to land!" he shouts. "We won't survive in the sky. There are too many of them. I can make a gap for you!"

A single downward glance tells me that the creatures are swarming beneath us, flying parallel to Blackbird.

My eyes widen as I realize that they're not only following us, but also forming barriers around us. Soon, it won't matter how quickly Blackbird darts and weaves—we'll be surrounded.

"Asha." Erik draws my attention back to him. Back to his solemn eyes and the grim press of his lips. "I need your permission."

I told him that my hammer won't kill.

I transformed Blackbird instead of killing him.

But it will be impossible to transform all of these creatures. There are simply too many of them.

They'll kill me before I can save them. And if they swarm toward the city, they could do extreme damage to the humans there. Wherever the humans are hiding, they won't be safe.

I cling to Blackbird, painfully aware that the longer I take to decide, the more danger I'm putting us in.

"Let me do the cutting," Erik says so quietly that I nearly don't hear him.

Let Erik do the cutting.

My heart hurts, heavy with my decision. "Do it."

He gives me the quietest nod. "Get to the ground. Stay alive. I'll come to you."

With that, he propels himself away from me, leaping from Blackbird's back and out into the storm.

He draws his sword as he jumps.

My breath catches as he lands on the back of the nearest creature—a beast with antlers—his sword slicing neatly through its neck before he jumps off it again. He catches the wing of another beast but swings himself—impossibly—beneath its belly, striking up through the underside of its scaled chest before dropping onto the back of the flying beast below the first and cutting its head clean off.

The creatures were closing in around us, but Erik's already created a gap for Blackbird to dive through.

Blackbird doesn't waste our chance. He heads straight for the gap, sailing through the clear space before it closes again behind us.

My heart is in my throat as I twist, trying to look back to see Erik through the swarm of feathers and malformed bodies.

I need to see him!

But the flying creatures are clearly aware of the threat in their midst. Half of them have closed in around the location where I last saw Erik.

The other half have broken away to follow me.

We have a few seconds' head start, and Blackbird isn't squandering them.

He tucks his wings to his sides, covering my legs with them, before dropping into a dive so steep that all I can do is cling to his back.

If I had a medallion right now, I'd be strong enough that holding on to Blackbird would be easy, but I'm relying on my human strength to fight the force of our descent.

He angles toward the northern end of the wasteland farthest from the city, and all I can do is hold my breath while the ground rushes up at me, anticipating the moment when he levels out enough that I will be able to reach back for my weapon and leap to the ground.

Soon...

Soon...

The angle of our descent eases just slightly, and I tell myself it has to be enough.

My hand whips back. My fingers close around my hammer.

The movement upsets my position, but it no longer matters.

Strength surges through my body.

Every muscle feels like it's on fire.

Power floods me, and with it, the world changes.

With my power, I am whole.

Blackbird spreads his wings, releasing my legs, and at that, I leap from his back.

I gain enough air to twist mid-jump and smack my hammer into the neck of the creature that's first on our tail.

It screeches, the sound of a bird of prey, as it tumbles through the air, crashing into the top of a nearby skeletal tree and sending charred pieces of wood flying around it before it hits the ash with a *thump*.

Another creature is right behind it, but that one swerves to avoid the other's tumbling body, its speed taking it right by me.

I fully anticipate that it will circle right back.

I land safely on the ash, now hundreds of paces from the city's northern wall, and in a clear patch of ash that will give me the space I need to fight.

My boots meet the rain-sodden mud before I spin to face my next attacker, only to discover that the creature is farther away from me than I expected.

But, damn, that isn't a good thing because they're coordinating their movements.

While half of them have remained in the sky, a moving mass that conceals Erik's location from me, the other half has formed three separate groups.

Each group descends toward me in a tight spiral—one to my right, one to my left, and another behind me.

The formations are eerily similar to the tornados of snow that raged through the air up on the mountain.

They create a dizzying pattern that makes it incredibly difficult for me to anticipate which creature from which group will reach me first.

I crouch low, ready to fight, my hammer in my left hand while I draw Thoren's dagger into my right.

Oh, for a medallion.

If nothing else, this situation has already proven to me that I can't go up against Thaden Kane without forging medallions first.

I can only hope I'll survive long enough to make them.

Blackbird has flown farther to my left and is circling back toward me as if he will scoop me up again, but a fourth, smaller group of creatures breaks off from the nearest spiral and races toward him, cutting him off before he can reach me. He's forced to veer away from me, ducking and weaving through the air as he tries to get back to me.

For now, I'm on my own.

The first creature reaches me.

My reflexes fire.

My hammer sweeps the air, connecting with feathers and fur as I use it, not to crush or hit, but to push and pull and pin so that I can slash instead with the dagger in my right hand.

Within seconds, the dagger's blade is covered in dark blood.

Every move I make is a blur. A spin, a kick, another slash. I ram my hammer down on a neck so I can cut it. I use it to shove a creature's wings back so I can stab its heart.

But with every dead beast, another creature takes its place.

For long minutes, I fight and still they keep coming, and even though I try to use my hammer defensively, now it's biting back.

It doesn't like what I'm doing.

I don't like what I'm doing.

When I jab my hammer into the next creature, a sharp energy strikes back at me. And after that, with every swing of my hammer, pain travels up my left arm.

It only grows worse with every death, until I'm screaming.

I tell myself to hold on. Erik will fight his way through the swarm that has remained in the sky. He will reach me any second now, and I won't be alone.

He will remind me that I have no choice.

He will tell me that I have to live.

When a group of snake-skinned creatures races toward me, I leap upward, trying to upset their formation, trying to get them to scatter, only to swing my hammer into a smaller beast with a *crunch*.

Terrible pain strikes through me. It's so sharp that I double over midair. A deadly loss of concentration.

A second later, talons tear across my left hand, a furred body rams into my right side, and a tusk impales my left thigh.

For a horrifying moment, I'm crushed between multiple bodies, my own pinned in midair.

I can't breathe. Can't think.

And then the monsters separate and I'm falling, only becoming aware while I plummet to the ground that my left hand has opened and my hammer is tumbling away from me.

Every bone in my body crunches as I hit the ash. Worse, I land on the side of the toolbox because the satchel slipped to my right during the fight, and pain strikes through my ribs before it slips out from under me.

My left leg is bent at an odd angle. My black pants are ripped across my thigh, and hot blood gushes from the wound in my upper leg.

I scream at myself to get up, but my body won't obey me. I must be going into shock, but there isn't a damn thing I can do about it.

The flying creatures seem to be re-grouping and closing in once more, but for a few moments, there is a gap of clear air above me.

My heartbeats slow as multiple things seem to happen at once.

Fresh lightning flickers softly in the boiling clouds overhead, and I'm confused by the golden color of it since the lightning before now has been crimson red. Thunder rumbles, and my heartbeats seem to thrum with it, and then—

Crack!

A new bolt of lightning, a thick cord of it, bursts from the clouds directly down into the ground somewhere near my feet.

I don't see exactly where it hits. I only know that it has lit up the air around me so clearly that I can make out every detail of the attacking creatures, whose claws and talons are striking toward me.

Their eyes are filled with anger and confusion. They're screeching and crying. They came into existence fully grown and with nothing but a tumult of predatorial impulses to drive their behavior.

It's clear they want me dead.

The slit of the sky above me disappears as they close in.

CHAPTER 24

The nearest beast is suddenly wrenched backward.

Then the next.

The air above me rapidly clears, only to fill with black threads, each one arcing through the space above me like living ribbons as they wrap around every beast near me.

The spiderweb of razor-sharp ribbons rips backward, and the creatures are torn apart.

I try to focus on the male silhouette standing nearby, his arms raised, but a female figure rushes to my side, demanding my attention.

The golden light around them both is so bright that I can't see more than their outlines.

"Asha!" The woman's face comes into view. Silver hair frames her face, and her pale green eyes are filled with worry as she rapidly assesses me, quickly focusing on my wound. "You're hurt!"

My lips part as I try to breathe. "Tamra?"

My sister presses her right hand to my cheek. "Lie still. I'm going to heal your leg. Then we need to move."

I can't seem to form coherent speech. I don't understand how she's here. "Tamra..."

There's a flash of silver metal. It's the medallion wrapped

around her right hand as she leans toward my leg. Hurriedly, she rips the material, peeling it away before pressing her palm to my skin.

The pain stops instantly, allowing me to focus more clearly on the man in the background.

He weaves his metal in the air like threads, forming a perfect pattern. Just like my mother used to do. Shredding, cutting, creating deadly spiderwebs...

He must be Gallium. I *will* him to be my brother, even though I know Gallium's metal isn't black.

"Tamra?"

Her right hand remains pressed to my leg. The pain may have stopped, but I sense the wound isn't healed yet. Blood still leaks from it.

It takes time for flesh to knit.

"We don't have much time," she says. "I need you to listen. This land has turned, Asha. Something triggered it. We felt it all the way in the east. There's no saving this city now. Do you understand?"

I shake my head. I don't understand at all. "How are you here?"

She slows down. "I'm sorry, it's a lot..." She glances at the man, who remains nothing more than a golden silhouette in my vision. "You saw the darkness in the east. That's what's happening here now. This land will be consumed soon. There's no stopping it."

I only saw the eastern blight from a distance, but it was a darkness that filled me with dread.

"The humans." I gasp. "This city—"

"The dragons will help them." Tamra's voice is earnest, but again, she pauses, pressing her lips together, her forehead creasing. "Asha... Whatever you did to trigger this event—and I'm certain it was you—every supernatural within hundreds of miles will have felt it. The fae, the dragons, the Valkyries, even the Einherjar in the north. They will have all felt it."

Wake up.

Three Valkyries were present when I used my hammer to bring Erik back. So was Graviter Rex. And even a Celestial Star—

The Celestial Star! I can only hope she flew clear of the storm up in the mountain.

I struggle to rise, but Tamra presses her left hand to my shoulder. "Don't move. You're not healed yet. Just listen." Her eyes bore into me, compelling me to lie back down. "They all felt it, do you understand? It's the kind of power that can start wars. Do you understand?"

"What..." My brow furrows as I try to straighten my thoughts. "No, I don't understand..."

She glances up at the man, and I'm suddenly aware that the air around us has fallen silent. The cries of dying creatures that I've been desperately blocking out have finally stopped.

The black, metal ribbons that were dancing across the air and delivering swift death finally retract. They slip back to the man's right hand before he steps out of the golden light.

His features come into view, and there's no mistaking who he is.

Thaden Kane Ironmeld.

His right arm is covered in bronze scales that spread across the right side of his chest and halfway up the side of his neck. They're fully visible since he's bare-chested.

The first time he came to me in a blast of energy that mimicked lightning, he swayed and stumbled within the crater he'd created in the earth, seeming disoriented, but this time, his footsteps are certain.

I recoil at the sight of him, flinching backward, seeking the location of my hammer. It's only a short distance away from me behind my head, which is why I couldn't see it before.

At my reaction, Thaden stops moving, maintaining his distance. His lips press together for a moment, but he sounds resigned when he murmurs to my sister, "Asha must have spoken with Milena."

"Or the dragons," Tamra replies quietly.

My brow furrows deeply, confusion swirling within me.

Before I can demand answers, my sister turns back to me. "I don't know what you've been told, Asha. I don't know what has happened to you since we were separated. But there are things you need to know, and we don't have time to tell you. If you believe nothing else, please know that I love you, and I'm so sorry I hurt you."

My eyes are wide as she lifts her hand from my leg. I can finally move without pain, lifting myself enough to see that the skin across my thigh is perfectly knitted. I'm certain there won't even be a scar. But it isn't my wound that concerns me.

Before I can speak, Thaden raises both of his hands. "You don't trust me. That's okay. But please, trust your sister."

His expression is so fucking sincere.

Far more sincere than he has any right to be.

"You lied about who you are," I snarl at him. "You lied about the dragon you killed."

His lips press together, but he appears far less concerned about my accusation than I thought he might. I expected him to freeze or react aggressively or, at the very least, exhibit some guilt, but he doesn't.

"This metal is mine," he says, his expression clear and open as he closes his fingers around his medallion. Then he taps the hammer at his belt. "This hammer is mine. I'm Malak Ironmeld's son. And yes, Graviter Rex's son was killed. I wish I had time to explain everything to you, but I don't. So all I'm going to do is ask you a question, Asha."

I consider him warily. More so when Tamra rises to her feet and steps toward him, as if she trusts him completely.

I, too, lift myself to my feet, inching back toward my hammer. "What question?"

His bronze eyes search mine. "If someone you loved was about to die, is there any darkness you wouldn't embrace to save them?"

I already know the answer.

On the night the Blacksmith race was annihilated, I offered my life in exchange for the lives of my little brother and sister. Every time I wore Malak's metal, it was because I had vowed to keep my siblings alive. When that dark metal was fused to my hand, it was because I was trying to save Erik's life. I used that same dark power to remove the device from his heart and give him back his life.

And then, when I refused to accept Erik's death, I used my power to bring him back.

It isn't a dark power.

But it seems the consequences might have been far more severe than I ever anticipated.

"There isn't," I say.

There is no darkness I wouldn't embrace to save the ones I love.

"Then you know my heart," he says. "And that's what matters."

I stumble back a step, shaking my head at how simple he makes it sound.

How can I possibly know Thaden's heart?

I know Erik's heart. I know my own heart. I know that I'm terrified right now because I can't see Erik anywhere. He hasn't jumped to the ground. There's still a swarm of creatures in the sky —I'm certain they will descend on us soon—but I can't see Erik among them.

I don't know where Blackbird is, either.

Now Thaden Kane, the man I'm certain is my enemy, is standing right in front of me, and he's asking me to come with him as if I wouldn't fear and distrust him.

I take another step back from them both. "Where's Gallium?"

Tamra takes a deep breath. "He's in trouble, Asha. But no worse than the danger we're in if we don't move quickly."

Her focus shifts to the sky—but not in the direction of the boiling clouds and the monsters spilling from them.

She looks northwest, her face rapidly paling and her voice suddenly a whisper. "The dragons are coming."

Without my power, I can't yet see what she can see, but in the next moment, dots appear in the distant sky.

Many dots. Rapidly growing larger.

I've only met two dragons: the dragon king, Graviter Rex, and a forest dragon named Torva Viridia, but judging by the number of creatures flying toward us, I'm about to meet at least ten more.

Tamra's focus flashes up to Thaden. "They'll kill you. We need to leave. Now."

Despite Tamra's urgency, Thaden's studying me quietly, remaining at a non-confrontational distance where I could easily get to my hammer before he could stop me.

Even now that I know who he is, the *pull* toward him is as strong as it always was.

Power attracts power.

More specifically, *Blacksmith's* power attracts itself.

What I can't reconcile are all the different accounts of him...

His own presentation of himself as a human when I first met him. Graviter Rex's hatred of him over the death of his son. Milena Ironmeld's account of how she fought him on the clifftop and her admission that she'd once lied to him.

And Torva Viridia, who said that before all of this happened, Thaden Kane had been *peaceful*.

Then there's Torva's puzzling account of the fight she'd witnessed between Thaden and Milena in which he had claimed that Graviter's son had given him no choice. He'd told Milena he would find me and free me from the Vandawolf. He'd said that *I* would listen to him, even if nobody else would.

And finally, there is the Valkyrie, General Glass, who asked me to protect him.

As Thaden watches *me* watch *him*, a resigned expression settles onto his features.

"Tamra," he says softly. "It took a lot for you to trust me. It will take more for Asha to believe that I'm not her enemy. Maybe, if I'd been honest with her from the start, things would be different." He shakes his head. "She won't come with us now."

"I'm not giving up!" Tamra cries so earnestly that it tugs at my heart and makes me doubt my own judgment.

She spins to me, reaching out for me. "Asha, we need you. *I* need you. Gallium needs you. I know I pushed you away. I hurt you. Badly." Her eyes brim with tears. "I was trying to protect you, but I got it wrong! Please, will you come with us?"

She swallows hard as she stretches out her hand to me. "Please, sister, will you take up your hammer and come with us? Will you stand beside me? Will you trust *me*?"

It's the fact that she asked me to pick up my hammer that freezes me to the spot. Neither of them has tried to stop me from retrieving it. Quite the opposite.

I take a beat too long to answer her.

In the distance, the dragons cross the mountains, only minutes away from us now.

I recognize Graviter Rex even from this far away. He's a powerful golden figure at the front. When I look at the others, I'm surprised to see that they appear to have riders. The Fae Queen Karasi spoke of human riders and the alliance between dragons and humans, so I assume these riders must be human, too.

Tamra's outstretched hand has dropped to her side.

With a dismayed cry, she turns to Thaden. "We need to go!"

He moves fast, lifting his right hand into the air, his medallion instantly splitting into multiple ribbons again.

I tense and snatch up my hammer, preparing to defend myself, but the ribbons don't appear sharp this time. His hands move through the air, both of them, the metal forming threads that he quickly weaves, using his left hand to nudge them this way or that, to form floating symbols, one after the other.

The golden light that was fading around him intensifies again, little flickers of it turning into streams. Then all of the streams pull toward his metal, somehow attracted to the changing shape of it.

It's so bright that my own power merely adds to it, two golden energies merging together.

While Thaden works, Tamra looks to the sky, her fear palpable.

I may not trust Thaden, and I don't understand why my sister would ask me to go with him, but her fear is warranted.

Graviter Rex has vowed to kill Thaden Kane.

I have no issues with Thaden being taken into custody, but I can't allow my sister to be hurt in the process.

Graviter knows how much I care about her. He understands I need to keep her safe.

I move out in front of her and Thaden.

The dragons are still far enough away that I have time to plan.

Or so I thought.

A moment later, Graviter's roar breaks across the distance, a roar so loud that it feels as if he could be standing right in front of me.

"Thaden Kane!" he cries. "You will pay for the death of my son!"

I freeze, shocked, when flames billow from Graviter's mouth, a hot stream that scorches the air even from a mile away—a gap that's closing fast.

It's a warning shot.

He's going to stop. I'm certain he is.

But then Graviter's fire continues to stream across the sky, a deadly heat that billows across the plain, obscuring everything in its path.

I can't imagine that he can sustain his fire for long, but to my shock, its heat only increases.

He's coming straight for Thaden. But Tamra's also in his path.

So am I.

"Graviter!"

He's going to stop. Surely, he is. This dragon has seen my memories. He knows what must come to pass. He talked of my death, but this can't be it. Not at his doing. I still have a chance to jump free of the flames, but a single glance back at Tamra, the way she stands resolutely at Thaden's side, tells me she won't leave him to save herself.

Surely, the future that Graviter saw doesn't involve my sister's death?

Please, not my sister's death.

My voice becomes a scream. "Graviter Rex! *Stop!*"

Thaden's voice sounds quietly behind me. "There is no beast more capable of mindless rage than a fire dragon."

When I turn to him, his concentration hasn't wavered, his focus remaining on his symbols, but still, he speaks to me.

"Graviter Rex doesn't see you right now, Asha," Thaden says. "He doesn't see Tamra, either. All he sees is me."

Another symbol forms in the air, even more intricate than the one before.

"This is the last one we need," he murmurs, but he's still crafting it, and the beads of sweat on his brow tell me he needs heartbeats longer than he's going to get.

Tamra throws her arms around his waist, her face upturned to his, her chest rising and falling with her rapid inhalations.

Graviter Rex is only two hundred paces away and closing fast.

I have a choice.

I can grab Tamra and pull her away from Thaden. I can force her to save herself. After all, Graviter wants Thaden dead, not her. She is simply collateral damage.

But I can't shake the Valkyrie's plea.

"Protect him."

I cast a downward glance at my hammer, this powerful conduit that refuses to kill.

Death is final.

Life... well... it carries hope.

I exhale my doubts and fix my resolution in my mind. Then I adjust my grip on my hammer and prepare to jump—this time *at* Graviter Rex.

I may not be able to hurt him, and I certainly can't and won't kill him with this hammer, but I sure as fuck can whack him across the side of his head and force him to change course.

I can make him miss his mark.

But I will need to time it perfectly. If I jump too soon, I'll miss his head and fall into his flames.

If I leap too late, well, I might jump clear of the flames, but I won't save my sister.

The heat is unbearable now. The wall of fire raging toward us, tearing up the ashen ground and flooding it with lava, is beyond anything I've ever experienced or even imagined.

But still, I stand my ground, counting down the final heartbeats as the distance between me and Graviter closes.

Now.

My muscles bunch, and I prepare to jump.

Just then, a flying creature hurtles in from my right.

Blackbird!

He soars over Graviter's head, and from his back, Erik leaps.

Erik's black claws are fully extended, and he's shouting, but I can't hear what he's saying above the roar of Graviter's flames.

In that instant, I take in the way he's covered in blood, the tears in his clothing, the fact that he's badly wounded, the gashes across his chest and arms and legs.

Despite that, the ferocity of his attack stops my heart.

I may not be able to kill a dragon, but Erik can.

His claws can cut through anything.

As he lands on Graviter's neck, he rams both sets of his claws down through the dragon's scales and into his neck.

Graviter jolts, his eyes fly wide, and his head snaps to the side. Whatever nerve Erik must have hit along Graviter's neck, it seems to have forced Graviter's body to respond reflexively.

The wall of fire rushes toward me—

And then off to the left.

The edge of it is so close to my position that its heat beats into me, stealing the breath from my chest and making it nearly impossible to draw air.

Too hot. So hot.

I use my already-coiled muscles to jump back from the edge of the fire, every hint of moisture on my body evaporating in the heat, my skin burning like a hundred suns are beating down on me.

Every rational thought leaves my mind.

All I have at this moment is the instinct to escape and survive.

I thump into a warm body behind me.

I recognize Thaden's scaled right arm as he wraps it around me, pulling me close.

My head was tipped back, my focus on Erik, but I caught only the barest glimpse of him as Graviter veered away from us. The briefest moment to take in Erik's anger and fear before golden magic blasts around me.

Around *us*.

Thaden, Tamra, and me.

A cascade of runes forms within the wash of light, every symbol Thaden was creating somehow appearing in front of me before they're consumed within the rush of magic he created.

It grips my body, tearing at my chest, and then everything goes black.

CHAPTER 25
ERIK THE VANDAWOLF

The dragon king's blood spills around my hands.

Graviter's fierce roar sounds in my ears. But it's his fire that I fear.

Only moments ago, Asha stood in the path of his flames, her hammer gripped in her hand as if she would defy the inferno that was coming for her.

Now, she's gone. Vanished in a burst of lightning so bright, my vision swims with golden spots.

I couldn't look away from her. I can't shake the fear I saw in her eyes before she disappeared. But I also can't deny the certainty that she wasn't afraid for herself. She was afraid for *me*.

The connection between us is unbreakable, but that makes it dangerous.

She will stop at nothing to keep me alive.

Just as I would give everything for her.

I wrench my claws from Graviter's back and leap to the ground before he can throw me off, risking being trampled in the process.

Landing in a clear patch of ash, my boots finally hit the ground for the first time since Asha and I took to the air.

I sprint toward the city wall, away from Graviter Rex as fast as I can.

My father's sword is safely sheathed at my back, but I no longer have a bow and arrows. I used up all of my arrows fighting the flying creatures in the sky, after which I snapped the bow in half and used the broken pieces of wood like daggers.

An upward glance tells me that the other dragons and their riders are making short work of the flying creatures that remain in the sky.

None of those dragons are breathing fire, but they don't seem to need it. Within seconds, they plow through the swarm of beasts, sending monstrous bodies falling to the ground.

The dragon flying at their head has crimson-red scales, eerily similar to the color of the clouds, which camouflages it against the sky. It's especially difficult to make it out since I still have bright spots in my vision from Thaden's magic, but its rider—

Damn!

My eyes widen as the female silhouette riding that dragon jumps up from her seat, leaps off her dragon and out into the air, and slices through the body of a nearby beast with a weapon that I can't quite make out—*Is it a sword?*—before her crimson dragon safely catches her.

Seconds later, she does it again, executing a fearless display of life-threatening attacks that send monsters falling to the ground.

My eyes narrow.

She can't be human.

But I don't waste any more time studying her because Graviter's roars continue behind me, along with his thudding footfalls.

He's coming after me, as I expected he would.

Blackbird has soared ahead of me, nearly reaching the city wall, and is circling back, his frightened eyes seeking me across the distance. But then his focus flies past me to the dragon coming after me, and he veers away again.

Blackbird is right to keep his distance.

Graviter can't see past his own rage right now. The fact that he came close to burning Asha to death is evidence of that.

My arms and legs pump as I race toward the stone wolf that rests on its haunches in front of the city. If I can reach it in the next few moments, I'll have time to jump all the way to its head, where I can call Blackbird to me. He can circle behind the monolith, protected from the dragon's attack for the few seconds it will take me to leap onto his back.

We can fly away from here, and I can find Asha.

Above me, the sky has remained dark. The flying creatures may be nearly completely annihilated, but soft flickers of lightning remain, and the scent of blood is strong in the air.

This land...

Something has changed.

I don't have time to figure it out.

The stone wolf is still fifty paces away. The last time I took shelter in front of it, I was more badly injured than I am now.

Ever since Asha removed the device from my heart and made me whole, my ability to heal my physical wounds has increased exponentially.

I can feel my skin knitting together across my thighs and arms and chest, but even so, it seems it's impossible to outrun a dragon of Graviter's strength and speed.

His paw swipes across the air, and I'm forced to duck and roll to avoid it, coming up in a crouch to face him head-on, prepared to use my claws again if I have to.

He rages at me, his roar so loud that it hurts my ears. "You protected Thaden Kane Ironmeld!"

But at least he hasn't taken another swipe at me, his front paws digging into the ash and his talons clawing the ground.

No matter how loudly I shout back at him, I can't compete with the volume of his voice, but I take a deep breath and shout all the same. "Fuck Thaden Kane! And fuck you, dragon king! I protected the woman I love!"

"The woman you—" Graviter jolts back from me, his forehead

suddenly creasing, his scales rippling with the change in his facial expression. "The woman—"

A deep fury rises within me, an unearthly growl beyond that of a wolf. "Were you so intent on revenge that you didn't see her, dragon?"

It's as if my voice is a whip.

Graviter flinches.

I don't stop, prowling closer to him, close enough that he could burn me to ash with a single puff of fire. Also close enough that I could leap up to his neck again and do a significant amount of damage to him.

"The woman whose hammer I made," I roar. "The woman I died for!"

He shakes himself and takes a step back from me. "No, that's not... Asha wasn't there..."

He seems so confused that my eyes widen and my voice lowers. "You really didn't see her?"

He stumbles back another step, teetering to the left before he drops to his haunches on the ground. His gaze has become unfocused. Maybe he's replaying the last few moments within his mind. Maybe he's realizing just how close he came to killing my hope and depriving this land of Asha's power.

He is deathly pale, his scales blanching to an unsettling shade of ivory. I wait for them to revert to their previous golden color, but they don't.

His whisper sounds horrified. "I nearly killed Asha Silverspun."

My claws slowly retract, my arms now hanging loosely at my sides as I contemplate a dragon king brought low by his own rage.

When Graviter first came upon Asha and me up on the clifftop where we had found Milena Ironmeld, Graviter was mindless with rage.

Asha tried to reason with him. She told him she wasn't his enemy. She didn't want to hurt him.

He roared back at her that his son's death had stolen the light from his heart. He told her he would not stop until all Blacksmiths were wiped from the face of the Earth.

He would have killed Asha then if I had not attacked him like I just did, using my claws to open up long gashes in his back.

Like now, it was only because of the physical pain I caused him that he seemed to regain clarity.

If nothing else, these experiences have taught me that a fire dragon's rage is all-consuming.

He literally couldn't see past it.

"What have I done?" he whispers.

The consequences must be dawning on him.

He threatened her. She wasn't his enemy before, but now?

Graviter remains hunched on the ground while the other dragons land around us, all ten of them.

The crimson-scaled dragon drops to the ground first, its female rider immediately jumping from its back. The other human riders are only moments behind her, dismounting from their dragons right after she does.

The dragons and their humans take up a formation that arcs around me in a semi-circle. They block off any possible escape other than back into the city, and even then, I would need to run to one of the gaps in the wall since the gate is closed.

Of course, there's always Blackbird.

I don't have to take my eyes off the humans to locate him in the air behind me. Judging by the faint beat of his wings, he's flying over the very northern end of the city, wisely keeping his distance from the dragons. He has nothing on their size.

The female rider of the crimson dragon reaches me.

She has dark-brown hair, chestnut-brown eyes, light-brown skin, and a pale-brown birthmark that extends down her left cheek and across her jaw. She's wearing simple leather armor—protective plates across her chest and thighs—but is otherwise dressed in a black tunic and pants.

Her right hand and forearm are covered in what looks like a long, black metal glove.

"Kneel!" she roars at me.

I probably shouldn't be surprised by her hostility, but I'm not inclined to obey.

"Get on your knees, or I will put you down!" She makes a swift movement with her gloved hand that looks like a mere twitch.

At the gesture, a blade appears in her hand, glinting, sharp, and the length of a hunting knife.

She continues coming at me, now only five paces away, and I anticipate the way she plans to immobilize me by the way her muscles tense.

She's fast—I'm impressed—but I have a wolf's reflexes.

I evade the sweep of her leg and the swing of her blade, a combination of moves that would have been intended to drop me to a knee and then get the blade to my neck. If she'd succeeded, I wouldn't dare make a move for fear she'd cut my throat.

Instead, I step to the right to avoid her leg and lean back to evade the blade. "I don't kneel!"

It isn't because I'm too proud.

My chest suddenly hurts.

Out of the blue, a sharp pain strikes through my heart. The intensity of it squeezes my chest and steals my breath, and I find myself snarling through a moment of confusion.

My wounds should have healed by now.

I'm certain I don't have any life-threatening injuries.

All I know for certain at this moment is that I shouldn't kneel, or I might not get up again.

She snarls right back at me. "You attacked a dragon, Vandawolf. A crime punishable by death. You're lucky I haven't spilled your blood already."

She gives another flick of her hand and the blade she was holding elongates, now the length of a sword.

Whatever that contraption is on her arm, it's capable of changing itself, but I'm certain it's mechanical, not magical. Every time she changes it, it makes a clicking noise.

I take a step back from her, gritting my teeth against the pain until, just as suddenly, it stops again.

My head clears, the sharp sensation fades, and I quickly reassess my chances against these riders and their dragons.

The other humans are also wearing long, black gloves on one of their hands, which makes them all as much of a threat as the woman who continues to prowl after me even as I take careful steps away from her.

It won't be long before I run out of space.

"You know who I am, but I don't know who you are," I say to the woman.

"My name is Catalina Shield. I am the champion of the human Queen Isabella Exalted."

I'm not overly familiar with the customs of the humans who live in the northwest, but it sounds like Catalina holds a similar position to Elowynn of the Dawn, who is the Fae Queen's Champion.

These humans swooped in here, presumably following Graviter on his way back to Asha and swiftly taking care of the threat in the sky, only to quickly become my opponents. I need to know if they came here already intending to force Asha and me to kneel to their Queen.

I think I know what Asha would say to them in that case.

"Is it your Queen's wish to make an enemy of me?" I ask, seeking clarity. "Or do you want to punish me solely because of my actions toward the dragon king?"

Catalina's jaw clenches, and I'm not sure how to read her momentary silence before she retorts, "Your actions led to the death of Milena Ironmeld," she says. "Milena was our ally. Even before you attacked the dragon king, you made yourself an enemy of our Queen."

I narrow my eyes at her.

Our actions didn't harm Milena. We rescued her and tried to keep her alive.

Graviter knows it was Thaden who was responsible for Milena's death, but he remains frustratingly silent, hunched over at the far side of the group, his scales still an alarming ivory color.

"Will you surrender, Vandawolf?" Catalina asks, her

expression increasingly dark. "Or will we find out if you can survive a fight with a *thunder* of dragons?"

By a thunder, I think she means the whole group.

Certainly, each dragon is shifting where they stand, baring their teeth at me, their scales gleaming.

Their riders all step forward, flicking their gloved hands in the air, at which blades of varying lengths form.

I consider my chances and rank them low.

As fast as I am, surviving a fight with dragons would never be easy. Blackbird can't get in close. And the sky continues to flicker with lightning, threatening another downpour and, most likely, another swarm of monsters.

What's more, the longer I'm separated from Asha, the angrier I become.

She brought peace to my heart. She made me whole. She gave me back my life and my mind and my future.

Now, she's been taken from me.

Thaden Kane has her.

And these... fucking dragons... are responsible for that.

Graviter Rex may as well have delivered her to darkness.

For the last ten years, I made sure I was always two steps ahead of everyone else, assessing my moves and countermoves, always prevailing, always achieving my goal, even if I experienced losses along the way.

But I didn't intend to survive beyond making Asha a hammer.

Nothing I do will be according to plan now.

It's time to make it up as I go along.

I extend my claws and bare my teeth, satisfied when my canines grow sharp enough to rip out throats.

I stare down at the small army of humans and dragons I'm facing.

Fuck them.

If they want a fight, they've got it.

CHAPTER 26

J ust as I prepare to leap forward, a slender figure appears in the corner of my vision.

I recognize her instantly, and that makes me freeze: Petra.

She's the daughter of Nero, the leader of the metalworkers who led the attempt to kill me outside this very wall.

I'm not sure if she's here to finish the job or to defend the city.

She's wearing the armor of the Wasteland Warriors and carries a sword at her back and a dagger at her waist. Her oval face is pale, and her lips are set in a determined line. The streaks of dark purple in her hair that mark her profession as a healer appear blood red under the crimson sky.

I'm baffled that I didn't sense her presence sooner, let alone detect her approach.

Where did she come from so suddenly?

My focus shifts to the weapon she's holding in her hands, and my concern only grows.

It's a crossbow, and it's loaded with an iron bolt that's tipped with a glistening, crimson powder.

It looks like the weapons Asha described from her altercation with the humans before she'd escaped this place.

The powder on the bolt could be crimson coal.

I'm not sure if the dragon riders will realize the extreme volatility of the weapon Petra's aiming at them.

Because, yes, as Petra takes another step forward, it becomes clear that she's aiming her weapon squarely at *Catalina* and not at me.

Catalina takes a hasty step away from me, her head swiveling from side to side as she attempts to keep both me and Petra in her sights.

The dragons and their riders all tense up, each one of them also dividing their attention between Petra and me.

"Hello there," Petra says to Catalina. "Unless you want to die, I suggest you move farther away from the Vandawolf."

At that moment, four more women appear, but not from behind Petra.

My eyes widen as they rise up out of the mud around the base of the stone monolith, shaking off the dirt as they jump to their feet.

It's a trick of camouflage that I taught the Wasteland Warriors in case they ever needed to conceal themselves before a fight—a tactic my father had taught me, although we could never use it in the freezing snow.

Fuck me, how long were they hiding in the muddy ash?

I recognize all four of the women, and I'm relieved to see that they're alive.

Nearest to me is Councilor Genova. She tips her chin at me before she pulls a hunting dagger from a holster at her waist and brandishes it at the nearest dragon riders, fearlessly ignoring their dragons.

Her skin is light brown and weather-beaten, her frame lean and muscular from her work as leader of the farmers. It isn't her blade that draws my eye so much as the small, but clearly full, pouch attached to her belt.

I'm concerned about what could be inside it.

More crimson coal?

The woman next to her is Mother Solas. Her hair is silvery

gray, and her eyes are faded brown. Her normally rosy cheeks are pale, and the smile lines around her mouth and eyes are nowhere to be seen.

She glares at the newcomers while her granddaughter, Rachel, takes position on her other side. Rachel's eyes are the same shade of brown as her grandmother's, and her skin is just as pale. She, too, grips a dagger and carries a pouch at her waist.

Nearer to Petra is Maybelle, who also holds a knife. She and her husband, Kedric, took Asha's siblings in and treated them like their own.

They stare down dragons without a hint of alarm, and it worries me a little.

Only those who have already faced their worst fears could look into the eyes of dragons and find nothing to be afraid of.

Catalina seems to have taken quick stock of them. "You're all human."

"So are you," Petra retorts. "A human with no power here."

"On the contrary," Catalina says. "Our Queen rules over all humans. Therefore, you're now under her jurisdiction."

"Like fuck we are," Rachel speaks up, her savage retort taking me by surprise. She was always reserved, concealing her compassion beneath a stoic façade. "We govern ourselves."

"By what authority?" Catalina demands to know.

"By the royal line of Solas," Rachel replies. "Which is to say, by *my* authority."

The other four women, including Petra, give Rachel firm nods.

I may not know what happened within this city while I was gone, but if Rachel has claimed her crown, then much has changed.

Catalina lowers her weapon slightly. "You're descended from King Solas?"

Rachel returns her glare. "I am."

Catalina's eyes narrow. "Can anyone verify that?"

"I can," Mother Solas says, her grip on her blade unwavering.

"And you are?" Catalina asks.

Mother Solas's lips twitch upward, and for an instant, I glimpse the power she keeps hidden. Not magical power. It's the power that comes from knowing herself.

"*My* name is Isabella Solas," she says. "I believe your Queen was named in my honor."

When Catalina's eyes only narrow further, Mother Solas continues. "Your Isabella was born and named five days before Malak took control of this city. The last communication I received from outside these walls was from her parents. They told me how happy they were and how they hoped she would grow to have the strength and wisdom of her namesake. I have their letter still."

Catalina's guard finally seems to lower, but she doesn't appear any less wary.

She takes her eyes off the women to look at her dragon, who edges forward, its focus on Mother Solas and Rachel. Its nostrils flare as it inhales so deeply that the air shifts around me.

It speaks in a distinctly male voice when it says, "They have the blood of the Solas royal line. I can smell it."

At that, the two riders who were closest to Catalina also step forward. One of them is male, tall and lean, while the other is female with blonde hair—an unusual color, at least among the humans in this city, whose hair is predominantly brown.

They circle in close beside Catalina, speaking in such low murmurs that without my wolf's hearing, I wouldn't be able to pick up what they say.

The man speaks first. "If these women are of the Solas royal line, we can't afford to antagonize them."

"We need them," the woman with the blonde hair says bluntly. "Not only them but every human in this city capable of fighting the fae. And damn, you have to admit, the way they hid in the ash was a little impressive."

"More than a little," the man says. "We need fighters like that."

"Desperately," Catalina finishes, speaking the single word in a hushed exhalation.

She turns back to Rachel and Mother Solas, takes a deep

breath, and then gives her gloved hand a flick, at which her weapon fully retracts.

The other dragon riders follow suit, all of them putting away their weapons and folding their arms across their chests. It seems that's their way of indicating they aren't going to attack.

Catalina presses her lips together and gives her shoulders a little roll as if she's recalibrating before she steps forward again, this time with her hands raised, palms out.

"I apologize for the tone of our initial greeting," she says. "But we weren't sure what we would encounter, and we had to be cautious." Her focus flickers to me. "Setting aside the situation with the Vandawolf, we didn't come here for a fight."

She points to the sky before she continues. "It's important that you understand: this land has turned. It has reached its tipping point, just like the land in the east did. You can't stay here any longer. You have to come with us—"

Petra snaps back. "You can't make us leave our homes. We've fought too hard for them."

Unlike the other women, whose daggers have lowered, her crossbow hasn't wavered. All she needs is a spark and she could kill every human in this clearing, although the dragons would most likely survive. And kill her in retaliation.

But it seems Petra isn't alone in her view of the situation.

Councilor Genova also speaks up. "*You* don't understand," she says to Catalina. "For the last week, we've fought a war within these city walls. We brought down the tyrants who would have subjugated us once more. We are finally free from the hatred of the past. We won't give up our freedom without a fight."

My eyes widen at what she said.

They fought a war against tyrants.

If the fight was against Petra's own father and his allies, then it would have been particularly painful for her. The tear sliding down her cheek and the press of her lips tell me it was.

"We have no wish to make you give up your freedom," Catalina says, her tone placating. "We can offer you new homes. A new life. Simply in a new place." She looks at the sky. "But if you stay, your fight won't be with us. It will be with the beasts that won't stop coming."

The crimson dragon speaks up from behind her, its voice a deep rumble. "We have witnessed the devastation in the east. Whole cities were razed to the ground. Endless dust storms. Blood-rain that clogs the air when the dust doesn't. Even if you can hold back the monsters for a time, the soil will sicken, and illness will spread. Very soon, you won't be able to breathe. It will take your children first, and then it won't stop."

I'm impressed by the way that none of the city's women flinch in the face of the dragon's ferocity, but their pensive expressions tell me they're thinking about what he said.

They won't be able to ignore the way the sky is boiling, and the lightning hasn't stopped flickering.

It was Genova herself who said that the crops were starting to fail. The darkness must be seeping in from every direction.

"If you ask us to leave, of course, we'll go," Catalina says with a shrug of her shoulders.

She won't.

Her whispered discussion with her comrades made that clear to me. She needs more bodies in her army, and these women have proven how hard they'll fight to protect what they love. Any commander would want them in their army.

But Catalina hasn't finished. She jabs her finger first at the clouds churning in the sky behind her and then at the wasteland. "But those creatures won't. There's no stopping them now. The people in the east tried and failed."

I narrow my eyes at the way she used the term 'people' instead of 'fae'.

This city has been walled off from the rest of the world for a long time. Thirty years under Malak's rule followed by ten years under mine. The first news we had of a war in the north between the human Queen and the Fae Queen was when Thaden arrived.

He gave that information to me and Asha. I didn't try to stop it from getting out, but I'm not sure how informed Mother Solas or

Rachel may be about the war they'll step into if they go with the dragon riders.

I draw breath to speak, and then I pause.

I can't influence their decision one way or another. It isn't my place. If they want my thoughts, they'll ask for them. It's up to them to make decisions for themselves now.

"You will do us the respect of giving us time to decide," Rachel says to Catalina.

Catalina nods. "Of course. But don't delay. If you want your people to survive, you must all come with us by the time the sun reaches its zenith. We can't linger here any longer than that. Our own people need our protection. We're risking their lives the longer we stay."

With that, she focuses on me. "However, there is one matter we must determine immediately."

Rachel stiffens. "What is that?"

"Regardless of what you decide for your people, the Vandawolf will come with us. He attacked a dragon." She gives me a cold smile. "He must face the consequences."

CHAPTER 27

Petra raises her crossbow again. "Like fuck he will."

Despite being the first to step between me and the riders, she hasn't looked at me until now.

The turn of her head reveals what I couldn't see before.

A savage cut extends all the way down the left side of her face, from her temple to her jaw. It's been stitched up, but it was undoubtedly made by a blade.

My anger rises to see it. I want to ask her what happened, but again, I still my tongue.

She has control of this situation, and I respect that.

"The Vandawolf stays with us," she says.

"No," Catalina snaps. "And before you object again, know this: I will fight you for him."

Petra gives Catalina her full attention again. "Try it. You'll enjoy a fiery death."

Catalina's lips rise into a smile. "Oh, sweet girl, you seem to be missing a spark."

Catalina has a point. None of the city's women appear to be carrying any kind of flint. Nothing to light their coal—if, indeed, that's what's in the pouches.

Petra gives a chilling smile as she very slowly extends her left leg, turning it slightly so that the side of her knee-high boot is visible.

It's covered in some sort of abrasive material.

"All it takes is a scratch," Petra says, her voice low and soft and completely in control. "And *boom.* Up you go."

She steps toward Catalina, who—wisely—takes a step back.

"My father didn't believe I'd do it either, but trust me," Petra says, "I've burned down whole buildings filled with assholes, and I will not hesitate to set fire to anyone who thinks he—or *she*—can take away my choices."

Her eyes brim with angry tears. The crossbow wavers in her hands, but it only serves to make the situation more volatile.

Once again, I nearly step forward.

It isn't worth her life to try to defend me, but then, with sudden clarity, it dawns on me that it might not be me she's doing this for.

She was there when my brother died. She formed a bond with him. She and I were never friends, never even allies, but she stayed close to me over the years.

I suspected it was because she was feeding information back to her father, but now...

My chest hurts again. Not the sharp pain I experienced before, but it smarts all the same.

"You will release the Vandawolf to us," Petra says. "Right fucking now. He may be a beast, but he was never a tyrant."

Her expression softens when she glances my way, her gaze passing rapidly across my face but pausing on the left side. That's where my eye was once amber, and a single tooth used to protrude between my lips.

"Actually," she says, "he may not be a beast anymore."

Catalina gives a snarl, but Graviter Rex finally speaks up, his voice muffled from behind his paw. "Let him go."

"But—"

Graviter raises his head so suddenly that Catalina jumps.

"Let the Vandawolf go!" Graviter roars, startling every rider. But not the city's women. They don't budge or flinch and again, I wonder what could have happened that they are acting as if they have nothing left to lose.

"You cannot make him fight for you, Catalina Shield," Graviter continues to snarl. "He answers only to his own conscience."

Catalina's jaw clenches and she replies through gritted teeth. "We need the Einherjar. He can get them for us."

I'm surprised by her admission.

Moments ago, she whispered with her comrades that they needed more fighters, but they must be in a dire situation if they want help from the northern clans.

Graviter raises himself further upward. "You've spent too long holding back the darkness, Catalina Shield, trying to counter the manipulations of the Fae Queen. You would try to coerce the Vandawolf to join your cause because you have forgotten how to ask for help."

"Nobody helps!" Catalina shouts back at Graviter. "Not unless they're forced to. Not until their homes are threatened. Or their children die. Or they have nowhere else to turn."

She may have jumped back from Graviter before, but now she storms toward him, even though her dragon lurches after her.

"No, Catalina," he says, but she doesn't stop.

"We are holding back the horde!" she screams at Graviter. "The fae want us dead. And *nobody. Fucking. Helps!*"

Graviter stares her down, a hint of gold returning to his scales. His response to her anger is a stern silence that extends for a long minute, stretching into the silence, and seems to subdue her more effectively than a verbal rebuke.

Her shoulders gradually slump, and the anger fades from her face. "Nobody helps unless we make them."

Behind her, the other riders are nodding, and their dragons appear grim. Catalina's dragon has hunched to the ground.

Graviter's hard expression softens.

He nudges his head toward Catalina's chest, his voice a low murmur. "Catalina Shield. Bright Heart. I think, perhaps, in this situation, you could give these courageous women the benefit of the doubt. You could try telling them the truth. And then maybe they, and perhaps even the Vandawolf, will understand why you need them."

Catalina shakes her head, but it's a slow movement until she turns back to the city's women, who are all watching her with growing concern, their foreheads puckered and lips pursed, not in anger but with clear worry.

Even Petra has finally lowered her weapon. "Try us," she says.

Catalina swallows visibly, chews her lip, and then says, "What I'm about to tell you must not spread to your people. We've managed to keep it quiet, although the truth will come out eventually."

She closes her eyes for a long moment, making herself completely vulnerable to attack, but none of the city's women makes a move.

Catalina opens her eyes. "Our Queen is dead."

Mother Solas gives a cry, her free hand flying over her mouth. "How?"

"I... can't..." Catalina exhales a shaky breath, at which the blonde-haired rider steps up beside her.

"The fae lured us to what was supposed to be a negotiation for a peace treaty," the blonde-haired rider says. "The moment our guard was down, their Queen killed ours."

My jaw clenches as my anger rises. When I was in the fae castle, Queen Karasi spun a tale that the human Queen refused to agree to a peace treaty. Her voice reeked of insincerity, but I didn't guess the extent of her lie.

Tears spill down Catalina's cheeks as she speaks up again. "The fae are fleeing the darkness in the east. Their homes are gone. Their children are dying. Isabella wanted to help them. She didn't want a war between us. But she underestimated how far their Queen would go for power."

"Their Queen is what is called a Solstice fae," the blonde-haired rider explains. "She has power over sunlight, which means she can create fire—and then control the fire she created. She blasted a hole through Isabella's beautiful heart."

"I failed to protect my Queen," Catalina says. "Now that Thaden Kane has betrayed us, we've lost Lysander Rex, and Milena is dead... the fae have started conducting targeted attacks, destroying human villages, and gaining control of our outposts. We no longer have the numbers to oppose them. I don't know where to turn."

The other dragon riders all abandon their posts, stepping up behind Catalina, each of them reaching in to press one of their palms to her back and shoulders as if to give her strength.

"We're here," the blonde-haired woman says. "You have us."

Catalina takes a deep breath and raises her head, facing the city's women again. "I know you have questions. You've been isolated here for a long time, but I wasn't lying about the monsters. This land is poisonous now. There was an intense influx of magic, and it's triggered an unstoppable change.

"I know I haven't done anything to deserve your trust, but I can offer you safe passage away from here. These riders are fearless." She inclines her head at the group standing at her back. "We can keep you safe on your journey. Wherever you decide to go."

Mother Solas maneuvers around behind Rachel to reach Petra. "Dearest, it's time to put away our weapons. These people won't harm us."

"How can you be sure?" Petra asks, distrust written in the tense lines around her eyes and mouth. Her weapon remains lowered, but she could just as quickly raise it again.

"Because Rachel is now the last of both royal human lines," Mother Solas says. "And these dragon riders? Well, they answer to Rachel now."

Mother Solas turns from Petra to Catalina with a stern declaration. "The northern army is now Rachel's to command. Is it not, Catalina Shield?"

Catalina's face floods with relief, all of the tension fading from her forehead and mouth. "It is. Yes. If she's willing to claim it."

At that, she takes a knee. Each of the dragon riders does the same.

Rachel's eyes are wide, and her lips part. She glances at her grandmother, who gives her a firm nod.

"I am," Rachel says.

"We have our Queen!" Catalina announces, at which the other riders thump their chests.

Rachel doesn't waste a moment. "You *will* help us leave," she says to Catalina. "And we will..." She turns to the other women, who all give her nods until she gets to Petra. "Petra?"

Petra points her crossbow at the ash at her feet, disengages the bolt, and rams the bolt's point into the dirt, where it can't harm anyone.

She raises herself upright and says quietly, "We will make a new home."

Rachel gives Petra a smile before turning back to Catalina. "A home we will fight for as hard as we fought for this one."

CHAPTER 28

For the next few minutes, I stay out of the way.

Rachel and Catalina are instantly engaged in discussion, Catalina asking how many people are still within the city and how many of them will need help moving. Petra and the other women stay close, and Rachel frequently consults them.

I listen carefully while remaining sharply aware of the way Catalina's dragon homes in on me, moving closer even when the other dragons and their riders take to the air to guard the city's walls.

It's clear I'm not meant to get past him.

I back away slowly, headed for the monolith, where I can rest against the stone wolf's front legs. When Asha recounted to me what had happened outside the city walls after the humans had tried to kill me, she said that she had turned several humans to stone.

I don't see those statues here, so I assume someone must have removed them at some point.

Or... possibly... smashed them up...

There are a couple of mounds of rubble nearby, the dust

blowing off them in the wind, but I can't be certain they're the remains of those statues.

The dragon follows me, maintaining a close proximity that confirms he's guarding me.

I am not Rachel's first priority, and I shouldn't be, but I need to get back to Asha. I made a choice to let these people decide their own future. None of it is mine to control now.

I just need the right moment to get away from the dragon without upsetting the fragile peace that's formed.

From the snatches I hear of the conversation, I learn nearly a third of the city's population is dead. They have twenty prisoners, but Rachel doesn't name them. Petra's expression remains stony, giving no indication as to whether or not her father is one of them.

A few moments later, I'm aware of a shadow flitting toward me. Maybelle's steps slow as she draws closer to me.

"Vandawolf?"

She sounds uncertain. My face has changed a lot since she last saw me.

"Maybelle." I focus on the question that matters. "Is Kedric okay?"

"Yes," she says quickly. "He's guarding the prisoners. Several of the Wasteland Warriors are helping to guard them too, but..." she hesitates. "Many of the Warriors perished in the first fight."

I want to tell her I'm sorry, but it will only sound hollow.

"What of my children?" she asks quietly.

She means Tamra and Gallium.

"Safe," I say, even though it could be a lie.

I didn't see Gallium, but the brief glimpse I caught of Tamra— the way she moved around Thaden—made it appear as if she were with him by choice.

"Thank you," she whispers. And then, "Stay there. Don't go yet."

My forehead creases at her words, but she flits away again before I can question her.

A moment later, I spot Petra hurrying toward me. She's coming from a different direction than the main group, so she must have broken off from them while I was speaking with Maybelle.

"You're hurt," she says, placing a basket on the ground that I recognize as her healer's kit. "Let me help you."

"I'm not hurt," I growl. My wounds have all knitted. I have no need of bandages.

She plants her hands on her hips and glares at me. "You are."

"I'm not."

"Then what is that?" she asks, gesturing at my chest.

I glance down and pause.

Fresh blood soaks into my already torn tunic beneath the location of my heart.

"Shirt off," she commands. "I need to see the damage."

My brow furrows as I pull off the tunic, puzzled by the wound that rests across my uppermost left rib. I remember a stabbing pain after I jumped away from Graviter Rex, but there was no reason for me to be hurt at that moment.

Petra sets to work, ordering me about—hold this, put pressure on that, stay still, stop moving—and I scowl back at her, focusing my energy on the annoyance of being tended to and away from my confusion about the injury itself.

She's quick and efficient, making short work of stitching and bandaging the wound.

When she finishes, I expect her to move away, but instead, she remains.

When I look up, I find her studying me.

It's startling to discover that she's looking directly into my eyes.

Before Asha made me whole, no human would look me in the eye.

Every part of my beastly countenance was fixed. Hideous reminders of what had been done to me. The humans couldn't look at me, so I let my hair grow wild and allowed it to fall across the side of my face, reminding them of what I was and what I'd done to give them their freedom.

But now...

Petra contemplates me for a long moment, and I'm reminded that she knew me before I was changed, even if she didn't know my name or where I came from.

"You're you again," she says.

I try to find my voice. "Asha did this."

Petra gives a nod. "She loves you."

I'm startled for a second time. I know Asha loves me. Now, that is.

But Asha didn't love me when she was my captive—which was when Petra knew her—and she shouldn't have. My power over Asha's life was too complete.

Love can only live in freedom.

"Oh, don't look so surprised." Petra scoffs. "If she didn't love you, she wouldn't have risked her life to drag your dying body away from my father's men. Or fixed your face." Petra shrugs. "She hated you before that, of course." She bends to her basket, pushing her instruments back into it. "I hated you, too."

"I know."

"You reminded me of him."

My brother.

More softly, I repeat, "I know."

She closes her basket but stays crouched beside it, her focus on it, her hands pressing to its top. "When you asked me to heal Asha, I didn't refuse because it would hurt her. I refused because it would hurt *you.*"

She looks up at me again, and now tears glisten on her cheeks. "You saved me. You didn't save him."

I try to find my voice, but it's nearly impossible. "He should have lived," I whisper. "Not me."

She nods, a harsh movement. "Yes," she says. "But then you left."

She rises to her feet, but her face is pale again, and she sways a little. I reach out to steady her, my hands closing around her shoulders. She doesn't shake me off.

"Within a single day of you leaving, I had the horrifying realization that nothing truly bad happened here when you were around. I thought it was because the people in this city were good. They would never hurt each other. But it turns out... you were stopping it."

She takes a shaky breath. "You would think, since I was Nero's daughter, that I would be safe, but power changes people."

She closes her eyes and falls silent.

I don't break her silence. It is her right to speak or not to speak.

Her lips purse as she gently breathes out. "I made it to Genova's home. We gathered together as many of the people we cared about as we could, and we barricaded ourselves in the southwestern quadrant." Her eyes open, and now there is a steely glint in them. "Then we made a plan. And then we made my father and all his men pay."

"Good," I say.

She studies me for a long moment, another extended silence while the dragon remains quiet in the background.

"You found peace," she says. "I'm glad for you."

When she steps back, I quickly open my hands, releasing her.

She pulls out a fresh tunic and pants from her basket. "Clean clothes. You can't go after Asha looking like that."

Before I can take the clothing from Petra, she darts forward, wraps her arms around me, and presses her head to my heart. "I wish you were him."

I'm frozen, my arms lifted from my sides as I try to process all the hurt in her voice, the lost life she could have had if my brother had lived instead of me.

I want to speak, but there are no words for this pain.

She releases me as quickly as she darted forward, pushing the clothing into my arms before she lifts her chin and looks me in the eye. "Goodbye, Vandawolf."

She only takes a step before she pauses again. "Don't let that dragon stop you. I don't think he's as coldhearted as he looks."

Then she turns and hurries away.

The finality of her farewell isn't lost on me.

Either she believes that she won't survive long enough to see me again or that I won't.

Or maybe there is a world where we both survive, and it's the past that is finally put to rest.

I quickly pull off my torn clothing and dress in the fresh garments Petra brought me.

As for *that dragon*, he chooses that moment to speak.

"It will take you weeks to find Asha Silverspun," he says. "Even with the help of your bird."

I'm not sure exactly where Blackbird could be right now, but I'm certain he would have flown clear of the dragons.

"Do you have a point, dragon?" I ask. "Or are you trying to provoke me?"

"I will make you a deal."

I consider him warily. In the past, *I* was the one who made deals and always to my own ends. "What deal?"

"Convince the Einherjar to join our army, and I will tell you where to find Asha Silverspun."

I narrow my eyes at the dragon. "But she's with Thaden Kane. If you knew where to find him, you would have gone after him already."

The dragon gives a *humph*. "I would not."

"Why not?"

"More than one reason."

I can't stop a growl from entering my voice, my frustration rising at his evasion. "Name one."

He tips his chin at me. "Your wolf's voice is very effective, Erik, but it doesn't work on me."

My eyes were already narrowed, but now my brow furrows because he called me *Erik*. "You know my name."

"Of course. Graviter told us. You should get used to hearing it."

I ignore his suggestion. "I don't know yours."

"I am Vargo Vanem."

My forehead creases as I attempt to interpret his name's meaning. "'Wise Light'?"

"Simply translated, yes. Now that Lysander Rex has perished, my son will be the next dragon king. When he hatches, that is."

It takes me a second to remember that dragons hatch from eggs.

Vargo continues. "He will not hatch for another three hundred years. So until then, we must guard our future carefully."

I'm surprised by Vargo's admission of vulnerability. "That's a long time."

"We count our generations in centuries, not decades." Vargo shakes his head, a surprisingly forlorn movement. "Graviter and his mate have two more eggs. They are twin boys, both fire dragons. They should have been next in line, but they will not hatch for another seven hundred years. We cannot wait that long for our next monarch."

"Convincing the Einherjar to join your human army will be impossible," I say.

Vargo doesn't seem surprised by my abrupt change of subject. "Why impossible?"

"They're separated into clans that are at war with each other. They don't fight for any cause but their own."

"You can unite them."

I can't stop my growl. "The son of a traitor? They will vie for the honor of killing me."

Vargo makes a rumbling sound in the back of his throat. "Not now that the Valkyrie Queen has reserved a place for you at the head of the table."

"Even more so now." My lips twist with bitterness. "The Valkyrie Queen may as well have painted a target on my back. The Einherjar will come after me simply for the fight. To die at my hand will guarantee them a place in the Hall."

"Well, you were dead." The dragon shrugs. "She didn't do it deliberately."

He isn't wrong. Even so, I succumb to my frustration and give another growl.

"You have no choice, Erik the Vandawolf," he says, staring me down.

No choice?

Oh... Fuck.

The Einherjar strive only for glory in death. They will come for me no matter what, and if I'm with Asha...

Ah, but if I'm with Asha.

I can't stop the rumble of laughter in my chest.

She would say, *Let them come.* She will fight beside me. We will take them down together.

But my humor quickly fades because her hammer will not kill.

Her power is limitless, but only for the light.

I armed her with everything good in my heart. Every wish I had for her. The life she deserves.

I gave her nothing of darkness.

A roar of frustration builds within me because I made her vulnerable, and now Thaden has her. It will take me weeks to find her, and I'll only bring the Einherjar with me.

I have to deal with them. And quickly.

My father's creed has become part of my soul: Protect the people you love at any cost.

I make the only decision I can. "Take me to the Einherjar," I say to the dragon. "I will make them join your army."

If I don't kill them first.

CHAPTER 29

Vargo carries me into the deep north, his crimson wings and body casting a daunting shadow across the mountains, forests, and plains we pass over.

Before we left the city, we stopped briefly in the forest in the west to retrieve my warm clothing since I'd need it where we're going.

As for Catalina, she didn't seem fazed by being without Vargo. When we left, she and the other riders were already escorting prisoners through the western gate. Each of them was in chains, and even from a distance, I recognized Braddock, the human who once looked out for my brother and me but came to hate me.

Within seconds, they were mere specks behind me, as tiny as the treetops we pass over.

By the time we reach the edge of Einherjar territory, the sun is setting, and the freezing wind plucks at my hair and chills my face. I can't feel my nose. It's been a long time since I've experienced cold like this, but it's the least of my concerns.

Arriving at night should be to my advantage since my eyesight is even sharper in the dark, but the Einherjar guards will be more suspicious of strangers arriving in the night, and as such, more inclined to kill me on sight.

We approach the first village, nearest to the south, where Vargo finally descends to a clearing within a rocky outcrop. The strongest clan always lives closest to the border. They can experience more attacks, fight more battles, and grow stronger in their deep light that way.

A vast plain stretches out in front of me with a gentle incline to a slightly higher plateau in the distance. The village sits on that plateau, surrounded by a wooden wall. The wall is high but still only half the height of the wall that surrounds the human city, which was built by Blacksmiths and reinforced with metal.

This was my father's old clan. The most powerful clan.

If I can persuade them to join the humans, the other clans will follow.

My father described this place to me, and it doesn't appear to have changed since he was here.

Barren fields stretch out on either side of a well-trodden path that is lined with spikes. Every spike has a head on it, some of them now skeletal.

In the distance is a high wall made of wood, with wooden spikes jutting from it. Neither the wall nor the spikes will be a problem for me, but the men patrolling the wall will be.

From this distance, I count at least twenty. The urgency of their movements tells me they've already spotted the dragon, although they can't possibly attack him from this distance.

If I kill even a single one of them, any alliance with the humans will be impossible.

I have to subdue, not kill.

"You will either emerge from behind that wall or you won't," Vargo says to me, his voice a soft rumble. "You're on your own now, wolf. If I get close, they will see the chance for a glorious death, and Catalina wants them alive."

I give a soft snort. "Understood."

If I appear weak, they will try to kill me out of contempt. If I appear strong, they will try to kill me for the sheer glory of it.

Pulling up my hood, I step out from behind the rocky outcrop and proceed along the wide path, ignoring the gruesome spikes along the way.

It doesn't take me long to identify every weapon the men on the ramparts are carrying or how much of a threat they pose to me. Each of them has a bow and arrows with multiple daggers at their waists and a sword at their backs. They're all dressed in furs, but not all of the furs are from wolves.

The man standing front and center wears the pelt of a bear.

He won't be the one with ultimate power in the clan, but he will have the most power of the men on the wall.

I raise my hands out from my sides, leaving my sword at my back, and continue along the path with my arms raised.

It will be no fun to shoot me with an arrow this way. Too easy to kill me, which would be shameful.

I can tell how much it annoys them from the snarls on their lips, easily audible to me even across the distance.

From within the village, I make out the sounds of life: crackling fires, laughter, a faint cheer every now and then.

According to my father, an Einherjar village works during the day but comes alive at night.

"Identify yourself!"

The shout comes from the central man wearing the bearskin. He isn't the tallest of the men guarding the wall, and he certainly isn't the oldest, but the scar down the side of his face tells me he's seen serious battle.

Also, the others wouldn't let him speak first if he didn't have status among them.

I stop in the middle of the path, now thirty paces from the gate. I leave my hood up, concealing most of my face while I keep my arms raised from my sides.

"I am Erik, son of Bjarne Haakonsson," I call, keeping any hint of a wolf's growl from my voice. "I request an audience with your chieftain."

The man laughs. "You are *Bjarnesson?* You do not look like the son of a *bear.*" He peers at me. "You look more like a stray dog."

He looks to his men, who all snort and guffaw.

I let them laugh, maintaining a steady focus on the central man beneath the shadow of my hood. "You will tell your chieftain that I have returned."

"Returned?" The central man's mirth vanishes, and his eyes narrow. "Returning implies that you were once here. But that could not be true. A runt such as yourself would not have been allowed in here."

"Friend," I say, lifting my hands a little higher, a little closer to my hood, "you would be wise to do as I ask."

"Why, *stray?*" he asks, smiling down at me.

He isn't being thickheaded. He was never going to let me simply wander inside.

He's keeping me talking.

I sense movement behind the wall. At some point, one of the men on the wall must have signaled for reinforcements. I'm impressed I didn't notice them do it. But this isn't the dominant clan for no reason.

I slowly slide back my hood. "I've come for what's mine."

The central man's smile grows, and his eyes become brighter. The barest hint of sapphire light—undoubtedly his deep light—gleams around his fingertips as he forms a fist and thumps it to his heart. "So you have, wolf."

At that, the gate creaks open, both doors opening inward.

A hush has fallen over the village. In the distance, multiple fires still crackle, but there's no longer any laughter.

When the gates open all the way, it becomes apparent that there's a line of men standing on either side of the path leading into the heart of the village. Each line has twenty men.

I will have to walk between them—and survive whatever beating they give me along the way.

From the ramparts, the central man shrugs down at me. "Of course, you will have to survive first."

With that, he takes a step backward, moving right off the back of the rampart before he drops from view.

A moment later, I hear the soft *thud* as he lands. He

reappears, shrugging off his fur as he heads all the way to the end of the two rows, where he takes up position, blocking the gap between them.

It's fucking freezing, but they'll see it as a weakness if I don't remove my own fur, so I carefully slip off my coat before repositioning my sword at my back.

I take a breath.

Exhale it.

As the moment extends, a sapphire haze builds around the warriors standing between me and the rest of the village. They're all calling on their deep light.

If any of them can take me down, they will be revered.

As far as they know, I'm here to kill them, too.

Draw blood, I tell myself. *Don't kill.*

Cut, don't maim.

Dominate, don't destroy.

I take a careful step forward. Then another, keeping my eye on all the men—including the ones who remained on the wall—as I continue forward, conscious of the arrows that could fly my way any second now.

I count my footsteps, all thirty of them, before I reach the gates, and then I count my heartbeats, taking a long, deep breath.

An arrow slices through the silence. My reflexes fire, and my fist wraps around it.

Plucking it from the air, I break it in half one-handed.

Snap!

The inertia breaks.

CHAPTER 30

In the first two heartbeats, I dodge a man's fist, break the next warrior's wrist, swipe the legs out from under another man, and dodge three separate arrows.

In the next ten heartbeats, I crack ribs, disarm four men, and punch another two so hard that they fly back into the wall.

After that, I lose count of my heartbeats.

My fists and feet fly, blood splatters, bones break.

If I were aiming to kill, the bodies would be piling up around me, but I've made it ten paces along the line, and I'm surrounded by a chorus of groans that tells me they're all very much alive. Their reflexes simply aren't supernatural like mine.

It's hardly a fair fight, but they chose it.

Despite the haze of sapphire light in the air, none of them has chosen to burn out their deep light, and I'm grateful because if any of them makes that choice, my chances of any kind of deal with them will be over.

As for the man at the end of the line, I'm not so sure. As I fight my way toward him, sending men flying and others straight into the ground, I catch glimpses of him rolling his shoulders, his dagger cutting the air in a rhythmic sway that tells me he intends to use it to full effect.

I'm not about to give him the chance.

I charge forward, feinting toward his left before switching to his right at the last moment, such a rapid change that he doesn't have a chance of following it, even with the force of his deep light, which bursts around him.

My left hand closes around his wrist, wrenching his arm outward and pushing his hand backward in a near-bone-breaking move that forces him to let go of the dagger. At the same time, my right fist collides with his exposed ribs, hard enough to make them *pop* and triggering him to bend reflexively. It's a tribute to his strength that he barely flinches, but it's enough for me to get past him and spin back.

Within seconds, I've kicked the back of his right leg, forced him to his knees, and wrapped my arm around his neck.

It's the same maneuver I used to subdue Thaden Kane when he first arrived in the wasteland.

I'm crushing his windpipe, and he's struggling to breathe, but I only have heartbeats before he fights back.

Allowing my wolfish nature to enter my voice for the first time, I growl a command. "Yield, and take me to your chieftain!"

I'm certain he isn't going to comply. I'm compressing his throat too hard for him to speak, but he gives no sign of yielding. If he intended to give in, he would have let his body weight drop already.

Worse, the sapphire glow around him is growing stronger, a dangerous sign that he's going to choose to burn out his light.

"Don't do it," I warn him, my grip tightening even further, enough to knock him unconscious if I have to. "Don't fucking do it!"

A loud voice shouts from the side of the clearing. "Son! You will *not* join the Vandawolf's father before I do."

I don't know who the newcomer is—and it's difficult to see him because he has cleverly chosen to stand right at the corner of my vision—but he clearly has authority.

Those men who are still standing all shuffle backward as the newcomer approaches, finally stepping into view.

He has startlingly blue eyes and hints of gray hair at his temples, although he can't be more than forty years old.

He doesn't carry a weapon, and his hands are turned palms-up in a sign of peace.

He keeps his eyes on me. "Vandawolf, if you wanted to kill my son, you would have done so already. Just as you would have killed every other man here. Yet you have not. This tells me you are here for reasons other than revenge, and I'm curious as to what they could be."

He inclines his head at the man I'm subduing. "That is my son, Eyolf. It would be a great honor for him to be killed by you, but it would be an insult to me if he were to meet your father in the Hall of Warriors before I could."

At that, the fight drains out of Eyolf, and the threatening sapphire light disperses from around him.

I release him immediately, stepping back from both men.

Eyolf jumps to his feet. It must be taking everything he's got not to press his hand to his lacerated throat, but he raises himself upright and glares back at me.

"It is an honor to fight the Vandawolf," the chieftain announces to his clan before he turns to me and lowers his voice. "Do you know my name, Vandawolf?"

"No," I say honestly.

I suspect that he was the man who challenged my father in the fight that led to our departure from this clan. But I don't know that man's name.

"Pity," he replies without enlightening me. "This way. We will talk."

I glance back at the warriors before following him, taking a quick look at the carnage I'm leaving behind.

Damn, I may not have succeeded in my *don't maim* goal.

But nobody has any limbs missing, only badly broken bones, and I'm certain they will be able to heal themselves with their deep light.

As the groans behind me fade, a hush seems to fall around the village again. I follow the chieftain along the path to the main hall—a longhouse similar to the one my father built on the mountain.

Despite the way the other buildings appear shuttered, I make out the turrets in the roofs from which arrows are pointed my way.

"Your timing has placed me in a dilemma," the chieftain says as we reach the door to the longhouse. "I would not dishonor you by making you speak with me out here in the cold. Yet inside my home are two of the most important people to me in this world. My son took it upon himself to defend them, and I'm proud of him for doing so."

The chieftain pushes the door open and I'm met by the spilling warmth of a hearth fire and the scent of herbs, along with the aroma of a cooked meal that makes me aware of how empty my stomach is.

"You've met my son," the chieftain says. "Now, you will meet my newborn daughter."

He gestures me inside first, which is an overly trusting action for him to take if I were intending to attack his family.

Up ahead, a woman sits on the hearth rug, a baby swaddled in a sling that wraps across her right shoulder, leaving her arms free. It's difficult to predict how tall she is while she's sitting down, but she has lustrous, hazel eyes while masses of wavy, dark-brown hair frame her shoulders.

She appears far more relaxed than I was expecting, taking a look at me before returning her attention to her baby.

I very slowly unclip my harness at the door, leaving my sword within its sheath and placing it against the wall. "I'm not here to harm you."

She arches an eyebrow at me before she rises to her feet, the baby remaining snugly held against her chest.

"Vandawolf, I appreciate your sincerity, but you are the one who should be afraid."

As soon as she finishes speaking, silver wings shoot out from her shoulders, wide and strong.

Every feather catches the firelight in dazzling rays before she wraps her wings around herself, cocooning the child at her chest, along with most of her body below her neck.

"It's lucky we are friends." She gives me a relaxed smile before she settles herself back down on the rug, adjusting her wings like a blanket. "Join us for a meal. You must be hungry."

Hungry? I'm certain my hunger has now given way to my need to survive an encounter with a Valkyrie.

She eyes me when I hesitate. "Or do you intend to reject the offer of a meal as dramatically as you rejected the place I chose for you in the Hall of Warriors?"

Her question tells me she isn't just any Valkyrie, but their Queen herself.

Her forehead crinkles in the beat that I hesitate, but the smile remains on her lips as she continues. "Most Einherjar drop to their knees when they find out who I am."

The chieftain steps past me with a laugh. "I didn't."

Her cheeks flush. "Yes, well, I made it clear I wasn't there to kill you."

"I'm glad you didn't kill me," he rumbles, reaching her side and settling down on the rug to stir the pot steaming over the fire.

Within moments, he's ladled out three bowls of stew, one of which he holds out to me.

I reach for a cloth hanging beside the door and wipe my hands and face. I broke bones cleanly. There isn't much blood on me, but it could be disrespectful to bring it near her baby.

She gives me a smile, as if she approves, before I approach the hearth and accept the bowl of food.

I settle on the other side of the hearth, keeping it between us. Of course, we're all capable of leaping over it if we want to, but it provides a barrier that gives the illusion of peace.

We eat quietly.

The baby fusses a little but settles back down quickly.

"Maybe we should call her *Fojan*," the chieftain murmurs, serving himself some more stew. "Since she has a strong voice."

The Queen wrinkles her nose. "It means *loud*, not *strong*. My daughter will not have to shout to be heard."

He makes a humming sound in the back of his throat. "Then what about *Placida*? Since it means *quiet*."

The Queen snorts. "She will not be that, either."

I listen quietly and bide my time, taking small mouthfuls so I can swallow them quickly. I need to respect the chieftain's position and allow him to direct the conversation. I'm certain he will draw us back to why I'm here, but only on his terms.

Halfway through the meal, and without even a hint of a change in his tone of voice, he says, "When Bjarne left, I lost a man I considered my brother."

I swallow my mouthful, but still, I remain silent, waiting for him to go on.

"I didn't blame him," the chieftain says. "He thought our clan could not change. Our former chieftain had no honor, and by the time Bjarne finally killed him, his brutality had festered. But the change Bjarne set into motion allowed me to continue his work after he left. This clan operates under different rules now."

As much as I should probably accept his claim without question if I want to achieve my goal here, I can't resist testing it. "The heads on spikes tell a different story."

The chieftain's blue eyes gleam. "Don't get me wrong, Erik. We love a good slaughter. But only of those who come looking for trouble." He casually stirs the pot again before he asks, "Are *you* here looking for trouble?"

Now we get to it.

I step through the opening he's given me, choosing to respond as frankly as I can. "The fae are pushing west. They will soon push north, too. The human Queen seeks an alliance with you for the purpose of protecting both her land and yours."

The chieftain makes another humming sound in the back of his throat. "That's a subtle way of saying she wants us to fight for her."

I shrug. "I thought it sounded better the way I put it."

He shakes his head with a low laugh. Then he leans back on his heels. "What would *you* do? If you were chieftain of this clan."

I snort. "I would tell them to fuck off."

I wish I could answer differently, but he would hear the lie in my voice.

"Then why are you here doing their bidding?" he asks.

"Because they have information I need."

"Ah." He studies me for a minute. "Will they give you this information merely for trying? Or do you have to sway us to their cause to fulfill your end of the deal?"

"You must agree to fight for them."

He grimaces. "Well, that is unfortunate."

I consider the way he looks at the Valkyrie, how they communicate silently with each other, and how grim their expressions suddenly are.

"We cannot join this fight," the chieftain finally says. "The Einherjar exist between the worlds of humans and supernaturals. We can't and won't take sides."

I understand his position. I even support it. But I can't leave knowing I accepted his answer and did nothing to test his reasoning.

"What of glory?" I ask. "There hasn't been a war like this for decades. It would give your warriors an unparalleled chance to build their deep light—or burn it out in a battle that will be recorded in history."

"We will find glory elsewhere," he replies smoothly.

My next question is a growl. "When the fae come for your homes, will you *give up your land* and find glory elsewhere?"

He watches me closely as I speak, and his response throws me. "I hear your mother in your voice. You have her heart."

My father told me the same.

Before I can reply, the chieftain continues. "I'm glad there is nothing of your father in you. Bjarne raised you well. But it will not change my decision—"

Wait.

"What did you say?" I replay his speech in my mind, his odd choice of words. "*Nothing of my father?* What do you mean by that?"

The chieftain freezes, exchanges a glance with the Valkyrie, and then peers at me. "Who is your father, Erik?"

"Bjarne Haakonsson," I reply without hesitation. "The man who raised me."

The chieftain's shoulders slump. "Clearly, he never told you... he was not your father."

That can't be true.

I push back against the tumult of confusion within me. "I have his eyes."

"You have the same gray eyes as your father because his sister also had those eyes."

The tips of my claws are suddenly protruding, and I fight to hold them back. "I don't understand."

The chieftain is stony, but his speech is clear. "Your mother was my wife. But you are not my son. As I said, our former chieftain had no honor. I went to kill him, but it was Bjarne's sword that struck him down. When your mother later died, Bjarne vowed to raise you."

His words reach me as if they're coming from far away. A place that can't exist. That shouldn't exist.

Suddenly, what he said to me at the gate takes on a whole new meaning. He spoke of me coming for revenge, and he commanded his son not to join my father in death before he could.

"Why didn't *you* raise me?" I ask, a snarl in my throat. "If she was your wife."

"Because there was too much anger in my heart," he says. "Bjarne was right to keep you away from me."

"And Thoren?" I ask. "My brother?"

"He was Bjarne's son."

"Erik will do the cutting."

My father never stopped me from throwing myself into battle, but he always kept Thoren safe. Always, he would say to Thoren, *"Stay back, shoot from a distance, let Erik do the cutting."*

Maybe, one day, if I live long enough, I will come to terms with his reasons. After all, he couldn't stop me from charging into danger. But right now, all I feel is anger that he used me as a shield for his own flesh and blood.

Why wouldn't he?

Finally, I have a reason for my greater aggression, my larger physique, and the fact that I dealt out death to an entire population of Blacksmiths, covering myself in blood and gore, and somehow, I survived it.

War is in my blood.

My chest hurts.

When I glance down, blood seeps through my tunic. The wound must have opened up again.

My voice is hollow as I rise to my feet. "I have your answer. I will tell the human Queen that there will be no alliance."

I make it to the door, where I retrieve my sword before I turn back to ask, "Do I have your assurance that I will be allowed to leave without incident?"

The chieftain gives me a firm nod. "You have my permission to kill any fool who tries to stop you."

But that's not all I need. I came here to protect Asha from the bloodshed these clans could bring into her life, and I won't leave until I'm certain I've done everything I can. "Do I also have your assurance that no Einherjar will come after me seeking glory?"

This time, the chieftain defers to the Valkyrie Queen, who considers me with more empathy than I was expecting, her lips pursed gently and her eyes soft. "I will make it known that any willful fight with you will not be counted in the Hall of Warriors," she says. "Go in peace, Vandawolf."

I pause at the door. "You could consider Amalia. For your daughter's name."

The Queen's forehead puckers. "It sounds pretty, but it means *work.* Toil. Why would you suggest it?"

"Because that is what a leader does," I reply, reaching for the door.

I haven't made it another step before the Queen suddenly tenses, her focus snapping to the left. "Wait!"

The chieftain responds immediately to her alarm. "What do you sense?"

"A power," she whispers, her eyes growing wide. "It's coming this way. And fast." She spins back to the chieftain, her eyes glowing silver. "Prepare your warriors. Darkness comes."

PART FOUR
THE CHOICE AT THE END OF THE BEGINNING

ASHA SILVERSPUN

CHAPTER 31

ASHA SILVERSPUN

I wake to the scent of ash and flames, a shout on my lips.

Gentle hands press on my shoulders before I can lurch upright.

My eyes fly open to find my sister leaning over me, an exhalation of relief on her lips. "Oh, thank the saints, you're awake."

I quickly assess my surroundings, checking for threats, surprised by what I see.

I'm lying on a thick rug at the side of a small but comfortable-looking room. A gentle fire glows at my back. My hammer rests on the rug beside me, within easy reach.

The nearest furniture is a simple wooden table, small and low, with two wooden chairs next to it. A flask of water rests on top of it, along with my toolbox. The satchel the box was in has been neatly folded and lies beside the box.

To the left of the room is a cooking area, but on the right, the entire wall is lined from floor to ceiling with shelves filled with metallic objects, each one more intricate than the last. My focus lands on a small, metal figurine. It's cloaked but faceless, smooth metal where its facial features might be.

"Where am I?"

Tamra's hands haven't left my shoulders. She's kneeling on the rug beside me. "This is Thaden's home, but we thought it would be best if he wasn't here when you woke up."

"How long have I been out?"

"An hour," she says. "It shouldn't have affected you that way, but we think it might have been because you'd lost a lot of blood. Your body went into shock."

My focus is on the first part of her speech. "We?"

"Thaden and me," she says, the tension growing around her eyes and lips. "Asha, I'm so sorry for what I said to you."

I'm not sure that my hurt feelings are the most important thing we need to talk about right now, but my sister always had her priorities straight. If this is where she wants to start, then it must be important to her.

"You're nothing like Malak," she says. "But I knew the accusation would hurt you enough that you'd walk away from us. I was trying to protect you because I'd figured out who Thaden Kane was."

"A Blacksmith," I say, slowly pushing myself upright. "Malak's son."

Her hands fall away from me, and she sits back on her heels. "I expected him to hurt you. I wasn't going to let that happen. I was determined to get him as far away from you as possible."

She gives me a steely look that defies her compassion.

Her power may lie in healing, but my sister is made of metal.

"But now, you're here," I say, my voice wary, my mind filled with questions.

"I got it wrong," she says.

Her cry back in the wasteland echoes back to me: *"I'm not giving up."*

"It wasn't my fault," she says with a shrug. "Thaden lied through his teeth, but he didn't do it for the reasons I thought."

I study her carefully. "Why am I here, Tamra?"

"Because this is where the answers are." She rises to her feet but doesn't reach for me. "There's water on the table. A bathroom over there—clean clothes are inside. Come out when you're ready."

"Wait, Tamra." I push to my feet. "What about Gallium? You said he's in trouble."

She takes a deep breath, and I don't miss how suddenly shaky she is. "The Fae Queen has him. She will use him as a bargaining piece. She sent a message to me—but only because she believed I would pass it on to you—to tell you that you will do what she asks when she asks it."

I'm reaching for my hammer within seconds. "She means to keep me on a string?"

By the time I straighten, Tamra must have swallowed her fears, because now she appears impossibly quiet. "The messenger didn't say what Karasi will ask you to do, Asha, or when. Only that you will have to make a choice."

I fight my frustration. "It's all a game to her."

Tamra inclines her head. "The longer she keeps you waiting, the more your fear will grow and the more power she has over you."

I consider the truth of that. "Which fae brought the message?"

Tamra clasps her hands together, and I don't miss the way her knuckles turn white. "It was Dusana. She followed us all the way here. There were others with her, but they turned back once they had Gallium."

Dusana is the fae warrior who was publicly beaten and cast out for attacking me.

"Karasi sent a message within a message," I murmur. "Dusana is the lowest of the low in fae society. Karasi means to tell me she will bring me low, too."

My grip on my hammer only tightens, but when I look at Tamra, she's studying me with a grave expression.

"The choices you make will determine all of our fates, Asha," she says. "You, alone, have the power to end all of this. Whether or not that end involves our deaths will be entirely up to you."

My eyes widen. She speaks with such gravity that my

heartbeats become heavy, and my hammer feels like a weight in my hands.

"No matter what Karasi wants you to do, no matter what decisions await you, for you to choose your path wisely, you need answers. When you're ready to step outside, the answers are waiting. Then the choices you make will be up to you."

My blood is thumping in my ears by the time she slips through the door and out into the sunlight. It's such a sudden influx of light through the door, especially after the night on the mountain and then the morning under the crimson sky, that my eyes have trouble adjusting.

A glowing line remains in my vision even as the door closes behind her. The golden light only serves to remind me of Graviter Rex's scales. His fire raging toward us. The sight of Erik leaping onto his back, forcing Graviter off course.

I press the heel of my palm to my chest.

I'm afraid for Erik. As strong and determined as he is, he attacked the dragon king in full view of other dragons and their riders. Graviter Rex had clearly lost his mind to rage, and the other dragons will see Erik as an enemy.

Fuck answers. I need to get back to him!

It takes a mental clamp around my heart to stop myself from rushing to the door and trying to leave this place immediately. It's only because of the way my sister spoke that I pause.

The fact that she talked of our deaths and laid them squarely at my feet...

I struggle to breathe out my fears, telling myself that Erik is the Vandawolf. He survived Malak. He will survive the dragons.

Reaching the table, I first check the contents of my toolbox, refraining from touching anything but verifying that nothing has been removed. Malak's tools are still in there.

Next, I reach for the water flask on the table and drink my fill, and then I head cautiously to the bathroom, finding it as simply laid out as the main room.

When I emerge, I'm dressed in a clean tunic and pants, much better-fitting than I expected.

I pause at the wall of metal objects. If I had to guess, I'd say they were set out according to when they'd been made. The ones on the bottom shelf are rudimentary, simple cones and cubes, but still beautifully made.

The ones on the higher shelves are fantastically intricate. One of them looks to be some kind of timekeeper with moving parts that make a soft, clicking noise. Then there's a figurine of a stag, every piece of its body made of tiny cogs that I suspect might move if I were to bump them.

And finally, there's the cloaked figurine without a face.

"That's you." The soft rumble sounds from the doorway a second before light spills into the room.

Thaden's form is so tall and his chest so broad that he must have blocked out most of the sunlight, and the glow from my hammer will have done the rest to conceal his presence before now.

He continues. "I didn't know what you look like, so I left the face blank."

My hand was raised toward the figurine, and now I lower it, turning to him. "Why me?"

"Because you're the linchpin of my life, Asha Silverspun. Without you, it all falls apart."

I'm not sure what to make of his statement or the seriousness of his tone, the same solemnity with which Tamra spoke.

All I can do is consider him with increasing wariness.

He's dressed in a short-sleeved tunic but pants of a heavier material, along with leather boots. There's a smudge of ash across his left cheek and several smears on his left forearm. He smells like a forge, but a regular one, the kind the human metalworkers used. There is no honeyed scent clinging to the air around him.

Importantly, he isn't holding any weapons. No hammer. No medallions.

He's dangerous enough without them.

He leans forward to push the door wide open, letting sunlight stream inside. I squint, unable to focus beyond the opening to see what lies beyond it.

"Tamra told me to wait," he says. "But time isn't on my side."

I approach him cautiously, pausing a few paces before I reach the door. I can now make out sounds from outside. Murmuring voices. Running water. But also clinking and tapping that I can't quite identify...

"Step back," I say to Thaden.

He complies, letting the door slowly shut again.

I grab it at the last moment, pull it open, and step through it, remaining aware of his location as he continues to move back, giving me space.

Suddenly, he isn't the center of my attention.

My jaw drops. "What is this place?"

CHAPTER 32

I struggle to take it all in at once.

Immediately in front of me is a large courtyard with a fountain in its center. All around it are circular rows of plants that teem with all sorts of fruits and vegetables.

People are quietly tending to the plants. Pumping water from the fountain. Pruning. Picking food. But not all of them are working.

A group of children sits off the right, circled around a woman who's reading to them from a book.

None of them gives me anything more than a casual glance, although an older woman pruning what looks like a tomato bush arches her eyebrows at me in a way I can't interpret.

But it isn't the idyllic scene that has caused me to catch my breath.

Every person has a metallic limb.

The little boy who runs up to Thaden has a metal foot that clacks on the cobbled stone. The older woman who arched her eyebrows at me has a metal hand. The man pumping water from the fountain has a metallic arm. The woman reading from the book has a metallic knee—startling, given that much of the rest of her leg is flesh and blood and I can't imagine how everything was knitted together in a functional way.

Each limb is an intricate series of cogs and pieces that are so complex and detailed that I can't possibly identify them all—or understand how they fit together to function like living limbs.

"Welcome to *Myrkur Fjall*." Tamra's voice sounds from behind me where she leans up against the wall of the cottage beside the door I stepped through. "A sanctuary in the shadows."

I'm speechless. If I weren't seeing it, I wouldn't believe it. "What...? How...?"

I turn to Thaden, my focus dropping to the young boy with the metal foot who ran up to him. He tugs on Thaden's hand, and Thaden leans down to him, listening to his whispered speech for a moment.

"I hope so," is all Thaden says before the boy runs back to the group of children.

He doesn't elaborate on what the child said, and I don't ask. If the boy had wanted me to know, he wouldn't have whispered.

"What happened to these people?" I ask.

Thaden keeps his distance from me as he replies. "Life happened," he says. "Accidents. Attacks. War."

"They heard about what Thaden can do, and they came here for help," Tamra says. "Or their families brought them if they couldn't bring themselves. Many of them ended up staying—mostly because it isn't safe out there for them."

I struggle with my competing feelings of suspicion and wonder. "So they came to you, Thaden, and you created..."

Arms. Hands. Legs. Feet. Joints. All perfectly fitted to the person and completely functional.

This is what Blacksmith magic was meant to do.

This is what our people once did.

But I can't reconcile what I know about him with what I'm now seeing. "How is this possible?"

His lips press together into a grim line. "You mean, how could Malak's son help anyone?"

I grimace.

I, too, was judged by the actions of my parents.

But it hasn't been his parentage that bothered me so much as what he's been accused of doing—and the fact that he masqueraded as a human.

"You lied to me, Thaden," I say. "*Convincingly*. For all I know, you could have imprisoned these people, experimented on them, and then brought them out here into the sunlight to make it look as if you're helping them. None of this could be true."

Even as I speak my fears, they don't really hold up. These people are tan. Their eyes are bright. None of them appears to be wasting away from malnutrition or mistreatment. My gaze lands on a group of teenagers who are tending to the plants in the farthest row back from us. It looks like they're spending more time chatting than anything else. One of them nudges another, who scoffs, while a third rolls their eyes at whatever was said.

They look normal. Happy. Comfortable. Far more comfortable, in fact, than the humans back in the city.

"In almost any place, I could pull off such a deception," Thaden says, drawing my attention back to him. "But not here. Here, lies can't flourish. We fight for our existence with every breath we take. Every hour is another hour of life not to be wasted. All you have to do is look up to be reminded of how close to death we are."

I consider the wispy clouds in the sky, the way they're blackening at the edges.

The sun continues to shine, but I'm suddenly unsettled.

There's a scent in the air, something dank and *wrong*, and I'm not sure what to make of it.

"Asha." My sister's voice is quieter now. "I need to ask you to leave your hammer behind. It's important that you don't stay in contact with your power. Nobody will mess with your hammer. Or with you. I promise you."

Like Thaden, Tamra isn't carrying her tools.

But putting away my hammer will leave me vulnerable.

It requires trust I don't feel.

"If you don't trust me, then trust your instincts," Tamra says.

"You can sense it, can't you? That feeling of foreboding. A scent like death in the air. That wasteland out there is filled with uncontrolled energy. It's only because of this mountain of rock that the darkness hasn't spread to this village, but your power jeopardizes that."

Carefully, I allow my hammer's handle to slide through my hand until it rests on the ground, testing her claim.

The moment I unclasp my fingers from around my hammer, the dread lifts from my stomach.

"You can leave it right there," Thaden says. "Nobody who lives here touches anyone else's metal."

"Because that would be extremely rude," Tamra says with a smile.

The nearest humans snort but continue with their work.

I give my hammer another glance.

My reluctance is only because of trust—or the absence of it.

Taking my hands off my hammer feels like leaving Erik behind. When I blanked out in the wasteland—right as Thaden brought me here—I felt the disconnect like a blade through my heart.

It isn't quite as sharp this time, but it worries me.

With great difficulty, I step away from my hammer.

Thaden gestures to the path running around the side of the clearing. "Will you walk with me? I'll tell you everything. No lies. No stories. Some of it will make me look good. Most of it won't. You can make up your own mind."

"Okay," I say cautiously. "I'll listen."

"Thank you."

He leads me around the garden while Tamra follows behind us.

"I came out here when I turned sixteen," he says. "Until then, Milena had me making weapons for the humans in the west. It was a task I relished, figuring out the mechanisms needed for warriors to manipulate the form of metal without magic. I saw it as a challenge.

"What's more, I could prove my loyalty. I was not my father. I

236

would not turn to darkness like he did. I would help humans, not hurt them. But I came to regret it."

"What happened?"

"I saw my weapons in action," he says. "There was a fight on the border. It was one of the first fae attacks after they fled their homes in the east. Lysander was my dragon. We were patrolling nearby, and what I saw—"

He clears his throat, and I let him take his time.

"I had created blades that could kill cleanly," he says, his voice now rasping a little. "You wear them as gloves. With a punch to the heart, the blade will extend for a near-instant death. But that wasn't how the human army was using them."

He falls silent again for a long moment and again, I let him take his time as we continue toward the edge of the garden.

"I understand that there's chaos in battle," he says. "It's a fight for survival. There are no perfect strikes. But the humans had somehow figured out that if they cut off a fae's arms, they could stop them from using their power. Very similar to Blacksmiths. It was horrifying." He shakes his head, his lips twisting. "I will never forget their screams as long as I live."

We reach the edge of the garden, where the path continues, and I catch a glimpse of a much larger village beyond it. It seems that the clearing we're standing within is more elevated than the rest because the path slopes downward.

But Thaden gestures to the side of the rock instead.

As I step closer, I make out a platform wide enough for several people to stand on, which is positioned hard up against the side of the rock, and a length of metal extends all the way up the cliff face next to it.

"What did you do?" I ask. "After that fight?"

"I refused to make another weapon," he says. "Milena was angry with me, but I was old enough by then to stand up to her, so I did. I convinced Lysander that there had to be a better way, and I came out here. I wanted to know what was causing the fae to flee their home."

"We're in the east?" I ask, taking an educated guess.

Tamra nods. "You need to see it. This pulley system will take you up, but you can't stay up there for long. Even without your hammer, the darkness will seek you out."

I can't stop my shiver. I haven't even seen what she wants me to see, but the scent I caught earlier has put me on edge.

"Tamra will show you," Thaden says.

"You don't want to go up with her?" Tamra asks him quietly.

He gives her a wry smile. "I don't think Asha would appreciate being in a confined space with me."

"True." My sister reaches for me before she steps onto the platform, and I step on it beside her, uncertain what to expect.

Thaden pulls up a section at the front of the platform, multiple flat pieces that click into place to form a railing on all three exposed sides. Then he reaches for a winch set into the rock and begins winding the handle.

The platform rises rapidly into the air.

The higher we go, the heavier the air feels. Somehow, the light seems to fade until the platform stops several feet from the top of a rock ledge, high enough for me to see over it but low enough that I can't step out.

The landscape beyond this mountain is a garish mix of blood red, black, and white.

Dark clouds fill the sky for as far into the east as I can see.

An ash-filled plain spreads across the distance, dust storms swirling across it. Tornados, just like the ones that whipped snow across the mountain in the east.

Within the storm down on the plain, shapes form, crashing against each other, countless beasts tearing each other apart.

My hand has flown over my mouth. "Tamra..."

"Creation magic did this," she says. "*Our* magic did this."

"We have to stop it," I say. "It has to be stopped."

But she's shaking her head. "Our magic—even our presence here—only makes it worse." Then she twists away from me to call down to Thaden. "Bring us down!"

I can see him turning the winch. He didn't hesitate, but our descent feels too slow.

There's a *pull*. A terrible, horrible pull.

Out on the plains, the dust storms change direction. They are, all of them, suddenly headed in our direction.

Tamra's speaking, but I can't hear her because my ears are buzzing with the echo of my own scream.

Wake up, wake up, wake up...

And then, even that echo is drowned out by the cruel impulses that used to assail me when I wore Malak's tools.

Take control of the light and the dark.

Fight the old and find the new—

"Get me down!" I gasp for air, desperate to breathe. "Get me down. Now!"

My vision blurs, and all I can hear, all I can feel, is the darkness pressing in on me until a final whisper sends a chill down my spine.

You will come to me. You won't have a choice.

CHAPTER 33

"It's okay." My sister's voice breaks through the buzzing in my ears. "You're okay!"

Her arms are around me. My legs must have given way because we've sunk to the platform, and she's half-crouched beside me.

There's a *thump* as the platform reaches the ground.

"Water!" Tamra calls. "We need water!"

Thaden's already running, pumping water from the fountain before returning to hold out a ladle of liquid to me.

I gulp it down, attempting to clear my thoughts.

"What happened?" he asks Tamra.

Her eyes are wide. "She went white, and then she collapsed."

His brow is furrowed as he crouches to me. "Asha? Are you okay?"

I can't possibly explain the awful pull or the impulses that felt like they were both a part of me and outside me at the same time.

"I'm fine." I groan as I try to push myself upright. "I'm okay."

Thaden and Tamra give each other worried looks.

"Maybe the rest of it needs to wait," Thaden says, a question in his voice.

"The rest of what?" I ask, wondering how there could possibly be more than what I just saw.

"It can't," Tamra says. "It took us days to locate Asha."

Thaden is quiet, his expression pensive.

I take another sip of water, drawing deep breaths and finally steadying myself. "I'm fine. Really. Whatever you need to show me, show me."

Thaden doesn't question me again. "This way," he says. "But I need to warn you that I'm about to take you to the darkest place in the village. I don't want you to think I'm leading you into a trap."

"Okay," I say, accepting my sister's help to stand. "Let's go."

Thaden sets off slowly at first. Instead of leading me down the incline toward the main village, he heads to the left, along a wide ledge that leads to the mouth of a cave.

He was right. It's filled with darkness and looks like a trap, but it doesn't reek of death or whisper within my mind.

He takes up a fire brand that rests in a metal loop at the mouth of the cave before he strikes a flint across the rock wall itself, lighting up the brand.

Tamra doesn't hesitate, going in first even without the light, and Thaden follows her, saying to me, "Stay behind us. That way, you can be assured that your way out is clear."

The mouth of the cave forms a tunnel that stretches far into the distance.

Halfway along, once we're engulfed in the dark and only the fire brand gives us light, an opening appears on the right, a soft glow emitting from it.

I think we're going to head inside, but Tamra and Thaden continue past it.

Still, I pause at the door, surprised by what I see—or rather, what I *don't* see.

The room contains a forge, fully enclosed except for the doorway. The fact that it's enclosed is surprising enough, since all forges need large openings to allow smoke to disperse.

But the coal glowing in the forge isn't crimson coal.

I don't see a single lump of crimson coal, and it's not as if it could be concealed. This forge is tidy and clean. Everything has a place. The wall is lined with regular tools—the same ones that human metalworkers use—although when I lean closer, I make out tools I've never seen before.

"Did you make those yourself?" I ask.

A moment later, the circle of light returns to me, and Thaden stands in the doorway beside me. "Make what?"

"Those tools." I gesture to the wall. "Did you make them yourself?"

"I did."

"I don't see any crimson coal."

"Because I haven't forged with it for years," he says. "I don't use my hammer to forge here. It's too dangerous."

He gestures to the metal box sitting on a pedestal on the far side of the room. "I keep my tools in that iron box and only get them out when I have no other choice."

He's already turning away, but I stop him.

"You used your tools when you came for me before," I say.

He gives a short nod. "Like I said, only when I have no other choice."

"But if you don't forge using your power, how have you helped those people?"

How does he make such intricate limbs?

He gives me a fleeting smile. "With hard work."

I persist. "None of them were made with Blacksmith magic?"

His answer is firm. "None."

I'm left with a sense of confusion. If I hadn't seen his forge and all its neatly lined-up tools with ordinary coal smoldering in the bowl, I wouldn't have believed him.

Several steps farther along the corridor, my eyes widen again. The firelight catches the walls, bringing into view intricate symbols carved into them.

"What are these?" Even as I speak, I miss a step, my eyes widening when I recognize one of the symbols: *Courage*.

The same rune is carved into my hammer.

"Did this place belong to the Einherjar?"

Thaden's steps slow. "Can you read the runes?"

I shake my head. "Not really. I only know a few."

He pauses to point to the wall, his hand trailing along the air beside the intricate lines. "According to the story written here, this was the birthplace of Fenrir, the monstrous wolf of war. He is one of the gods revered by the Einherjar."

"A wolf," I murmur.

"Also according to these runes, he now walks this Earth in the form of a man."

"Did Malak ever come here?" I ask.

Thaden's forehead creases. "Why do you ask?"

"He wanted to be a god," I say. "Perhaps this was his inspiration."

Thaden seems thrown, his shoulders tensing. "Milena said that members of her House were often sent out on diplomatic missions to dangerous territories. Their house was considered the lowest, so its members were dispensable."

"That's why he was sent to the fae east of here," Tamra says, speaking up from Thaden's other side. "Right?"

Queen Karasi told us that she met Malak when he visited her people, but everything she said is suspect, as far as I'm concerned.

Thaden nods. "Milena mentioned it to me when the fae first started pushing west. And yes, before you ask, he did kill their previous Queen. Karasi wasn't lying about that."

He turns back to the runes. "He also spent time in the north with the Einherjar. He taught himself to read runes. Then he taught Milena, and she taught me. I never imagined he might have been here, in this cave. Possibly even standing right here..."

He gives himself a shake, but his forehead remains creased and the tension around his eyes is more intense, as if the thought of stepping along here now unsettles him.

Tamra moves into his path, tipping her head back to see Thaden's face. "You are not him."

He gives a snarl. "You know I am, Tamra. Exactly like him."

"But not for the same reasons. Not for hatred or malice."

His shoulders slump. "Yet the outcome is the same: death and pain."

"No," she says, her small hand folding around his forearm. "*No.*"

He glances back at me. "How about we let Asha be the judge of that?"

Tamra's worried eyes meet mine, but for some reason, her expression softens. "Asha will judge."

Then she turns on her heel and hurries forward into the dark as if she doesn't care that she's leaving the light behind.

Thaden follows her, but the tension doesn't leave his shoulders.

I walk close behind him, my gaze flitting to the runes a final time before they come to an end.

That's when we reach a set of steps.

They're steep and I can't see what they lead down to until we're nearly at the bottom, and then my footsteps falter again.

Soft growls reach me, floating up through the air like a whisper from my past.

I'm suddenly transported back in time within my mind. The silver throne is once again pressed to my side. I'm desperately trying to hold Tamra and Gallium close, their young bodies trembling with fear as we listen to the approaching growls, the fierce snarls of a beast who would tear us apart and change our lives.

I stop right where I am, unable to descend, even though Thaden has moved ahead of me, and the light is a mere circle at my feet, illuminating the final two steps.

The growls sound again, but this time, they're even softer, more plaintive somehow.

Thaden's voice is quiet. Controlled. "How is she doing today?"

A woman's voice replies. Not a voice I'm familiar with. But it's equally gentle. "Maybe a little better. Precious thing, she caught a mouse but let it go instead of eating it."

I find the courage to descend, my focus landing on Thaden

first, taking in the tension around his mouth, the terrible vulnerability in his eyes.

Then I focus on the woman sitting on a chair in the far-left corner. She begins rising out of her seat but stops when she sees me. She has kind eyes and hair that might once have been auburn, but it's mostly gray now.

Then my focus falls on my sister, who has retreated to the wall on the far left and watches me with an intensity that fills me with dread.

Finally, I turn to the right.

To the large cage filled with children's toys and a soft bed and books that have had the corners chewed off them.

And then to a little girl with ink-black hair and sharp teeth, who watches me with bright green eyes as she slowly, very slowly, extends her black, metal claws.

She can't be any more than two years old, if that.

I can barely breathe, my heart hammering in my chest and my left hand curling into an unwitting fist, seeking the hammer I didn't bring with me. "Thaden... who is that?"

He steps between me and the cage, blocking my view of the little girl. "She's my daughter."

CHAPTER 34

The fear in Thaden's eyes hits me hard.

So hard that the horrified cry that was rising to my lips vanishes instantly.

His chest rises and falls rapidly, and his voice is strained. "Do you remember the question I asked you in the wasteland before you came here?"

"What darkness would I not embrace," I say, trying to breathe out my own fear and my confusion and my dread.

He nods urgently, and the terrible vulnerability in his expression only gets worse. "Her heart wasn't working. When she was born. You can't imagine, Asha. You can't possibly know... To hold your baby daughter in your arms. To listen to her mother weeping. To have all this power at my fingertips and not be able to do anything—not a damn thing—to save her."

He swipes at the tear trickling down his cheek, words tumbling from his mouth. "I made a choice. A split-second decision."

He swallows hard, his throat visibly constricting. "Every other time I helped someone, I had time to plan, to design and then to construct what they needed, but even then, metal doesn't grow, Asha. That boy out there with the metal foot—he'll need a new, bigger one soon. Which will be easy enough. Feet and hands and joints must function, but a heart?" The tension in his face only increases. "A heart must live."

My question is a bare whisper, barely an exhaled breath. "What did you do?"

How did he turn his daughter into a wolf?

"Milena had given me my father's first prototype," he says. "The one she stole from him when she fled with me."

I know about that device. Erik told me about it. Malak had confessed to him the details of his sister's disappearance. Malak had discovered that his prototype device had been missing—the one he eventually perfected and used on Erik. When he'd gone looking for his sister, believing she had taken it, he'd discovered that she'd fled the city.

Malak never knew that she'd taken his son, too.

In his rage and to save face, he'd destroyed a section of the city and invented the story about a human rebellion in which his sister had supposedly been killed.

"Milena gave me the prototype as a reminder of what I must not become," Thaden says. "But within that device was already the soul of a wolf. A living creature whose life force would ensure that the metal could grow."

I quickly recall what Erik told me about his own change. Malak had embedded the device in Erik's heart, but Erik's heart had been fully functional and intact, and Thaden is telling me that his daughter's *wasn't*.

He seems to anticipate my question. "I used a piece of one of my medallions," he says. "I commanded it to take the shape of the tiniest heart I could fashion, and then I fused the prototype to the base of it and—"

"But the pain, Thaden." I'm horrified. "How did you expect her to survive the implantation?"

"I didn't." His voice is bleak. "By the time I did all that, she was already dead." His eyes meet mine. "So you see, I had nothing to lose."

He finally steps away from me. "The prototype took hold

immediately. The metal heart attached to her damaged heart so fast, it was fucking frightening. The power in that device was—" He closes his eyes for a second. "But she healed up, and within seconds, she was alive."

I consider the little girl in the cage. "But not the same."

He shakes his head. "She's growing at the speed of a wolf cub. She's only two months old, but her body is beyond that of a baby already, and her mind can't keep up. She acts on instinct, not reason. She looks old enough to speak, but she can't. She's..."

"A predator," I whisper, steeling myself. "May I move closer to her?"

"Yes, but be careful. Her claws—"

"Can cut through anything." I take a cautious step toward the cage before I lower myself into a kneeling position.

"Caught a mouse and let it go, huh?" I murmur, recalling what I heard the woman say when we first arrived.

I'm still not clear who that woman is—she certainly appears too old to be the child's mother—but she isn't my greatest concern right now.

The little girl watches every move I make.

Her nostrils flare when I settle into position.

No doubt she's inhaling my scent.

With a brief narrowing of her eyes, she darts forward, pressing her nose between the bars, drawing an even deeper breath.

Her eyes brighten, and she makes another growling sound, this one questioning.

"You can smell the wolf on me, can't you?" I ask her softly.

Erik's scent will be all over me. I don't know what wolf Malak may have used for the soul of that prototype, but it's possible it was from the same original pack as Erik's wolf, Skirra.

"If only I knew how to speak to you like Erik could."

As the little girl continues to peer at me, I look up at Thaden again. "What happened to Lysander Rex, Thaden?"

I still don't know how Thaden killed him or why. When I challenged Graviter Rex to a fight, staring him down, I convinced myself that if Thaden could kill a dragon, then I could, too. *Somehow.*

I was so confident at that moment that I think even Erik believed I could do it.

Thaden lowers himself down onto the floor beside me, crossing his legs and hunching. "He saw her, and he thought I'd turned to the dark. He thought I was conducting experiments like my father had. And on a child, no less."

I consider what I know of fire dragons and their rage. The way they don't see anything else around them once their fury takes hold.

I also remember the mind-destroying heat I felt the first time I touched Thaden's scaled arm while I was in contact with my power. That was the first time I sensed Lysander's soul. He was majestic, but his fury had no limits.

"He truly believed you'd betrayed him," I say.

Thaden inclines his head. "All my life, Milena and the dragons have watched me, waiting for signs that I would turn. They treated me as if it hadn't been so much a question of *if*, but *when*. Lysander was my dragon, but I knew he'd been assigned to me because of his strength. His fire was more destructive even than his father's. He was powerful enough to end me."

"What happened, Thaden? How did he die?"

Thaden is quiet for so long, focused on his daughter for such an extended moment, that I suspect the answer even before he speaks it.

"She happened," he finally says in a bare whisper. "I took her out into the sunlight for the first time. We were walking down the path toward the village. At that time, only a handful of people knew that I had a child, but even fewer knew what I'd done to keep her alive. Milena certainly didn't know. Neither did the dragons.

"But then Lysander arrived. I wasn't expecting him. He must have seen her from the sky because he was already in a rage when he landed and blocked the path. The heat from his mouth was burning us. He was shouting at me, but his fire was hurting her. She was terrified, screaming, and then—"

"Then?"

He takes a deep breath before the corners of his mouth turn down. "Then she was covered in dragon blood." His expression is haunted, his eyes shadowed. "Fuck me, she was barely as big as his paw, but she went straight for his throat and—"

He glances back at the woman in the corner, who has turned pale.

"I was there," the woman whispers. "Precious thing, but that dragon was dead within seconds."

"Trust me, Asha," Thaden says, turning back to me. "You don't want me to describe it."

I lift my hand. I really don't need to know.

"And then?" I ask, knowing that what happened next matters, even though I can already see it playing out. I can already guess why Thaden asked me how far I would go to protect the ones I love.

"A dragon was dead," he says, his expression now blank. "I knew they'd come for me. So I made another decision."

"You took his soul." But my forehead crinkles. "But you aren't left-handed. How did you do that?"

He is grim. "My father never took souls with his Blacksmith magic. He used his Blacksmith magic to create the devices and transplant them into living flesh. But the taking of the soul was dark magic."

"I don't understand..."

"Dark magic drains life. It exists in every murder. All I had to do was take another medallion, fashion it into the shape of a dragon, and let go of the good in my heart. I accepted the dark. Then Lysander's soul was mine."

I shake my head, speaking with certainty when I say, "It wasn't that easy."

I remember again the pain Erik described to me of his transformation, of having his heart opened, and how he would have embraced death because it was better than the agony he was experiencing.

"You're right." Thaden's gaze is steely as he looks me in the eye. "It wasn't that easy. But it made me strong enough to protect my daughter. And that's all that fucking matters."

I lean back on my heels. I don't need him to tell me the rest. He went to Milena. They fought. Then he came to me.

I have only a few questions left now. "How did you create the devices that you used to entrap Milena on the clifftop—the one for the snow bear and the other for the tree?"

"The tree was easy," he says with a suddenly dark grin. "I killed a giant spider. Actually, the bear was easy, too, since I have a dragon's strength. For both, I used a medallion and the death force of the dying creature."

"But Blacksmiths only have three medallions."

I've already counted to four.

"I had seven," he says. "*Now* I have three."

I shouldn't be surprised. It's not as though he grew up within the same system of rules that I did. It sounds as if he was making weapons well before the usual age of sixteen.

I fold my hands in my lap. "You said you needed my help."

"*She* needs your help." His gaze hasn't wavered. Where before his eyes were full of fear, now they're full of hope. "I can't do what you can do. I can't help her mind or make her whole. Even before you healed the Vandawolf, I believed that you alone could heal her, but once I watched you pull that device from his heart, I was certain. Asha, she needs you."

I try to breathe through my emotions: fear, anxiety, uncertainty. So many times since I stepped into this cave, I've caught my breath and tried to calm my heart.

"My hammer isn't like any other," I say. "When I helped Erik become whole, I had a medallion. He believes I can do anything with my hammer, but... I can't exactly clobber her with it."

I shake my head, frustration rising within me as I continue before Thaden can argue with me. "To help her, I need a medallion. But you've both warned me against using my power here. You, yourself, have stopped forging, and I can only guess that even changing the shape of your medallions was a considerable risk. Am I right?"

He nods. "There was a real danger that I'd draw the blight here. But—"

"A medallion takes days to forge," I plow on, "and that's once I have the right metal. Days of risk. I'd also need crimson coal, which you don't seem to have."

I try to rein in my frustration, try to slow my speech, but all I'm left with is a horrible sense of hopelessness. "How can I possibly help her?"

"Because you're not going to do it here," he says quietly.

I blink at him for a moment. "What?"

He shuffles closer to me, and I'm startled when he reaches for my hands. "I'm asking you, Asha Silverspun, to take my daughter away from here. Away from me. And do whatever you need to do to heal her."

"Thaden, that's..." My voice fails me. He can't possibly mean what he's saying. Not after he did so much to keep her safe.

"The dragons think that I killed Lysander," he says. "Only the people in this village know I have a daughter, and only the people in this room know what she is—or that *she* killed the dragon and not me. If you take her with you—"

His voice suddenly breaks. He takes a shaky breath and then snarls against the tears gathering in his eyes. "If I give her up, you can keep her safe."

I'm struggling to speak, to comprehend the complexity of his request, let alone to foresee its consequences. "There are no guarantees I'll even be able to help her."

"All I ask is that you try. You're the only one with a chance. Worst case, she'll have someone in her life who understands her wolfish nature and can communicate with her."

"The Vandawolf," I whisper.

Because suddenly, he isn't alone.

And neither is this little girl.

Thaden nods. "If you agree to do this, she must never know

that I'm her father. Do you understand? You can't tell her who I am or what she did. As far as anyone knows, I killed the dragon, not her."

I'm alarmed by his suggestion. "Thaden, healing her will be hard enough. She has a right to know who she is."

"She has a right to live with love and trust in her life," he says. "She will never have that if she's living in the shadow of her grandfather's legacy. I'm begging you, Asha. She needs to be free of it."

How can I possibly make this decision, let alone do what he asks?

The danger and responsibility involved are immense.

I find myself recalling one of the first things Thaden said to me when he was chained up in the Vandawolf's prison, and I'd asked him: *Why are you here, Thaden Kane?*

He had turned the question back on me, asking me why *I* was there. Why was I doing the bidding of a wolf when I could raze the city to the ground?

Now, I ask him, "When you were in the prison, back at the city, you were testing me, weren't you?"

"I needed to know if you were the person I hoped you were," he says. "All I had was Milena's account of you. Even when she cut off her hand, I couldn't be certain of the real reason why she refused to make you a hammer."

"It was because she couldn't," I say. "There was too much darkness in her heart."

"And none in yours," he says.

"Oh, but there has been," I whisper, remembering the pull of Malak's tools and the malice within them. "Too much darkness."

"Which is why you will understand my daughter," he says. "The Vandawolf will understand her wolfish soul, and you will understand the battles of her heart."

I contemplate the little girl, who has pressed her cheek forlornly against the bars. She looks up at me for a moment before her gaze drops as if she thinks I'm going to reject her.

But of course, she will hear the pounding of my heart and probably even smell my turmoil.

It's startling to me that, despite hearing how she cut down a dragon, it's only now dawning on me that she could have easily cut through the bars if she wanted to.

There must be a part of her that chooses not to.

I wonder if her world feels safer within the confines of this space. After all, on her first outing into the sun, a fire-breathing dragon tried to burn her to death.

I turn back to Thaden. "You said that only we know about her, but you haven't spoken of—"

I was about to say *her mother*, but at that moment, Thaden's daughter turns away from the bars, and I have my first full view of her back.

Fuck me.

"Dear saints," I whisper. "She asked me to protect you."

General Glass told me very clearly that her people had little room for compassion and none for weakness.

Now I see the stumps protruding from the little girl's shoulder blades and the beginnings of a single, deformed, silver feather.

No wonder she could plow through a dragon.

Her mother is a Valkyrie.

"What is her name?" I ask him.

He replies in a hush, as if speaking the child's name aloud can only threaten his hope. "Galeia," he says. "It means *new life*."

I come to a decision, even though it could be the most dangerous vow I've ever made. "I will help her."

CHAPTER 35

That afternoon, I kneel in front of the little girl's cage again.

This time, I'm alone with her, but I also have my hammer and toolbox with me.

Over the course of the day, Thaden told me everything he knows about the blight, the way it feeds off death, and how dangerous it is to travel near it. He told me about his human mother, although he refused to name her, and the way Tamra shook her head indicated she doesn't know his mother's name, either.

He also explained how he traveled from here to the wasteland the first time—and again this morning.

It's a journey I'll experience again soon.

I've asked Tamra to come back with me, but she has yet to make a decision.

As for my choice to raise Galeia, it doesn't feel as overwhelming as I thought it might. I raised my siblings until they were nine years old and were separated from me. I know how to care for children. And I won't be alone. Erik is the only other person in this world who will understand Galeia.

I won't force this choice on him, but I know his heart. He won't turn her away.

I've prepared myself for the journey back to him, right down to the weapons harness I'm wearing, but right now, I have a much harder task in front of me.

"Child," I murmur to Galeia as I settle down on the hard rock. "Come out of that cage."

I don't expect her to understand me. Thaden made it clear that Galeia lives by her instincts. If Erik were here, things might be different, but I'll just have to do my best.

Of course, Thaden could bring her out of the cage to me, but I need her to trust me.

I need her to choose to come with me.

If she doesn't, I have no hope of surviving her claws if she gets frightened.

I breathe out my anxiety because, damn, I'm putting my life on the line.

Galeia's forehead crinkles at me from where she sits in the middle of her cage. One foreclaw has speared through the arm of a straw doll, pinning it to the floor.

She doesn't budge, but that's okay. I have a plan.

Very carefully, I open the lid to my toolbox and make a show of peering inside it. She won't be able to see its contents from where she's sitting.

As I hoped she would, she cranes forward, trying to see what I see.

I have to be careful not to touch any of the dark metal inside the box, but I reach into it as if I will pull something out.

She darts forward, pressing her face to the bars, inhaling deeply again.

Her green eyes are suddenly even brighter than before.

She makes an urgent growling sound in the back of her throat, and I do my best to interpret it.

I tip the box toward her so she can see into it. "Something you want?"

She moves much faster than I was expecting. So fast, I nearly drop the box in shock.

With astounding speed, she shreds the bars in front of her, her black claws slicing through them as if they were nothing but air before she leaps at the box.

I've barely caught my breath before her little hand darts into it and then retracts again. She's now crouched right in front of me, her fist closed around whatever she took. She presses it to her heart, making another growling sound that begins with force but ends plaintively.

The corners of her mouth are turned down, and she looks up at me with that same forlorn expression she gave me when she pressed her cheek to the bars earlier today.

I don't dare make any sudden movements.

She's out of the cage, which is what I wanted, but my task only gets more dangerous from here.

A piece of metal that was still clinging to the bars behind her falls to the ground with a *clang*, but I don't react.

I swivel my eyes to the box, taking a quick look at its contents. The device that was in Erik's heart is the only thing missing.

She holds it up to her nose, inhaling deeply, and I make out the wolfish faces in its design.

"I can take you to him," I murmur, keeping my voice low and very slowly gesturing to her closed fist before pointing to myself. "You can come with me."

She leans toward me, inhaling deeply, dragging in my scent before her focus falls on my hammer. She crouches lower to sniff that, too, but she looks puzzled, tilting her head at me.

I can't for the life of me figure out what she wants, but I take a risk, carefully brushing my fingertips against the hammer's handle.

Light glows around my weapon, and I'm aware of the way my skin and hair and body light up with it.

Galeia's eyes widen. She takes a quick breath, another deep inhale, blinking rapidly before she looks at me again.

She sneezes. Her little nose wrinkles. Then she edges toward me, and I stay very still as she climbs onto my lap.

My heart beats hard, not only because of the danger she poses to me, but also because she's holding the dark device near me—a device made out of metal that Graviter Rex warned me never to touch again.

But she keeps it pressed against her chest, her fist closed around it.

I'm certain this is the best I'm going to get.

Very slowly and carefully, I lift my hammer and slide it into the scabbard at my back.

I'm concerned that once my light is gone, Galeia will move away from me, but she snuggles more closely.

My arms close around her before I very carefully reposition her on my hip.

I'm relieved when she nestles into me as I stand.

I've left my toolbox on the floor, so I use my foot to close its lid. I won't take it with me. This dark metal stays here. I'm saddened to leave my grandmother's pin behind, too, but it also touched the dark metal, and I can't risk that it's been contaminated.

I would have chosen to leave the device Malak used on Erik, but it seems Galeia has other ideas.

Now that she's safely tucked into my arms, I don't delay, striding from the room and along the tunnel, past the Einherjar runes to where Tamra and Thaden are waiting for me.

What I didn't see the first time I passed through this tunnel was another opening opposite Thaden's forge.

It leads into a chamber that's only a little higher than Thaden is tall and barely wide enough for three people to step inside.

The walls have been carved with the same sequence of symbols that Thaden formed with his medallion before he brought me here.

The woman who was watching over Galeia—a woman who has evaded every effort I've made to find out her name—stands at the entrance. During the day, Thaden explained that it was she who told him how to carve the symbols, tapping into the dark magic needed to transport him instantly to the wasteland.

With a grimace, he told me how it didn't work to plan the first time. He had intended to take his tools with him. With them, he could have snatched me up and brought me back here right away.

It explains why he had looked at his hands and cursed so loudly when he first appeared to me in that blast of lightning.

Everything he did after that was improvised.

Now, his relief when he sees Galeia in my arms is palpable. "She came with you."

I wait for him to reach for Galeia, to kiss or hug her, but he doesn't.

"I can't hug her," he says, his eyes filling with tears. "I took on the soul of the dragon that tried to kill her. If I step near her, it triggers her fear."

"I'm sorry for your pain," I whisper.

He shakes his head rapidly. "I'm grateful, Asha. You can protect her in ways that I can't. Sending her away is hard, but knowing she has the chance of a life free from the past means everything to me."

I blink away my own tears, turning to my sister, but she, too, is crying.

I can read her decision in the way she presses her lips together.

"You've decided to stay," I say softly to her.

"I'm needed here," she replies. "I may not be able to use my power, but I can help these people." She bites her lip. "If I go back out there, I'll only be used as leverage against you."

Just as Gallium will be.

"I'm safe here," she says. "The blight is growing so much that even the dragons will think twice about coming here, and if they do... well... we'll be ready."

I thought I was prepared for her decision, but it turns out that I'm not.

I try to keep my voice steady, fighting the burn behind my eyes. "I'm going to miss you."

She purses her lips, softly blowing out a breath as tears trickle down her face. "I miss you already."

She leans into me, pressing her cheek to mine.

I'm certain she would hug me, but for the little girl I'm already holding. As Tamra stays beside me, Galeia reaches up with her free hand, brushing her fingertips through the tears trickling to my chin.

The corners of her mouth turn down, and she makes a sad, growling sound in the back of her throat.

I close my eyes, trying to hold on to this moment. "I promise you, Tamra, I will find Gallium. I'm fighting on my own terms now, nobody else's."

"I know you will," she says. "You have always kept us safe."

I don't want to say goodbye.

I promise myself it won't be long before I see my sister again.

Forcing myself to move, I step back toward the chamber.

The older woman gestures inside it. "I've modified the symbols," she says, pointing to one that sits lower than the others. "The dark magic should now take you to the wolf who holds your heart."

She doesn't sound confident.

"'Should'?" I ask.

She grimaces. "Dark magic serves only itself. Even when you think you control it, you don't."

I consider this carefully. "Is that why Thaden's hammer remained behind the first time he used this chamber?"

She nods. "Undoubtedly."

I try to exhale my anxiety as the woman steps away. Anything could happen once this magic takes hold of me. I could arrive without my hammer, or worse, Galeia could end up in a different place than I do, or—

I take a deep breath and stop my thoughts in their tracks because this is still the safest way for me to travel.

Thaden reaches for me. "Asha, thank you."

"I will look after her, Thaden," I say. "No matter what happens. I promise you. She will have the life you couldn't have."

I want to believe it, and, in this moment, I'm certain of it.

He swallows hard, giving me a nod, and that's all before he rakes his forefinger against the small blade embedded just inside the entrance to the chamber.

His blood spills across the wall, splattering the side of the first symbol. It lights up, quickly followed by the second, each one seeming to trigger the next in sequence, all of them glowing and sharp.

But I'm unsettled to see that it isn't a golden light this time, not bright and dazzling like the burst of lightning around Thaden when he first arrived in the wasteland.

A dark light presses in on me, growing blacker with every heartbeat.

I catch a glimpse of Thaden, where he startles outside the chamber before the light closes around me.

His eyes are wide with alarm and his shout is panicked as he lurches toward us. "*No!*"

Then, the magic takes hold.

I flinch against the freezing cold darkness, instinctively crouching low, holding Galeia close to my chest.

She gives a cry, filled with fear, a second before sharp pricks of pain across my arm tell me she's extended her claws.

For the shortest moment, my heart stops.

So, too, does my ability to breathe.

Then the pressure lifts, and I open my eyes.

I take a breath, but in the next instant, the air is filled with ash, and all I inhale is dust.

A scream rises to my lips.

I'm crouched in the center of a vast plain. Tornados of dust whirl around me. Hard things *crunch* beneath my boots and when I look down, there are bones protruding from the ash.

In the distance, monstrous forms crash against each other, the impact thudding through me.

I was prepared to arrive somewhere other than Erik's location, but I was not prepared for this.

We can only be in the heart of the darkness and the pull... Oh, the *pull*...

Pain stabs at my side. Galeia's claws are digging deeper. I try to hold her closer even as she screams in terror, her cries whipping away in the shrieking wind that drowns my thoughts.

I promised I would keep her safe.

I promised I would help her.

I promised Erik we would never break.

From within the swirling darkness up ahead, a figure takes shape, dust, and ash drawing together into a form I refuse to recognize.

The whisper that reaches me across the distance chills me to my bones.

Come to me, Asha. You don't have a choice.

CHAPTER 36

I do the only thing I can.

Remaining crouched to the ashen ground with Galeia pressed to my right side, I reach back with my left hand and draw my hammer.

Power surges through me, my light gleaming through the shadows, throwing my surroundings into sharp relief.

The ash looks like flecks of gold swirling across the landscape. The outlines of the monsters in the distance become clearer, giant bears, wolves, and stags clashing and tearing each other apart—until my light reaches them.

And then they stop, dropping to the ground and turning in my direction.

The figure gliding toward me is bathed in brilliance, her features more beautiful than any I've ever seen, her form swathed in silver silks, her pale hair flowing in the wind, every step she takes making her seem oblivious of the danger around her.

I'm filled with horror, a terrible, shattering fear, because saints help me...

I know who she is.

"Take control," she whispers. "Take the power you want.

Banish the dark, punish the wicked, and make the world as you want it to be."

My heart pounds, but my blood is running cold as the shadow-woman smiles, and her voice slithers around me like chains tightening with every heartbeat. "Let go of your limits."

A denial slips past my lips, drowned in the fury of the wind and Galeia's screams.

My grip on my hammer loosens, and I leave it in its scabbard because my one choice—to fight back—is not a choice at all.

Tamra warned me that this darkness wants me dead.

Thaden warned me that using my magic would only feed the blight. Even the nameless woman who was watching over Galeia warned me that dark magic only serves itself.

It brought me here, and I have no choices.

None at all.

Because, if this darkness claims my power, it will be unstoppable.

A scream rises to my lips, a snarl as fierce as a beast. "I will never be you!"

"Oh, but you will, Asha," the shadow-woman says, her serene smile gleaming ever brighter with every step she takes. "There is no darkness you won't embrace to save the ones you love."

I'm frozen, rendered still where I crouch with no way out.

No way at all.

"Do it," she whispers more forcefully than before. "Use your hammer. Fill this ash with power. Bring the dead to life. Wake... *everything.*"

Her smile grows, and her eyes gleam. "All will bow to you. Every creature, living and dead, will revere—"

She stops speaking abruptly, her focus on something behind me. A snarl rises to her lips, the smile drops from her face, her beauty slips, and dark cracks suddenly appear across her skin.

I don't dare take my eyes off her, but at the corner of my vision, there's a light, and it's getting brighter. Fast.

A high-pitched hum comes with it, the kind that's made by

something moving so quickly through the air that it's defying the laws of nature.

It happens so fast that I have no time to prepare.

A bright orb shoots across the space between me and the shadow-woman before it crashes into the ground.

The moment it hits, it explodes.

Heat and light and fire ripple out from the impact point, a wildfire raging toward me and there's nothing I can do to get out of its path.

For a heartbeat, I'm surrounded by an impossible silence, and then the explosion reaches me.

The impact knocks me backward so hard that I gain air, my arms closing ever more tightly around Galeia, whose screams have suddenly stopped.

For two more heartbeats, I'm suspended in the air, caught in the force rippling out from the impact point.

There's a crater in the ground, filled with a raging fire so bright, my own light pales in comparison. I could be looking at a thousand stars all exploding at once.

Within the circle of light is a girl.

She can't be more than ten years old, dressed in white, her hair as pale as the moon, and her skin paler. So pale, she's almost translucent. Luminous. Nothing but light.

Opposite her, the shadow-woman was thrown into the air, just as I was.

The girl punches her right hand forward, light spearing from her palm, slicing right through the shadow-woman's screaming, splintering form.

And then she's nothing more than splashes of dark light shrieking across the air.

The girl turns, racing toward me.

Her feet are bare. Of all the things I could notice at that moment, it seems the least important, but my head is buzzing, and my thoughts are wooly.

She's screaming something at me.

I don't have a hope of understanding her because now I'm falling.

The ground rears up at me, but the girl is leaping toward me, her hand outstretched, her body flying through the air, and right before her hand brushes mine, I'm certain of the command on her lips.

Jump!

My feet barely touch the ground before I reach deep for control and compel every muscle in my body to obey, throwing myself upward.

A split second later, a feathery body appears beneath me, flying low to the ground. At the exact same moment, the girl's hand closes around mine. She flips herself around behind me, and we both land safely on the bird's back, and then we're rising into the air.

I can't process it all at once.

My mind is only now catching up with my body as I register Blackbird's frantic wing beats. The lightning sizzling through his body. The panic in his flight. The way the girl leans out to the side, punching her hand out again, spearing light across our path head, separating the shadows even as they try to close in around us, and then—

We soar into clear air.

Oh, it's dank and copper-filled and reeks of death, but it's practically sweet compared to the suffocating darkness that looms so close behind us.

I don't understand what just happened—or who the girl who crashed into us is—but my concern now is for Galeia.

She's limp in my arms, her little limbs loose. Her head would be lolling if I weren't supporting her.

"Galeia?" I can't tell if she's breathing. It's all I can do to stay secure on Blackbird's back while we're moving so fast. "Galeia!"

She gives no response.

No, no, no...

"Galeia!"

In the next heartbeat, I detect the smallest rise and fall of her chest.

"She's alive." I can't stop my sob of relief, but it's short-lived. Galeia might be alive, but she isn't conscious, and the longer she remains that way, the more worrying it will be. "I don't know what's wrong."

"My magic hurt her." The girl speaks behind me. "I'm sorry. She is dark magic, and I... am something else."

I don't have time to wonder what 'something else' could be. This girl certainly came out of nowhere, and her power is immense, but I'll figure out what her 'something else' is later.

"We have to set down," I say. "I need to know where she's hurt and figure out how to help her."

"We must not land," the girl replies firmly. "We must fly straight and true to my home in the west—"

"The west is hours away!" I can't turn to the girl, or I'll upset my precarious balance, but I need her to understand how worried I am. "Galeia can't wait that long."

"Galeia?" The girl's voice is soft but carries a clear note of curiosity. "That is an unusual name for such a dark creature."

"She isn't a creature," I snap. "She's a person, and she's very important to me."

How did that become so true so quickly? How did Galeia burrow her way into my heart in such a short time?

Blackbird's ears are pricked. He's clearly listening to what we're saying, but for now, there's an extended silence behind me.

No immediate retort from the girl.

Then she leans forward, reaching past me to point into the distance.

"Do you see the thunderbirds up ahead? The fae have spread their defenses wide. We must evade them at all costs. Even if you weren't already their enemy, this child is *Darkness*. They will sense her nature and attack you on sight.

"That means we have two choices. We must either head due west along that mountain ridge where they do not yet patrol, or we must turn sharply north, circle around them, and *then* travel down along the coastline."

If we travel west from here, we'll fly through the airspace above human territory. They're allied with the dragons, who will also no doubt carry out air patrols, and most likely react even more badly to Galeia's presence.

But if we go north first...

My eyes widen. The deep north belongs to the Einherjar and the Valkyries. They are Galeia's people. Her mother lives in that direction. She told me to protect Thaden, so I assume she will want to protect her daughter, too.

Even if we don't reach her, the north is still far safer for Galeia than the west.

But first, I need to know more about the girl's intentions. She got us out away from the blight and Blackbird clearly trusts her—even if I have no idea how they crossed each other's paths. I don't want to dismiss the possibility that she has good reasons for wanting to take us directly west.

"Why do you want me to come to your home?" I ask.

"Because that is where the end begins," she replies.

"The end of what?" I ask, my heart suddenly beating harder.

"The end of the beginning."

Too fucking cryptic.

"We fly north," I declare. "Blackbird? Do you understand?"

He shows me that he does when he banks steeply to the right.

The sun is setting up ahead, but the natural darkness will help us stay hidden. We've already traveled far enough toward the west that Thaden's village is a mere speck in the east, although the dark plain is still very visible.

On our other side, to my left, I can make out the heaviest concentration of thunderbirds, their lightning flickering through the air, as well as the castle where Queen Karasi is situated.

But the white-haired girl was right. The path we're taking right now sits cleanly between the two.

She gives a loud sigh at my choice, but then she points toward the east—a final look back. "Do you see the edge of the dark plain?

It has spread farther west even in the last day. Now my magic has fed it even more."

My forehead creases. "Your magic pushed it back."

"No, Asha," she says so quietly that I nearly don't hear her. "I've made it worse. Saving you was my only purpose."

I risk another glance back—a final glance. Even from this distance, it's clear that blight has extended farther along the wide plain.

The girl clears her throat. "It will spread even faster now, and the fae will become desperate soon. They will push west, and the humans will go to war."

I wish I could deny the girl's prediction, but Tamra described to me how badly the fae are hurting. I'm certain Queen Karasi will only act in her own best interests, but she won't let the blight reach what remains of her people. After all, she can't be a queen without people to rule over.

I wish I could ask Blackbird where Erik is. The last I saw of them both, Erik was leaping off Blackbird's back onto Graviter Rex's neck. They must have been separated somehow...

My heartbeat quickens at the possibility that Erik's in trouble.

With my heart in my throat, I monitor Galeia's breathing—shallow but constant. The ground beneath us is rocky and sharp, impossible to land on, and I pray we reach a safe spot soon.

As the air becomes colder, I fight off the chill, shivering in my tunic and pants and trying to keep Galeia warm, too.

I don't mind when the girl presses in behind me, but she seems to be doing it more for my benefit than hers. She isn't shivering at all despite wearing nothing more than a dress. Actually, I'm not even certain how she's keeping it from flying up in her face. Still, the darker it gets, the warmer she gets.

"What should I call you?" I call back to her, my teeth chattering.

"In my original tongue, I am called *Caoilainn Liadan*."

I try to repeat it, but it's nearly impossible while I'm shivering. "C-C-C..."

"How about you call me *Cailey*," she says, seeming to pick

some of the most prominent sounds from her name and piecing them together.

I give her a nod, and that is all before I concentrate on staying alive.

Finally, I spot firelight ahead, along with the outline of a wall that appears to surround a gathering of buildings.

It looks quiet, with only a few silhouettes of people patrolling the wall.

I don't imagine that our welcome will be warm, but I'm prepared to invoke General Glass's name if I have to. The Einherjar may be savage, but they revere the Valkyries. I'm certain they won't risk harming the child of one.

"Down there," I say to Blackbird. *Finally.* "On the flat land next to those rocks. We can set down and—"

A sudden gust of wind rushes up around us, coming out of nowhere, its force snatching the words from my mouth. At the same time, an enormous, scaled body shoots into the air right in front of us.

I don't have time to wonder how we didn't see it.

Blackbird shrieks and attempts to evade it, but the new beast knocks into us.

I catch a glimpse of fierce reptilian eyes and crimson scales and then we're tumbling toward the ground.

CHAPTER 37

My only goal in those awful moments as I tumble through the air is to land on my back.

I have to take the brunt of the fall and protect Galeia's unconscious body. Not easy when I'm spinning uncontrollably and have no way to control my fall without letting go of her.

Somehow, I manage to hit the ground on my side, sliding across stones and dirt and then grass before coming to a stop facing away from the village. Galeia has remained cradled in my arms, her shallow breaths warm against my neck.

Thank the saints.

Cailey must have landed on her feet because she's a bright spot in my vision, already sprinting toward me, screaming, "Get up!"

Thud-thud-thud.

A rapid succession of thumps sounds directly behind me, and all it takes is a glance to see three arrows protruding from the ground right at my back. An inch farther toward me, and they would have impaled my back.

But they aren't the last.

My eyes widen at the thick rain of arrows that are pouring

down toward me. If the first three were to gauge the distance, then these ones will hit me.

Fuck!

I roll to my feet, leaping away from the spot where I was lying —a space that seconds later fills with arrows.

I launch myself into a sprint, running as fast as I can, following Cailey's path while I hold on to Galeia.

There's suddenly a cacophony of sounds behind me, such a chaotic blend of noises that I can only identify the loudest of them...

The heavy beat of massive wings high in the sky.

The lighter beat of smaller, but no less powerful, wings closing in on me.

Another *thud*, something landing only paces behind me and then a beastly roar that silences everything else.

"Hurt her, and I will rip out your fucking throats!"

I miss a step, dropping to the ground in a crouch before I twist to see the scene behind me.

I gasp for breath, trying to take it all in.

In the sky, a majestic dragon with crimson scales coasts in the air, appearing almost suspended in the sky above us.

In the distance, at least thirty warriors appear on the wall, all of them with arrows nocked and pointed in my direction.

Much closer to me, a woman is in the process of alighting on the ground, her silver wings sweeping inward as she lands.

She is undoubtedly a Valkyrie, but her focus is on the figure standing between her and me.

Erik.

He casts a brutal shadow, every muscle in his body visibly tense, his claws extended, and his warning growl fierce. He's wearing different clothing, but I don't miss the blood splatter on the back of his neck.

Why is he here? What happened while I was gone?

As relieved as I am to see him, I don't have any chance of getting answers right now.

"Step aside, Vandawolf," the Valkyrie commands him, her

hazel eyes flashing with silver that tells me she is accessing her power. "It is not your place to deal with this darkness."

His snarl is full of fury. "Asha is not darkness."

"Of course, she isn't," the Valkyrie snaps. "I speak of the creature in her arms."

Creature?

A rush of disappointment fills me.

How naïve I was to think that the Valkyries would protect Galeia—or at least help *me* to help *her*. My impression from my interaction with General Glass was that she believed her daughter had died. I should have realized from the depth of her grief that, even if she thought Galeia was alive, she had no hope of seeing her child again. Her people would not allow it.

Erik takes slow steps back and toward my right, taking a careful but quick path to stand at my side instead of in front of me.

We are most powerful fighting side by side.

I'm certain the Valkyrie will realize it, and we will back away now.

But my hope of a quick retreat shatters at the look on his face.

Since I made him whole, I haven't seen a glimpse of the beast that he was turned into. Not once.

Now, there is nothing of peace or calm in his expression.

Only a seething fury.

Oh, Erik, what has happened since we were separated?

"You told me to go in peace," he growls at the Valkyrie, low and dangerous, and despite his talk of peace, he draws his sword as if he wants a fight. "Do you plan to make an enemy of me, after all?"

"You forget I am the Valkyrie Queen!" she snaps. "That creature has Valkyrie blood. Blood that has been corrupted by dark magic. She is my concern, not yours. She's certainly not worth dying over."

"*Child,*" I grind out, wishing I could reach for my hammer right now, but I'd risk dropping Galeia. "She is a *child*, not a creature."

"She is Darkness," the Valkyrie Queen snarls, taking a step toward us, her eyes glowing more silver with every passing second.

All she has to do is lay hands on me—or Erik, for that matter—and she can deal out death in an instant.

I brace for her attack, knowing that I can fight her if I can reach for my hammer, strategizing how I can possibly do so, but at that moment, Cailey steps forward.

She is a picture of serenity, a calm force that contrasts sharply with Erik's fury, as she takes up position a step ahead of me and to my left.

Pure-white light sparks around her hands as she raises one hand toward the warriors on the wall and the other toward the Valkyrie Queen.

The Queen's forehead creases, and she takes a step back. "What are *you*?"

"Something that should worry you," Cailey replies. "I saw what you did on the battlefield in the abyss. I saw what you sacrificed to defeat the primordial deity. I know the future you fought for. A future for your newborn daughter. So believe me when I tell you: This child"—she inclines her head at Galeia— "must live."

The Queen's eyes are wide. "You saw the battle in the...?"

"I did."

"Then you're—"

"I am."

The Valkyrie Queen takes another step back, her face suddenly ashen. "Then it will soon be the end of the beginning."

She stumbles a little as she turns in the direction of the village as if she's seeking something back there. Her silver wings sweep around her body as she turns, providing a protective shield while her attention is diverted. Cailey mentioned something about a newborn daughter. Perhaps the Valkyrie's child is back in the village—I'm not sure—but it's clear that what Cailey said has startled her.

Erik doesn't waste his chance to step to my side.

274

His furious, gray eyes now flood with worry. He retracts his claws before his free hand closes around my shoulder. "Asha—"

Maybe he was going to ask me who Galeia is, or maybe he was going to tell me that now is our chance to leave, but at that moment, his fingers brush Galeia's arm.

A dark light sparks between them.

The shot of energy bites so hard that I gasp for breath.

Galeia jolts in my arms. Her arms and legs stiffen, her head shoots up, and her eyes fly open.

She's suddenly wide awake and snarling, her quickly darting gaze rushing from me to the dragon in the sky to the Valkyrie Queen, whose wings catch the moonlight as she begins turning back to us, and finally to Erik.

I try to hold on to Galeia, but she launches herself out of my arms with a shriek.

"Galeia, no!" My cry of warning strangles in my throat as she jumps, not toward the Valkyrie or even at the dragon, but right at Erik.

She collides with his chest, her little arms wrap around his neck, and then she clings to him, growling and whimpering and snarling, her wide, green eyes turned up to his.

He's frozen where he stands, his arms half-raised, his sword arm slightly bent, which I'm not surprised to see since she flew at him so fast he was no doubt ready to defend himself.

Still, she keeps on growling, more softly now but also more fearfully as she presses her face to his neck. Her legs dangle until he seems to remember himself, catching them with his free arm so he can support her.

Erik looks stunned, his eyes wide and lips parted. His forehead crinkles. Then clears. Then crinkles again.

Finally, he interrupts her with a short, sharp, commanding snarl, his head tilted so he can glare at her.

She stops whimpering, blinks at him, and then she smiles.

A giant, beaming smile.

Her lips purse, and new sounds comes out, clearly formed with difficulty but identifiable all the same. "Wo...l...f."

Wolf.

Erik looks at me and I can't possibly identify what he's feeling. Anger. Sadness. Disbelief. Desolation. "Asha."

"We have to protect her," I say, the most important thing I need him to know.

The Valkyrie Queen is already making moves toward us again. Cailey hasn't lowered her arms, but the threat will only increase. Erik must have so many questions, just as I have questions for him, but neither of us has time to answer them right now.

His reply is instant, and my heart warms to hear it.

"Yes," he says emphatically. "We will protect her."

With that, he turns back to the Valkyrie Queen with narrowed eyes.

"We're leaving," he says to her. "All of us. We can do it with or without bloodshed. It's your choice." His voice becomes low and dangerous as he asks, "Which will it be?"

CHAPTER 38

I'm surprised when the Valkyrie Queen's wings droop and her hand rises urgently. "Wait," she cries. "Please."

She was moving toward us, and I thought it was because she intended to attack us, but now I'm not so certain.

"I misjudged this moment," she says, her gaze passing from Erik, to me, to Galeia, then to Cailey. And finally to the dragon, who has risen even higher into the sky but continues to hover above us.

She swallows visibly. "I need to speak with Asha Silverspun."

I'm conflicted. The longer we stay here, the greater the risk that a twitchy bowman will shoot an arrow at us. Or that the Valkyrie Queen is about to orchestrate some ploy to take Galeia from us.

I'm also very concerned about the dragon.

It's showing signs of landing—or at least approaching the ground—and Galeia may not react well if it comes near her.

It coasts toward the rocky outcrop that now sits behind me, the same outcrop it shot up in front of when it knocked us into a spin.

There's no sign of Blackbird, and I hope he's staying low and isn't hurt.

"It's up to you," Erik murmurs to me.

Cailey gives me a reassuring nod. "The Einherjar won't make a move while I'm here," she says as if she reads my fears. "Neither will the dragon."

Turning to the Valkyrie Queen, I say, "I'll speak with you."

As I step to the side, I take out my hammer, making it clear I won't hesitate to use it.

As my power spills around me, her eyes narrow at me.

I arch my eyebrows right back at her. "You carry your wings. I will carry my hammer."

"Very well. Over here." She gestures to a clear patch of grass not too far from Erik, who doesn't take his eyes off me. Neither, for that matter, does Galeia, her little lips pursed into a snarl that's clearly directed at the Queen.

Only now, I take in the pathway leading up to the wooden wall around the village. It's lined with spikes, each one more gruesome than the next. I was lucky I didn't fall on one.

"Speak," I say to the Queen, keeping my distance from her.

She folds her hands in front of herself but doesn't retract her wings. "My generals told me what your hammer did to their feathers and their armor. They also told me you tried to revive the Vandawolf and failed. Clearly, they were wrong about that."

She stops speaking and peers at me as if I have some answer for her.

I don't.

All I have are accusations. "You forced General Glass to give up her daughter."

"We do not tolerate weakness," she replies without a hint of regret.

"You mean you don't tolerate empathy," I say. "Or perhaps you fear divergence."

"I fear extinction," she says, her voice strained. "It begins with the kind of dark magic that has kept that creature alive."

"You mean *my* magic," I say, giving her a pointed stare. "Only when combined with Blacksmith magic can dark magic achieve such a thing."

Her hands unfold, a potentially threatening move, but she proceeds to firmly cross her arms across her chest as if she were determined to chain her reactions.

I'm certain she rarely engages in an argument that she can't win with a show of force.

The muscles in her jaw clench before she blows out a slow, firm exhale. "Every Valkyrie Queen passes on a warning to the next," she says. "I don't know when the warning started or if it holds any truth, but I can't ignore it."

I consider her warily, uncertain of her change of topic. "What is the warning?"

"When a star falls, it will be the end of the beginning."

Cailey said something similar about beginnings and endings, but it didn't make any more sense then than it does now.

My forehead creases. "What does that mean?"

"I didn't understand it, either. Not until just now." The Queen takes a deep breath. "I believe it's a warning that the days when supernaturals can walk openly on this Earth will come to an end. One day, we will have to hide who and what we are."

The gravity of her tone gives me pause. Just as she did moments ago, I look to the dragon perched majestically on the rocks, then to Cailey's bright form, then to Galeia and Erik, taking in their wolfishness.

"My daughter is only a baby, and yet I fear for her future," the Valkyrie Queen says softly. "Now that you also have a child, you too must surely fear what will come to pass."

Well, at least she's stopped calling Galeia a creature.

"I've lived with fear my whole life," I say. "But why are you expressing your worries to me?"

"Because I need to know which side you will choose in the coming war: human or supernatural."

Neither.

"I will not take part in any war."

She arches her eyebrows at me. "Clearly, you don't know what the Vandawolf came to ask us."

I'm wary. "Enlighten me."

"The human Queen wishes to form an alliance with the Einherjar. She wants them to fight for her against the fae. My mate, who is the chieftain of this clan, declined her request. I know where *he* stands. What I need to know... is what you will do."

I consider her carefully. "Why me, in particular?"

The tension in her posture increases. "Because you have the power to force the Valkyries to follow you."

Her focus falls to my hammer. "Until my generals told me what you did, I believed that there were only two kinds of supernaturals who posed any threat to the Valkyries. One kind are the Keres, but they are our allies and would never betray us. The other kind are the Furies, but they are built to exact justice, so if a Fury comes for a Valkyrie, well, that Valkyrie *deserves* to die. But Blacksmiths..." She gives a sharp exhale. "Even when Malak came to the north, I didn't fear him. But *you*..."

Her voice is filled with dread as she steps toward me, closer than she should. "I fear what you will do to us."

I'm astounded that she would admit this to me. "What do you want from me?"

"I need to know: Will you force us into this fight?"

Once again, I find my focus on Erik. He came here to ask for the Einherjar's support, but his reasons for doing so can't be simple. I can't assume he has pledged his support to the human Queen.

Although... anything could have happened in the last day.

After all, here I am with a child I didn't know existed.

All I can tell the Queen is what I know to be true.

"War won't solve this." I turn my attention back to her. "I've been pulled into the heart of the darkness in the east. The blight is spreading. Even if I believe that the fae are the aggressors in this situation, darkness is the real enemy, not the fae."

The Valkyrie gives me a suddenly wry look, one eyebrow arching a little. "Have you met Queen Karasi?"

I let out a laugh. "Oh, there's no doubt she's a shrewd leader."

"*Shrewd* is a generous description," the Valkyrie Queen

replies before her smile fades. "Her people are suffering. Mine will, too, if the blight reaches us. I'm not a fool, Asha. We will soon have to fight for our homes."

"It's the darkness that has to be stopped," I say.

But she shakes her head at me. "You can't use magic to stop a darkness that feeds on the life force of dead magical beings. Even humans, who all have a small amount of magic in their bodies, can feed it. The more magic you pour into the blight, the darker it grows." She gives a frustrated sigh. "It is self-sustaining."

"Then there's no hope," I say, but my words are a challenge, not resignation. "We should all simply give up, walk into it, and let it be."

She narrows her eyes at me.

I stare back at her.

"Oh, I think we might have been friends," she says, her voice quiet.

"Perhaps we still can be."

She gives me a nod, but she waits, and I know she needs more. She needs to know if I'll force her to take action she doesn't want to take.

"I will not force you into this war," I say, but I hold up my hand. "But I want something in return."

"What is it?"

"Leave us be. *All* of us."

Her focus is suddenly on Galeia, but I'm not finished.

"And tell General Glass that her daughter will be loved."

The Valkyrie Queen's eyes are now narrow, silver slits.

There's no doubt in my mind that she's struggling with my demands, and I'm really not sure what she'll choose.

"Or we can fight," I say calmly. "And I will win. After which, I'll force the Valkyries and the Einherjar to fight on the side of the humans."

The Queen eyes me with such resentment that I'm surprised by her response.

"We would most certainly have been friends," she says. "I agree to your terms."

Without another word, she sweeps her wings back, rises into the air, and lifts her voice to a commanding shout. "Fall back! Let them leave."

The warriors on the wall immediately lower their weapons.

Now that I'm holding my hammer, I can make out their features. One of them, an older man, catches my attention. He has the brightest blue eyes, glowing sapphire in a way that makes me suspect he is somehow in constant contact with his deep light.

He gives the Valkyrie Queen a firm, supportive nod, which draws a soft smile to her face before she soars back to him.

Within moments, she has disappeared into the village, and only a few warriors patrol the wall.

A hush falls around me, broken only by Galeia's soft snarls, but she sounds less fearful now.

I find myself taking a deep breath.

Across the way, Erik's expression is no less fierce, but there's something in his eyes, something lost...

I hurry toward him, reaching him as fast as I can, wrapping my arms around him and Galeia, my power glowing around all of us. "Erik—"

Cailey's voice interrupts me. "We don't have time for reunions. We must move." She's already spinning to the dragon, addressing him as if she has authority over him. "Vargo Vanem, you will carry Erik, Asha, and Galeia. I will ride the wolf-bird. We will go west. To my home. You know the way."

The dragon inclines his head, an unexpected show of reverence. "Yes, Caoilainn Liadan. As you request, it will be done."

Blackbird appears at that moment, sweeping toward Cailey. She launches herself into the air and onto his back in one seamless move as he soars past her. "Hurry!"

I take Erik's hand, meeting his eyes. I suddenly can't find words. Some of the ferocity in his expression fades. I press my cheek to his, and that's all we have time for.

The dragon soars from the rock to the flat plain beside us, sending a gust of wind around us that nearly knocks me off my feet. I quickly put my hammer away and reach for Galeia, but her arms only tighten around Erik's neck.

"Okay?" I ask him, and it feels like I'm asking for far more than that he carries her on the journey.

I'm asking him to protect her. To accept my choice to bring her with me. To support me in trying to help her. All without knowing anything about who she is and why she's here with me.

He nods. "I'll look after her."

Within minutes, we're seated in the saddle on Vargo's back, Erik holding Galeia in front while I sit behind him. This way, I can lean forward and tell him everything.

Then we're rising into the night, and once again, I cling to the hope that wherever Cailey's taking us, it won't be into danger.

CHAPTER 39

As we fly through the night, I tell Erik everything that's happened since we were separated, including all of Thaden's revelations and who Galeia is.

Because I'm sitting behind Erik, I can't see his reactions, but I can feel every time his body tenses, along with the rumbling vibrations of his surprised growls.

It's difficult to have a full conversation while the cold wind seems determined to snatch every word from my mouth, but somehow, I answer all of his questions.

Then he answers all of mine.

He tells me about what he heard and saw back at the human city and why he went to the Einherjar. He tells me about the dragon rider Catalina Shield, as well as Rachel's decision to lead the humans. Also, that the human army is depleted.

Although he speaks openly about all of those things, I sense he's keeping something back. I'm not sure how to ask him what it is or if I even should.

By the time the first glimmers of sunlight lift the darkness behind us, we've fallen silent.

Galeia is asleep. Erik deposited the device she was clinging to safely into a pocket of his coat, where I won't come into contact with it.

I struggle to keep my eyes open.

I can't remember the last time I slept, and exhaustion is becoming my enemy.

Just when I'm tempted to reach back for my hammer and draw on my power to keep myself awake, the air changes.

Suddenly, I taste salt on my tongue.

With it comes moisture, a dampness in the air that I've never experienced before.

In the distance, I can hear a strange sort of crashing sound. "What is that?"

"I don't know," Erik says, sounding wary.

The dragon speaks for the first time. "That is the ocean."

Ocean?

My eyes widen as a massive expanse of water comes into view. It stretches left to right and westward as far as I can see, a seemingly endless mass of liquid right at the edge of the land.

Directly below us is near-constant forest, but along the way, I've made out human villages and outposts. We even spotted several dragons in the distance, but none approached us.

Now, we're heading toward a large clearing that seems to sit right at the world's edge. The earth falls away in rocky cliffs while the water crashes into them, sending spray high into the air.

Blackbird can't fly as fast as Vargo, so he's still some way behind us, but I can make out Cailey's form on his back. She doesn't appear so bright now that the sun is rising behind her.

Vargo angles toward the ground, descending in a rush before pulling up to land.

I stumble from his back while Erik slides down his side, keeping a firm hold of Galeia.

The clearing is vast, but so is the forest that surrounds it. The only structure, situated right before the edge of the cliff, is a black rock that looks from this distance to be several paces wide and as high as my waist. Otherwise, the clearing is bare of anything other than grass.

Blackbird lands behind us, and Cailey slips from his back. She moves more slowly than she did when we left the Einherjar village, leaning for a moment against Blackbird's side.

"This is your home?" I ask, crossing the distance to her, even though I want nothing more than to slide to the soft grass and fall asleep.

"We're safe here," she says, sounding more breathless than I was expecting. "It's time to rest."

"Safe from what, exactly?" Given her need to get here in such a hurry, I'm surprised by her suggestion that we should now rest.

"Safe from the blight," she replies. "We are now as far from it as we can be. Right at land's edge."

"But you said—"

"I've bought you time, Asha. Time is what you need. But first, so is sleep. You must be strong for what lies ahead."

I'm about to demand answers, but her legs buckle, and I find myself catching her instead.

She feels lighter than air. Nearly insubstantial. Her pale hair falls across my arm, and her eyes rise to mine.

"I have no strength during the day," she whispers. "Please. Help me out of the sun. Accept your need to sleep. Tonight, you will forge your medallion."

"I'll... what?"

I can't see how I can possibly forge anything when I don't have crimson coal or any metal I could use, but her attention has already turned to the Vargo, who watches us with a grim expression.

"Vargo Vanem," she says, her voice increasingly weak, "please speak with Graviter Rex. Tell him what you have seen. He will know what must be done." Her expression hardens despite her apparent exhaustion. "Warn him that if he comes here with rage in his heart, he will only invite his own death. The dragons must come in peace."

Vargo gives her a solemn nod. "I will do as you ask."

He immediately rises into the air, the wind from his enormous wings bending the nearby trees and knocking me back a step.

I bump into Erik's chest. His arms close around me, strong and warm. Somehow, he caught me while also holding on to Galeia. She's still sound asleep, her head nestled in the crook of his neck.

"Exhaustion only leads to mistakes," he murmurs, his voice solemn. "The world must be spinning around you right now, Asha. You need to rest before it will stop."

My eyes burn with his assessment.

In the last day, I found out about Galeia. I learned why Lysander Rex died. I survived the blight—but only because Cailey came for me and... *bright saints*... I don't know who or what she is, except that she seems able to demand respect from all supernaturals. If my experiences have taught me anything, it's that I must question everything. I could be making a terrible mistake by trusting Cailey so easily, and yet...

I have no fear that she will hurt me.

Neither must Erik, or he wouldn't be supportive of her suggestion that we rest.

I give him a tired nod. "Let's find a place to sleep."

The forest is full of trees with such wide trunks that they must be hundreds of years old. Within an hour, we've not only found a shaded place to sleep with a thick layer of moss to lie on, but also a fresh water source in the form of a nearby stream.

My stomach grumbles, but my hunger isn't too bad since I ate before I left Thaden's village.

I curl up in the shade with Galeia nestled against my chest and Erik at my back, his arm curled around me.

Cailey has already slid to the ground only two paces away, curled up in a bed of moss, and closed her eyes, her chest rising and falling deeply.

Within moments, I'm asleep.

I wake to darkness, jolting upright before I place myself.

I'm still in the clearing beneath the giant trees. Everything is quiet and still. Soft moonlight filters through the gaps in the canopy of leaves overhead, telling me I slept all day.

Galeia is still fast asleep, but she appears to have gravitated toward Cailey. Or maybe Cailey gravitated toward her. Either way, Galeia is now snuggled against Cailey's side.

I relax a little. She wouldn't do that if she didn't trust Cailey.

For a moment, I take them both in. Galeia with her black hair, such a tiny form capable of such destruction, and Cailey, who looks no more than ten years old, with her white hair, also capable of immense power.

They both look so young and so old at the same time.

I reach back before I realize Erik isn't lying behind me.

A new fear strikes through me before I catch sight of him through the trees.

He's standing at the edge of the cliff, where the waves crash against the rocks.

Leaving Galeia beside Cailey, I retrieve my hammer and step quietly through the trees out into the open. The glow my power makes is subdued but no less powerful.

It feels as if the more familiar I become with the force within me, the more I can control its visual effects.

To reach Erik, I pass by the rock that sits near the cliff's edge, getting a closer look at its structure. As I estimated, it sits at my waist height, has both flat and curved sections across the top, and is wide enough that it takes several steps to pass by.

Erik is aware of my approach because he turns slightly in my direction, but he doesn't say anything.

I settle in beside him, letting the silence sit between us. It's an unusual sort of non-silence, since it's filled with the crashing of waves while also, somehow, feeling calm.

He finally speaks, his question low and soft. "What if I was meant to die on that mountain?"

All of my calm flees in an instant. I fight to keep the shock from my voice. "Erik?"

What could possibly make him ask such a thing?

"War is in my blood." He finally turns fully to me, his gray eyes shadowed and his jaw tense. "You have been my anchor since my family died. What will I do if there is peace?"

I want to tell him that the idea of peace is so far out of our reach that I don't believe we will ever attain it.

I want to tell him that even if we find peace, darkness will never end. Life will always hold battles for us.

But more than anything, I want him to know that there is no peace for me without *him*.

Before I can respond, the sound of wings reaches me—too many for either of us to ignore.

Erik spins to the sound, and I do, too, easily making out the thunder of dragons coming our way.

I count ten dragons, all approaching fast.

CHAPTER 40

I'm immediately on my guard.

The dragons soar through the air above us, heading out across the ocean before circling back and landing in what looks like a well-practiced cascade.

None of them has a human rider, and I'm not sure if that's a good or bad sign.

I make out Torva Viridia's form among them. She is the forest dragon who flew us to the mountain. She and I didn't exactly part on good terms—I threatened to give Milena's body to the fae, at which she snatched up the body and flew away—but I hope Torva has realized that's what I wanted her to do.

Graviter lands first, his golden scales catching the moonlight. Torva Viridia is right behind him. Then Vargo Vanem. Followed by seven other dragons whose names I don't know, each one settling down on the grass. Even in this vast clearing, they take up a lot of the space.

Graviter takes cautious steps toward me before stopping a solid twenty paces away.

Without thinking, I've gripped my hammer more tightly, and my power spills more brightly around me. Erik hasn't reached for his sword, but the tips of his claws are visible where he stands to my right.

Galeia is currently hidden in the forest with Cailey. The dragons don't give any indication that they can see or sense her, but I'm prepared to defend her with my life if she emerges and they react badly to her presence.

Graviter can't miss our defensiveness, but he remains subdued.

"Asha Silverspun." He greets me formally, dipping his head in what appears to be a bow. "I have come to make amends. If you will let me."

I consider each of the dragons carefully. Graviter is their king. For him to come to me like this...

"How?" I ask him.

How does he intend to make amends?

"You need to make a medallion," he replies. "But your medallion must be forged from metal that is given, not taken. We are here to give you what is needed."

With that, he lifts his right paw and extends a single talon.

It only makes me tense. Erik gives a warning growl beside me, his claws extending fully, but Graviter continues slowly.

He presses his extended talon to the scales that rest across the top of his other paw, leveraging the talon beneath one of his scales.

He grimaces but doesn't make a sound as he pulls a single scale off the top of his paw.

It's one of his smallest scales, but it's still the size of my palm.

"For when you need fury," he says.

I consider him warily, but before I can question him, Torva Viridia steps up. She is small compared to Graviter, her scales alternating green and blue. While Graviter is a picture of fire and fury, she radiates only with intense calm.

One of her talons extends and within seconds, she too leverages a scale off the top of her paw, this one emerald.

"For peace," she says.

Vargo Vanem is already attacking his own paw, quickly succeeding in removing a single, crimson-red scale. "For wisdom."

Each of the dragons in the background scratches at their left paw, leveraging up a scale and speaking, one by one.

Patience. Justice. Honor. Compassion. Discipline. Inspiration. And finally...

"Water," the last dragon declares. She has a distinctly feminine voice and her cerulean-blue scales catch the moonlight even more brightly than Graviter's.

When the other dragons turn to stare at her, their eyebrows raised, she stares right back at them. "What? All that discipline and justice. She's going to get thirsty."

She winks at me across the distance. "I'm Lily Verago. Water dragon. If there's a fire, I'm the one you need."

When Graviter continues to glare at her, she rolls her eyes. "Okay, fine. *Resilience*." She smiles. "Like water that keeps on flowing."

Nearer to me, Torva gives a nod of approval, a smile flickering around her mouth, and it's clear to me that she and Lily are friends.

Then Torva takes a deep breath, blowing gently across the air.

The loose scales lift up off the dragons' paws, caught in the stream of her breath, and waft like flower petals toward me.

Before they would reach me, they veer to my left, cascading down onto the surface of the rock that sits at the edge of the cliff.

I don't know how to point out the flaw of their gifts without sounding ungrateful. "They aren't metal," I whisper.

"You don't need metal," Graviter calmly replies, as if he'd been prepared for my question. "It is the basic tenet of your power that you can mold *anything*. It's time to test how far your power can go."

"What of the fire I need?" Then my forehead creases. "Do I even need fire?"

"I don't know," Graviter replies. "Do you?"

I study the ten scales of different colors neatly piled on the top of the rock. Then I consider my hammer.

I close my eyes and imagine forging a medallion for the first time.

Within my mind, I can hear myself instructing Thaden that day in the human forge.

My own voice is so clear in my memory.

Count the heartbeats. One... Two... Three...

"Yes," I say, my heart sinking a little because I'm certain the dragons haven't brought crimson coal with them—I can't smell its honeyed scent on the air. "I need fire."

Graviter gives me a solemn nod. "Then allow me to give you the flame you need. If you will step aside."

The dragons stiffen behind him. Torva edges forward. "Graviter?"

He has already stepped up to the rock.

His scales ripple with an intense heat that sends me back a step and propels Torva away from him. A visible flame rushes from his chest through his throat, burning so brightly that it glows startlingly within his body.

It reaches his mouth, and I prepare for the burning heat.

He puffs out a single, perfect flame. It fills the concave section in the rock's surface and then—impossibly—it stays alight, glowing serenely even as the wind rushes around it and the waves send spray into the air that would surely dampen it.

The other dragons give a collective gasp.

"Graviter!" Torva cries, jolting toward him again. "*No...*"

I cast anxious glances between them, aware of the way Erik has stepped up to my side. "What's going on?"

Graviter takes a step back, stumbling a little, but quickly rights himself. "Every fire dragon has an eternal flame," he explains. "It can only be given once, and once given, it will shorten my life by hundreds of years."

He gives Torva a reassuring smile before he turns to Vargo. "I will live long enough for your son to be born, but I will not be able to teach him what he needs to know. You must do that."

Vargo's eyes fill with tears that leak down his crimson scales, but he gives a firm nod. "I vow it."

Tears roll down Torva's cheeks. "Graviter, your twin boys

won't be born until after Vargo's son. They will never know you now."

Graviter turns to the other dragons. "Which is why you must all promise me: You will watch over them."

Words fail me. "Graviter..."

But he is already swinging away from me, this time toward the trees.

"I am not the only one who has given their life for this," he says.

At the edge of the trees, Cailey appears, her silhouette bright again. Galeia is propped on her hip, not a small feat, given that Cailey is only small herself.

Galeia's growls can be heard above the crashing waves, and with a quick glance at me, Erik hurries across the distance toward them, taking Galeia from Cailey before Galeia can leap from her arms.

Even with my power, I can't hear what he says to Galeia—or if it's spoken in growls or words—but she calms immediately. Even so, they stay at the edge of the trees while Cailey steps forward.

All of the dragons bow low to the ground, each one murmuring her name. "Caoilainn Liadan."

Once again, I wonder, *Who is she?*

Torva edges toward me, her emerald eyes bright as she whispers, "She is your Celestial Star."

My breath catches.

Oh... Of course.

She came to witness the making of my hammer. Then she stayed while I fought the Valkyries. She saw Erik revive. We were separated from her when she gave us some space, and then the storm hit us.

Graviter told me that she was as old as the Earth. She had seen the births of gods and titans and had, until now, watched over the Valkyries in the End Lands.

It makes sense to me now that the Valkyrie Queen reacted so intensely to Cailey's presence.

But the Celestial Star was an orb of light, and now she stands before me in the form of a girl. A sense of foreboding fills me as I take in the sadness on the dragons' faces and the way Graviter told me his wasn't the only sacrifice made for me.

A wash of new sadness fills Torva's expression as she continues. "She chose to burn out her light to save you. It was the only way to pull you out of the darkness. She has become mortal and will perish soon."

I shake my head, a cry of denial rising to my lips.

No.

It's too much.

I fight the sob filling my throat and the pain filling my heart.

First, Erik chose to burn out his deep light so he could forge me a hammer. Then Graviter gave me his eternal flame. And now I'm told the Celestial Star fell to the ash to pull me from the darkness.

It's too much.

Graviter Rex swings back to me and his eyes are suddenly filled with fury. "Sacrifices have been made, Asha Silverspun, and they won't be the last."

His voice is a command that I can't deny. "It's time to forge your medallion."

CHAPTER 41

"We will be your witnesses," the dragon king says.

With that, he steps back from the rock that has become my anvil. He joins the other dragons, who all settle down under the moon to wait.

Erik remains in the distance with Galeia while Cailey steps to Graviter's side, reminding me of the way she floated at his shoulder when Erik made my hammer.

"I don't have tongs," I whisper, even though it feels like such an insignificant hurdle after everything that has been given to me.

"You don't need them," Graviter rumbles. "The eternal flame will not burn the one to whom it is given. You alone can plunge your hand into this fire and remain unharmed."

I'm relieved to hear this. Brushing my fingertips across the tops of the scales, I take in the different textures and colors, even thicknesses. Torva's scale is smooth. Graviter's is rough. Lily's is flexible. Vargo's is opaque.

They have given me different strengths, but also different perspectives, the collective gifts of a dragon family.

At one end, I place fury, and at the other, I place peace. I line them all up side by side, each one as important as the other. Each one influencing the other. All of them are parts of a whole.

Then I scoop them up in my right hand, gratified when they slot neatly against each other in my palm.

I pause before I would extend my hand into the fire.

All I have is the echo of my mother's long-ago commands as she ordered her students to plunge their strips of metal into the fire and then beat them. She would order the students to heat and forge until they were collapsing from exhaustion, creating their medallions with cruelty. *For* cruelty.

It can't be her voice that I follow.

It has to be my own.

To do this, I need to listen to my own heart and accept all of its needs as well as its flaws.

"Heat," I whisper.

Slowly, I extend my hand into the fire, aware of its warmth and the impact it has on the scales.

Each one begins to glow, the same way dull iron will blaze a lustrous amber when heated correctly, except that these scales were already luminescent.

Now, their beauty is both terrifying and astonishing.

I count my heartbeats, feeling calmer...

And calmer.

And *there*.

I remove my hand from the fire, placing the pile of scales carefully onto the flat part of the rock, my hammer already in my left hand.

I don't wait. I can't allow the scales to cool.

But I will not force them, either. I will respect their structure and allow them to be what they wish to be.

I give them the lightest tap. The contact rings out clear across the clearing, a soft, mesmerizing chime.

Clang!

My power flows through my hammer like a newly released stream. Golden light spills through the scales, filling every tiny crack between them.

With the next hit, the scales compress, the energy from my

heart streaming down through my arm, through my hammer, and into the scales.

And now the work begins.

For the next hour, I beat the scales with my hammer and fold them with my hands, beating and folding, over and over. At intervals, I plunge my hands into the fire to reheat the scales before I start all over again, beating and folding, pouring my power into the scales, making them mine.

I work to a rhythm of my own making, molding the scales into one whole piece that I fill with all the parts of me, strong and flawed. My medallion will not be perfect, but it will be true.

The perfect conduit.

I expect the process to take days, but within the hour, the scales are no longer scales.

They are gold.

I lift my hammer, intending to beat the metal one last time, but I stop.

Wisdom is knowing when something should not be entirely mine. There is still a thread of the dragons' natures in this metal.

It's the finest possible thread, nearly invisible, practically imperceptible, but I don't want to beat it out.

It's the same thread that has given me purpose and kept me alive: a sense of family.

I lower my hammer as a hush settles around me.

The dragons have remained quiet, and now they hunch low to the ground, their focus on me becoming even more intense.

Now, I must claim the medallion as my own.

The final clangs echo in my ears, a melody that washes away in the wind, whipped out to sea.

The golden band I've created is wider than any other medallion. It will cover more of my palm.

Lowering my hammer to the ground and leaving it there, I lift my left hand, hovering it over the medallion for a moment.

You belong to me.

My power is mine.

I press my palm down onto the golden band. The metal I've

created responds instantly to my touch, wrapping itself around my palm, fitting itself to my skin, and sealing across the back of my hand.

I inhale and exhale, breathing through the moment, letting my power settle, taking in the ebb and flow of it and the way it changes how the world appears to me.

First, the wide expanse of water, countless droplets churning with energy, then the makeshift anvil itself, all its striations and grooves, and its ability to take the force of my hammer and carry the heat of the eternal flame without breaking.

Then the dragons and the immense energy rippling through their scales, the life-force in their hearts so powerful they could set the world on fire.

Followed by the fading glow from the heart of a dying star that fills me with sadness.

And then, at the edge of a massive forest, which itself carries so much life, stands the man I love.

He is holding on to Galeia and protecting her, simply because I asked him to.

He is the storm in my calm, a force more powerful than every dragon here because he, alone, has the power to break me.

"It is done," I whisper.

CHAPTER 42

The dragons lift their heads, and it isn't lost on me that they now consider me with expressions ranging from relieved to fearful.

They have given me the ability to constantly access my power and I could just as easily use it against them.

Cailey, on the other hand, is beaming, her pale cheeks glowing. And moments later, Blackbird slinks from the forest on the other side of the clearing, taking wary glances at the dragons before he prowls toward me and plonks himself down at my back.

His casual response to my power seems to break the tension.

Cailey hurries toward me, Graviter's steely gaze becomes calm, and the other dragons begin murmuring among themselves.

Torva edges toward me first, her emerald eyes soft in the moonlight. "We left our posts so we could be here. We need to return to the other dragons and help the humans. But I hope you understand, we will return here soon. War is coming, and we need your help."

"War may already be here!" the alarmed cry comes unexpectedly from Cailey, who has pulled up sharply only a few paces away from me and has spun toward the forest in the east.

My focus snaps to the sky, my senses taking in so much more now that my power is constant.

A thunderbird soars toward us, its amethyst-colored lightning sizzling through the air around it. It's a mighty beast with inky-black feathers and a dark-purple beak. It isn't approaching quietly, beating its wings and sending multiple cracks of thunder echoing across the clearing.

"That's Concord," I whisper, my eyes wide. "She belongs to the Fae Queen's Champion, Elowynn."

Even from a distance, I can see that Elowynn isn't the one riding her. The woman on Concord's back has a more petite frame and golden hair, distinctly different from Elowynn's nearly black tresses.

"She isn't alone," Cailey murmurs.

Two more flying creatures appear behind her, but they aren't thunderbirds.

Dragons as big as Vargo spear through the air after Concord, and for a moment, I think they're chasing her until I realize that they're maintaining a formation at her back that allows them to flank her.

"Are they escorting her?"

"We'll find out soon enough," Graviter growls before he swings to his family. "Dragons! I will guard this plain. The rest of you, back to your posts."

I'm forced to crouch low so I'm not knocked from my feet by the force of the wind as all of the dragons except for Graviter take off at once.

I'm aware of the Blackbird gripping the ground with his claws, digging in while Cailey is buffeted across the ground and against Blackbird's side.

Within seconds, the dragons have risen into the air and taken up a formation that allows them to circle the clearing before heading back past the oncoming trio. Several of them take their time circling again, a show of force that the fae rider won't miss.

I cast an urgent glance at Erik, but he is already stepping back into the shadows of the forest. Galeia will be on edge, and it's incredibly important that she doesn't react badly to the rising tension.

By clearing the ground, the dragons have allowed Concord to land, along with the two dragons who were following her, while Graviter moves off to my right like a guard.

One of the incoming dragons has a single rider, while the other has two.

I recognize the two human women who leap off the back of the second dragon—Mother Solas and her granddaughter, Rachel—but not the woman who jumps from the back of the first dragon.

Cailey's murmur sounds at my shoulder. "That is Catalina Shield. She is the champion of the human Queen, who is now the younger woman, Rachel Solas."

Erik told me what happened back at the city. Mother Solas and Rachel didn't treat him like an enemy, but they have new responsibilities now. Rachel will now bear the weight of an entire human population on her shoulders.

Catalina surges ahead first. She has dark-brown hair, consistent with most of the humans I've met, light-brown skin, and a birthmark across her left cheek and jaw. Her armor appears to be made from leather, but she's wearing a black metal glove on her right hand. I consider it with some wariness, since it looks like the type of glove Thaden designed for the humans.

She quickly reaches Concord and shouts a command up to the fae woman who has remained on Concord's back. "Get down on the ground. Slowly!"

I recognize the fae as Dusana. She was the one who attacked me in the mountains before Elowynn escorted me to the fae castle.

My sister told me it was Dusana who delivered the message to her at Thaden's village. That message had no real substance but contained a clear threat: If I want my brother to live, I will do whatever Queen Karasi asks.

Now, it seems Dusana is finally here to tell me what that is.

But the dynamic between her and Catalina tells me that Dusana is certainly not in control of this situation.

She slides from Concord's back without waiting for the bird to extend her wing, wobbling during her landing and taking a long minute to right herself.

"Walk!" Catalina orders her, at which Dusana stumbles toward me.

"Stop," Catalina barks. "Down on your knees. Keep your hands where we can see them."

Again, Dusana obeys.

When I first encountered Dusana, she was wearing raven-black armor and carrying multiple concealed weapons. She held her head high. Now she's dressed in an old, stained tunic and tattered pants. Her hair is matted, and her cheeks look gaunt.

She shivers in the wind, and her eyes are hollow when she looks up at me.

I take a closer look at Concord, unhappy to make out missing feathers around her neck and red marks on her exposed skin. She was either beaten or chained. She sinks to the ground, her head low.

I may not be friends with any fae, let alone Concord's rider, Elowynn, but Concord chose to help me at a time when I desperately needed it.

"We've brought you to Asha Silverspun, as you demanded," Catalina snaps at Dusana. "Now speak your message."

"No," I say before Dusana can open her mouth. "Do *not* speak."

Not yet.

Catalina blinks at me. I've surprised her, but she will rally soon enough.

"Cailey," I say, quickly drawing the star to me.

"Yes, Asha?"

"Will you bring some water from the stream?"

Cailey doesn't question me. "I can do that."

She darts away toward the edge of the forest.

Then I incline my head toward Blackbird. "Concord must be thirsty, too. Blackbird, can you show her to the stream?"

Blackbird makes a growling sound in his throat before edging toward Concord. I learned early on that fae thunderbirds understand speech, even if they can't speak back. Only the Dusk fae have the power to commune with them fully, reading their minds and speaking silently with them.

Dusana is a Dusk fae.

It means she doesn't control sunlight or wind or other elements that could kill a person, but she could silently command Concord to lash out...

I watch her carefully while Blackbird moves toward Concord. The female thunderbird glances at Dusana before she turns her attention to Blackbird, blinking slowly at him.

His half-bird, half-wolf form is a lot to take in, but Concord doesn't startle.

When he veers toward the forest, looking back at her, she follows him without hesitation.

"Was that a test?" Dusana asks, her voice raspy and more subdued than I've ever heard it.

"Maybe." My focus is now on Catalina, whose darkening features tell me she isn't in the mood to be patient.

In contrast, Mother Solas and Rachel have stayed well away from me. Probably something to do with the golden band clearly visible on my palm. Rachel was young when Malak died, but Mother Solas lived through his reign. She saw firsthand what an angry Blacksmith is capable of doing.

"Explain to me why you're here," I say.

Dusana heaves out a weary breath. "I bring a message—"

"Not you," I say to Dusana before I turn back to Catalina. "*You.*"

Catalina gives me a once-over before she seems to rethink her position. Her focus flashes briefly to the sky, where Vargo coasts through the air. Erik told me she's Vargo's rider. He also told me she's willing to do anything for her people.

I need to know if that will make her reckless.

My brother's life may turn on her choices.

"Late yesterday, the fae started withdrawing their forces from the western border," she says. "That continued today. All of the fae are falling back. Then, this fae arrives, claiming to have a message, but she will only deliver it to you. I knew where you were because of the dragons."

My forehead creases. "Queen Karasi is withdrawing her troops? But she has nowhere to go. She can't go north. The Einherjar and Valkyries would stop her."

Catalina nods. "And she can't go farther south because the blight has now spread across the way and blocked the pass. Even if it hadn't, she wouldn't be foolish enough to head into the deep south, where the dark elves would make a feast of her."

"Then where is she going?"

Dusana speaks up. "East."

Impossible. I keep my expression blank. "The darkness is in the east."

"She doesn't care," Dusana snarls. "She would rather march us back into darkness than watch us starve to death."

I hear the lie in her voice. I saw for myself that Queen Karasi has plenty of food. At least for herself and her chosen favorites.

I slowly sink to my knees, putting myself at eye level with Dusana before I rest my hands on my thighs, turning my left hand palm up.

"Do you see my hammer?" I ask Dusana.

Her focus flickers to it before she nods.

"My hammer refuses to kill." I watch the cogs turn in her mind before I continue. "But my medallion has no such limitations."

I have no proof of my claim. I haven't tested it. But it's a certainty I feel with every beat of my heart.

"I can force you to speak the truth," I say.

The corners of her mouth turn down before her lips draw back, revealing her gritted teeth. "Then do it!"

I stay where I am for now. "Deliver your message."

She stares defiantly back at me. "Queen Karasi does not wish to go to war with the humans and their dragons. She offers an alternative resolution to the conflict."

"What alternative?"

"A fight to the death," Dusana replies. "Between the fae

champion and the human champion. The winner takes all for their Queen."

I process this for a moment, aware of the way Catalina—as well as Mother Solas and Rachel—are casting glances at each other. They're clearly thinking it through.

But Dusana herself is peering at me, which tells me it's my reaction that matters to her.

"Anything else?" I ask, keeping my expression blank.

"As a show of faith, Karasi has withdrawn her army from the western border to give the humans time to prepare. At dawn in three days' time, Queen Karasi will assemble her army on the eastern plain. Either the human champion will meet her champion in a fight to the death, or the fae army will push west and kill every human in its path."

Catalina murmurs beneath her breath, "A single death or outright war."

"It won't be that simple," I say.

Catalina is so caught up in what this proposal means for herself and her people—and why wouldn't she be, since they are her largest concern?—that she has missed the obvious.

"Dusana of the Dusk," I say to the fae, "why did you bring this message to *me*?"

Her eyes are dull, not a hint of malice, as she says, "Because your brother's life depends on it."

CHAPTER 43

My brother's life.

I don't react, even though I'm fighting my rising anger and frustration.

I finally have all the power I could ever ask for, but my family is still in danger.

"Explain," I command Dusana.

"If the humans agree to a fight between champions, your brother will be returned to you on the battlefield. If not, he will be killed."

My mind whirls as I try to sort through Karasi's motivations. She clearly wants me to convince the humans to agree to the fight, but why?

Karasi has maintained an appearance of strength, even though her army is depleted. A fight to the death will ensure she doesn't have to reveal how weakened her army has become. It would also mean she doesn't have to pit her people against dragons because defeating them would be extremely difficult.

But to pin her life on the outcome of a single fight, she would have to be confident that her champion would win.

Unless... there's something I'm not seeing. Information I don't yet have. A game with pieces I can't yet see.

Dusana hasn't stopped studying me, and now her hands twitch nervously. "I've delivered my message," she says. "I will leave now."

I arch my eyebrows at her. "How do you propose to do that?"

Concord hasn't returned. There is still a massive dragon guarding the clearing along with a very unhappy human champion who looks like she would rather dispatch Dusana to the saints than listen to another word she says.

There's movement at the edge of the forest, but it's Erik. He carries a wooden bowl.

I experience a moment of concern that Galeia isn't with him, but he wouldn't leave her unless she was safe.

Dusana's shoulders sink at the sight of Erik. She must be estimating her chances of leaving here alive and, judging from her resigned exhalation, have now gauged them to be very low.

I asked her how she intended to leave and now she replies. "I guess I won't be leaving after all."

"Why did Queen Karasi choose *you* as her messenger? Why not Elowynn?"

Now, Dusana flinches. She edges backward, shuffling on her knees, even though that only takes her closer to Catalina and her ominous, metal-gloved hand. "I can't... I'm not allowed..."

I wish I could force her to tell the truth. But my power is in transformation. I can create something from something else.

I don't have the power of compulsion.

Of course, I could change her nature to one of truthfulness. But that could be inherently dangerous. She could tell the truth to the wrong person, and it could get her, or us, killed.

On the other hand, here I am with a golden medallion unlike any other Blacksmith's, and Dusana may well believe I'm using its power, even if I'm not...

My left hand snaps out faster than Dusana can take a breath, connecting with the side of her face. "Speak the truth."

She freezes, her eyes flying wide, but they fill with tears. "I *hate* you! If you'd only died in that cave, like Karasi wanted—"

"Like Karasi wanted? Karasi made a show of keeping me alive."

"She's always playing two games. One in plain sight and the other in the shadows. Officially, her orders were to give you safe passage. Unofficially, I was sent to kill you."

I wish I was surprised by this. "You failed."

"Which is why I was publicly beaten. Not because I disobeyed an order."

"Did Elowynn know?"

Dusana snorts. "Elowynn knew nothing."

"Where is she now?"

"Chained in a filthy prison."

"Why?"

Why would Karasi chain her own champion?

"Karasi told me to follow your brother and sister into the east. I was to make sure they never made it to their destination. I simply had to drop some apple seeds from the sky, and the darkness would come for them." Dusana exhales heavily. "My orders were to scoop Thaden up before the darkness got him and bring him back to Karasi."

"Why Thaden?"

"Because he was changed into a dragon. He must know how it was killed."

Of course, the Fae Queen would be desperate to know how to kill a dragon. Erik didn't reveal his claws to me until after we'd left the fae castle and only a handful of people know about Galeia.

"I didn't realize Elowynn was following me," Dusana continues. "She saved Gallium and got in my way before I could get Thaden. When we returned to the castle, Karasi flew into a rage, called us traitors, and imprisoned us. She only released me to send me here."

"What of my brother?"

Dusana's shoulders are slowly sinking. "The last I saw of him, Karasi was keeping him like a pet. If he does something she doesn't like, Elowynn pays the price."

My blood boils. I don't know enough about the dynamic

between Gallium and Elowynn, but I know how much it will kill him for someone else to be hurt in his stead. "What about Elowynn's sister, Gliss?"

"Also in prison. She's refusing to tell Queen Karasi what the dragons are thinking."

Before I left the fae castle, Gliss revealed to me that she alone could slip into a dragon's mind and decipher their thoughts. She explained that dragons aren't like other creatures. Their thoughts are complex and concealed with light magic, the purest kind. She told me that she was withholding information from her Queen and that if Karasi found out, she would be punished for it.

I want to ask Dusana more, but even if I'm not forcing her to tell the truth, my contact with her mind tells me she's exhausted.

I will only get one more answer out of her.

"If Elowynn is in prison and you are now our captive, who will be Karasi's champion?"

"I don't know," Dusana whispers, meeting my eyes. "I fear she might fight for herself."

I remove my hand from Dusana's face, and she slumps to the ground.

Erik has reached my side and his grim expression tells me he heard everything.

He lowers himself to the ground with a quick, murmured reassurance. "Galeia is with Cailey. They're playing with Blackbird and Concord near the stream. They're safe and happy."

He hands me the bowl of water. It looks like a piece of tree trunk and, judging by the scrape marks on the inside, he used his claws to hollow it out so he could fill it more deeply.

I hold it out to Dusana. "Drink."

She leans away from the bowl as if it could contain poison.

I give a soft sigh. "Karasi's message was thorough. It included a way for the humans to respond that doesn't involve you returning with their answer. Karasi doesn't expect you to make it back alive."

"She expects you to kill me." Dusana's brown eyes appear faded, but she doesn't look away. "She told me she hopes you will.

I've outlived my usefulness. I'm a liability. My people will have been ordered to kill me on sight."

I believe her.

"Well, then," I say, inclining my head at the bowl. "You've got nothing to lose."

Her brow furrows.

Hesitantly, she reaches for the bowl.

Maybe she thinks I'll throw it in her face before she can drink it.

She doesn't take her eyes off me as she lifts it to her lips and gulps down the liquid.

I turn my attention to Catalina. "Dusana is now my prisoner. She is no longer a threat to your people."

Catalina's lips press together. I imagine she's trying to decide if she can trust me.

"I understand you're not accustomed to relying on others," I say to her. "Rachel knows I'm true to my word."

"Far more than any person I've met," Rachel says, finally stepping forward. "Lady Asha."

It's what she used to call me. I'll never forget the day she helped me up the stairs to my tower, gave me water when I couldn't lift the cup myself, and sat in the wooden chair in the corner of my room, protecting me while I slept.

"I'm glad to see you, Rachel," I reply. "And you, too, Mother Solas."

The older woman steps closer to me than Catalina or Rachel do. In the moonlight, her silvery-gray hair looks whiter than it did when I last saw her, and the smile lines around her mouth and eyes are fainter, her expression more strained.

"If the Fae Queen plays two games," Mother Solas says, "one we can see and one we can't, then she will have a plan within a plan. No matter which option Rachel chooses, we must also have a plan of our own."

Rachel nods, her intelligent gaze taking in Dusana as well as me and Erik. "Gallium's life is in danger. Maybelle's heart will break if anything happens to him. Whatever plan we devise, rescuing him has to be part of it."

She focuses on me. "Queen Karasi has proposed a fight between champions. Catalina is my official champion, but I don't have to choose her for this fight."

I'm wary of where Rachel might be going with this. I also expect Catalina might have something to say about it, but her response surprises me.

"Karasi has placed Lady Asha's brother in danger," Catalina says. "She will expect Lady Asha to insist on going into the fight herself. After all, Lady Asha is a Blacksmith with power unlike any other. Who better to destroy the fae?"

Catalina studies me carefully, no doubt trying to gauge my reaction to her theory. I don't blame her. The weight of countless lives rests on her shoulders, and my choices could endanger them.

"It can't be me," I say quietly. "Queen Karasi has fallen back to the eastern plain. That's right at the edge of the darkness. She knows I can't fight there, or I will only draw the darkness to me and doom everyone around me."

Erik has been quiet, but now he reaches for me. "Queen Karasi takes delight in holding power over others. She forced you to hunt Milena Ironmeld simply because she could. Of course, it benefitted her to have Milena dead, but you told me how she waited until the last possible moment to offer help."

I close my eyes against the memory of the moment when I held a nail to his heart and prepared to drive it into his chest to end his suffering.

"Yes," I whisper. "She waited until I was preparing to end you."

"She took pleasure in your pain and grief, and then she seized power over you. Despite the fact that you could have killed her without any effort." Erik's eyes grow hard, the same kind of fury that was etched into his face when he recounted to me how his brother had died and how powerless he'd been to stop it.

He glares at Catalina and Rachel and Mother Solas and even

at Graviter, who has remained resolutely quiet, but I know Erik's anger isn't directed at them.

"Do not try to put logic to Queen Karasi's plans," he says. "What she wants is to watch you destroy yourselves, trying to protect the ones you love. She will win, and she will enjoy it."

My heart is sinking with every word Erik speaks because the connection between us is so strong that I can feel his pain.

Only a short time ago, he told me that war is in his blood.

His message was clear: He was not built for peace.

"Erik." My throat constricts. "No."

He turns his furious gaze on Dusana. "Who will rule the fae if Karasi dies?"

Her eyes widen. "Queen Karasi doesn't have any children—no daughter to whom she can pass the crown—so her champion will inherit the crown. That would be Elowynn."

"Elowynn," Erik growls. "Who has already proven she will fly into darkness to protect Gallium—a Blacksmith who could be her enemy. She is a fae with a conscience and a heart."

He turns his glare on Catalina, his teeth sharpening, and I'm impressed when she doesn't flinch at his ferocity. "The human army will assemble in multiple positions," he says to her. "One on the front line, another two in defensive positions behind it. And yes, Catalina Shield, I'm telling you how to assemble your army, and I appreciate how offensive that is."

She arches an eyebrow at him. "Just a little."

Erik's voice lowers as he turns his focus back to me. "Asha will free her brother. I will fight for Rachel." He takes a breath. "Queen Karasi won't miss the battle, even if she isn't fighting for herself. Either way, I will kill her."

"Erik—"

His hand closes around my arm. "You will *not* lose your brother, Asha. I won't allow it."

He's gripping my left arm, and my power surges at his touch, but I clamp down on it.

I want to convince him that he doesn't have to do the cutting.

But I can't deny that he has the strength to end the Fae Queen.

Neither, it seems, can Catalina.

"Once you kill Karasi, the fae will come after you," she says.

Erik nods. "Their forces will be split until Elowynn can take control."

Catalina appears to chew on this, but she defers to Rachel.

"I have no wish to annihilate the fae people," Rachel says. "Erik, do you believe Elowynn will accept an offer of peace?"

Dusana interrupts before Erik can answer.

"Accept peace and go where?" she snaps, glaring at the humans. "My Queen wants the fight to happen near the darkness because it doesn't discriminate. Dragons, humans, fae... As soon as any magic floods the air, we will all be lost. All it will take is one thunderbird cracking its wings, or a Solstice fae panicking and using the power of sunlight, or stars forbid, a Frost fae snatching hold of the dark wind by accident and dragging it toward us."

She stares at the humans. "Don't you see? Nobody can win. Any fight is doomed! Nobody..." Her shoulders slump. "Nobody can win."

"Then that's what she wants," Rachel says, her voice clear but resigned. "It's clear that Queen Karasi delights in power. She knows she can't win a battle against dragons, no matter how strong her thunderbird riders are. The darkness is closing in on her. She's going to die, but she will make damn sure she takes us with her."

"In fact," Catalina says, her gloved fist clenching and unclenching, "this whole proposal could be a ploy. She proposed three days, but she won't have that long. Not when she's pulled her people so far back. It has to be a diversion. She's planning something, but there's no way for us to know what it is. We need to fortify our position so that we can defend against any attack she may make. And we need to do so quickly."

Mother Solas gives a resigned sigh and nods. So does Rachel.

Even Dusana inclines her head, although she mutters, "A human thinking like a fae. I've seen it all."

But Erik... I study him closely.

He is always two steps ahead. Always planning his moves and countermoves, understanding another person's motivations and remaining a step ahead.

I used to believe that his machinations were for himself. Then I found out they were all for me. Whatever he did, no matter how harsh it seemed, was to keep me alive.

Now I can see the outcome of his words here. The moment he told Catalina how to maneuver her army, he nudged the humans to push back against his suggestion.

"Vandawolf," Rachel says, addressing him formally, "I have no choice but to reject entirely the notion of war on that battlefield. I respect your suggestion that the human army assemble and be ready to fight, but that will only play into the Fae Queen's hands. The only way I can keep my people safe is to employ the same methods that kept us alive in our lost city. Our new home is free of darkness. We will fortify our defenses, dig in, and stay alive. If there is a war, we will fight it on our own terms."

Her expression softens. "But I can't ignore the plight of Asha's brother. If you are willing, you will go as my champion. Not in three days, but at dawn tomorrow. You will call out the Fae Queen's bluff and make it clear you are ready to fight her champion. And if you have the chance..."

Her voice becomes a snarl. "You will kill that fucking queen."

CHAPTER 44

I have never been more aware than I am at this moment that loving someone and protecting them can't mean making their choices for them.

Every part of me wants to intervene.

To stand in Erik's way and tell him: *Don't do this.*

But I could no sooner stop the waves crashing against the cliffs behind me.

Within minutes, Graviter has agreed to Rachel's plan. He quickly rises into the air to mobilize the dragons to help fortify the human villages against an imminent attack.

Rachel and Catalina hurry back to their dragons—but not before Mother Solas murmurs something to Rachel, who pauses but then nods.

Erik goes with them and I should be listening for what they say, but when I try to stand, my world spins.

I find myself sinking back to the ground.

If Erik goes to this fight at the edge of the darkness, I won't be able to help him because my power—my mere presence—would endanger him.

Even Gallium's presence on that battlefield could be a trigger for the darkness. I can only pray that Karasi will ensure my brother's tools are nowhere nearby. Or... she might bring them with her just to taunt him and tempt fate.

I want to scream at the unknowns. All the games she could play while she risks the darkness and her people's lives.

I consider for a moment that if I take off my medallion and leave my hammer behind, could I go with him then?

But the whisper in the darkness returns to me.

The way it called to me. The way it pulled me...

It knows me.

I can't go near it without endangering myself and anyone with me.

My heart is suddenly thumping hard in my chest.

Erik glances back to me across the distance as if he senses my disquiet.

I wrench my focus back to Dusana and then to Mother Solas, whom I'm surprised is approaching me instead of leaving with her granddaughter.

Taking a deep breath, I finally rise to my feet, easing myself upright through the moment of dizziness.

I will face my fears soon enough.

Dusana remains kneeling on the grass, but judging by the dark rings under her eyes, it's because of exhaustion, not obedience.

"If I may, Lady Asha," Mother Solas says to me, folding her hands in front of herself, "I'd like to stay with you for a short time."

Since the moment I met her, Mother Solas has been open and honest with me, so I have no hesitation in speaking my mind. "Your granddaughter needs you now more than ever. Why would you stay here?"

Mother Solas waits for the dragons to lift into the air and fly away, watching them leave before she answers me. "She trusts me to keep her informed if Erik changes his mind, but that isn't why I want to stay."

She has my full attention. "Mother Solas?"

"Rachel doesn't know this, but the smoke from the crimson coal back at the city has damaged my chest. Breathing isn't easy.

I'm not in a good way." She gives me a brave smile. "For some reason, I can breathe more easily here. Maybe it's the moisture in the air, but I feel it may ease my passing."

My eyes are wide. "You're dying?"

"It won't be long now. A few days at most." Then, with the stoicism that must have seen her through Malak's entire reign, she turns to Dusana. "Your Queen is certainly something, isn't she?"

Dusana tips her head back and returns Mother Solas's frank stare with a shrug. "She is the center of her own world."

Mother Solas extends her hand. "Right, then. Up you get."

Dusana scoffs at her. "A dying human woman offers me her hand? You would sooner drop me and blame it on your bad breathing than help me. We are enemies, old woman. Don't try to make me your friend."

"Why not?" Mother Solas asks. "You wouldn't be here if you weren't a dead woman, too. You said as much."

Dusana scowls. Muttering under her breath, she takes Mother Solas's hand and wobbles to her feet.

"Also," Mother Solas continues, "my chest may burn with every breath I take, but that makes me even more determined to live the remainder of my life to its fullest."

At that moment, Blackbird appears at the edge of the forest. Concord is close behind him. They both peer up at the sky as if to check that the dragons are gone.

A second later, two smaller figures burst from the tree line, darting between the birds. Galeia is a giggling blur, her tiny legs moving astonishingly fast, while Cailey is a streak of bright light chasing after her.

Seeming satisfied that the threat is gone, Blackbird bounds after them while Concord steps regally through the trees, checking the space around her before darting forward and pouncing after him.

Beside me, Mother Solas plants her hands on her hips. "Food," she declares. "They'll be hungry." She eyes Dusana. "I'm certain you must be hungry, too."

Dusana gives a groan. "I'm famished." She brushes the grass

off her pants, but she quickly glares at Mother Solas. "Sharing a meal doesn't make us friends."

"As you like." Mother Solas strides away, calling loudly, "Little Wolf and... uh... Bright Child, who wants to go berry hunting in the moonlight?"

Galeia pops her head up above the grass, which is taller where she's crouched, so all she reveals is the top of her face and her bright eyes.

I'm certain she heard *hunting* and not *berries*.

Oh, dear.

Mother Solas and Dusana are already ten paces away. I move to follow them, but Erik has prowled back to me.

"Asha."

At the way he says my name, my heart is instantly heavy, and all my peace vanishes.

I speak my fears without hesitation, knowing that he will hear and listen to me. "You're choosing a path that could tear me apart."

He shakes his head, his dark hair falling across his eyes so much like he used to wear it to hide his wolfish features. "I made you a promise, Asha. I will never hurt your heart again."

I fight the burn behind my eyes. "You can't make a promise like that and then run toward death."

In the distance, Galeia's giggles float across the wind, along with the soft chatter of women who have somehow gathered together in this place, such a powerful combination of sounds that I can hear them above the crashing waves.

Erik takes a step toward me. "You removed the device from my heart. I can fight Karasi with the strengths I gained without risking the darkness. At least not any more than another human would risk. I can do what I was destined to do."

"Die in battle?" I ask, unable to keep the bitterness from my voice. "Like your people?"

"No," he whispers. "I can do what you need me to do."

He's now right in front of me, one arm sweeping around my

back. "There isn't anything I won't do for you, Asha. You are my family. You are the one I would embrace any darkness for—"

"And yet you would break me."

"Never," he says, his voice a deep growl.

He sounds so certain, and yet his actions are a deep contradiction to his promise.

He presses his forehead to mine and his voice lowers even further still as he asks me a question I wasn't expecting.

"If you could create any future for us, what would it look like?"

Tears burn behind my eyes, and I let them fall.

"A home," I say. "Not in the mountains. Not in the snow. Not in the wasteland. It would be here where the grass is green and the trees give shade and the sky is never red."

My anvil is within reach of my left hand, and as I speak, my palm brushes up against it. My feelings are so strong that I can't possibly contain them.

I don't *want* to contain them.

My power is mine now. To use as my heart and my conscience dictate.

"And our house?" he asks.

The pain of the past floods me, but with it comes moments of connection and change that I will always cherish. There are good memories among the bad, and it's those good memories that tug my lips into a smile.

"Not a house," I say. "A *tower*."

A rush of energy flows through my hand into the anvil, and with it, all my wishes take shape around me.

Faster than a heartbeat, the black rock spreads beneath our feet, and the grass transforms into stone.

Walls spring up around us. Strong walls that can't be breached with a ceiling that's open to the sky. And still, my power flows as the rock we're standing on rises upward, more walls and more rooms forming beneath it, giving it strength and structure. I can't see them from where I stand, but I feel them form, as certain of their existence as I am of Erik's nearness.

Our upward momentum slows and then it stops, all so effortless that we don't lose balance.

A window forms in the wall opposite us, letting the moonlight in while the rush of the ocean sounds far away.

The view from the window is breathtaking. Stars sparkle in the distance, and the moon sits high in the sky.

Erik hasn't taken his eyes off me, but his voice is soft as he asks, "A cage in the sky?"

It won't have escaped him that there may be a window, but there are no doors.

"Does it need to be?" I ask him, a challenging tone entering my voice.

He shakes his head, a slow, resolute movement, but it's the tears filling his eyes that freeze me.

"I won't die in this battle," he says.

My voice is a whisper. "How can you possibly know that?"

"Because it won't come to pass."

My forehead creases and my question is quiet. "What?"

His arms tighten around me, strong arms that are suddenly shaking, while his eyes... his deep-gray eyes that once held so many secrets, are leaking tears he doesn't try to hide.

His voice is ragged. Raw. *Hurt.* "You believe I'm the one in danger, but, Asha... precious Asha... why do you think the dragons gave you their scales? Why did Cailey fall to the Earth to save you? Why did Thaden Kane hand you his only child? And even the Valkyrie Queen asked you which side you would fight on, and you said—"

"The darkness is the real enemy."

I can barely breathe.

A storm of fear and dread builds within me.

Only an hour ago, Erik and I stood quietly at the cliff's edge, and he asked me if he should have died on that mountain.

He told me I was his anchor and that he feared what he would become if there was peace.

And now, a terrible realization dawns on me.

He fears what he will become without me.

"You can do what nobody else can," he says. "You can banish the darkness."

He slides one arm away from me to press his fist to his heart. "The battle you're facing, your fight with the darkness, is the one on which our future turns. And it will take everything—" He draws a shaky breath, and his voice becomes ragged. "Stopping the darkness will mean giving *everything*. All of you. Your power, your mind, and your heart."

He turns his hand from his own chest to mine, pressing his palm to my heart in the same way I pressed my hand to his chest on that first night in the throne room.

"Everything," he whispers, and then he falls silent.

When he presses his cheek to mine, his tears dampen my skin.

Outside, the wind picks up, beating against the walls of the tower I created while inside this room, there is a peace that is destined to break.

"I made you a promise, Asha. I will never tear you apart. But you can't promise me the same."

"No." My denial is instant. "I will find a way. All this power..." My breathing is rapid, my heart thumping, my fist closing around my medallion, my other hand pressing over his. "I will find a way."

I crush my lips to his, vowing that no matter what it takes, I will survive.

CHAPTER 45

We sink to the floor, where it takes a mere press of my medallion for me to create a soft rug and cushions for us to lie on, tangled in each other's arms.

His kiss is as deep as mine. I taste his tears on my tongue, and I want nothing more than to forget what awaits us.

My body has heated at his touch, but when I pull back to catch my breath, I can't ignore the dark circles beneath his eyes. "When did you last sleep?"

"Uh..." His brow furrows for a long moment.

"Too long ago," I murmur, my upper arm slipping around his side, my hand stroking his back. It takes everything within me to deny the need that was growing within my body, but my concern for his wellbeing is more powerful right now. "You need to rest."

The corners of his mouth hitch upward. "I'd rather do other things."

I answer him with a smile. "So would I, but you told Rachel you'll leave at dawn. You need to sleep first."

His eyes are already closing. "Sleep first," he mumbles. "Other things second..."

I continue stroking his back, my fingers finding all the knotted muscles, easing them as best I can.

Within minutes, his breathing is deep.

He falls asleep so quickly that it speaks to his exhaustion.

I stay with him for an hour, allowing my own heart to calm, folding away these peaceful moments within my memory.

Finally, I rise from the rug and tiptoe to the solid wall where a door should be.

Pressing my hand to the rock, I consider what sort of staircase I should make to reach the bottom of the tower. Before I've formed a clear thought, the rock melts away from my hand, vanishing and forming an opening.

A corridor already exists, along with a room opposite this one.

Both are lit with golden orbs that float near the ceiling. The floor is inlaid with sparkling jewels that catch the moonlight from a window at the end of the corridor. And at the other end of the corridor is a staircase that glows sapphire blue.

Huh.

It only takes ten steps down before I reach the bottom of the stairs, which let out into a homely-looking cooking area.

A glance through the window on the left tells me I'm at the bottom of the tower, but... I'm certain I was much higher up in the tower only moments ago.

I'm a little surprised that I constructed so much, but then... I'm not.

I wanted a home, and that is what I made.

The scene within the kitchen is peaceful.

A fireplace glows on the other side of the room.

Beside it is a large rug on which Cailey sits cross-legged while Galeia is snuggled against her side.

Mother Solas sits at the far end of the large table near the fire, a bowl of food in front of her. She's slowly chewing while Dusana sits on the long side of the table, one foot on her chair, her knee bent. The bowl in front of her is empty, other than a few smears of food. A pile of wildflowers rests on the table beside the empty bowl.

None of them startles or seems surprised when I appear.

I try to find my voice. "Uh...?"

"We saved some for you and the Vandawolf," Mother Solas says, pushing two bowls toward me across the table. "It's rabbit stew. Galeia caught the rabbit."

The little girl tilts her head back to give me a grin around the bone she's gnawing.

"She left *some* of the rabbit for us." Dusana rolls her eyes, briefly glancing up from the wreath of wildflowers she's constructing. I'm not sure if it's intended for Galeia, Cailey, or herself, but I'm sure I'll find out soon enough.

I pull up a chair and can't deny how hungry I am.

Within minutes, I've consumed the stew, and I lean back in my chair.

Across the table, Dusana holds up her wreath, assessing it with a scowl before she reaches for more flowers and starts reinforcing the middle. "We know what the humans plan to do, and we know what the Vandawolf plans to do, but what is your plan, Asha Silverspun?"

I arch my eyebrows at her. "Do you really expect me to tell *you*?"

Dusana puts down the flowers and huffs at me. "As the old lady pointed out earlier, I'm a dead fae. If you tell me something and later regret it, it won't be hard to kill me."

She has a point.

I'm aware that Mother Solas and Cailey are both looking at me while Galeia continues to suck happily on her bone.

"I have an impossible task," I say.

"We know," Cailey replies. Despite her appearance, her voice carries the weight of years. "You need to stop the darkness."

"Ha!" Dusana snorts. "I thought you were going to say you need to free your brother. I was going to tell you nothing is impossible, believe in your dreams, but stopping the darkness? *That*'s impossible."

"For any other supernatural," Mother Solas says. "But is it really impossible for you, Asha Silverspun?"

When I respond with an uncertain grimace, she gestures to the tower around us.

"I would have said this structure was impossible," she says, "but here we are enjoying the fireplace while two lightning-powered birds snuggle on the overly large perch you made for them."

"Perch?"

"You'll see when you go outside. Two perches, actually. One on either side of the tower. Although I fear you've made them large enough for dragons to land on, which they may view as an invitation."

"That was a mistake," Dusana says, widening her eyes at me.

I ignore her. "Creating a tower is very different than extinguishing a power that is fueled by the very magic I would use to stop it."

But Cailey's forehead has creased. "How do you stop a fire?"

"You pour water on it," Dusana quickly replies.

"Sure, but how else?"

Dusana's forehead crinkles. "You can smother it or stomp on it."

"How else?"

Dusana gives her a stare. "You clearly have something in mind. Say it already."

Cailey's eyes are brighter than they've been in hours. "You take away the fuel source."

My forehead creases. "How would that apply to the darkness?"

"It feeds on the magic of the dead," she says. "The more death there is, the more magic there is, the stronger it grows, and the faster it spreads, creating more death. And so it goes on."

"Self-sustaining," I say.

"But what if there were a way to leach the magic from the ground?" she asks.

I give the matter serious consideration. "You mean something to pull the magic away? But then it would simply go somewhere else and fester there instead."

Mother Solas holds up her hand. "Not if the place it went was capable of containing that magic."

Like Cailey, she, too, is suddenly animated. "You created a tower in the blink of an eye. You did it for a purpose: a home. You gave it doors and windows and warmth and light and all the things that living beings need to thrive. But what about a place where its entire purpose is to constrain the churning magic that fuels the darkness?"

"Like a prison," Dusana says with a delighted smirk. "But for magic."

"A place that can't be breached," Cailey says. "Or even found. You can't risk that someone would open it up."

"With all the properties needed to counter the dark magic, you siphon from the land and *extinguish* it," Mother Solas says.

"As well as any other magic that is festering within it," Cailey adds. "After all, the darkness is the result of dark magic acting on other kinds of magic: elemental magic from the fae, light magic from dragons and humans, and original magic like Blacksmith magic and my magic, too. Whatever object you create to siphon away the darkness, it would need to attract all of the magics that have been corrupted."

"And be strong enough to tether them," Mother Solas adds. "To keep them contained."

"Forever," Cailey finishes.

I take a breath and calm my beating heart, thinking it through. All the moving parts: a tether, a prison...

But I find myself circling back to one thing, and it brings dread to my stomach. The same dread I saw in Erik's eyes.

"The darkness feeds on death," I whisper. "It generates monsters and has a life of its own. Stopping it won't be as simple as using a siphoning object and creating a prison. Not if I am to stop it from reviving and happening again. When any magic dies, it would need to be claimed and kept safe."

Mother Solas reaches for my right hand and gives it a squeeze. "Think on it, Lady Asha. The answer will come to you."

Across the table, Dusana positions the wreath on her own head. "More importantly, what do you think of my flowers?"

She holds her head high, and I remember how happy she'd looked when she thought Karasi had given her an elegant gown.

"Beautiful," Cailey says brightly. "Let me get a closer look."

She pops Galeia onto the rug to rise to her feet and reach Dusana, pursing her lips. "Actually, I think this one needs to be... not there."

With a cheeky smile, Cailey plucks the central flower from the front of the wreath and darts backward, reaching the other side of the room before Dusana can stop her.

The wreath immediately separates where Cailey broke the circle, and the two sides fall to either side of Dusana's head.

She scowls.

Cailey pokes out her tongue. "It looks better that way. *Wilder*. More like you."

"It does," I say to Dusana. "Really."

She huffs before she reaches up to pat the flowers, following their path down her hair.

Across the way, Cailey holds up her prize—a single wild rose —her fingers glowing for a moment before she turns the flower a pure white color. She pushes it into her own hair.

On the rug, Galeia gives a yawn. Her dark hair is matted from the wind and—I grimace—what is probably some blood splatter from hunting.

She needs a bath, but more than that...

I rise from my seat, circle the table, and kneel on the rug.

She immediately crawls into my lap, her green eyes raised to mine.

For a long moment, I can't look away.

Despite Thaden's parentage, there is nothing of a human or a Blacksmith in Galeia's nature. From what Erik told me of the Valkyrie on our flight here, it doesn't matter what race of man they mate with; they only have daughters, and their daughters are always pure Valkyrie.

But Galeia was given the heart and soul of a wolf, and it's because of that heart that she's still alive.

There is such a push and pull of energy within her. A cold

indifference to death because of her Valkyrie nature, while her wolfish heart is desperate to connect, to be part of a family, and to be loved.

When I press my left hand to her back, she doesn't flinch.

I used to fear touching other people when I was in contact with Malak's tools, and I was right to be afraid. His dark power was cruel and malicious.

But my own power is fully within my control, and it only does what I want it to do.

It's easy for me to sense the sections of Galeia's heart and to distinguish the original biological part from the metal pieces. Within all of them is the capacity for hope and compassion and forgiveness and anger and strength, but they all pull against the darkness of the living metal that's pumping blood around her body and keeping her alive.

Even though her Valkyrie parentage obliterated her Blacksmith nature, the strength of the metal device means she carries an enormous amount of Blacksmith magic within her body. Just as Erik used to carry Blacksmith magic, too.

She is unique. I'm certain there will never be another like her.

She remains calm in my arms as I assess her.

The others are hushed around me.

"Galeia," I say quietly. "I can give you a voice and a mind that's all your own. But you will need to make a choice."

Her bright green eyes remain focused on me.

If I'm not certain she understands me, I will wait until Erik wakes up. I can ask him to communicate with her.

"What do you wish to be, Galeia?" I ask her. "A Valkyrie or wolf?"

Her answer is astonishingly clear.

The moment I say *Valkyrie*, she bares her teeth with a sharp growl, but at *wolf*, her snarl fades, and she gives me such a wide grin that the bone falls from her mouth.

She purses her lips. "Wo... l... f."

I have all the certainty I need.

"Then so you will be," I say, pressing my left hand to the location of her heart.

Be a wolf.

The color of her eyes changes, amber flecks appearing while the emerald green darkens to the shade of the forest.

The *thump-thump* of her little heart calms beneath my palm, less frantic. Now stronger, steadier.

I sense the metal within her chest fully merging with the remaining parts of her natural heart, all of the intricate pieces becoming whole. A part of her that belongs to her and that she can control.

Her entire body relaxes, every shred of tension vanishing.

The streams of cold fury I saw before—the tension that spoke of a Valkyrie nature—vanish, and so, too, do the stumps and the single feather on her back.

Her chest rises with a deeply inhaled breath, and her eyes grow wide.

For a moment, I'm afraid that I've hurt her, and my heart is in my throat.

Then she releases her breath with a slow whisper, "I am a wolf."

She closes her eyes, her dark head sinking to my shoulder and her breathing deepening.

I check her heartbeat, making sure she's okay while she snuggles into me.

Within seconds, she's asleep.

A sense of peace fills me.

It's the first peace I've felt for days.

The hush continues around me for long minutes while the fire crackles and the scent of wildflowers lingers.

My peace extends...

Until I break it.

"Malak wanted to be a god," I say. "He wanted to create life and take it at a whim. He wanted to control the light *and* the dark. The heart within this child is both, and it made me realize..."

I meet Mother Solas's eyes. Then Cailey's. Then Dusana's.

"The darkness began with Blacksmith magic, and it hungers for Blacksmith magic more than any other magic," I say. "Only an object made from the most powerful Blacksmith magic could tether it. An object of pure darkness."

I close my eyes for a moment before I continue. "Creating a prison will be an easier task. All I have to do is make a new home, but without any windows or doors, and I need to place it outside the boundaries of the natural world so it can't be found."

I try to breathe while none of them speaks.

"Creating the siphoning object will be harder. First, because it must be made from the very same tools that caused the darkness in the first place. And second, because I will have to forge it at the source. Only then can I be sure it will take hold of every shred of darkness. None can remain."

I am suddenly cold but no less determined.

"But that isn't all," I whisper. "To keep the darkness from reviving and to ensure that this never happens again, all magic that dies in the future must be claimed and kept. The darkness must have a living keeper."

"Lady Asha..." Mother Solas is on her feet, her face pale. "What can we do?"

"Look after Galeia until Erik can return for her." Tears burn behind my eyes. "I won't leave without him. I will ask him to come with me as far as he safely can. I won't waste a second of the time I have left with him. But when I'm gone, he will need people around him who can keep him anchored."

I force myself to my feet, carrying Galeia to Mother Solas's waiting arms. "I know you don't have long. Please tell Rachel what has happened. Ask her to find a place for Erik." I swallow against the constriction in my throat. "Galeia will take up much of his time, but once she's grown, he will need a purpose."

That's all I can manage before I slip from the room.

CHAPTER 46

When I reach the top of the tower, Erik is still fast asleep, and I don't want to wake him.

Maybe I should rush away. There are people who need me. But Erik needs me, too. And I need him. The moon is high, and dawn is several hours away. I will stretch out these final moments with all my might.

I press my hand to the wall, closing the doorway once again. This tower answers my needs so I trust that Galeia and the others will be safe within it.

Slipping back to the rug, I nestle against Erik's side and close my eyes.

He stirs, his upper arm sliding around my waist, pulling me closer, but his breathing remains deep.

I close my eyes and let myself dream about a life here with him. He and Galeia can hunt in the forest. I can use my power to create everything we need. In that dream world, the darkness wouldn't exist, and nothing could tear us apart—

"Asha." Erik's panicked whisper meets my ears a second before his arms clamp around me.

Only moments ago he was sleeping peacefully, but now he crushes me to his chest, one of his hands tangling in my hair.

His heart is pounding so hard I can feel it.

"Fucking nightmares," he rasps before his lips press to mine. His other arm has slipped beneath me, and my body weight must be pinning it, but he doesn't seem to care.

His eyes are wide open, and right now, he is pure *wolf*.

"Don't go," he snarls at me, a command that echoes with all the ferocity of the beast he used to be. "You've given enough. I've given enough."

The pain in his voice is like a knife in my heart.

I want to tell him that I won't leave him. That the darkness unleashed by the actions of those who came before me is not for me to banish. But I can't lie to him...

Tears slip down my cheeks, and I don't try to stop them.

He watches their downward path, his hands stroking my back, his fingers finding the gap between the bottom of my tunic and my waistband and tugging them apart, caressing the bare skin he exposes.

"Give me permission," he says, more softly but no less intensely than before, "and I will make you want to stay."

The pressure of his hands lightens, tantalizing strokes now swirling across my lower back, and I can't deny the desire heating my body.

"You have my permission," I whisper.

Slowly, he lifts himself and me into a sitting position, first pulling me up onto his chest, then using his stomach muscles to sit up before guiding my legs around his waist. His hands don't stop kneading my back, easing the sore muscles across my shoulders, all the while tugging on the material of my tunic.

"This room needs a bath," he says without taking his eyes off me, brushing his lips to mine.

I lean back toward the edge of the rug, taking my time to reach out with my left hand, my movement causing my back to arch and pushing my core against his hard length. My new position draws a growl to his lips, and I can't stop my groan as pleasure spikes through me at the contact.

It takes everything in me to focus on my task and not rock against him.

Finding the edge of the rug, I press my palm to the hard floor, a vision of a big, white, claw-foot bath filling my mind. The rock forming the floor in the left-hand corner of the room ripples and extends upward until the bath that I imagined forms, complete with cloths to wash and dry ourselves with.

Erik barely glances at them. One of his hands continues supporting my arching back while his other slips around to my stomach, stroking upward between my breasts, stopping at the base of them, his fingers splayed but not stroking. It's a promise of pleasure that only feeds the heat growing between my legs.

Before I can give in to my impulses and rock against him, he sweeps both of his arms around me, lifting me while my legs are wrapped around his hips.

When he carries me to the bath, I'm not surprised that it begins to fill at our approach, gentle steam floating up off the surface of the water.

He turns me to face the bath, remaining close behind me as he pulls up my tunic, taking his time to lift it over my head, his fingers stroking the skin across my back as he exposes every inch of it. Then stroking down my thighs as he pulls my pants to my feet, undressing me slowly, planting kisses against the backs of my legs on his way back to a standing position.

He breaks the contact between our bodies only for a moment to remove his own clothing, swiftly dispensing with his tunic and pants before closing the gap between us again. His kisses swirl against my left shoulder, stopping at the base of my neck where he pushes aside my hair so his mouth can travel higher, gently nuzzling my earlobe.

With every touch of his hands and tongue, shocks of pleasure strike through me, forces of energy that make my thighs clench and my breathing hitch. Especially when his hands brush across my stomach again, easing upward a little, then downward a little, caressing the base of my breasts and the top of my pelvis but refraining from traveling any higher or lower.

My nipples are hard, aching for his touch, and my core feels heavy with desire.

Slipping his hand around mine, he steps into the bath before reaching over to lift me into it. In the moment before his arms capture me, I take in the full nakedness of his body, all of his muscles, and the hard need that he must be keeping at bay.

Easing us both down into a sitting position, he maneuvers me so that I'm facing away from him and resting between his legs, at which he reaches for a cloth and begins washing me. Starting with my back, he runs the wet material around my neck and shoulders, trickling water down across my breasts, nudging me forward so he can rub my back before easing me back against his chest again.

With long, maddening strokes, he washes my arms before finally reaching down to clean my thighs, but only the outside of them, before he pulls my knees to my chest so he can reach my calves.

It is both thrilling and agonizing.

How slowly he touches me. How he avoids any part of me that might ease the intense burn that has built in my core. How he takes his time running his tongue from my ear to my shoulders, pressing me forward again so he can kiss my lower back.

Despite the water lapping at me, threatening to sweep my own wetness away, my core is only growing wetter.

My breathing is rapid by the time he growls, low and soft. "Move to the other end of the bath."

I trust him completely, sliding through the water to the other side and turning to face him.

As soon as the contact between us breaks, he sets about cleaning himself, washing his hands, scrubbing at the hints of blood on his neck, even leaning forward to immerse his hair in the water.

But when he emerges, he stares ruefully at the water. "I should have told you to get out."

It's true.

He must have cleaned the worst of the blood off himself in the stream because I didn't realize until now that there was still so much blood on him.

Now, it's swirling through the water toward me.

Without fuss, I rise to my feet, lifting myself away from the evidence of his battles moments before the bloodied water can reach my pelvis. Now, only my calves are immersed.

"Better?" I ask softly, staying right there in full view.

The regret leaves his eyes and his heated gaze passes from my face all the way down my body to the water's surface and then back up again. "Much."

He, too, rises upward, shaking himself off like the wolf he is, standing opposite me, droplets of crimson water dripping off him.

As I take in the scars on his body and the moisture on his skin, my eyes widen.

In an instant, I'm transported back in time. I'm standing on the balcony outside my tower. He's there with me, and we are enemies again. Him and me. Wolf and Blacksmith. Droplets of blood falling between us.

I'm suddenly sobbing.

I want to go back, even more desperately than ever. I need to go back to the moment when he found me unconscious in the snow. I want to have woken up. I want to have seen him.

I want to have run away with him, choosing a different future and leaving all the darkness behind.

"Asha." His voice is broken.

I'm crying too hard to see past my tears, but I hear the water *swoosh* as he gets out of the bath.

He reaches for me, lifting me up and out so smoothly that I wish he could pull me from my future so easily.

My legs wrap around his waist, and my arms close around his chest.

"Why can't I let the world burn?" I cry against his neck.

"You can," he snarls, the intense pain in his voice reaching me through my grief. His lips press to my forehead, then my cheeks. "Let it all burn, Asha."

The need within me bursts back to life. Using my muscles to raise myself up, I demand his kiss, pressing my lips to his, seeking his tongue, tasting every part of his mouth, hungry for his body, needing him, heart and soul.

He responds with the touch I crave, turning and lowering me back onto the rug where he can kneel between my legs and reach every inch of my body.

He balances on one hand, while his lips close over my breasts, one at a time, drawing each nipple into his mouth, his free hand stroking my other breast as I arch into his touch. Cries leave my lips as the heady ache in my center eases and builds with every demanding stroke of his hands and tongue, and a world of pleasure bursts alive within me.

He moves closer to my pelvis, his kisses heading lower, but I take hold of his shoulders.

The wetness between my legs is already intense. His own needs must be beyond his limits.

"Fuck me," I groan. "Don't make me wait."

I need the connection with his body. I need to believe that nothing can ever separate us.

He pauses for only a moment before he positions himself at my center.

His deep, gray, wolfish eyes meet mine as he says, "Stay with me."

In this moment, I convince myself I'm speaking the truth. "Always."

The first thrust sends me over the edge.

I scream with pleasure as my world spirals and my body strains to contain the release, to deny the crash as long as I can.

He doesn't take it slow, thrusting into me with a hard rhythm that my body welcomes, every muscle in my core accommodating him, every sensitive inch of me burning with desire.

I reach my arms back to the rug, gripping it, bracing, pushing myself against him as firmly as he's thrusting into me.

Pleasure explodes within me, long, long moments of an

orgasm that extends beyond anything I thought possible. My mind lifts with it, filling with every memory of him.

All the times he pushed me away. All the times he commanded me. All the times I defied him and challenged him and fought to keep him alive when he was ready to let me go.

All the pain and all the love.

I will hold onto him for as long as I can, and I will never, ever, forget him.

The crash takes him, and both of his hands hit the rug, his command thrumming through me. "Stay with me."

I gasp for breath, trying to speak through the ripples of pleasure still raging through me. "*Always.*"

I pull him to my chest, wrapping my arms and legs around him, needing his weight like an anchor, refusing to let go.

He rolls us over so he's lying on his back, and I'm resting down on him, my head resting against his heart.

Thud-thud. It's rapid, like his breathing, and I close my eyes, memorizing the beat.

"I will love you forever, Erik Vandawolf."

His response is a growl. "It took a dragon to keep you from me when I made your hammer."

I remember it.

I struggled against Graviter's hold so hard, trying to get to Erik, to stop him from giving his life for me.

Now, he's warning me that he won't let me go easily. The strength of his arms around me only emphasizes his words.

"Then we'll have to find a dragon on the way." My voice is a bare whisper, and my heart aches so badly I can't force myself to move.

For long minutes neither of us moves or speaks.

Then, finally, the thumping of his heart eases, and I know that if I don't move now, I will never do it.

Pushing up off him, I disconnect our bodies and slip from his arms, heading straight to the side of the room where a tap of my hand against the wall provides me with a bathroom.

My movements are wooden as I wash up.

My body doesn't feel like it belongs to me.

For a moment, I lean forward, gripping the edge of the sink, my eyes closed, my jaw clenching.

The hurt... I can't stop it.

I have no choice but to throw myself into a future that requires my own destruction.

CHAPTER 47

When I emerge from the bathroom, I find Erik already dressed.

He's quiet as he hands me my clothing and helps me pull on my weapon harness again, placing my hammer into it.

He pulls on his own harness and slides his sword into the scabbard at his back before he bends to the discarded coat on the floor, retrieving from its pocket the dark device that was once in his heart.

I didn't ask him for it, but he holds it out to me.

I will tell him everything on the way, but for now, the hollow look in his eyes tells me he guesses what I have to do.

It takes me a mere second to pull a thread from my shirt and transform it into a pouch to hold the device. He drops the device inside it. Then I tie the pouch to my harness.

"I need to go to Thaden's village for the rest of Malak's tools, as well as Thaden's tools," I say, my voice rasping in the silence between us. "I can't leave any dark metal behind. All of it must come with me."

And now for the harder part. "But the village is much closer to the darkness than you need to go to reach Queen Karasi. Traveling there is extremely dangerous—"

"I don't fucking care," Erik growls, pulling me close again. "I will come with you to the edge, Asha."

Erik promised he would present himself to Queen Karasi today in the guise of being Rachel's champion. He hasn't told me exactly what he plans to do yet, although his ultimate goal is to end the Fae Queen.

He will need to travel toward the darkness either way. Even though I'm determined he won't get near it, I whisper, "Okay. Let's go to the edge. Together."

Within minutes, we've descended the steps, which, astonishingly, let out onto one of the perches Mother Solas mentioned, as if the tower knows where I want to go.

Concord and Blackbird are huddled together against the ocean wind, their feathers ruffling in the breeze, their necks curved against each other.

For a moment, I don't want to disturb them, but they both look up a moment after we appear in the arched doorway.

I want to take Blackbird, but Concord will be well-known to the fae. At a glance, the fae won't question her presence in the sky. It's possible we could even fly right through fae territory unhindered as long as nobody gets too close to us.

Even so, I go to Blackbird first. "I need you to stay here and watch over the people in this tower. Look after them. I promise we will look after Concord. We won't let anything happen to her."

Blackbird gives me an unhappy growl, and I understand his reluctance, but Concord is already extending her wing to me.

Despite her apparent willingness to carry us, Erik approaches her slowly. "We're flying toward the darkness. Are you sure you're prepared to take us there?"

Concord tosses her head in the affirmative, and moments later, we're in the air.

~

We travel straight ahead.

The air is clear, and it's the quickest path, but once we reach the edge of human territory, it will become more dangerous.

The sun is rising over the horizon by the time we reach fae territory. I would have preferred traveling in darkness, but there's nothing we can do about it now.

The fae castle is a speck in the distance, where it sits on the side of a mountain.

A flash of light draws my focus to the airspace beside it.

I lean closer to Erik. "Did you see that?"

"I saw it."

Another flash flickers across the air. Then another. The faint sound of thunder reaches me. And then we're close enough that I can make out more specks, a mass of them flying above the plain.

"Monsters?" I ask, my eyes wide. But I discount that possibility immediately. The sky isn't blood red across the plain. There are no churning clouds. The air isn't filled with the copper scent that accompanies the darkness.

And yet there's a hum of shouts and thunder and clashing steel while flashes of lightning and fire split the air.

In the next moment, we're close enough to see.

I gasp. "They're all thunderbirds."

"They're fighting each other." Erik's shoulders are tense. "The fae are fighting each other."

I look to the ground, where the rows of tents used to be. They're gone. The plain is bare.

Oh, no.

My heart is sinking.

"Erik, what if Karasi's people turned on her? What if they wanted to follow Elowynn?"

I point to the ground. "She didn't move her *troops* back. Those tents were full of families. Not warriors. She's forced them toward the darkness so she can use them as leverage. Any fae warrior with a family at risk would do whatever she says."

"Against those who no longer have any family to lose," Erik snarls, his growl an angry rumble through his body.

We'll reach their battle within minutes.

Concord gives a soft squawk, and I suspect she wants to know what to do. She's Elowynn's bird, and it must be taking all of her restraint not to try to find her rider right now.

To Concord, I say, "Take us across the mountain ridge above the forest. We need to pass north of the castle to avoid the main battle."

But to Erik I murmur, "You have to stop the fight. The fae don't need to fear the darkness. I will deal with it. Their families will be safe. They don't have to kill each other."

His body is tense, his jaw clenched. He hasn't yet agreed, and I understand why.

It means leaving me.

It means that the final moment he has with me will be right here, right now, and it can't be enough.

We're hurtling toward a goodbye that neither one of us wants, and it's too soon.

Up ahead, on the western side of the castle, a fight becomes visible on the ground.

My heart stops when I make out a flash of copper metal and a male figure whose silver hair is identifiable even from this distance.

"That's Gallium."

"I see him," Erik says. "Gliss and Elowynn are with him. But they're surrounded."

I close my eyes for a moment, breathing out my pain.

Then I raise my voice to Concord again. "Concord! Swoop toward that tree."

Erik glances back at me. "Asha?"

"You'll see."

Concord dips toward the nearest tree, which is still at least two hundred paces from Gallium's position.

I reach out, stretching as far as I can, plucking a single leaf from its branches before she lifts higher again.

I close my fist around the leaf and send a quick command to it.

A bow and quiver of arrows form in my hand, and I nearly lose hold of them before Erik twists to grab them.

"You won't run out of arrows," I say. "The quiver will refill itself."

"I won't shoot to kill," he says. "They're fighting for their families. They don't deserve death for that."

I press my lips to his cheek, inhaling his scent, needing time that we don't have.

"Go, Erik. Fight this war. And all the wars that come after it. I will be with you. Always."

He turns to press a kiss to my lips.

It's angry and hurt and full of love.

Then he throws himself off Concord's back and into the air, landing safely on the ground before he breaks into a sprint, racing toward my brother.

I try to keep them both in my sights, desperate to know that they'll be okay.

But then Concord shrieks.

My focus snaps forward just as fire explodes around us.

CHAPTER 48

Concord ducks and weaves, narrowly avoiding the flames.

I can't tell where they came from—the ground or the sky—or even if we were the intended target, but in the next moment, we're surrounded by chaos.

Flames shoot across the air in front of us, followed by a barrage of icy air that's sharp enough to strip the skin off my face. To avoid the ice and fire, Concord has dipped closer to the ground, from which vines whip upward, wrapping around my left leg.

I transform my medallion in an instant, the long blade slicing through the vine and freeing me before the rope can tug me down.

Concord shrieks, her cry full of fear. She will have been trained to fight against dragons, not other thunderbirds.

The internal conflict she must be feeling right now, seeing the thunderbirds fighting each other, must be immense.

I lean low over her neck. "Focus on staying alive. Get us through this so you can return to Elowynn and help her."

She dips again, veers to the left, evades another shot of fire, and then a series of daggers made from ice before we shoot through the chaos and into the clear air beyond.

Concord doesn't pause, beating her wings and picking up speed, racing away through the air as fast as she can.

I can't look back.

The darkness is ahead of us—and so is the mountain ridge that Tamra described, which appears to be the only safe path through the storm now.

My heart sinks to see the rows of white tents all lined up across the plain so dangerously close to the edge of the wasteland. A wall of darkness rises up behind them, no farther than two hundred paces away from the back row.

There's practically nothing between those fae and death. No ridge, no barrier.

All it will take is a single fae death... Hell, even a trail of dead apple seeds... and the darkness will breach the gap.

The dust storms alone will kill the rest of the fae in those tents.

My blood boils at how recklessly Karasi is risking her people's lives in the name of power.

While Concord flies bravely on, my chest fills with the coppery scent of death, and a moment later, the sunlight vanishes.

We're flying beneath crimson clouds.

Far across the valley to the right of the ridge, the dust storms rage, enormous tornados spinning across the ground and crashing into the mountains on either side.

Enormous beasts battle each other in the middle of the plain, the flow of ash across their bodies so thick that it looks like water rushing over them—and then through them when they smash to pieces.

I focus on the way ahead, urging Concord closer to the ground, where Tamra said the dragons had burned everything away. It should be safer there.

Sweat builds across my brow, and I fight against the panic rising within me. It's a nameless panic fed by the whisper of the wind and the scent of death that enters my chest with every breath.

Finally, I make out the curve of the mountain's ridge ahead, the circle of cliffs that protect the village that shelters within them.

"Concord," I say, "don't land. Fly low to the garden that sits in the shadow of the rock ledge. I will jump off your back. Turn as quickly as you can and return to Elowynn."

She makes a low, keening sound. I don't know how to interpret it other than I hear sadness in it.

"Thank you," I say, pressing my face to her neck. "For helping me."

There isn't time for more. The garden appears below me, and I jump, calling on my power to ease my landing so I don't break anything.

I expect the clearing to be filled with people, but it's deserted, which worries me until I make out the lights in the village down the incline.

It's barely past dawn. The village must still be waking up.

Thaden's cottage, situated close by on my left, is also dark.

Concord banks swiftly overhead, turning back the way we came and in the next moment, she's gone.

I've landed next to a patch of green vegetables circled by a row of herbs, and my boot must have crushed some of them when I landed, because their fragrance rises into the air.

I take it in. This fresh scent. Along with the soft hum of sounds in the distance. Sounds of life that have persevered despite the threat of darkness looming over it.

A soft, clanging sound reaches me, and I follow it along the path at the side of the clearing, entering the long tunnel that Thaden took me through when he first brought me to Galeia.

His forge is located within this tunnel, and the clanging sound draws me to him.

He's standing at his anvil on the other side of the forge, tapping at a small piece of silver, shaping what must be intended to be a cog or maybe a hinge. A very small fire burns in what looks like a specially designed box next to him, emitting only the barest amount of smoke.

I allow myself a moment to appreciate how hard he has

worked to help the people around him—all without relying on his power.

His concentration must be intense because he doesn't notice my presence until I've taken a step inside.

His head shoots up before he spins to me, his bronzed eyes widening.

"Asha!" He puts down his tools and hurries toward me. "You're okay!" Then he looks past me. "Galeia?"

I hold up my hands, a placating gesture. "She's safe. She's well. She's... healed."

My gesture shows him that I'm wearing a medallion, and it stops him in his tracks.

All of the tension leaves his shoulders. "You helped her."

"I did."

"Thank you." He gives me a small smile that contrasts sharply with the fierce physical traits of the dragon whose soul he claimed. But his smile fades as he refocuses on me, suddenly searching my eyes. "Asha?"

My voice is a strained whisper. "I know how to stop it."

His hands drop to his sides, and his broad shoulders seem to grow heavy again. The way he looks at me tells me he knows what it will cost.

His gaze lowers to the floor before he takes a deep breath and looks me in the eye again. "I will never forget what you said to me when we first met. You told me you wouldn't hurt me because you only kill monsters."

I exhale quietly, attempting a smile. "And you asked me: What if I am one?"

He nods.

Then, without hesitation, he crosses the room, picks up the toolbox I left on the pedestal there, and brings it back to me. "My hammer and medallions are inside. I put them away after you left."

"Thank you." It is the smallest thing I could say after everything that has led us to this point. All the threads connecting our destinies that had been weaving years before we were even born.

I force myself to turn away, preparing to leave, but he stops me.

"Asha, wait. There's one more device."

I pause, sharply aware that the device that currently rests within Thaden's chest is also constructed from dark metal.

So, too, is Galeia's heart.

I have already chosen not to take her heart. It wasn't even a question in my mind. She can't live without it. Removing it would kill her.

I have to believe that Malak's tools and Thaden's tools and all the dark magic those tools contain will be enough for me to create the object that will banish the darkness.

But as for the device in Thaden's chest...

He's suddenly right behind me, his presence as powerful as fire. "Will you make me human?"

My eyes widen at his request. "What?" I turn back to him, unable to keep the disbelief from my voice. "You would give away all of your power, all of the dragon's strength, never to use it again?"

He's quiet for a moment. "Real power is overcoming the past. Strength is finding my purpose. I don't need magic or a dragon's soul to do either of those."

I consider him carefully, even more afraid of his request than I was of healing Galeia. She is a child with a brain and body that will develop with her nature, but Thaden is a fully grown man with entrenched beliefs and decades of memories.

His voice lowers. "Even if I didn't believe with my whole heart that I am meant to be human, there's no other path that keeps Tamra and the people of this village safe. Graviter Rex believes I killed his son, and I can't tell him otherwise. Once the darkness is gone, he will be able to come for me. I will go out to meet him, try to lead him away, but I fear for my people."

Thaden catches his breath, and I understand his concern.

A fire dragon's rage is without constraint.

"If you strip me of my power," he continues, "Graviter Rex may consider justice served."

I take another moment, thinking it through. "I don't know what you looked like," I say, as if his appearance is my biggest concern.

"I think you do," he says, his lips pressing into a grim line. "Milena told me how much I looked like my father."

Oh, I remember Malak well.

Black hair, inky-blue eyes, pale skin, and high cheekbones. But the chill that I would feel when I was in his presence... I've never felt that around Thaden.

"With one distinct difference," he continues. "My skin was light brown like my mother's."

Slowly, he begins removing the tunic he's wearing. Then he points to a spot right beneath his left pectoral muscle. "This is where I drove the device into my heart. I expect removing it will be just as painful, so I'm going to back up and brace against the wall."

He does as he says, even though I haven't agreed to anything, and there he waits.

I make a decision.

It's formed from instinct alone, but I have to trust myself and the power that Erik allowed me to access. I need to trust this medallion that I forged from a hammer made of his deep light, a forging in which I poured every part of myself.

"You are not your father, Thaden," I say, placing the toolbox on the floor and striding toward him, drawing on my power in a flash, a surge so strong that the moment I press my left hand to his heart, he jolts.

His fists slam back against the rock wall, his teeth visibly gritted.

With a swift wrench, I pull the device from his heart, fully aware that it's slicing through flesh and bone and causing him unbearable pain.

But I also sense he needs to feel it.

He needs to know that it's gone and that all the grief that came with it is finally over.

The dragon device slices through his skin and drops to the floor, but I'm already pouring my hopes for him through my metal.

Heal. And be human.

Be all the things that humans can be. Loving and kind like Maybelle and Kedric. Intelligent and loyal like Rachel. Compassionate and strong like Mother Solas. Talented and resilient like Genova—

Genova.

My eyes widen as a very real possibility occurs to me.

Genova was the one who walked me through Malak's orchard. She pointed to the dark cottage and asked me what must have happened within its walls to turn Malak into such a monster.

She was a midwife for the Blacksmiths and the one who told me about the baby Milena took away. The baby who was Thaden.

I may never know if she is Thaden's mother, but oh, he is so much like her in so many ways. Smart, loyal, thoughtful, strong.

As I pour my power into his heart and body, the dragon scales vanish from his skin while his body shape remains the same, tall and broad-shouldered. His bronzed eyes shift from amber and yellow to green and finally inky-dark blue. His hair color changes at the same quick rate, the strands becoming black, and his skin transforms to light brown.

Now that the device is gone from his body, he doesn't appear to experience any pain. All of the tension leaves his face, his jaw unclenches, and his shoulders relax.

The reversion to his previous appearance happens so easily and seamlessly that I'm under no illusion that it's entirely because of my power. His body knew what it was before he forced the dragon's soul to merge with his, and it must have been ready to change back.

The changes happen smoothly until he's standing in front of me, wholly changed. But also... the same.

Even though his coloring is different, he is still Thaden.

Quickly, I do a final check of the wound across the location of his heart, keeping my left hand pressed to him for another few seconds until his skin fully heals.

His heart resumes beating normally, a strong *thump-thump* before he slumps forward, and I catch him, lowering us both to the floor.

His head comes to rest on my shoulder, and his breathing deepens. Erik slept for hours after I made him whole, and it occurs to me that I probably didn't think this through. I should have ensured we returned to Thaden's cottage first.

"It's okay," he murmurs in my ear as if he reads my regret. "This is where I wanted to be. In my forge, where I found my purpose. I'll just sit here a while. I'll be fine." His forehead creases. "Hopefully, Tamra won't get a fright when she sees me."

And then he says, "She's a good person. The best person. Maybe even the family I didn't think I would ever have. I'll keep her safe. I promise."

I ease him back into a sitting position, giving him a small smile as I take a final look at his new appearance.

I don't know how Milena could say he looked like Malak.

Every part of Thaden's features, from his dark eyes to his jaw and even the crease in his forehead, all are alive with feeling.

"Asha," he says, reaching for me, even though his hand doesn't make it halfway up before he has to lower it. "When you come back from this, will you do something else for me?"

I'm not returning from this. I nearly say so, and then I stop.

He knows.

The solemn tilt of his head and the way his lips press together, the sadness in his expression, tells me so.

"Whatever it is, ask me when I come back," I whisper.

Scooping up a pair of tongs from the workbench, I deposit the dragon device into the toolbox and hold the box close as I hurry away.

Back along the corridor to the little chamber that sent me into the darkness last time.

Before I step into it, I upend the pouch I was carrying into the toolbox, too, the wolf device that was used on Erik clanking softly as it hits the others.

I count the pieces. They're all there now.

Malak's hammer and medallions. Thaden's hammer and medallions. And all the devices that brought so much pain.

Along with them is my grandmother's pin. A single bright spot amid the pieces of dark metal.

Taking a deep breath, I cut my finger on the blade at the side of the chamber and let the darkness take me.

CHAPTER 49

Ash and dust choke me.

I open my eyes to the vast plain that stretches around me, to the tornados of crimson dirt that whip at the air and monstrous beasts that crash against each other in the distance.

I can barely breathe. All I can do is take short, sharp gasps while the scent of blood and death threatens to drive every rational thought from my mind.

You don't need to feel afraid.

The whisper reaches me across the wind, far closer to me than it was the first time I was pulled here.

A woman's figure takes shape within the darkness, sections of dust peeling from the sides of tornados, ash rising from the ground, all of it pulling together to construct her body. Ash streams across her head and down her sides like hair.

This darkness belongs to you.

She glides toward me, her features all too clear. A mirror to my darkest fears.

She is me.

"Take control," she whispers. "Shape the living to your needs. Command the dead to do your bidding. Fight the old—"

"Find the new," I say, rising to my full height. "Oh, I will."

I will create something that has never existed before.

A keeper of all the magics.

A keeper who will wear a dark crown and live forever in a prison.

But to do it, I must first take a terrible risk.

I must lure the darkness to me. The only way to do that is by feeding it. I must trap it before it knows it's trapped. And only at the last moment will I imprison it.

Reaching for my hammer, I slip it free in one smooth movement, taking hold of it in my left hand, right next to my medallion.

Power bursts around me, sending rays of golden light spearing through the air around me.

The shadow-woman's smile grows broader as I raise my hammer above my head and prepare to drive it into the ground.

"Come to me!" I cry as I ram my hammer into the dust and bones in the ground.

Energy explodes out from me, rippling visibly across the crimson ash. The impact shudders through me, and my bones feel like they've become dust, too.

"Come to me!" I scream again, raising my hammer and hitting the ground once more.

This time, lightning streaks across the sky and thunder booms. Blood-rain splatters my hair and falls onto the shadow-woman.

Memories of all the times I ran through this rain assail me.

All the times I cut down monsters, only for more to rise.

Until the magic is cleaned from this soil and every other part of the land that's affected, this darkness won't end.

In the distance, the monsters have stopped fighting and now they converge on me from all directions.

All of them are enormous beasts. Many have tusks. Others have claws. Still more have teeth. They are vicious and deformed, but not by choice.

They prowl toward me, giant beasts that stop to gather in a wide circle.

"I have come to claim you," I cry, lifting my voice above the rumbling thunder, tasting blood on my lips from the raindrops that continue to fall. "I will give you purpose and strength. I will be your Queen."

With that, I return my hammer to the harness on my back and bend to the ash at my feet.

There are so many bones beneath this soil, all waiting to be transformed. It takes mere seconds to find a large one.

"Become an anvil," I whisper, voicing my command, even though I don't need to speak it aloud.

The bone reshapes itself into white rock, taking the same shape as the black rock on the cliffs beside the ocean, providing a wide, flat surface on one side with an indented section on the other.

Drops of blood-rain gather in the indent.

I press my palm to them. "Become fire."

Black flame bursts to life, its heat rising into the air. It, too, smells like death.

While the shadow-woman glides slowly back and forth nearby, an embodiment of all my worst fears, the beasts wait quietly, and even the tornados of ash have settled, becoming calm, the wind merely plucking at the ground in places.

All of them, waiting.

I open the toolbox and carefully tip its contents onto the anvil.

Graviter warned me never to touch this dark metal again. But he didn't say what would happen if I did.

He didn't need to.

Whenever I picked up Malak's hammer or wore his medallions, I lost myself to them. When Erik and I were traveling through the forest to find Milena, I conquered the power of Malak's medallion over me, but I didn't extinguish its malice and cruelty.

Now I will welcome them back.

Because I can't make a dark crown with love in my heart. This crown can only contain hatred and savagery and death.

Very carefully, I separate my grandmother's pin from the

other pieces, sliding it to the side of the flat surface. I will incorporate it at the end, once the core of the crown is solid and strong.

My hands shake as I lift them over the black metal, preparing to take hold of Malak's hammer again, to use it one last time before it, too, must be melded into the crown.

I can't do this without my own medallion, so I leave it on my hand. Between my medallion and Malak's hammer, I will have all the power I need.

My heart becomes cold as I banish my happiness, all my memories of Erik and my siblings and Galeia. All the warmth and love. I take a mental knife to it all and cut it apart so that none of that happiness can wrap around my thoughts and find a way into the crown.

"Find the new," I whisper to myself.

Take control.

In those final heartbeats, I tell myself I'm limitless.

Then I take hold of Malak's hammer and embrace its malice.

CHAPTER 50

I am cold.

The fire burns my right hand as I plunge the first pieces of dark metal into it without using tongs.

Pain strikes through me, and Malak's medallions quickly burn red hot before I wrench them out of the fire and position them on the anvil.

My mother's voice screams in my memory, telling me to forge until my hands bleed.

I strike Malak's hammer down on his own medallions, and then the work begins.

Over and over, I reheat the metal before beating and folding it, adding the pieces one at a time, beating and folding them until only Malak's hammer and my grandmother's pin remain.

Hammering the mound of dark metal into a flat circle, I take the black hammer in my right hand and thrust it into the fire.

My hand is already red and raw from the fire, whatever pain sensors existed within it having burned away so that I feel nothing in that hand now.

When Malak's hammer glows red hot, I place it down on the circle of metal and fold the edges up around it, kneading it like dough, using my left hand to press with my power as well as my increased physical strength until the metal is flat and smooth once more.

A hush has fallen around me, the same as when I forged my medallion, but with every move I make, the scent of copper grows stronger in the air, and lightning flickers more brightly in the sky. The dark pall around me grows so dense that the monsters that have gathered to watch are black silhouettes, practically formless.

My arms shake with exhaustion. My mouth is beyond dry. I'm not sure how I'm breathing because even though the tornados have calmed, there is more ash in the air now, drifting like snowflakes all around me.

The spokes of a crown come together within my hands, each one tall and sharp, while the crown's base is a thick, black band.

Finally, it rests, fully formed in my hand.

All of the dark metal has been melded into a single object.

But my grandmother's pin is now a problem I don't have a solution for. It rests on the anvil, a bright spot in the dark.

My fear is that it will bring light into this crown—a light that will undo all my work.

Maybe I need to leave it be. Simply take the pin with me in its current form.

I'm preparing to reach for it and slip it into my pocket when a cold hand wraps around my wrist.

My head snaps up.

The shadow-woman leans across the anvil, her fingers gripping my arm.

At her touch, my mind empties of everything except...

Screams.

My parents are dying, and I can't help them. A beast covered in blood has torn them apart, and now he is coming for me.

He will kill me, too.

My heart is suddenly pounding. Within my mind, I'm seconds away from death.

But *I* have the power now.

This dark crown is everything I need.

I don't have to be afraid.

Why was I worried?

My forehead creases because I can't remember now.

I can destroy whatever I want to destroy. I can walk out from this dark plain, dragging the ash with me wherever I go, and I can make the world what I want it to be.

Nothing is beyond my reach.

And nothing... not one fucking thing... will ever hurt me.

The shadow-woman's lips rise into a smile. "*Now* you are me."

She unwraps her hand from my wrist and draws back, but before she goes, she slaps the silver pin from the anvil, sending it flying into the dust, where it quickly disappears beneath falling ash.

I pay it no mind.

It's no longer important. All that matters is this crown and the power that comes with it.

I turn my left hand over, palm up, giving my golden medallion cold consideration as I decide what to do with it.

If I take it off, I can merge it with the base of the crown. That way, I can turn its light to dark and wear all of my power like a queen—

An explosion of white light blasts across my vision, knocking me backward. The light pours through the shadow-woman, ripping her figure apart, silencing her screams, and cutting through the beasts that stood behind her.

The air shrieks as a black-feathered creature soars across the space above me, and three figures jump from its back.

Each one is swathed in light that radiates out from them, disintegrating every dark thing nearby.

When a monster tries to ram into them, it shatters into dust.

When I step closer, pain strikes through my heart, cutting so sharply that I scream in agony and jolt backward, away from the light.

"The darkness has her!"

I recognize that voice. It belongs to a girl named Cailey.

She crouches where she lands, her hands outstretched,

pouring white light into our surroundings, cutting down any monster that tries to approach.

"Dusana!" she cries. "You have to reach Asha or we're lost!"

One of the other figures runs toward me. It's Dusana, her golden hair forming a halo around her face, the flowers she was weaving still entwined in the strands.

Her steps slow before she reaches me, and her face drains of color. "Asha?"

I clutch the crown to my chest, keeping to the darkness, ready to strike out if I have to, prepared to turn her to stone or dust or blood to protect what's mine.

"Oh, no." Dusana's brown eyes widen as her gaze rushes over me. "Cailey! Mother Solas!" Her desperate scream fades as she whispers, "I think we're too late."

"It's never too late," Mother Solas says, striding through the light toward me, her form backlit in a way that makes her white hair shine silver like mine used to.

The strands of hair now billowing around my face are the color of the darkest night. More than black. They are streaming strands of darkness pouring down my sides. My arms, where I can see them, are charred and my nails are sharp.

I have become the darkness.

Just before she would reach me, Mother Solas bends to the ground, scooping something up.

She stops and holds it out to me.

Her hand is wrinkled with age, but it doesn't shake.

Within her fingers is the silver pin, shaped like a crescent moon. Its glistening, silver surface is as bright as Cailey's power.

"We're here with you," she says, her voice quiet even though the wind is picking up around us. "You don't have to do this alone."

Her voice reminds me of a small moment in time, when Erik stood beside me, his hand brushing mine. Mother Solas had given me this very same pin, but it wasn't the gift that mattered.

It was the fact that Erik had made sure it had been kept safe for me.

Erik.

My thoughts are suddenly splitting apart.

I have power.

I am powerless.

I will kill them all.

I have to save them.

My heart is pounding so hard it's about to tear in half. One part yearning for the light, the other for the dark.

Take control. Take control. Take control…

I stumble back a step, clutching my head in my hands, and then I sink to the ash, the black crown gripped in my left hand, its cold surface pressed against my temple.

"We're here," Mother Solas says, lowering herself to the ash in front of me, her intelligent, compassionate eyes refusing to look away. "Asha Silverspun, you know this in your heart: We are the magics you need. It will take all four of us. You will not die alone this day."

I take a deep, shuddering breath, tasting the awful, blood-filled ash on my tongue, my voice broken and sounding far away in my own ears. "I don't want to go."

Tears fill Mother Solas's eyes. "I know."

I gasp against the pain in my heart. "I have the power to stay."

"You do," she whispers. "The choice is yours."

In the distance, Cailey lowers her arms, backing up in our direction, drawing in toward Dusana and Mother Solas, all of them reaching for me, their arms slipping around me.

Cailey's light continues to glow around us, but her face is drawn and pale.

I sense that her energy is almost gone.

The darkness will swallow us all soon.

"We're here," Dusana murmurs, the scent of wildflowers filling my chest as she bends her head to mine.

"We're here," Cailey whispers, resting her head on my other shoulder.

"We're ready," Mother Solas says. "Light magic, elemental magic, original magic, and dark magic."

"The four of us," Dusana says. "Together."

I bow my head, finally letting go of my fears.

In my mind, I hear Gallium's long-ago voice telling me he will fight beside me. I hear Galeia asking me to make her a wolf. I hear my sister telling me she loves me and Thaden taking his first breath as a human.

And I hear Erik when he growled at me, telling me... he just wanted to do one good thing before he died.

I close my eyes and inhale the scent of starlight and wildflowers.

Then I rest the black crown on my lap so I can raise my left hand to Dusana's shoulder.

Softly, I say, "You will be the keeper of elemental magic. You will wear flowers in your hair and a tiara on your head, and you will live in a bright realm, tethering elemental magic for eternity."

She gives me a smile. Possibly the first she's ever bestowed on me. The twinkle in her eyes tells me she's pleased. "As you like."

Then she fades from view, her form disappearing. But not into nothing. I sense the power I created, a force that will only grow stronger as I create more keepers.

Mother Solas reaches for me again and I take the hand she offers. Within it, she's holding the silver pin. I close her fingers around it and then I place my left hand over the top.

"You will be the keeper of light magic," I say. "Your years will fall away, and you will be the warrior that I suspect you were in your youth."

This brings a smile to her face, and she nods.

"You will have golden armor, and this pin will become your weapon," I continue. "You will live in a peaceful realm, tethering light magic for eternity."

She speaks as she fades from view. "As you like."

I turn to Cailey, conscious that her light is fading fast. The darkness is pressing around us, and the monsters are swarming inward.

Until all four of us have taken our place as keepers, nothing is safe.

"Cailey."

When my voice chokes, she wraps her hand around mine, her head remaining on my shoulder.

"Don't be sad for me, Asha Silverspun," she says. "I may look young, but I am as old as time. In my lifetime, I have witnessed the births of gods and battles against titans. I am ready for my next adventure."

"You will be the keeper of original magic," I say. "You will live in a starlit realm with a never-ending night sky and all the silver roses you could ever desire. You will tether original magic for eternity."

She lifts her head to give me a soft smile. "As you like."

Her form slowly fades.

Tears slide down my cheeks, but I'm ready now, too.

Lifting the dark crown to my head, I exhale and speak my final command. "I will be the keeper of dark magic. I will live in a dark realm strong enough to hold the very worst of all magic and never let it loose."

I take a final breath while the scent of starlight and wildflowers lingers in the air, and the dust storms rage toward me.

There is only silence as death comes for me.

Lowering the crown to my head, I accept all of the darkness that will change me forever, as I say, "I will tether dark magic for eternity."

CHAPTER 51

The darkness around me fades.

I expect to become surrounded by the shiny, black realm I imagined for myself, but instead...

A wash of blue spreads across the air above me, the most beautiful sky I've ever seen.

White clouds blossom within it and a bird soars beneath them.

The ground I'm kneeling on becomes soft with grass, a thick field of foliage spreading out all around me.

To my right, the ground splits open and a tree trunk pushes up through it, sprouting strong branches and emerald-green leaves and bursting with flowers. Within seconds, the tree is fully grown, white petals floating toward me on the breeze.

I'm frozen, my breath stilling because I'm... not...

I'm not in the dark realm I'm certain I created.

I am still in the valley, the vast plain where, only moments ago, the darkness raged and dust storms whirled.

My hands fly up to my head, reaching for the dark crown, only to find—

It's gone.

The dark keeper's crown is gone!

My hands snap back down, but my medallion is still there,

wrapped around my left palm. So, too, is my hammer, strapped to my back.

But while my surroundings have healed, I have not.

The strands of hair falling at my sides are blackened and my arms remain charred. The dark magic I took into my soul still whispers within my mind, a chilling cruelty that doesn't belong in this renewed environment.

Panic fills me, a horrible, overwhelming, terrifying panic.

I am not the dark magic keeper.

But my magic worked. The land around me is restored. The air is clear, and the darkness is gone.

If I'm not the dark magic keeper, then... who is?

Who was taken instead of me?

I stumble to my feet, whirling to my surroundings, a deep dread filling me as I seek an answer in the tree, the flowers, and then higher, my focus rising to the bird that was soaring across the sky and is now diving toward me.

A crack of thunder sounds as it rages at me, a shriek emitting from its beak.

I don't recognize this thunderbird. It certainly isn't Blackbird or Concord.

I leap backward and crouch to the ground, my left hand extended, ready to defend myself.

A single figure somersaults from the bird's back, landing lightly on the ground while the bird itself soars away.

I may not know the bird, but I recognize this woman.

She is beautiful, her skin dusted with gold and her long, blonde hair falling in waves around her shoulders. Her eyes are a glistening yellow, like the color of sunflowers, but they're also filled with hatred.

"Witch!" Queen Karasi snarls at me, her right hand rising and heat building around it. "You ruined everything."

I once watched her light a flame with a mere flick of her fingers. The fire she could pour at me may not be able to match that of a fire dragon, but she could burn me to ash just the same.

I don't wait for her to reach me.

My medallion responds to my instincts, a golden shield forming, protecting my body as I reach for my hammer and throw myself forward into a slide, aiming for her right side.

Her fire shoots across the air where I was standing, but I've already reached her and she doesn't adjust her balance in time.

My hammer smacks into her legs, knocking them out from under her. She falls forward but twists midair, the heat from her flames pouring toward me.

My shield transforms and my muscles obey my commands, a golden blade forming in my hand as I also twist, aiming for her exposed side.

My blade impales her all the way to her heart.

Her eyes widen as she drops to the ground. "You..."

She doesn't say another word, landing with her legs twisted beneath her, the life fading from her eyes.

Still crouched, I retract my blade with a whisper. "Go to your keeper, Fae Queen. Dusana will be delighted to claim your magic."

I lean backward, relief filling me.

It's over. The Fae Queen is dead. The darkness is gone. Peace has finally fallen.

A quiet fills the valley while the sun shines overhead.

I tip my head back to its rays, soaking them in until my vision blurs and my forehead creases because when I try to take a deep breath, I discover...

I can't.

I gasp for air, desperately trying to make my breathing work. But something's wrong. Terribly wrong...

I look down at my chest, finally focusing on the gaping wound that cuts through my ribs.

Her fire burned right through me.

It must have happened the moment my shield retracted.

I tell myself to cover the wound with my medallion, to reach for it, heal it, and use my power to save myself, but my arms don't obey me.

I topple to the side just as I make out figures in the distance.

There are more thunderbirds in the sky, all of them flying toward me. And people on the ground, all of them running.

Two are ahead of the others.

I recognize Erik, his muscles pumping, his dark hair flying as he sprints toward me. But I don't recognize the little wolf that races at his side, keeping pace with him despite his incredible speed.

I try to hold on, but my head is swimming, and my thoughts are murky.

"Asha!" His roar reaches me from a distance. "*Asha!*"

I don't have air to speak.

Death has come for me, after all.

My body hits the soft, green ground, and my vision fills with nothing but the crisp, blue sky.

The air blurs, becoming a swirl of indigo, and then I'm gone.

CHAPTER 52

Everything sharpens again.

A beautiful, shiny, black realm comes into view around me.

And for a long, terrible moment, my world tears apart.

CHAPTER 53

I jolt upright with a scream on my lips.

Tears pour down my cheeks, and my heart is filled with anguish. "What have I done?"

Strong arms cradle me, holding me close. Erik's scent fills my chest. I recognize his arms and his worried eyes.

I also recognize my surroundings—I haven't moved from the place where I fell to the grass. Queen Karasi's body lies only a short distance away from me.

But pain is tearing at me, ripping at my body and my heart, pulling at my soul.

I'm screaming, and I can't control it. "What have I done?"

"Asha." Erik's voice is raw as he holds me close. "Asha, what is it? What's wrong? Tell me!"

"It shouldn't have been him." I rock with pain, unable to stop my cries. "Erik... It shouldn't have been him."

Erik's face is deathly pale as my cry echoes around us. "Who, Asha?"

I'm barely conscious of the other people around me, of the relief on their faces that's quickly turning to concern.

My brother, Gallium, stands beside Elowynn. They're both injured with countless cuts and bruises on their faces and arms, and their expressions are strained. Behind them are the dragons Graviter, Vargo, and Torva, along with the humans Catalina and Rachel.

Blackbird and Concord rest on the grass beneath the nearby tree, their feathers ruffling in the breeze, but they are anything but peaceful, their eyes wide.

Elowynn's sister, Gliss, kneels closer to me, her dark hair shining in the sunlight, and I register the way her hands are withdrawing from me. She likely healed me like she'd healed Erik.

I don't care about my wound.

I *can't* care.

"I saw him." I grip Erik's arms as hard as I can. "I saw the dark magic keeper. He took all of the darkness from my heart. He freed me from it."

I press my hand to my chest, where the darkness lodged within my soul as soon as I had taken hold of Malak's metal again.

"He took the darkness. He saved me from it, and then... and then..."

But it's slipping away from me.

I try to hold on to the memory of the keeper's face, trying to fix his features in my mind, but they've already vanished.

I can't see him anymore.

I can't remember him.

All I remember is the flash of pain in his eyes because all of his light was stolen.

And now...

I press my lips together. "I don't... I can't..."

"It's okay." Erik pulls me close to his chest. "Asha, you're alive. That's all that matters."

His heart thuds loudly at my ear, telling me how much fear he felt. How much pain he would have experienced to lose me, even though he was prepared for that outcome.

"I'm alive," I whisper.

And so is he.

So is my family.

As Erik holds me close, a furry body pushes between us,

squeezing onto my lap and reaching up to press its paws to my chest.

It's the little wolf I saw running beside Erik.

She has the softest black fur but such anxious amber eyes. Also, the roughest little tongue as she licks at the tears sliding down my cheeks.

A moment later, she transforms, her furry body changing nearly instantly into the little girl I recognize.

"Galeia," I whisper as she presses both of her hands to my chest, her eyes searching mine.

Fresh tears fall down my cheeks.

"I'm okay," I say, pushing back against my sadness as I try to reassure her. "I promise."

She seems to accept my words, resting her head on my chest before she tugs Erik closer to me.

His arm slides around me, his cheek pressing to mine, his hold encircling us both.

We are alive.

We are safe.

The darkness is gone.

The fae and humans will have a lot to work out. My siblings need to be reunited. But for now, there's only one thing I need.

I take a deep breath, inhaling and exhaling, before I whisper to Erik, "Please, will you take us home?"

He draws back a little, lifting one hand to cup my cheek before answering me with a kiss.

Then he lifts us both up, me and Galeia together, carrying us to Blackbird, who immediately separates from Concord and offers his wing.

Within minutes, we're airborne, and the beautiful landscape and all its sacrifices are far behind us.

CHAPTER 54

For many days, I remain in the black tower.

It seems empty without the women who made it feel like a home, but I can't bring myself to leave it.

Galeia decorates every room with flowers and random twigs that she finds in the forest, and at one point, she brings home a frog, which she eventually, reluctantly, returns to the stream.

Erik takes her hunting with him, teaching her to use discipline and setting firm rules about what she should and shouldn't catch and how to kill without causing undue fear or pain.

Her growth has slowed since I made her a wolf, but her mind and body continue to develop at twice the rate of a human child.

Her laughter and bright eyes tell me she's happy.

While I don't leave the tower, others come to me.

My brother is the first to visit. He brings Tamra, and my heart lifts to see them.

Gallium tells me everything that happened to him after he and Tamra were separated, how he survived Karasi's machinations, and how he and Elowynn kept each other alive.

Tamra speaks more carefully, never mentioning Thaden by name, but she slips into the conversation that the leader of her village is doing well and that she is helping him construct new homes now that the darkness is gone and the village can expand.

I'm not sure how much Gallium knows about Thaden's real history, but it seems he understands enough that he gives Tamra a smile and doesn't prompt her for more information than she's willing to give.

Finally, though, Tamra's eyes widen when she tells me about the moment she felt the keepers' creation.

A force had traveled through the ground.

Apparently, even the humans felt it.

Gallium confirms her account, describing to me how the air filled with power and all of the thunderbirds were forced to the ground. The influx of energy seemed to sap the fae's power for long enough that they had no choice but to stop fighting.

My siblings tell me that already, the stories are growing about the keepers' creation and the women who made it possible, but when Tamra prompts me about the dark magic keeper's identity, I can only shake my head.

I can't remember. No matter how hard I try.

Around him, there is only silence.

A terrible silence.

It leaves a hole in my heart that I don't fully understand and I pray will one day heal.

Before my siblings leave, Gallium pulls me aside. He gives me a hug, a quiet one, but I sense he has something more he needs to say.

"Gallium?"

"I would like your blessing," he says, his eyes crinkling at the corners.

I'm surprised. "What for?"

He gives me a crooked smile. "Would it alarm you if there were a fae in the family?"

I can't help my answering smile. "Please, if you want to be with Elowynn, don't wait, Gallium. Life is too..." My smile fades and I blink away the burn behind my eyes.

Life is too fleeting.

"Yeah," he murmurs, hugging me again. "Thank you, Asha."

My heart feels lighter then, even when they leave.

My next visitor is far less relaxed.

Graviter Rex comes to me about Thaden Kane. He doesn't know the true story of how his son died, and I will never tell him, but understandably, his anger and pain about his son's death have not abated.

I meet him in the clearing at the base of the tower, grateful that he came to me before flying out to seek justice, but I also need to be clear about my position.

Turning my left hand palm out, I make my medallion clearly visible as I tell him, "Before I banished the darkness, I visited Thaden Kane Ironmeld and took retribution for your son's death. I have stripped Thaden of his Blacksmith power and made him human. He will remain powerless for the rest of his life. I consider this a far more severe outcome than the death I could have given him."

Graviter considers me quietly, his golden scales rippling and his eyes narrowed, but the heat from his mouth is subdued.

When he gave me his eternal flame, he revealed that it can never burn me. What he didn't say, but I now strongly suspect, is that none of his dragon fire can burn me. He could pour flames down on me from his mouth, and I would not be harmed.

"Justice is part of my medallion," I continue. "So are fury and wisdom. The dragons gave me these gifts." I peer up at Graviter. "Do you agree that justice has been done and no further retribution will be sought?"

He takes a long moment to consider my question, and I don't hurry him. He counts his years in millennia. His son was his world. The events that led to Lysander's death were tragic, and I can't disrespect the deep pain that Graviter will continue to feel for the rest of his life.

"Thaden Kane Ironmeld is human," Graviter says, seeming to chew his words as he speaks.

"He is."

"His power is destroyed."

I nod. "It is."

Graviter inhales deeply, his eyes filling with tears before he inclines his head. "Then justice has been done."

He is too proud to grieve fully in front of me.

When he turns without another word, I let him go.

Every day after that, other dragons visit me. As Mother Solas predicted, they appear to love the perches at the sides of the tower and make frequent use of them. It seems like each day, there is a different dragon resting on one of the platforms, quietly watching over me.

The humans also come to visit, and nothing can prepare me for how hard it is to tell Rachel about her grandmother. Somehow, I get through it, and Rachel hugs me before she leaves.

Things get quieter after that.

The fae and the humans broker peace.

The humans who were responsible for the anarchy in the Cursed City are tried and executed, including Braddock, the man who once guarded me.

I stay away from the trials, but Erik is conflicted. I sense he wants to be there in support of the humans he protected: Petra, in particular.

But for either of us to make an appearance could influence the outcome.

I am acutely aware that with one word, I could sway decisions. Any decisions. Simply because... as I come to realize... they are all afraid of me.

Just as the fierce Valkyrie Queen looked fearfully into my eyes and told me I could force her to join a war against her will, every leader fears what I could do.

The dragons gave me access to my power, but it seems they never expected me to survive the process of banishing the darkness.

Even Graviter, who told me he had seen the future, seemed thrown, as if, at some point, the future he claimed to have seen must have changed, and now it is all unknown to him too.

Soon the dragons' presence at the tower, their constant surveillance of me, becomes not a reassurance, but a caution.

I come to know what Thaden experienced.

The dragons are prepared for me to turn.

It won't help to tell them that I never will.

Whatever I experienced in the dark magic keeper's realm, I remember one thing for certain: When I died, he took every shred of dark magic from my body and soul, freeing me from it forever.

Whoever he was, he gave me a priceless gift of freedom, making my heart mine again.

Erik and Galeia are my balance against the quiet distrust of others. Erik is a constant strength, assuming the role of warrior for me, telling the dragons to fuck off when he senses I need space. Galeia is a source of joy, her dark, wolfish nature making her both mischievous and sweet in turns.

And then, something unexpected happens.

I wake one morning, four weeks after I created the keepers, and the first thing I do is vomit up every bit of last night's meal.

I barely make it to the sink in time.

My launch out of the bed is so fast that Erik is halfway up behind me, his hair tousled and the blankets tangled in his legs. "What is it? What's wrong?"

At the same time, Galeia, who sleeps on my side of the bed but frequently ends up at my feet, wriggles her way out of the blankets I accidentally piled onto her when I jumped up.

She, too, considers me with worried eyes.

I groan as I rinse out my mouth and splash my face with water. "I feel terrible."

Wobbling back to the bed, I nudge Galeia aside, but she climbs up onto my stomach, pressing her ear to it.

"Baby wolf," she declares.

"What?" I'm so startled that I'm halfway up out of the bed again before Erik's arms close around me, tugging me back down.

Galeia resettles herself on my chest while he makes a show of pressing his ear to my stomach like she did.

When he lifts his head to my questioning eyes, a smile tugs at the corners of his lips. "Baby wolf."

My eyes are wide. "Really?"

"He has a strong heartbeat."

"He?" I narrow my eyes. "Or are you guessing?"

Erik looks at Galeia, who nods in agreement before he confirms. "He."

I sink back to the pillows, trying to process what this means. I've changed our surroundings little by little over the last month, adding the things we need: a big bed, a fireplace, and a bath with endless hot water.

Also a separate bedroom that Galeia doesn't know about, since she insists on sleeping with us. She has a wolfish need for a pack that we won't deny her, but there are times... quite a few times... when we need our own space.

I can't stop my smile.

I guess a baby wolf isn't so unexpected if I think about it.

But pregnancy also comes with questions for me.

Thaden was the first child born to parents who were not both Blacksmiths. What's more, he was born a *Blacksmith*, not a human. I didn't expect to have children of my own for the same reason. I believed I could only become pregnant by a male Blacksmith.

My happiness fades, and my worries rise.

Erik seems to sense the change in my mood immediately. "Asha?"

"You called him a baby wolf," I say. "But could he be a Blacksmith?"

Within my question is a deeper fear.

Blacksmith magic can cause so much harm. Of course, my people are not alone in this. Every magic can cause harm. So can non-magical people. It's all about choices.

But I formed an assumption many years ago that my siblings and I would be the last of our kind. Once we pass, Blacksmiths would no longer exist.

While Galeia nestles against my chest, Erik pulls me closer to his side.

"This child is pure wolf, Asha. I can sense it." He nudges a kiss to my neck. "And since you've been wearing your medallion nearly constantly, I also sense he may be like Galeia."

"Able to shift?" I ask.

Erik nods. "We'll find out for sure when he's born."

I breathe out my tension. "Well. That's a good thing." I can't stop my smile. "Imagine not being able to keep up with her."

Erik chuckles. "I don't have to imagine. She makes me feel old."

Galeia's response is a toothy grin, but her delight at the idea of a baby brother is unmistakable.

The next day, Erik heads out to ask Genova to come and see me. She was a midwife for the Blacksmiths, and while she left that profession behind her, she's the only human I trust to help me through this.

When she arrives, she approaches me in her usual calm, insightful way, unflustered by the tower or the flight here on the back of a wolf-bird.

She asks me how I'm feeling and I'm honest with her.

"Powerful *and* powerless," I say.

She inclines her head as she checks me over. "You've walked a path I never could have imagined, Asha."

"So have you," I murmur.

She becomes still for a moment.

And then, "Is he...?"

She presses her lips together, falling silent.

Even here, she won't feel safe to ask about Thaden. The fact that she brought a Blacksmith child into the world... well... there are some who would kill her for it.

"My son will be a wolf," I say, acting as if she'd been talking about him. "Erik and Galeia are certain of it. But I think I should also seek my sister's opinion about it. She lives in the village known as *Myrkur Fjall* now, did you know?"

Genova shakes her head. "I didn't."

"She's very happy there," I continue. "The leader of the village is a good man. He's intelligent and honorable. He crafts metal limbs for those who have suffered terrible wounds. Tamra helps him. They look after the people who live there."

Genova raises her eyes to mine with the barest whisper. "Thank you."

Clearing her throat and wiping at her eyes, she steps back from me. "Everything seems fine. If you have any concerns, send Erik for me. Regardless, I'll visit each month to check on you, and I'll visit more often closer to the birth."

After that, the days pass quickly.

Weeks turn into months, and the stairs become my enemy.

I eventually set up a bedroom on the first floor of the tower, and that's where my son is born eight months later.

He is perfect and strong, his eyes already gray like his father's, a matting of wolfish hair across his head, and oh, he has lungs!

His roar as he takes his first breath sounds like a challenge to the world.

Erik holds my hand as tightly as I squeeze his.

Genova has barely wrapped our son in a blanket before Galeia darts into the room, her eyes wide.

She was waiting outside with Gallium and Tamra, who appear in the doorway behind her, looking a little helpless because clearly, there was no keeping Galeia from her brother.

She crawls onto the blanket beside me while Genova hands me my bawling son, laying him carefully down on my chest.

He quiets at the contact, his eyes barely open beyond slits, but he sees me. And I see him.

Erik nudges in on the other side of me, and then I'm wedged between the people I love most in the world.

The family I will protect, no matter what.

I close my eyes and whisper to them, "You are loved."

And so am I.

EPILOGUE
GALEIA – TWENTY-FIVE YEARS LATER

EPILOGUE
GALEIA

The ocean wind whips at my black hair as I stand at the edge of the platform high above the waves.

Far below me, in the clearing outside the tower, there is a bustle of activity. More than this tower might ever have seen.

I tug at the neckline of the black dress I'm wearing. It's made of silken material that's fit for this occasion, but I'd rather be dressed in leather and hunting in the forest than staring down at what will soon be a wedding ceremony for the oldest of my brothers.

Aksel is a small figure from this high up, where he stands next to Father and Mother, but he surpassed me in height years ago, now matching Father in stature and strength.

So, too, do all my brothers.

All five of them.

They are so fierce, and their black, metal claws are so renowned that some of the humans have started calling them the Iron Wolves. They shun the name, but it isn't their reputation that matters today.

Today, peace will finally be forged.

Aksel will marry Charlotte, the daughter of the human Queen

Rachel Exalted, solidifying an alliance between the human Queendom and my family.

If I were cynical, I would think it was arranged purely for political purposes, to finally put to rest the fear the humans have of my mother.

But Aksel loves Charlotte.

He would have claimed her as his mate years ago if it weren't for all the human customs he had to navigate, which matter even more because she's the heir to the human throne.

He's had to be careful.

Today is the culmination of years of cautious, patient steps.

For a moment, I teeter on the edge of the platform overlooking the clearing, my balance perfectly placed to keep me from falling.

It's the kind of balance that only winged creatures have.

Not surprising since I was born to be one.

Sometimes, I catch Mother glancing at me as if she expects me to ask her questions about my origins.

I don't remember much. My mind seems to have blocked out much of it and I've never tried to open those doors, but I know that I was born as a Valkyrie. I remember the uncomfortable stumps on my back and the single deformed feather that itched horribly. Sometimes, I remember the scent of fire but nothing else to give that memory context.

I *do* know that I chose to be a wolf, and I have never, not even for a heartbeat, regretted my choice.

I also know that if I ask for more information, Mother and Father will tell me everything.

But I won't ask.

Because then I will know my full name, and names have power.

I will not tie my life to the past.

I'm about to step back from the edge of the platform when there's a stir in the clearing below.

A man approaches from the eastern side, fully visible to me from where I stand. He steps out of the forest as if he might have walked all the way here.

At his appearance, the nearby guests already gathered in the clearing immediately hush and veer away from him.

A path quickly opens up for him, but the tension I sense in the air tells me the guests are avoiding him out of caution, not reverence.

Who is he?

I peer down across the distance, wishing I could get a sense of his scent, but the wind keeps whipping it away.

He has black hair and a tall, muscular physique similar to Father's. His jaw is strong, his cheekbones high, and he has light brown skin. He *might* have blue eyes but it's difficult to tell from so far away and with the sun shining on his face.

He's wearing simple clothing, certainly nothing so fancy as the garments worn by the other guests, but what's no doubt concerning them is the weapon he carries in his right hand.

It consists of two sharp blades that sit on opposite sides of a pole that's as tall as he is. One of the blades is curved, while the other is a solid spike that could be used like a dagger. Interestingly, rather than brandishing the weapon, he's using it like a staff as he walks in Mother's direction.

She, Father, and Aksel remain where they are near the tower's base while he proceeds slowly toward them. They're facing away from me, so I can't see their expressions, but their posture indicates that they're far more relaxed about the newcomer's appearance than their guests are.

When the man reaches them, he takes a knee and lowers the weapon to the ground, but Mother quickly drops into a crouch opposite him.

I'm surprised when she throws her arms around him, hugging him tightly.

By the way he stiffens, her gestures seem to have startled him too, but he relaxes into it, his arms slowly rising to hug her back.

As hard as I can, I listen for their voices, determined to isolate their speech from the wind.

"Thaden," she says. "I'm glad you came."

"I wasn't sure if I should."

The wind is against me. As powerful as my hearing is, their speech is like whispers, and I can't be certain of their emotional states.

Briefly, I consider racing down the stairs to the base of the tower, but even at my quickest, it will take me a minute to reach the bottom, and there's no telling what I'll miss in the meantime.

"I can't stay," the man called Thaden says.

Mother pulls back a little. "Are you sure? It's been so long."

Her back is to me. I still can't see her expression.

But the way he focuses on her tells me she must be searching his eyes, the same method she uses to pull the truth even from a dark creature like me.

For some reason, he breaks her gaze, his head tipping back a little.

He looks all the way up to the tower's ledge, and for a moment, I'm certain he's looking directly at me.

"I came to give Aksel and Charlotte a gift," he says, even though his focus remains on me.

He does have blue eyes. I can see them now. They seem to shine with sadness and then, more powerfully, with peace.

He exhales deeply before his focus lowers to my mother again.

Slowly, he rises, drawing Mother to her feet at the same time.

Then he picks up the staff, carefully turning it horizontal before he holds it out to her.

"This halberd's handle is made from the first tree that grew in my village after you banished the darkness," he says. "Its blades are fashioned from steel that I honed for years. It will never rust, and with a little care, it will always remain sharp."

"And this emblem?" Mother asks, a little more loudly this time, as if she wants the onlookers to hear her now.

I crane to see what she's pointing at.

Thaden turns the weapon, the light catches the steel, and I can see what's carved into the curved blade.

It's a circular symbol. One side is a crescent moon, while the other side is splayed like the rays of the sun. I immediately recognize the two halves of the symbol—and I'm sure Mother did, too—even before Thaden explains.

"This crescent moon represents the Silverspun family," he says. "And these are the rays of the sun, which is the symbol of the Solas family. Together, they are united. This is my wish for your family, Asha."

Mother turns to Aksel, and I can finally see tears glistening on her cheeks. She presses her lips together as if she's having trouble speaking.

Aksel's voice is a deep rumble. "You have honored us with this gift, Thaden Kane Ironmeld."

Thaden Kane Ironmeld.

My eyes widen. The dragons whisper about him. How he once killed a dragon and how Mother punished him by making him human.

Mother and Father rarely speak of the time before the darkness was banished, but Mother certainly didn't greet Thaden like an enemy just now. He certainly doesn't seem to view her as one, either.

"Thank you for accepting my gift," he says, and that's all before he turns away.

Mother jolts forward as if she'll stop him, but then her hand drops back to her side.

She lets him go, her head tilted to the side, watching him as he makes his way carefully along the path the other guests have cleared for him.

Within minutes, he disappears once more into the forest.

I'm left with an oddly hollow feeling in my chest. A pang in my heart, which I can only put down to what today's event means for my family.

Aksel will start a new life today.

Change is happening.

Stepping back toward the opening into the tower, I enter a large alcove that's large enough for a thunderbird to shelter inside if the weather is bad.

At the rear of the alcove, a long, wide corridor provides a

direct line of sight to the second platform situated on the other side of the tower.

Now that I'm inside, I'm sheltered from the wind, and I attempt to pat my hair back into place as I quickly descend the stone staircase to the next level.

Torches spring to life around me before I enter the next corridor down. At the far end is the next staircase, but I pause halfway along.

I stop at the doorway to the room where Mother keeps the eternal flame. It burns in the middle of the floor, casting light all around it.

The walls in this room are white, but one side of them is covered with golden lettering that flows across the surface as if it were alive.

It's the rule of law.

At Graviter's request, Mother has started writing the laws that will allow supernaturals and humans to live in peace.

The first law they wrote together was the *Law of Champions* so that a fight to the death can never again be used as a ploy and only ever employed as a last resort.

Reading the laws written on the wall is like trying to catch one's own thoughts. They're designed so that the law someone might need is the one they will first see when they enter the room.

I haven't dared step foot beyond the door.

I'm fully aware of the darkness in my heart and I'm not sure that any of these laws would ever help me.

Walking on, I pause again, this time at the room to the left of the staircase.

The air inside this room always feels heavy.

Four statues stand at intervals in a circle. Their backs are to each other.

Mother didn't use her power to make the materials from which they are carved. She spent years looking for the right white stone, the darkest crimson wood, the heaviest gold, and the smoothest black onyx.

Then, she spent years carving and molding them.

One statue to honor each keeper.

Cailey is white stone, her young form appearing almost to float above her statue's base.

Crimson wood for Dusana, depicted with her head held high and flowers cascading through her hair.

The gold for Mother Solas, who is dressed in armor and carries a curved blade strapped to her back.

And finally, from the black onyx, Mother carved the statue of a man whose face is partially obscured by a black crown. The crown's wide band sits around his eyes while its sharp peaks extend up past his head. He is cloaked in a long, black robe that conceals his body, making him almost figureless.

I may have shunned my own past, but I've tried to find out who he was.

Each community—the fae, humans, and dragons—has kept alive the memories of Dusana, Mother Solas, and Cailey, but around the dark keeper, there is only silence.

Nobody knows his identity.

I don't want to stop searching, but at some point, I might be forced to.

Now, I consider carefully what each statue is holding.

Their arms are upraised, each supporting a book.

The books are closed.

Mother gave no explanation for the books, and my brothers didn't ask her. Neither did Father.

But I know what they're for.

Blame it on my dark nature, but I don't respect boundaries.

When I was supposed to be out hunting with Father and my brothers, I crept back to witness the pact made between Mother, her brother and sister, and the two dragons Graviter Rex and Vargo Vanem.

At a time of their choosing, Tamra and Gallium will bring their tools to the eternal flame and burn them.

Neither of them has children, and it's caused them both deep sadness.

For Gallium, in particular, it's problematic since he and

Elowynn don't have a daughter to whom Elowynn can pass her crown, and the fae's future is more tenuous because of it.

Regardless, soon the Blacksmith race will come to an end.

Tamra and Gallium have vowed that their tools will be destroyed.

As for Mother's tools, the eternal flame can't burn them—no flame can—so she asked Graviter Rex to ensure that the dragons take possession of her metal when she passes.

Graviter will store her hammer and medallion with his dragon's gold, which will be inherited by his twin sons.

His sons will believe only that the tools are powerful dragon's gold.

Vargo has vowed, since he will live longer than Graviter, that he will ensure that the tools' true nature is never revealed.

Both Tamra and Gallium were concerned about the risk of Mother's tools being misused, but Mother was adamant it was the only way.

"Dragons guard their gold jealously," she said. "They are best placed to protect these tools. There is no other choice."

I sensed Tamra and Gallium's reluctance, but they finally agreed.

When the others left, Mother asked Vargo Vanem to stay back for a moment.

He remained with her on the platform on which I was balancing only moments ago, and I will never forget what they spoke about.

"It's the end of the beginning." Mother's voice was strained. "Supernaturals won't be able to walk in plain sight forever. And dragons, well... You aren't exactly going to be able to hide in small spaces."

Vargo gave her a nod, his shoulders hunched. "We feel our mortality more keenly than ever."

She took a deep breath and I heard the determination in her voice. "I left a thread of dragon within my medallion," she said, holding it up to the light. "When I pass, and Graviter is gone, please use this medallion. Protect all dragons. Give them the ability to hide among humans."

Vargo's eyes had widened. "The gravity of your gift is not lost on me," he said. "But without a Blacksmith's heart to power this metal—and one as powerful as yours—it may as well be a trinket."

Mother gave him a soft smile. "Perhaps, one day, there will be a heart strong enough to overcome that difficulty."

Vargo gave her a nod, his expression deeply contemplative as he flew away.

As for the books, there's a part of me that vehemently disagrees with Mother's decision to create them, but I can't do a damn thing about it.

Those books can only be opened for the first time by a Blacksmith.

She and her siblings will make that choice.

Once opened, the books will take on lives of their own.

They will become powerful receptacles of magic, recording history as it happens, but their real purpose...

Within generations, the books will extinguish all knowledge about Blacksmiths.

Not too quickly. A little at a time. Until everything about my mother and her family and their ancestors is forgotten.

It will be as if they never existed.

I shake off my foreboding, turning away from the room with the statues, and slip down the staircase, heading for the back of the tower.

I'm meant to be joining my brothers already, but I don't follow the rules, so if I changed my behavior today, it would only alarm them.

Well, that's my reasoning.

I slip through a concealed door at the back of the tower that sits close to the cliff's edge, only to find Mother staring out across the ocean.

Her hands are folded in front of her, her golden medallion catching the light, while her forehead is lightly creased.

It isn't the first time I've found her standing here like this, as if she's trying to remember something.

She senses my presence right away and flashes me a smile, her eyes lighting up. "Daughter."

I slip one arm around her waist. For a moment, I consider asking her about Thaden Kane Ironmeld, but I want to focus on her.

She looks so... lost.

"You needed to escape?" I ask her.

She sighs. "No blood can be spilled while I'm here; I've made that very clear. I created every safety precaution I could think of, and still—"

"They look at you as if you're going to eat them." I bare my teeth dramatically.

Oh, those humans and supernaturals have no idea.

I'm the one they should be afraid of.

It doesn't escape me that Mother takes the brunt of their fear, bearing the weight of it so that I can live free of it. Well, mostly.

"This alliance will make things better," I say. A hopeful statement more than a certain one.

She presses a kiss to my forehead. "I hope so."

"I know so." Aksel's deep rumble meets my ears a second before his body casts us both into shadow.

He stands tall, wearing the confidence of an alpha, but his protectiveness of us shines through in his concerned gaze. "Everything okay?"

"No," I grumble. "This dress itches. Can't I get changed?"

He shakes his head with a laugh. "Into your smelly hunting clothes?"

Our wolfish noses are particularly sensitive, but I'm certain the humans wouldn't notice.

Still, I give an exaggerated sigh. "Fine. I'll stay in the dress."

Mother drops another kiss on my forehead. She looks beautiful in her violet-colored dress, her silver hair flowing around her face and shoulders.

As we make our way around the base of the tower, Father meets us there, holding his hand out for her.

The love between them is a tangible force that hits me hard.

Their connection will never break. No matter what battles they face.

I hang back a little, and when Aksel glances at me, I say, "I'll be there in a minute."

He catches up with Mother and Father, joining my brothers and the other guests at the front of the tower.

Charlotte will arrive soon, and then everything will change.

I find myself wishing it wouldn't.

As fiercely as Mother and Father have watched over me and protected me, I've also protected them.

My family is my world.

If my brothers have a problem, then I have a problem. If they need help, I'm there.

After today... it all starts to change.

It doesn't take me long to slip into the forest, finding a shadowed spot out of the light where I can take deep breaths and fix an expression on my face that says, *I'm happy for you.*

When I'm certain I've managed it, I prepare to head out into the light again.

Before I can take a step, my senses prickle.

I consider the nearby shadows, inhaling deeply, trying to pick out the various scents. Musky air, moss, a rabbit, and also—

A woman steps forward through the shadows.

She has green eyes, auburn hair, and a dusting of freckles across her nose, along with a slight cleft in her chin.

She looks about Mother's age, but she's very thin, practically a whisp. She's wearing a short-sleeved, leafy-green dress that stops at her knees and skims the tops of her brown boots.

Her appearance is extremely disarming, which only makes me distrustful, my eyes narrowing at her.

I'm certain I've never seen her before, but there's something so damn familiar about her...

"Hello, Galeia," she says. "Do you remember me?"

I remember her scent.

But the face I associate with that scent was much older than she now appears.

Carefully, I say, "You told me not to eat the mouse."

"Indeed." She breaks into a smile. "Precious thing, you let it run away without taking even a nibble of its tail."

I'm not sure if I should be offended that she called me a 'thing,' although it's somewhat unclear if she was referring to me or the mouse.

"You were much older," I say, standing my ground as she takes another step toward me.

I have no fear of her.

My claws are ready.

"That face suited my needs at the time." Her focus slips past me to the tower. "Oh my, that is a very impressive tower."

"People call it *the Spire*," I reply, gauging her reaction.

This place is well known in the supernatural community. If she's heard of it, then she will also know who lives here and that a single wrong move will get her hunted down and killed. My mother may be misjudged, but I have no boundaries when it comes to protecting my family.

The woman arches her eyebrows. "I can see why it has that name." Then she waves her hand at the gathering in front of it. "But it looks like we've come at a bad time."

"We?"

"My two brothers and I." She turns slightly and points in the direction of the shadows behind her.

Two men stand in the darkness, neither fully visible.

Their scents are strange to me. Magical. Certainly supernatural. But of a kind I haven't encountered before.

I peer harder at her. "Who *are* you?"

"I like to be called Halle. But my brothers, when they're being cruel, call me Hel. You can meet them if you like?"

I scoff. "With an introduction like that, I don't think so."

One corner of her mouth hitches up. "Let me try again. My

eldest brother was born in the cave where you once let a mouse go free."

Now she's the one peering at me, and she doesn't have to say more.

Even if I didn't remember that cave and all the runes etched into the side of it, Father has told me all the stories of his people.

I take another deep breath, pulling in the scent of the most darkly shadowed man.

Fuck me.

Is he the Wolf of War?

"My other brother, also older than me," Halle continues, gesturing to the other man, "well, he slithered his way out of a similar cavern. Right after he decided it would be more interesting to explore the world than to encircle it for all eternity."

I gasp. "The World Serpent."

Of course, she could be lying to me, but the energy I'm now sensing around all three of them tells me that, even if these supernaturals aren't the gods they claim to be, they're fucking powerful.

Halle gives me another smile, and for the first time since she arrived, the twist of her lips isn't shrewd or conniving. She considers me openly. "We've waited decades for you, Galeia."

"Why?"

She gestures to the clearing. "You don't belong here, tucked away in that tower. Not when you have such a long life ahead of you and the power to do anything you want."

She takes another step toward me, startling me when she says, "Come with us."

I should tell her an emphatic and immediate *No*.

But my senses are exploding with the increasing energy surrounding her and the two men standing nearby.

It calls to me, drawing me toward them.

I make myself stop. "My family..."

"I understand," Halle says. "They're your pack." She searches my eyes. "But are they your future?"

I look back.

At my brothers. At Mother and Father. At the life I've lived.

I tell myself they need me, but...

I have needed them more.

I needed their love, their support, their understanding, and their determination to bring peace to this land.

Halle doesn't seem to miss the way I angle in their direction.

"Your pack is important," she says. "We don't expect you to leave with us right now. But I hope you will understand, we can't linger here beyond tomorrow morning. Our presence may be seen as a threat."

My eyes burn with tears as I consider the choice I now face. Even as I think of leaving, I feel the tug of my future.

My destiny.

Of all the things Father taught me, destiny is not to be denied. He will understand my decision, perhaps even more than Mother or my brothers will.

"It's the end of the beginning," Halle says, her expression grim. "Will you stay in the past or step into your future?" She tilts her head, her eyes filling with power. "Will you come with us?"

With my heart in my throat, I say, "I will."

I won't leave without saying goodbye. I would never vanish on my family without explaining my reasons and ensuring they understand my choice. And, no matter how much I may hate this scratchy dress, nothing could drag me away from my brother's wedding.

Today, I will celebrate with my family.

Tomorrow, I will explain my decision.

Then, I will forge my destiny.

I will never forget the love I've been given or the battles that were fought to keep me safe. My destiny may claim my path, but my family will always be part of my heart.

Did you know that this book is part of a connected world? For more fae, enemies to lovers, and dragons, check out Bright Wicked.

If you would like to know the identity of the keeper of dark magic...

There is a bonus chapter at the end of this book. But please heed the spoiler alert! This chapter has been carefully placed at the end of this book to help prevent any accidental spoilers.

You can check out the full list of series in this connected world over the page!

DISCOVER THE EVER REALMS

Seven series. One world.

Suggested Reading Order:

Bright Wicked
Storm Princess
Assassin's Magic
Soul Bitten Shifter
Supernatural Legacy
Dark Magic Shifters
Kingdom of Betrayal

Related series:
Demon Pack

BRIGHT WICKED

A COMPLETE FANTASY ROMANCE

If you want more epic romantasy with soul mates, forbidden love, and dragons, check out the complete
Bright Wicked series.

One forbidden touch.

I am the Bright Queen's Champion. The only fae to control the power of starlight, I am sworn to protect my people from the dark Fell who live in the wilderness beyond our border.

But when a Fell more powerful than any other challenges me, I'm not prepared for his fierce strength and skill.

Or the dangerous desire in his eyes when he looks at me.

Two champions bound to destroy each other.

One misstep is all it takes for me to invoke an ancient law that binds my fate to his. Suddenly, my life is no longer my own.

I am tied to him in a promise of pain and destruction.

Three days to live.

Now, I have only three days before I must fight him in a battle to the death that will determine the future of our two lands.

Every heartbeat counts.

But how can I kill the only man who sees me for who I truly am?

Content information: Bright Wicked is high fantasy romance, the first in the Bright Wicked series, a trilogy told over three consecutive days. Recommended reading age for the series is 17+ for heat level.

ALSO BY EVERLY FROST

BRIGHT WICKED - COMPLETE

(Fantasy Romance)

1. Bright Wicked

2. Radiant Fierce

3. Infernal Dark

STORM PRINCESS - COMPLETE

(Fantasy Romance)

1. Book 1

2. Book 2

3. Book 3

ASSASSIN'S MAGIC - COMPLETE

(Urban Fantasy Romance)

1. Assassin's Magic

2. Assassin's Mask

3. Assassin's Menace

4. Assassin's Maze

5. Rebels

6. Revenge

7. Rogue

8. Assassin's Match

SOUL BITTEN SHIFTER - COMPLETE

(Dark Urban Fantasy Romance)

1. This Dark Wolf

2. This Broken Wolf

3. This Caged Wolf

4. This Cruel Blood

SUPERNATURAL LEGACY - COMPLETE

(Angels and Dragon Shifters)

1. Hunt the Night

2. Chase the Shadows

3. Slay the Dawn

4. Claim the Light

DARK MAGIC SHIFTERS

(Dark Urban Fantasy Romance)

1. Wolf of Ashes

2. Bond of Flames

3. Crown of Fate

KINGDOM OF BETRAYAL

(Fantasy Romance)

1. A Sky Like Blood

2. A Sin Like Fire

3. A Storm Like Iron

4. A Soul Like Glass

DEMON PACK - COMPLETE

(Dark Paranormal Romance)

1. Demon Pack

2. Demon Pack: Elimination

3. Demon Pack: Eternal

ABOUT THE AUTHOR

USA Today bestselling author Everly Frost writes fantasy romance and paranormal romance with badass female leads and morally grey heroes who fall first. When she isn't dreaming up spicy enemies to lovers romances, she's binge-watching Lord of the Rings, tending to her fur baby, or learning to sew. Subscribe to Everly's newsletter for a free novella today!

Join Everly's mailing list at: www.everlyfrost.com

amazon.com/author/everlyfrost

facebook.com/everlyfrost

instagram.com/everlyfrost

bookbub.com/authors/everly-frost

goodreads.com/everlyfrost

THE DARK CHAPTER 52
THE KEEPER OF DARK MAGIC

I am the keeper of dark magic.

The following pages contain my first memories. Make of them what you will.

But first, heed my warning:

These pages reveal my true identity.

My identity is a terrible secret known only to me.

Even my true love doesn't know who I am.

Have you met her?

She is a dark creature, too, even more dangerous than I am.

She will not take kindly to another being knowing what she doesn't know...

If you haven't read her story, you will find it in the completed **Dark Magic Shifters** series.

<u>Be warned: my identity is a major spoiler for that series.</u>

If you hate spoilers, you should not read on.

If you read on... well... I take no responsibility for any sorrow you might cause yourself.

Or perhaps I will welcome your torment. I am a dark creature, after all.

Did you heed my warning?
If you hate spoilers, do not read on.

One last thing.

By reading on, you solemnly swear that you will not share any part of this chapter with anyone, anywhere.

Not on any website. Not on your social media. Not in your DMs. Not on a scrap of paper quietly slipped to a friend. *Nowhere.*

Because you are not a dark creature. You would never devastate other readers by spoiling an entire book series for them.

You will keep my secret at all costs.

.

.

.

.

.

.

.

.

The following is a true account of my first memories.
Or... is it?
You may never know.
I am a dark creature, and dark creatures lie...

.

.

.

.

.

.

.

.

The Dark Chapter 52

The Keeper of Dark Magic

Pain tears through my soul.

My heart rends from my body at the same time as my body

comes into being, two simultaneous events that leave me unable to process where I am, what I am, or even who I am.

All I know is that my body is now fully formed.

I have a mind, and with that mind comes all the knowledge I require.

Thoughts and sensations bombard me, all within a split-second explosion that teaches me everything I need to know about my existence.

A moment ago, I was a collection of cells, life barely beyond conception.

Now, I am a man.

Around me, there is a never-ending darkness. It is beautiful and shiny, a dark prison that extends far into the distance in every direction.

The darkness seems to cling to my arms, intensifying as I raise myself from where I was lying, trembling on the cold floor, clothed only in a simple tunic and pants.

I push up from the black marble, acutely aware of the metal crown I'm gripping.

Power rushed into the crown at the same moment as my creation—the same moment that knowledge exploded through my mind.

It was enough power to burn the world to ashes, all now safely contained in this metal.

It's a power I can't touch. It is fully contained, and I am nothing more than the living guardian of it.

The flood of dark magic into the crown eases, and I relax my grip a little, becoming aware of how bloodless my hand had become.

My forehead creases as I consider...

Do I have blood?

Or is it a construct of my creation that I believe I am alive when I am not?

My heart does not beat. I know that much.

Having righted myself, I lean forward, peering at the reflective surface I'm kneeling on, trying to make out my features.

I have dark hair. Not quite black because it contrasts with my surroundings. The strands are the darkest gray. They sit around my head like a wolf's pelt.

The color of my eyes is harder to see.

As I tilt my head, attempting to make out the finer details of my appearance despite the darkness, my eyes appear pale green, then gray, then a combination of the two colors.

I test my ability to stand, rising upward. Without another being to compare myself to, I'm uncertain if I'm tall, although I sense I might be. My shoulders feel broad, my arms and legs bulky with muscles I've never used.

I feel strong.

Again, my forehead creases, because strength, like height, is relative.

My strength now lies in my ability to carry this crown.

Already, its weight is heavy.

I flinch when, far, *far* away, a dark magic creature dies. I catch a glimpse of its—*his*—final memories, as if I'm seeing them from his eyes.

Instantly, I know everything he knows. He is a dark elf. He betrayed his Queen, so badly that she, herself, wields the blade that dispatches him to me. For a moment, I glimpse the world around him. It's filled with dark wonders, glittering jewels, and—

My whole body wrenches because another death hits me.

This one is far more powerful.

As powerful as the moment of my creation.

It drives me to my knees again, a roar leaving my lips as the pain of my creation ripples through my soul once more. My shout echoes out around me as I scream out the agony.

I have to get up.

I have to reach her because, unlike all the other magic I'm tethering even at this very moment, unlike the other creatures who are at this very second experiencing their deaths...

She is here.

She has come to me.

I need to see her.

I have to ask her why.

Why did she choose this for me?

As I force myself to my feet, making myself run in the direction of her presence, I'm also living the memories of her death.

She's tipping her head back to the sun, telling herself the battle is over. She has finally secured peace. The Fae Queen lies dead on the green grass and won't hurt anyone ever again. The darkness is gone. She can return to the ones she loves...

But then, she realizes she can't breathe, and finally, she looks down at her chest to the gaping wound that cuts through her ribs.

The ground rears up at her as she topples to her side.

In the distance, supernaturals and humans are rushing toward her.

Ahead of the others is a man, and racing alongside him is a little wolf.

I don't want this memory to fade.

I need it as badly as she does. I need to see the man named Erik and commit his face to my memory.

But then her eyes close, and her memory blurs.

I fight the disorientation of seeing her dying moments while, at the same time, I'm trying to focus on my surroundings so I can locate her in the darkness of my realm.

There she is.

She's kneeling on the cold, marble floor, her shoulders hunched and her arms limp at her sides.

Her hair and body are charred, as if she dipped herself in soot.

The dark magic coating her soul calls to me.

Of all the magic I will tether, hers is the most important.

But these precious moments with her are more so.

I slow my steps as she raises her head, her eyes unfocused at first, then widening as I move closer to her.

Her lips part with an audibly sharp breath, and tears fill her eyes. "No," she whispers, her charred hair waving around her face as she shakes her head. "Please, no."

I lower myself into a kneeling position opposite her.

I wish I could put away the crown and set aside the cause of her pain, but I'm incapable of letting it go. It's part of my body now, regardless of whether it's in my hand or on my head.

"Hello, Mother," I say.

Tears slip down her cheeks. Her gaze travels from my hair, which is the same color as Erik's hair, to my eyes, which are a mix of hers and his.

Every angle of her face and posture embodies her grief.

We speak at the same moment.

She asks me, "*How?*"

I ask her, "*Why?*"

I search her eyes as intensely as she searches mine, and with heart-shattering clarity, I realize that *I* am the one with the answers. Not her. I know both how and why.

Within her dying memories was the last piece of information I needed. "You didn't know you were pregnant."

Her left arm slides slowly around her stomach. Her voice is a rasp. She rocks forward but doesn't take her eyes off me. "This is too cruel."

It is. But at the moment of my creation, the basic tenets of my existence were instantly clear to me. "That is the nature of dark magic," I say. "It serves only itself. Even with all of your power, you would never have been able to control it. It will always choose the path of greatest pain."

I reach for her hand—her left hand where her golden medallion rests. Her skin is cold, but she clasps my hand tightly, as if she will refuse to ever let me go.

"All it needed was an innocent life," I whisper, my own voice strained. "Your creation magic did the rest."

Her shoulders sink, her head lowering over our joined hands so that her tears drip onto them. "I don't want this."

For a long moment, I feel her pain, and it reflects my own. My life has been stolen. Of all the lives to take, the dark magic wrenched away the brightest, because that is what it will always do.

But I can offer her some solace. "My brother will thrive. I'm sure of it."

Her head snaps up. "Brother?"

"Twins run in your family." I tilt my head, holding on to all the knowledge I gained from her memories, along with my understanding of my own nature. "I would have been the Blacksmith. He is the wolf."

Her face pales beneath the soot. "You were the…"

"You won't remember that you're pregnant," I say, again trying to console her. "You won't remember me. When you return to the ones you love, your memories of this place will vanish."

That, too, is the nature of dark magic. It only takes. She may try to hold on to her memories, but she will not succeed.

Her eyes only widen further, her tears flowing more freely down her cheeks, but her jaw clenches, and her voice becomes determined. "I won't leave you here."

"They're healing you," I say. "You don't have a choice. You will be pulled back to yourself soon, and when you are, I will take all of the darkness from your heart and soul. I will free you from it. Once and for all. That is my purpose."

She darts forward, her left hand pressing to my chest, her voice urgent. "Your heart," she whispers. "It isn't beating."

My forehead creases. I know so much, can discern so much, but I'm not sure why she spoke of my lifeless heart.

Perhaps she can feel the tug of living energy that will wrench her back to her world, and the contrast of my empty heart is startling to her.

No matter what, we only have seconds now before I will never see her again.

I slip my free hand over her own, pressing her palm closer to my chest. "I won't forget you."

She's shaking her head, a frantic movement now. "No, I won't go. I won't leave you here!"

But, already, there's a backward tug on her body, the force of her life returning.

She fights it, trying to hold on to me, even as she's being pulled away. "No," she screams. "*No!*"

At the last moment, when only the very edge of her medallion is pressed to my chest, she cries, "The power in a heart. With the power in a heart, you can be free—"

Then she's gone. Vanished. Only the echo of her cry remains.

The power in a heart.

I press the heel of my palm to my chest, rubbing at the spot where my skin tingles with her magic.

What did she do?

More importantly, why are my cheeks wet?

With every passing moment, the dark magic that fueled my creation is growing stronger. The urge to place the crown upon my head is undeniable.

I was innocent. I would have been a Blacksmith more powerful even than my mother, because my father's blood also ran in my veins, the power of deep light.

I would have been born to the brightest light.

Now, I have paid the price for crimes that were not my own.

To the darkness around me, I whisper, "What greater darkness could there be?"

With that, I lift the black crown and settle it on my head.

It sinks past my forehead and down over my face, where it covers my eyes.

No more will I see hope or love.

From now on, there is only malice, cruelty, death, and maybe... one day... vengeance.

Because within my mother's dying memories, I saw the little wolf. She is the last descendant of the Blacksmith whose actions led to my imprisonment.

Her existence makes revenge possible.

I can't stop my slow smile, for I am now a dark king, and vengeance will be mine.

～

If you did not heed my warning and wish to know all about my vengeance, check out Dark Magic Shifters.

Or, if you would prefer to read this connected world in the chronological order of events,
check out the complete romantasy series, Bright Wicked.
Don't worry... I'm in it.

Yours in darkness,
The Keeper of Dark Magic

WOLF OF ASHES
(DARK MAGIC SHIFTERS #1)

Want more keeper of dark magic?

Check out Dark Magic Shifters.

His dark crown will be mine.

My mother was imprisoned for a crime she didn't commit. She was locked away in darkness, never to see light again.

I was born into that darkness. I learned to survive without sunlight and to thrive on the scraps that were thrown to me. All because someone didn't want me to claim my birthright.

Now I'm free. And I'm coming for what's mine.

I'll go deep into the nightmares of an empire built on blood and bones to find the man who stole my place among supernaturals. I'll do whatever it takes to slice his empire apart, piece by little piece.

Even if it means making a deal with a dark king whose thirst for vengeance exceeds my own. A broken king capable of wielding deadly magic. The darkest of them all.

In return for his power, he wants more from me than I can give:

He wants my heart.

Content information: Dark Magic Shifters is a dark paranormal romance series.

Recommended reading age is 18+ for sex scenes, mature themes, violence, and language. Ends on a cliffhangers with a happily ever after in the final book.

Tropes for the series include enemies to lovers, morally gray characters, wolf shifters, dragon shifters, anti-hero, with a touch of supernatural mafia.